Diam   ds

ESTHER KREITMAN

Translated from the Yiddish and with an introduction
by Heather Valencia

DAVID
PAUL

Published in Great Britain in 2010
By David Paul
25 Methuen Park
London N10 2JR
www.davidpaulbooks.com

First published by W. & G. Foyle in London in 1944 in Yiddish as *Brilyantn*

Translated from Yiddish by Heather Valencia
Translation copyright © Heather Valencia 2010

Worldwide distribution (except North America) by
Central Books, London E9 5LN

A CIP catalogue record for this book is available from the British Library

Front cover photograph: Paul O'Driscoll/Getty Images

ISBN 978-0-9548482-0-0

Printed in Great Britain

Acknowledgements

In the course of preparing this edition, I had the good fortune to make contact with some interesting and helpful people, expert either in the Antwerp/Flemish field, or in the diamond industry and its history. Herman Note, Yiddishist and fellow translator, gave me the correct spelling of Antwerp place names, and explained local dialect expressions in the text. He put me in touch with Leo Schumer, who solved many queries on the diamond industry. I am grateful to Rosalind Gold, who talked to me about her late father, the well-known Yiddish actor, Yidl Goldberg. He was also a Hatton Garden diamond dealer. Through her I also got to know Harry Karton, a London diamond merchant, and I profited from a discussion with him, at the London Diamond Bourse. Two researchers were kind enough to allow me access, to what was then, unpublished work: I was able to read parts of Carole Timms's dissertation on the London diamond trade, and an article by Faith Jones on Esther Kreitman.

Finally, Lucette Pilcer, herself a retired diamond dealer from Antwerp, gave unstintingly of her time and knowledge, and was kind enough to read and correct the sections of the introduction, and references in the novel, pertaining to the Antwerp diamond trade.

I am indebted to David Paul and Sylvia Paskin who carefully read every draft and helped me to make many improvements to earlier versions of the text. I am grateful to my husband Mike for his constant interest and encouragement.

To all these people I express my sincere thanks. Any mistakes or inadequacies in the final version are entirely my responsibility.

HV

Contents

Introduction   9

A Note on the Translation   28

Diamonds   31

Glossary   284

Bibliography   293

Esther Kreitman

Introduction

by Heather Valencia

Esther Kreitman: her background and literary fate

Esther Kreitman was one of a relatively small group of women novelists and poets writing in Yiddish. Long ignored or under-valued, their qualities are now becoming more widely recognised.

In Kreitman's case the disadvantage of being a female writer has been compounded by her position in the shadow of her more illlus-trious brothers, Israel Joshua and Isaac Bashevis Singer. Her oeuvre was more or less ignored, even within the Yiddish literary canon, and until recently she has been known outside Yiddish-speaking literary circles only as the author of the novel *Der sheydim-tants* (The Devils' Dance). This work was translated into English, with some alterations to the text, by her son, the writer and journalist Maurice Carr (Moyshe Kreitman), and published as *Deborah* in 1946, by Foyle's in London. This translation was reprinted by Virago Press, London in 1983, and jointly by the Feminist Press, New York, and David Paul, London, in 2004. In the same year her short story collection also ap-peared under the title *Blitz and other stories*, in the English translation of Dorothée van Tendeloo. The publication of this edition of *Dia-monds* means that all her books are now available in English transla-tion, so that her literary achievement can be assessed by a wider readership.

Hinde Esther Singer was born in 1891 in Bilgoray, Poland, the eldest child of the Hassidic rabbi Pinkhes Menakhem Singer and his wife Basheve; the Nobel Laureate Isaac Bashevis Singer took his mother's name in his *nom de plume* (in Yiddish he is known as Yitskhok Ba-sheves, i.e. Isaac, son of Basheve), a fact which hints at the important role the mother played in the family. Esther's father, who failed to take the required examination in Russian language, could not obtain an official post as a rabbi. He managed to find work in small, obscure communities. He acted as the rabbi of a village, Leoncin, then he became a teacher in the *yeshiva*, or Talmudic academy of the Hassidic community in Radzymin, and, finally, he obtained a position in Warsaw, where he ruled on points of Jewish law and mediated on disputes in the poorest Jewish district, around Krochmalna Street, where the family lived.

During this period, Hinde Esther had already begun to write, but her youthful writings were destroyed, just before her marriage, on the insistence of her mother, who feared that Tsarist police might find them seditious if they were discovered on her journey west. It seems that she entered unwillingly into the arranged marriage with a diamond cutter, Avrom Kreitman. They were married in Berlin in 1912, after which the couple went to Antwerp, where several of her husband's relatives already resided. In 1914, the Germans invaded the city, and Avrom, Esther, and their baby son fled to England, where they lived in a series of cramped attic rooms, at various addresses in North London.

There is little doubt that the marriage was extremely unhappy; Maurice Carr calls his father a *shlemiel*, a loser, and depicts his distant and tyrannical personality. His wife left him for several periods. After the Russian Revolution of March 1917, the British and Russian governments signed an agreement that Russian citizens of military age had to join the British army, or return to Russia, to do military service there. Avrom Kreitman took the latter option – whether out of enthusiasm for the revolution, like so many young Jews in the west, or to escape his unhappy domestic life, is not clear – returning to London some time after the end of the war.

Maurice Carr comments: "Henceforth, more than ever, *paterfamilias* Avrom and his unloving, unloved Hindele will be going their separate ways under one roof." Avrom was seldom in work, and his wife had to embroider blouses (which contributed to her very poor eyesight) and do other poorly paid piecework to provide for the family. In a letter written in 1944, Esther asked her celebrated brother

Isaac Bashevis in America to lend her some money, saying that her husband had not worked for two years – but to no avail. Her request was refused.

Decisive points in her life were two visits to her native Poland. In 1926 she spent several months, together with her son, at her brother Israel Joshua's *dacha* in the countryside near Warsaw. She may well have intended to abandon her husband and stay there, but her relationship with the other family members was strained from the beginning, and she returned to London.

In 1929, she returned alone to Warsaw, and stayed there for ten months. During this time, she translated two substantial works into Yiddish, Dickens' *A Christmas Carol* and George Bernard Shaw's *The Intelligent Woman's Guide to Socialism and Capitalism*. These were published in Warsaw in 1929 and 1930, respectively.

Significantly, it was after this second return to her old homeland that she once more began to write creatively, inspired no doubt by her encounter with her brothers and their exciting literary circle in Warsaw. The novel *Der sheydim-tants* (The Devils' Dance) was published by the Yiddish publisher Brzoza in Warsaw in 1936, and *Brilyantn* (Diamonds) appeared in 1944 under the imprint of W. & G. Foyle's Hebrew Department, London. The volume of short stories was published in 1950 by the Narod Press in London. The original edition took its title from one of the stories, *Yikhes* (a concept which conveys the honour or pedigree which comes from having family connections with pious and learned Jews). After this, Kreitman appears to have written very little. In worsening health and without any significant improvement to her economic situation, she lived in London with her husband until her death in 1954.

These are the well-documented events of her life. The woman herself is, however, an enigmatic and elusive figure. A great deal has been written about the dysfunctional Singer household and about Hinde Esther's personality and her physical and mental health. Much of this information must, however, be treated with caution. One difficulty is that Kreitman's first novel, *Der sheydim-tants* is treated by several critics as if it were straight autobiography, so that evidence

11

about concrete details of Kreitman's life is extrapolated from depictions of the life of the fictitious heroine. This leads to confusion between the real biography and the fictional work. Even though she undoubtedly draws strongly on her background and experiences, in this and in her other works, a work of fiction cannot be relied upon as a source of biographical information.

The principal non-fictional sources of information about her are memoirs by her relatives. There are accounts of her by both her brothers, who both, however, had their own agendas and differing viewpoints. Furthermore, these accounts were written long after the events they portray, by brothers who were younger than her: I.J.Singer, who was three years younger than his sister, published his reminiscences of his childhood and youth, *Fun a velt vos iz nishto mer* (Of a World That is No More*)* in 1946, thirty years after the period he is describing, while Isaac Bashevis Singer was thirteen years younger than Esther, so that the traumas of her adolescent years, which he vividly depicts in his memoirs, *Dem tatns bezdin shtub* (In My Father's Court, 1956) and *Di mishpokhe* (The Family, 1983) took place when he was a very small child, and the accounts were written when the author was looking back on events, which occurred at least thirty years before. There are also inconsistencies in the accounts of the two Singer brothers, with respect to their sister.

A further fascinating and little-known account of the writer's difficult life and personality can be found in the memoir by Maurice Carr, entitled *A Mother's Son: Early Memories*, which vividly reveals her feelings about her family and childhood. Carr describes his experience of his mother at different stages of his life and relays much information given to him directly by her. It is possible, where these three personal accounts are in agreement, to understand some aspects of her personality and feelings which had an influence on her as a writer.

It is clear that she had a very unhappy childhood and youth in a family which, quite apart from its constant perilous financial situation, was dysfunctional in many respects. Pinkhes Menakhem was an adherent of the Hassidic movement, which stressed an ecstatic, mystical relationship with God, rather than formal scholarship, while Basheve was from the rationalist or *misnagdish* tradition. She was a learned woman, unhappy with the lot of a traditional Jewish wife and mother, and seems indeed to have been the intellectual driving force in the marriage. Despite, or perhaps because of her own intellectual frustration, she supported her husband in his contention that a daughter was of less value than a son, and, indeed, had no hope of education or independence. Bashevis laconically states: "My father didn't bother with her because she was a girl and my mother did not understand her." Having a female as opposed to a male child was actually considered a shameful failure in Hassidic society.

This is brought out vividly in Israel Joshua's memoir, where he describes the muted celebrations, which he witnessed when a younger sister was born: "The Hassidim sniggered in the house of worship as my father named the new child, Sarah. Siring a female child was a shameful act, for which they occasionally flogged a young father with their belts. Naturally the birth wasn't celebrated at our house, except for serving egg cookies, and whisky, to the few men who bothered to drop in. For a girl, this was considered sufficient."

Hinde Esther was in fact sent away to a wet nurse for the first two years of her life, an experience which had a lasting effect on her psyche. She recreated it in one of her most impressive and moving stories, *Di naye velt* (The New World). The cold relationship between her and her mother appears to have persisted throughout her adult life. Maurice Carr witnessed the reunion with her parents, in Poland, in 1926, where they met for the first time since they had parted in 1912 on her marrying. "Bathsheva pauses out of reach of my mothers arms (which were) uplifted for an embrace. In a husky warble she declares, 'Why, Hindele, you're not all that ugly! I always thought you uglier than Lena. Lena, I knew from my mother's tales, is the Leoncin village idiot.'"

Hinde Esther was denied the opportunity to study which her younger brothers enjoyed. Her frustration and loneliness was reflected in her relationship with her two brothers, which seems to have been a mixture of jealousy and, particularly towards I.J.Singer, adoration, with which the latter was obviously very uncomfortable. Maurice Carr describes their reunion in Warsaw after an absence of many years:

"With a shriek of mingled joy and anguish my mother throws herself upon him in an embrace so passionate as to be more than sisterly. He struggles to disengage himself, takes a backward step and fixes her with a glare of mingled sorrow and revulsion." Similar passion characterised her possessive love for her son, which Maurice Carr evokes with tact and kindliness in his memoir.

Within the family she was regarded as odd and unpredictable, not least on account of the strange fits from which she had suffered since childhood. This condition seems to have been diagnosed as epilepsy only in the later twenties in London. According to Maurice Carr, these attacks abated during her later life, but were replaced by extremes of mood: "senseless furies and intemperate broodings." He ascribes his mother's lifelong mental torments to her rejection by her mother Basheve, who, as he put it, "mercilessly cast away an unwanted daughter." It has to be said, however, that Carr's interpretation is based on the stories his mother told him of her childhood, which must have been tinged by her own feelings about the events she experienced.

It can be asserted with confidence however that Esther Kreitman's family background and personal history influenced the generally dark view of humanity which underlies her fiction. Lack of understanding and communication, and strong passions, with often a hint of incestuous feelings, are prevalent in relationships between the sexes. This is particularly true of *Diamonds*, as we shall see.

Kreitman is, therefore, generally seen as a sad and vulnerable woman. It is only right to redress this balance a little by citing two instances from Maurice Carr's unpublished memoir which show other sides to her character. On little Moyshe's first few days at school he suffered anti-Semitic taunts from a teacher and physical bullying by some of his classmates. When he eventually told his mother, she marched along to the school and demanded to see the headmaster, whom she harangued in her "Yiddishy English" so that the offending teacher was forced to apologise to them. Secondly, after their return from Poland in 1926, the Kreitmans' landlady reported, with ill-concealed malice, that Avrom had been keeping company with a lady neighbour when Esther was in Poland. Kreitman was ready with a quick-witted ironic reply: "I'm sorry to see you in such distress, Mrs

Rosenzweig. Since there's no accounting for a gentleman's taste, you shouldn't be all that jealous!" In these and other incidents remembered by Maurice Carr, she emerges as a woman of courage and determination, with a wry sense of humour, not cowed by authority but capable of standing up for her rights. Indeed, the very fact of her having managed to find the space and time to write, given the exigencies of her life, shows great determination. When contemplating her work, as one critic has written: "One is confronted by two questions: how is it that such a talented storyteller wrote so little? And then, after deeper reflection on the circumstances of her life, how did she manage to write anything at all?"

Antwerp, the Jews, and the diamond trade

By the early twentieth century, the period in which the novel is set, Antwerp had become the world's foremost diamond centre. Its rise began in the sixteenth century, partly due to the arrival of Portuguese

Antwerp Diamond Bourse c 1904

Jews, fleeing the Inquisition, who brought with them their established trade, diamonds imported from India. Soon, Antwerp was handling almost half of the world's diamond trade. Its pre-eminence declined in the following century, but revived in the late nineteenth, with the opening of South African mines.

After 1880, another wave of immigration brought Ashkenazi Jews from Eastern Europe, who were fleeing from poverty and pogroms, or, as we read in *Diamonds*, from conscription into the Tsarist army, where Jews were very badly treated and forced to desecrate their religion. Other politically active secular Jews, like Leybesh, were escaping imprisonment for revolutionary activity. Many of these newcomers learned to be diamond cutters or polishers, and most settled near the main railway station, which is still in the diamond district of Antwerp.

From about 1880 onwards, the Antwerp trade was centred around the Diamond Bourse, the Diamond Club and the Fortunia, all to be found on Pelikaanstraat. The small dealers, however, operated from cafés and taverns such as the "Shenkl" described in the novel. As Kreitman depicts it, the business was a complicated network of formal and informal activity, with its own hierarchy and unwritten codes of practice. Merchants would carry valuable batches of diamonds or "parcels", as they are called, in their pockets, and a sale was – and still is – concluded only by a verbal agreement, a handshake and the Yiddish words *mazl un brokhe* (literally, good luck and blessing). At the top of the ladder were the large-scale merchants like Berman, who bought and sold both rough and polished stones. Unlike some who had factories employing cutters and polishers, Berman distributes rough stones to independent workers, after carefully weighing these parcels of diamonds – wrapped in small folded papers (*brivkes*). The weight of the stones is carefully controlled, before and after each polishing process, to check weight loss, and to calculate the price of the finished stones. Once they are polished, Berman sells them on.

Berman, the epitome of the successful Antwerp merchant, does a great deal of business from his own office, and from home, but he also employs the broker, Shapiro. Brokers, who usually invested in no stock of their own, used their knowledge of the market to obtain good deals for their clients. Though they might be financially as well off as merchants, they enjoyed lower status. Despite Shapiro's affluence, Berman consoles himself that "Shapiro was just a broker, and he, Berman, a diamond merchant."

The novel depicts the power of men like Berman, who decided the amount of goods to pass on to smaller dealers and to distribute to cutters and polishers, who, despite their craftsmanship, were considered as manual workers and occupied the lowest status. This aspect of the social structure is emphasised throughout the novel; it is shown, for example, in Berman's treatment of his workers in the opening chapter, and in the account of Dovid's attempt to become a polisher.

In the novel, Esther Kreitman also employs her knowledge of the technical processes which produce finished stones. In the case of larger stones, a highly skilled cleaver splits the rough diamond into two or more pieces, by scoring it with another diamond, and then using a metal wedge and a hammer; the aim is to remove any blemishes but to lose as little weight as possible. The cutter shapes the rough stones into a round shape. In both these processes a *dop* is used, a cup on a stick, in which the diamond is secured with wax, cement, or, as Kreitman describes it, lead. The splinters, dust and powder discharged by the cleaving and cutting activity were called in the Antwerp dialect of the time, *bakvuils*. This powder was used in the final process when it was mixed with oil and used to coat the *scaife*, a metal disc mounted on a polishing machine. The cut stone, secured on the *dop*, was held against the rotating disc and repositioned for each new facet. Although modern technology has brought many new developments, the basic processes have remained essentially the same.

The size, cut, colour and clarity of a diamond determine its value. Characters in the novel allude to the weight of polished stones (diamonds are weighted in carats, a carat being 0.2 of a gram) and the cut: there is mention of the small flat "rose cut" diamonds and of "full cuts" which have fifty-seven facets. In the early twentieth century the colour of the finest diamonds was designated "blue-white"; then, in decreasing value come: finest white, fine white, white, commercial white, top silver cape, silver cape, light cape, cape and dark cape (see chapter 13).

With the outbreak of the First World War and the German invasion of Belgium, the Antwerp diamond trade collapsed. A bombardment began on 28th September, 1914 and the city fell on 9th October. Kreitman depicts the evacuation ordered by King Albert on 6th October, which, in fact, brought her to London, with her husband and baby son. Diamonds being easily transportable, many merchants carried their stocks with them, and, as we see in the second part of the book, those who ended up in London were able to begin trading again in Hatton Garden.

The novel, *Diamonds*

Esther Kreitman's craftsmanship is evident in the accuracy with which she depicts the milieu, characters, and rituals of the Antwerp diamond trade, and the technical processes involved in the creation of finished diamonds. This is particularly impressive in view of the fact that her husband was a lowly cutter, who was not particularly communicative to his wife. Furthermore, the couple only lived in Antwerp for two years, so that her personal exposure to this world must have been limited.

The novel, however, is not merely a historical treatise on diamond trading. Diamonds have a strong, symbolic significance in the work. For those whose lives they touch all their personal worth is judged in terms of them and human relationships are transactions, with diamonds as the currency. Commenting on his brother's marriage to the daughter of a rich merchant, Jules Tsvaygnboym makes no mention of the person of the bride, but only remarks that, apart from the large dowry, the bridegroom has received a watch "with diamonds the size of hazelnuts." Berman even makes money out of his daughter's marriage. He forces the bridegroom, a prosperous diamond merchant in his own right, to buy his diamonds, for the jewellery that Jeannette will receive as a gift from her husband.

These glittering stones exert a powerful influence on the lives of all the main characters, shaping their destinies in various ways. To Berman, diamonds are more than a livelihood, he is in thrall to them, and his unbending character seems to reflect the hard coldness of the stones. It is through diamonds that he has become what he is, and his personality dominates the lives of all the family members. For Dovid, diamonds are a constant symbol of his failure to fulfil his father's expectations, and Jeannette is sold to the elderly diamond merchant in the same way a fine stone changes hands in the marketplace. Rochl has to be content with fake diamonds, while the real ones are buried in the safe; a telling image of her marriage to Berman and his treatment of her. Diamonds are the *leitmotif* underlying all the human relationships and unifying the work.

18

In this, her second novel, Kreitman shows her versatility as a writer. In its theme and form, *Diamonds* is very different to *Deborah*. Chronologically it overlaps and then follows on from the earlier novel, which ends just when war is declared. *Diamonds* begins a year earlier, in August 1913, during the annual fair or *kermis* in Antwerp. It spans the outbreak of war, with the Berman family's flight to London in October 1914, continuing until Jeannette's wedding, in the early spring of 1915, and the events of the following months. There is then a gap of three years, until Passover 1917. The final chapter follows Berman back to Antwerp, after peace is declared.

The outer framework and many of the scenes and characters, draw strongly on the author's own fate from 1914 onwards. But whereas *Deborah* had a female protagonist, whose early life replicated very closely the events of Kreitman's own, here the central character is a very ambivalent, and ultimately unsympathetic, male figure. The reader empathised with Deborah because of her plight and also, as a result of the restricted narrative perspective, the characters and events were seen exclusively through her eyes. Here, by contrast, the narrative perspective is fragmented: the omniscient narrator of *Diamonds* allows the reader access to the thoughts and feelings, not only of Gedaliah Berman, but of all the main characters, and permits us to eavesdrop on an array of different conversations and events. The multiple perspectives give rise to a panoramic and episodic novel. Kreitman, perhaps displeased with the reception of *Der sheydim-tants* as totally autobiographical, and possibly fearful of accusations of libel, stressed the fictitious nature of all the characters.

These invented characters are however situated in clearly recognisable and vividly depicted geographical locations and an accurate historical context. The author's own experience of Antwerp and London, coupled with her sharp perception, allow her to recreate vivid Antwerp scenes: the Bourse, the annual *kermis*, the streets and parks, the Jewish district and other recognisable locations. The atmosphere of London during the First World War is also wonderfully captured: Jewish Whitechapel, Hatton Garden, conversations in cafés and on damp and foggy streets, and the hubbub at Speakers' Corner.

No less authentic is the depiction of the political and historical reality of the period. The fusion of the lives of fictional figures with real events is, of course, the hallmark of the historical novel, and here Kreitman exploits the genre with great success. With a sure hand she evokes well-known situations: Antwerp as a refuge for Jews avoiding conscription into the Tsarist army, the political activities of Jewish socialists, the exclusion of Jews from trade unions, the progress towards war, the bombardment and evacuation of Antwerp, the flight of the refugees from Antwerp, and the activity of Mrs Pankhurst and the suffragettes in London. The historical material is interwoven with the lives of her fictional characters and often made vivid through sharply observed vignettes: scenes of argument and speculation in the streets, for instance, between Germans and Belgians, and Russian and Austrian Jews; the sudden enmity, on the outbreak of war, between ethnic groups who had previously co-existed peacefully.

Particularly convincing is Kreitman's recreation of experiences, which affected her most strongly: for instance the everyday life of Jewish refugees in temporary reception centres in London. Kreitman evokes these scenes with a light but sardonic touch, depicting the social hierarchies which still obtained, reinforced through memorable figures like the "potato king" and his consort, the snobbish "old maid" who is in charge of distributing old clothes to the refugees, and the condescension of members of the assimilated Anglo-Jewish community who run the establishments, including Frau Zederbaum, the pillar of the Jewish charity organisation, who lectures the assembled refugees on the iniquity of discarding a burnt milk pan. The humiliations suffered by the refugees, and the differential treatment of affluent and poor immigrants, are woven into the narrative to great satirical effect.

The novel has a large array of characters, who fall into three separate but connected, categories. The primary group comprises the central figure of Berman and those on whose lives he exerts an immediate influence: the other members of his family, and the couple Leybesh and Gitele. Then there are secondary characters, whose lives revolve around the main protagonists: diamond merchants and brokers, cleavers and polishers, Reb Beynish the matchmaker, Dovid's friend Jules, Jeannette's bohemian boyfriend, and the officials of the

Jewish charity organisations in Rotterdam and London. Thirdly, a host of figures flit across the scene, appearing only once, for an instant, either described by the omniscient narrator or observed through the eyes of one of the main characters, in the street, a park, a synagogue or a factory. They are, however, portrayed with loving attention to their physical appearance, their clothes and gestures, and are drawn with Kreitman's wry touch. Although these figures play no actual role in the development of the plot, they should not be regarded as superfluous to the fabric of the novel. On the contrary, these little snapshots of individuals, encountered by chance, provide rich colour, creating an impression of the vibrancy of real lives being led in the cities they inhabit, Antwerp and London. They also demonstrate Kreitman's delight in the panorama of ordinary life. Some of the characters and scenes in *Diamonds* have a distinctly Dickensian flavour: one good example is the personality and household of Mr Marks, with whom Leybesh lodges for a time in London. The fact that she translated *A Christmas Carol*, suggests that Kreitman was familiar with Dickens' work, and he may well have influenced her as a writer.

As with Dickens, it is often the attention to small details, in the vignettes of people and scenes, which subtly convey Kreitman's social consciousness and humanity - always present in her work. Through Berman's eyes we survey the Antwerp mothers out walking in the streets, some pushing elegant prams with lace pillows and plump babies, others with dilapidated prams, and babies with thin, wrinkled faces. There are the hairdressers in the East End of London, working till late, on the eve of Yom Kippur, because the poor women can never be sure, till the last minute, that they will have enough money to have their wigs washed and curled. We catch a glimpse of women at a London pawnbroker's trying to sell their threadbare bedding, feverishly laughing at the owner's joke at another's expense, in a desperate attempt to ingratiate themselves with him. The diamond cleavers, during a slack period, wear their best clothes on weekdays in an attempt to hide their poverty. Similarly the poorer refugees, for whom the move to London actually offers the hope of betterment, nevertheless join their more affluent travelling companions in bemoaning the loss of lucrative livelihoods in Antwerp, in order that their indigent state should not become apparent. In these and many other moments in the novel, Kreitman's understanding of the disadvantaged and vulnerable, and their essential human dignity, emerges strongly.

The most complex psychological portrait, the person around whom this human panorama revolves, is Gedaliah Berman, a most ambivalent figure. He is ruthless, rapacious, morally unscrupulous in his business dealings, and harsh and vindictive to his wife and son Dovid, making them into the scapegoats for his own failures and disappointments. He begrudges other dealers their successes, even when these do not adversely affect his own career. In business and family life he manipulates others for his own ends, and often, sadistically, for the pure pleasure of doing so. He treats Rochl with gratuitous cruelty, and the only family member to whom he shows affection is his daughter Jeannette, and here there are strong hints of feelings, which are more than fatherly. Though outwardly a pious Jew, his behaviour falls short of the moral standards of a good Jewish life. He handles stolen goods, and admits to himself that his reason for withstanding the temptation to have a sexual liaison with his maidservant is that it would generate gossip, which would be bad for business, rather than any moral scruples, or consideration for his wife.

If Berman were simply a monster, he would be less interesting. Kreitman's narrative strategy allows us, however, if not to empathise fully with him, at least to gain insight into the complexities of his personality. We see that he is a man tormented by guilt and self-doubt, and the long flashback in chapter 11 very convincingly suggests the psychological background to his later development. The catalyst for this flashback, in which Berman remembers the details of his unhappy childhood, is the arrival of his father from Poland. Significantly, Berman has failed to answer his father's letter, and forgotten about the old man's impending arrival. The reunion with his father revives in him all the suppressed memories of an impoverished and dysfunctional family, whereby the stigmatisation and isolation he suffered as a child, his alienation from his mother, who was shunned by many in the village as a witch and his father's psychosomatic paralysis, which caused him to lie in bed for eight years, are all understood by the

22

reader as traumatic circumstances, which contributed to the man Berman later became. Only through great determination was he able to overcome the legacy of his childhood and turn himself into a successful businessman, but he has never escaped from his past, and much of his ruthlessness can be attributed to the fragility of his sense of identity. The paralysis of his father, with its connotations of impotence, was brought on as an escape from his impossible situation and the relentless demands of his wife. Berman's parents' unhappy relationship may have shaped his own later understanding of the relationship between the sexes, and of what constitutes a real man: he is compelled to master women, and is, perhaps, subconsciously punishing Rochl, in order to purge the bitterness he still feels against his mother. Berman's overreaction to Dovid's failure can be understood in the light of the effect on him of his own father's inability to be a man and a provider.

The arrival on the scene of the old father, Reb Chaim Yoysef, brings into sharp focus two related themes, which underlie the novel: the collision of two worlds and the situation of the uprooted, Eastern European, Jewish immigrant in Western society. Chaim Yoysef and his fellow Hassidim in the two *shtiblekh*, prayer houses, he visits, represent the old, intact world of Jewish belief and culture. Suddenly thrust into the non-Jewish world and the modernity of the city of Antwerp, they are cast adrift in a society with different *mores* and values. As we see, from the end of the novel, Berman's father ultimately takes a stand. His refusal to have a tombstone purchased with the tainted money from diamonds, symbolises his rejection of his son's way of life in this modern secular society. Gedaliah Berman straddles these two worlds, which contributes to his insecure sense of identity: his consciousness and formative experiences are rooted in the old world, but he is endeavouring to carve out an identity for himself in the modern, commercial city. The two different sets of values are at war within him.

Again and again these tensions which underlie Jewish life in Antwerp are reinforced in the little thumbnail sketches of fleetingly observed characters. For example, the old woman, newly arrived from her *shtetl*, who used to weep when she saw her daughter and son-in-law working on *Shabbes*, the Jewish Sabbath, but who has now got used to amusing the grandchild, so that the parents can work undisturbed. In this little vignette, the combination of the *Shabbes* candles, which have been lit and blessed, and the whirring sewing machines, symbolise the uneasy co-existence of the two worlds.

Berman's children, born and brought up in Antwerp, have tried to cast off this legacy. Dovid has shaved his beard and no longer prays. We see his embarrassment when his pious diamond cleaver friend asks him if he has already said his afternoon prayers. Jeannette embraces the life of leisure and fashion, reading French novels, shopping for elegant clothes, and, later, mingling in bohemian and artistic circles, in London. In reality, however, they have not found a true identity or succeeded in freeing themselves from their domineering father. Only Jacques, the youngest, seems relatively unscathed.

It is significant that the two male members of Berman's family, Dovid and Jacques, do, finally, manage to break free, and create new lives for themselves, whereas the two women, Jeannette and her mother, do not. Jeannette's situation most closely resembles that of Deborah in the earlier novel, both girls submitting, albeit for very different reasons, to arranged marriages with men who are far from being ideal partners. In both novels the inappropriateness of the marriage is symbolised by a grotesque and painful incident at the wedding ceremony.

After the marriage and her abortion, Jeannette succumbs to a life of aimless indolence, idling at home all day in her dressing gown, playing like a petulant child with her maid and her little dog as if they were both toys. Her exuberant personality is turned into a grotesque caricature of itself, with clear signs of hysteria and a possible mental breakdown. At the end of the novel, this seems to have been either averted or overcome – we do not know what has happened in the intervening period – and she has obviously taken on the role of a fashionable, society lady.

Rochl is dominated by, and in fear of, her husband. Despite his having been in love with her, when they were both children and his passionate courting of her, when he first arrived in Antwerp, Berman's conception of the relationship between husband and wife is entirely self-centred. This emerges clearly in the comment by the narrator at the end of chapter 11: "He loved Rochl, who was very beautiful, and because of her, he always ate in the same restaurant, until one fine morning, he took her away from her aunt's pots and pans, married her and set her up in her own kitchen, so that she should cook good meals, as only she could, for him, instead of for the general public."

We see Rochl as a gentle and kindly woman, whose love for her son particularly knows no bounds, but her children, Dovid included, seem to show little real affection for her. The narrator's comment in the final chapter, that Dovid had loved his mother very much, seems almost ironic, in view of his apparent indifference to her during her life. The only person with whom she develops a warm and close relationship is Berman's father: both of them are alone in a hostile environment.

One of Kreitman's characteristic techniques is to invest moments of extreme pain with elements of the grotesque, as in the two weddings, already mentioned. She does this superbly in the macabre scene of Rochl's death, which is not without elements of black comedy. Like her life with Berman, even her death is characterised by misunderstanding and lack of communication. The letter which causes her heart attack is, in fact, just a business note about Berman's diamond dealings, so that ultimately her death, like her life, is bound up with the cold, glittering stones.

As in her earlier novel, Kreitman empathises with her female protagonists, not only in her depiction of the fates of Jeannette and Rochl, but in the glimpses of other female figures and their lives throughout the novel, and it is in her consideration of women's lives that she is at her most daring as a writer. In the early part of the 20th century, women writers, particularly in Weimar Germany, were using fiction as a forum for discussing issues of women's liberation: female sexuality, free love, contraception and abortion. In her presentation of all these issues, Kreitman proves herself worthy of inclusion in this category of early feminist writers.

A frank treatment of the taboo topic of female sexuality is infrequent in Yiddish literature. In Isaac Bashevis Singer's novel *Der sotn in Goray* (Satan in Goray), published in 1935, female sexuality, seen from the male viewpoint, is dark, dangerous and tinged with madness, whereas Kreitman depicts Gitele's passionate relationship with

Dovid from a woman's point of view. She describes Gitele's agonised longing for Dovid as she lies in bed in the refugee quarters in London, conveying the young woman's physical desire with tenderness and sensuality and showing it to be a natural female impulse. Gitele's feelings of guilt are not to do with her sexual urges but with her betrayal of Leybesh.

Kreitman's modernity is also seen in the portrayal of Jeannette's affair with Ronald, and the resulting pregnancy. She is, in fact, too daring for the taste of Morris Mayer, the editor of the London Yiddish paper *Di tsayt / The Jewish Times,* who, in his otherwise positive review of the novel, demurred that *"two* sinful love affairs is too much for one Yiddish novel."

Most impressively for a female Jewish writer of that time, she touches on the issue of women's right to control their own reproduction, as in the brief conversation between Jeannette and other married women in chapter 28. The implication that Jewish wives employed stratagems to prevent unwanted conception is very much at odds with traditional Jewish thinking - that women's primary responsibility was the production of children, and contraception and abortion were theoretically out of the question. In the treatment of the abortion issue, Kreitman does not explicitly campaign for legalisation, but in her sympathetic consideration, not only of Jeannette's situation, but also of the desperate economic consequences of unwanted pregnancy for working-class girls like Anneke and Jeannette's maid, we see to what extent she had broken free of the social and religious mores with which she grew up.

Kreitman presents a bleak picture of human nature. With very few exceptions, the central and peripheral characters, both Jewish and non-Jewish, are neither happy and fulfilled themselves, nor willing to show kindness to others. It is a dog-eat-dog society, where enmity and suspicion, rather than fairness and generosity, govern human relationships. Berman does not seem to have gained a great deal of self-awareness through his experiences. At the end of the novel he is ready to rebuild his life in Antwerp, and he gleefully plans to suggest to Gitele that she should get a divorce from Leybesh, who is in the fledgling Soviet Union, and marry him. Without hesitation he writes to the matchmaker, the symbol of the old order. Berman's powers of self-delusion are still so intact, that he does not conceive of the possibility that even the lure of diamonds might not suffice to persuade Gitele to marry a man old enough to be her father, from whom she has received harsh treatment in the past. Berman, it seems, has not moved on since the beginning of the novel. The ending is ambiguous. The reader must decide whether the letter from his father has at last opened Berman's eyes to the selfishness and dishonesty of his life and will lead him to some kind of inner peace, or whether he will remain alone and self-deluded.

Esther Kreitman is unusual among Yiddish female writers in having turned to the genre of the novel. The majority wrote poetry and memoirs. Her achievement in this work is to have depicted a Jewish family at a crucial turning point between tradition and modernity, setting it in the wider European context and convincingly linking the fate of the characters to the cataclysmic events of the First World War and its aftermath. Starting from the events of her own life, she has transcended the more immediate, personal and Jewish concerns, to create a modern novel of penetrating, psychological insight in a convincingly depicted historical and social milieu. Though her oeuvre is small, its scope does warrant Clive Sinclair's judgement that Esther Kreitman was "a writer of distinction."

Heather Valencia
Stirling, January 2010

Heather Valencia is an Honorary Research Fellow at the University of Stirling where she was a lecturer in German language and literature. She began studying Yiddish in the early 1980s, wrote her PhD thesis on the poetry of Abraham Sutzkever, since when she has edited and translated several Yiddish works into English and written numerous articles on Yiddish culture. She edited a bilingual edition of the London Yiddish play *Der kenig fun Lampeduse/The King of Lampedusa* (2003), produced an anthology of Yiddish literature for students entitled *Mit groys fargenign/With Great Pleasure* (2003) and translated stories by Lamed Shapiro in the collection *The Cross and other Jewish Stories* (2007).

A Note on the Translation

Yiddish was Esther Kreitman's mother tongue. It was the primary language spoken by the Ashkenazi Jews of central and eastern Europe till the Holocaust. Like English, Yiddish is a fusion language, which evolved from the medieval German of the Rhineland, where Jews settled from about the tenth century on. The language is written in Hebrew script and has a strong Hebrew component. It has developed over the last thousand years, incorporating many elements from Russian and Polish as its speakers migrated to Eastern Europe from the fourteenth century.

Esther Kreitman's Yiddish style is decorative and colourful, with a plethora of adjectives and a tendency towards rhetorical, "flowery" language. Moreover, like many other Yiddish writers, she did not have access to editors, who could have pruned some of the excesses of her prose, and weeded out inconsistencies or repetitive passages. This places the translator and editors in a dilemma, in that they must reconcile faithfulness to the author with the production of a version which reads well in English, so that the reader is not prevented from enjoying the novel by stylistic irritations. With the help of the editors, David Paul and Sylvia Paskin, I have endeavoured to walk this tightrope; we have kept as faithfully to Kreitman's text as possible, but occasional apparent inconsistencies or *non sequiturs* have been removed or explained. A few repetitive or superfluous descriptions, which slow down the flow of the narrative, have been slightly altered or shortened. Very occasionally, we have reorganised sentences or paragraphs, to give them a more logical order. In this way we have aimed to create an English version that does justice to Esther Kreitman.

Flemish names and expressions in the original text have usually been retained in the translation, and foreign-language terms in the original have been italicised, though some words in the translation are italicised for emphasis. Yiddish names and phrases have usually been transliterated according to the recommended transliteration of the YIVO Institute for Jewish Research, unless they have familiar forms in English, (e.g. Gedaliah instead of Gedalye). Yiddish, or Hebrew religious terms have been generally translated, unless they are normally used in their original form by English-speaking Jews (expressions, for example, such as *Shabbes*, *shochet*, *mezuzah*, *tefillin* etc). In this case they have been italicised, and given their familiar English spelling, rather than the YIVO transliteration. These and other terms explained in the glossary are denoted by an asterisk in the text.

All the characters in this novel are entirely fictitious
Esther Kreitman

Chapter 1

None of Berman's people came to his office in Pelikaanstraat that day. There was no one clutching small paper parcels of diamonds and smiling ingratiatingly at the frosted glass door that led from the long, dark corridor into Berman's Holy of Holies. The office was shut.

In the homes of the diamond cutters, the machines were silent, covered up like corpses. The women threw curtains or aprons over them, so that they didn't have to look at the cold, functional machines. At busy times, they sucked the lifeblood out of their husbands and sons, and, at slack times, they caused terrible tension in the household, when hunger and deprivation threatened.

Berman paced about agitatedly in his house, grumbling to himself. It was always the same. If there was some kind of holiday in the middle of the week, he would be overcome by a mood of black fury, which he was unable to shake off. Berman hated holidays, especially those Christian holidays, which had nothing to do with him. He was so used to his daily routine. In the early morning, Anneke, the maid-servant, would bring in his viscous red medicine, and, after taking it, he would lick his lips, as if it had been a glass of fine wine. Then, having piously said his morning prayers, he would stretch himself up to his full height, crack his smooth, olive-skinned fingers and admire himself in the long polished mirror, which stood between the windows. He was indeed a fine figure of a man, with a well-combed, neatly parted beard, a thick, silky moustache and intelligent, piercing black eyes. Anneke would be waiting for him in the corridor, holding a brush, in order to remove the nonexistent fluff from his best black overcoat with its elegant velvet collar; he would take a last look in the mirror of the coat stand in the spacious hallway. He then stepped through the polished white front door, which Anneke held open for him, and walked to work.

It is the same routine every morning: as soon as he opens the door of the anteroom to his office, about two dozen yes men surround him, with inane smiles of false humility on their faces, grabbing the "good morning" out of each other's mouths, so that they can be the first to speak to Berman.

Berman knows that they all hate him like the plague, but, nevertheless, he always gives the best work to those who manage the best smiles. "The poor can't afford to be proud," he says to himself. All the same, in his heart of hearts, he is annoyed with himself, because, even though he doesn't like the Galician Jews, he always gives them his best diamonds. He tries to justify it to himself: "I hate paupers who put on airs!" He spits out the word "paupers", and starts poking around with his tweezers, among the heaps of newly delivered diamonds, which look like small lumps of dried mud.

Berman carries on poking around until the men's hearts begin to sink and nervous blotches appear on their cheeks. Then he starts peering at the stones; he stares and stares, and if he doesn't find any blemish, if the stones have not been badly shaped by the cutter, he starts weighing them on his scales. Good, they haven't lost too much weight either. He pushes them to one side. Sometimes, he makes one heap out of all the smaller piles. Sometimes, he keeps the piles separate from each other, just as he keeps himself distant from the workers. Finally, he wraps up batches of rough diamonds in the little *brivkes*, or parcel papers. As a matter of course he warns the cutters to be careful the stones don't lose too much in the cutting. Then he holds out one parcel in the general direction of the crowd, who immediately rush forward like hens when the farmer scatters crumbs. Berman, however, doesn't let anyone just grab the package. His laughing black eyes flash, and he calls out: "Friedman!"

Little Friedman rushes up so fast that he almost lands on Berman's desk. The others stand there with outstretched hands. Eventually they are all crowding back down the narrow corridor, feeling that a weight has been lifted off their shoulders. "Thank God, got some work again!" they say with relief, although they know very well that tomorrow, and the day after, the whole procedure will be repeated. But it can't be helped and they are used to it.

Having got rid of the workers, Berman prepares himself to receive the brokers, whom he has sent out with his merchandise - his polished diamonds. He rubs his hands with pleasure. They appear one after the other. Berman greets them individually, with a special word for each one:

"Do sit down, Herr Rosenbaum! *Nu*, how are you, Herr Rosenbaum?", or: "Well, had any luck? No? What, still nothing? I beg you, Hatskelevitsh, don't play games with me. So? You really mean it? That's a fat lot of good to me!"

Berman enjoys hearing the brokers making flowery speeches, to persuade him to lower the price, so that it will be easier to sell the goods. He puts on a pensive air, his long nose gleaming and his black eyes smiling, and combs his beard with his fingers. The luckless brokers are swearing by their beards and side-locks, by the lives of their wives and children, by God Himself, but Berman just cuts them off abruptly, saying there is no question of that at all, and calls Rosenbaum back in:

"Tell me, Herr Rosenbaum, you've already made some sales, haven't you? That's very good! And at a good price, you say? Excellent! That's what I like to hear. What?! Is *that* what you call a good price?"

"Listen, Herr Berman, if you're not happy with that, I'll take the goods back. They weren't all that keen to have them anyway."

Berman is taken aback, but he hides it with an ironic smile on his ruddy lips, speaking with an air of indifference:

"You're just making excuses, Herr Rosenbaum! With goods like mine I don't need, God forbid, to beg."

And he puts on his coat as a sign that he has to go to the Bourse immediately, and has no time to waste on nonsense. Rosenbaum accompanies him. He gesticulates all the way there, trying to persuade Berman that if he doesn't accept the price that has been offered, he will never be able to make such a good deal again.

"Huh!" replies Berman.

In the Bourse the noise and clamour are in full swing.

"Herr Berman, a parcel of blue-white?"

"I have some fine stones for you, Herr Berman, you've never seen the like of them. Fine goods, eh? I should have such luck!"

"Herr Berman!"

But Berman doesn't raise his eyes. Here, too, he sits poking with his tweezers. He is so absorbed in his work that you would imagine he would need at least twenty-six hours in every day, just to sort out his piles of diamonds.

This is Berman's normal routine. "And now, out of the blue, a holiday! And a holiday like that, too! *Oy, oy*!

The Flemish people came out into the streets every year at this time, to celebrate their annual *kermis* under the open sky. Every town and remote village kept this national holiday, but in Antwerp the festivities were greater than anywhere else. People from the nearby villages set out over the flat, sunny fields. Dressed in their best clothes, lighthearted groups poured along the highways and byways: over fragrant, mown grass in the bright sunlight, past golden sheaves of corn and stacks of still-damp hay. Old grandmothers were swaying along in little carts, their wrinkled faces bathed in sunshine, a smile in every wrinkle. The young people simply danced into town.

Hardly anyone, apart from old or sick people, stayed at home. And if a dilatory Antwerp housewife had not yet finished scrubbing the grey flagstones in front of her house, she hastily swept away the soapy water with her stiff brush, and poured the last pails of water over them, at great speed, her wooden clogs paddling about in the wetness, like little boats, and tapping to the rhythm of her sweeping. Half an hour later, she was in the street, dressed up to celebrate the holiday.

Outside the cafés, on wicker chairs at green painted tables, stocky, red-faced Flemish men and women, both old and middle-aged, sat enjoying a glass of foaming beer. Infected by the gaiety of the young people, they joined in the singing of the popular Flemish song:

"*Oo-la-la!*
In het park van de nachtegaal
Ooooo-laaaa-laaaa!"*

The girls' coloured dresses dazzled the eye, and their ringing laughter delighted the ear. They threw bold, flirtatious glances and dimpled smiles, skilfully catching the eyes of the boys, and getting answering glances. The boys danced, played on mouth organs, strolled around among shiny automobiles, embracing and kissing different girls. Flags fluttered, ribbons streamed out, red, black and yellow.

Even the Bourse and the Diamond Club were closed, on account of the holiday. Rich Jewish diamond merchants had travelled abroad to the watering places. The middle classes had gone to Spa,* and the minor traders and brokers, who traded in diamond powder and *bakvuils* celebrated the Belgian holiday in Antwerp.

Berman was the only person who took no interest in the *kermis*. The singing in the street grated on his ears like the buzzing of an annoying fly. If he covered his ears with his hands, the muffled hum got on his nerves even more. He paced back and forth on the dark blue carpet of his dining room, which absorbed his footsteps and betrayed nothing. But his face spoke volumes. Every wrinkle told its story.

Suddenly, he stopped pacing about, and surveyed the furnishings, as if seeing them for the first time. The heavy silver pieces on the oak sideboard gleamed brightly at him. From the grandfather clock in the corner, came a calm, regular ticking. The padded, leather chairs stood solidly, and at ease, around the heavy table. A thin cobweb, which, in such a spotless room, you would only notice on a very bright sunny day, stretched from the window to the mirror, which hung above the white marble mantelpiece. The room looked affluent, tranquil and harmonious.

"Huh! I've wasted my money on that no-good son of mine! It was pointless to let him study ... thought he should get an education ... should be able to do something that would stand him in good stead. And what's the result? Nothing! Why have I let these devils of sons grow up? I should have buried them at birth!" Berman had apparently forgotten that only *one* of his two sons, Dovid, was a "devil". "I thought I'd take him into the Bourse and make him a member. I'd introduce him to merchants; he'd start trading, work his way up, eventually make a rich marriage, and so forth. Isn't that, what you'd expect? He's a good-looking, well-educated lad after all. And to marry into the Berman family is quite something! And with the big dowry he'd get, we could work as partners, and expand the business. You can't entrust a fortune to a novice." Berman's face broke into a smile, and he spread his hands, as if to measure the exact area, that the dowry would fill.

35

They would buy the largest parcels of diamonds; the very best merchandise. The biggest stones would fall into their hands. The most important merchants would regard it as an honour if Berman showed them a tiny parcel of blue-white. He wouldn't give the time of day to the small fry.

Suddenly, he realised that he was dreaming, and gave himself a shake; his face darkened in anger and shame. Why on earth was he indulging in these fantasies?

"I'll tear him out, root and branch, the good-for-nothing! I'll chase him away like a dog. Away, out of my sight!"

The idea of chasing his son away soothed his nerves a little. He paced back and forth more calmly, concentrating on keeping the anger from rising up again inside him.

Chapter 2

A knock on the door roused Berman from his gloomy thoughts. He started straightening the chairs round the table, even though they were already straight. He smoothed down his square, silken skullcap, combed his beard with his fingers, and called out in French: "*Entrez!*"

"Ah, it's you, Herr Shapiro! So pleased to see you!" he said, speaking elegant German, as he always did with business associates. He pulled out a heavy leather chair for his guest, and sat down at the top of the table.

"How are you, Herr Shapiro? Delighted to see you!"

Shapiro was a tubby little man with a black beard, trimmed into a neat, round shape. The whiteness of his plump face accentuated the blackness of the beard. He sat down, took out his spectacles, rubbed them with a piece of yellow chamois leather, held them up and examined them minutely, to see if they were properly clean. Then he set them on his nose with his podgy, white hand. His alert eyes took in everything in the room, and he quickly noticed that Berman was not in a good mood. "Aha! He's probably had another scene with that son of his. He thinks no one notices what's going on. Wait till I tell him the news, that'll really be the last straw!" He straightened his glasses and waited for Berman to begin.

"Well, how are things, Herr Shapiro?"

"Not bad, thank you. Thank God, one makes a living! And how are things with you, Herr Berman? Been doing good business?"

Berman looked sharply at Shapiro and gave a little sigh.

"No, unfortunately I've done no business at all! How can you do business when everyone has gone away. Damn these holidays!"

"You're absolutely right" agreed Shapiro, adding with a sly smile: "Have you heard the latest news, Herr Berman?"

"What latest news? No, I haven't heard any news at all."

"Oh, you haven't heard that Tsvaygnboym has made a match for his son?"

Berman trembled, and paled slightly. Shapiro looked at him over his glasses, enjoying his discomfort.

"*Azoy*? With Lieberman's daughter?" In his agitation Berman spoke Yiddish, instead of German.

"Yes indeed. And they *say* the bride is worth half a million francs. But I don't really believe that," said Shapiro consolingly.

Berman gave no answer, but he thought to himself that if Dovid were to appear at this moment, he would roast him alive. He started pulling at the fringes of the red plush tablecloth, then tapped on the table with his forefinger; but since the tablecloth muffled the sound, he started on the fringes again.

"So there you are!" continued Shapiro. "What a piece of luck for Tsvaygnboym. From now on he'll not have to worry about finding the money to buy diamonds. Heh, heh, heh!" And he gave a little laugh, which went right through Berman, grating on his ears, and jangling his nerves. He would have liked to have taken the roly-poly little man and thrown him down the stairs.

"Mind you, they say that the bride ..." began Berman, about to remind Shapiro that Lieberman's daughter had a slight deformity. But Shapiro didn't let him finish.

"*Ach*, people say all sorts of things when they are envious. It's always the same!"

Berman knew that if this went on much longer he would make a fool of himself. To stifle his anger, which was now directed more against Shapiro than Dovid, he called his wife:

"Rosa, have some refreshments served."

His wife Rochl, who was only called Rosa in front of important visitors, took off her apron, turned down the gas in the oven, where half a side of veal was roasting, and came into the dining room, with flushed cheeks.

"The maid's gone out. These holidays are *such* a nuisance!" she said, excusing herself to Shapiro for bringing in the refreshments herself. Shapiro stood up like a gallant gentleman and made a peculiar bow:

"*Guten Tag*, Madame Berman!"

"*A gutn tog, a gut yor!*" answered Rochl, speaking simple Yiddish in her confusion. She sat down at the table with them and smoothed her wig, which had been specially coiffeured for the holiday. She didn't know what to do next. Noticing that her husband was seething with suppressed rage, a situation very familiar to her, her heart began pounding. She prayed silently, begging God to spare her any embarrassment, by making Berman control his anger until Shapiro had left.

"Do take something, Herr Shapiro!"

"*Ach*, it *really* wasn't necessary. You shouldn't have gone to such trouble," said Shapiro, his darting eyes picking out the finest bunch of juicy, black grapes in the dish. He plucked at the grapes and told her the news about the engagement. Rochl blanched. She glanced at her husband and her heart sank. Shapiro's eyes glittered. He fixed his burning gaze on Berman, who sat rooted to the spot, staring into the distance. His thick, black eyebrows gave him the appearance of a wild man. He seemed transfixed, and with his large hand he pulled at the flesh of his own neck.

At last Shapiro got up to go.

"Well, don't forget, Herr Berman, I've got goods for you!"

This roused Berman from his stupor. He stood up, tried to smile, and asked Shapiro why he was in such a hurry, thinking all the time that it would serve him right, that Hungarian rogue, if he fell, and broke his arms and legs, on the way home.

His feelings of jealousy and rage at the news of the match, as well as shame at his weakness in letting Shapiro see his anguish, made Berman want to vent his frustration on someone. He looked round for Rochl, but she had gone downstairs with Shapiro and left the house. She went to the shop across the road to buy something she didn't need. When she realised that there was no way of avoiding the storm, she slipped softly back into the house. She peered through the keyhole of the dining room, her heart pounding. But her eyes lit up at what she saw; she could hardly believe her luck: Berman was sitting with his head on the table, both arms under his beard, snoring.

"Thank God for that!" she sighed with relief, and went into the kitchen. When she opened the heavy cast-iron door of the oven, a blast of heat reddened her face, and a delicious smell met her nostrils.

The meat had only started to burn on one side, and the rest was brown and juicy. "*Some* people get pleasure from their children," she thought, as she wiped the plates and prepared the dinner, remembering that her husband would probably wake up soon, and, if not, she would have to waken him for his meal. "If only he hadn't had the mad idea that Dovid should marry that ugly creature! A handsome lad like my Dovidl, and her, a cripple, God forgive me for saying it! And now that Hungarian Don Juan, that Shapiro, comes along to add to my problems. He's not fussy whether they're old or young, and there are some old maids who would have him."

From the hall came the sound of singing:

"*Oo-la-la!*
In het park van de nachtegaal
Oooo-laaa-laaaaa!"

Their daughter Jeannette ran up the stairs three at a time.

"Oh my God, she'll waken her father." Rochl wanted him to carry on sleeping, but Jeannette's singing did, indeed, waken him. Berman stood up, gave a huge yawn, rubbed his right leg, which had got stiff during his nap, stretched, and came to the kitchen door, where he stood for a few moments, motionless. Then he came to, crossed the threshold, washed his hands and face, dried them on a white towel, and looked in the mirror over the sink. Rochl watched his every move, and finally ventured to ask:

"Gedaliah, shall we eat?"

He didn't answer. That was the sign for the table to be laid.

"Jeannette darling, give me a hand, skip into the dining room, and set out the cutlery."

Jeannette made a face, but then she gave in, took a corner of her dress between her fingers and literally skipped into the dining room.

The clatter of dropped silverware and the sound of girlish laughter brought some life into the household. Jeannette came back into the kitchen, threw herself into the sagging armchair and carried on giggling. She had left the dropped cutlery on the dining room floor, and Rochl went and bent down with a sigh to pick it up.

The three of them sat at table, toying with their knives and forks. No one said a word. Jeannette knew that her father did not like anyone to talk at table. "No conversation at mealtimes," he always said. When they had finished, she went over to her father and took his head in her dainty hands. Berman trembled. The soft warmth of her young hands did him good. She kissed his beard, his moustache and his hairy cheeks.

"Promise you won't be cross, dearest Papa, if Mama comes with me to the Keyserlei?* I'm going anyway, and it would be nice if she came too. You don't mind, do you? You should really come too, it's great fun. Even the pious Hassidim* are out of doors today, winking at the girls. You should really come and see it."

"Listen to the girl! She doesn't know what she's talking about. Hassidim, winking at the girls? Fine sort of Hassidim!"

"What does she know? She thinks every man with a beard is a Hassid," said Rochl.

"Who are these Hassidim of yours, then?" asked Berman absent-mindedly.

"You see, Mama, I knew Papa would say yes. He's *such* a good Papa. *Dearest* Papa!" And Jeannette rewarded her father with a dazzling smile, just like she gave her young admirers.

"What do you say, Gedaliah, shall I go?"

"Oh well, I suppose even an old horse deserves a holiday!"

That meant Rochl could go.

Jeannette flew down the stairs. Her mother, holding onto the banister, followed her more slowly. She stole a look in the mirror of the coat stand, and her heart beat faster, as she thought, fleetingly, of the Hungarian Don Juan.

The youngest of her children, twelve-year-old Jacques, arrived, just as they were leaving the house.

"Jacques, you can eat in the kitchen, do you understand? Don't go in to Papa, he's a bit on edge. And for goodness sake, don't make a noise. Do you hear?"

"All right, I hear you." Jacques leapt up the stairs, like a hare.

The Keyserlei was still buzzing with activity. You couldn't find an empty seat at a coffeehouse table, for love nor money. The sun was scorching, and in the space of a couple of hours, women in low-cut dresses had red, sunburned chests. The air stank of roast pork, beer

41

and baked potatoes. Oceans of beer had been poured down thirsty throats. Boys were singing bawdy songs and girls were throwing themselves into their arms. They danced on the pavements and in the middle of the street. The older people at the tables, kept time to the music with empty beer glasses on tin trays, and, as they grew tipsy, they got daring enough to sing along, hoarsely:

"*Ooo-laaaa-laaa!*"

The Jewish women, all dressed up and wearing their best wigs, remained sober, but they joined in the fun with everyone else, laughing at the drunks. Jewish boys and girls walked openly, arm-in-arm, in front of all the rich women of Antwerp, not caring if they were gossiped about.

Rochl kept meeting acquaintances. "Well, what do you think of those *shnorrers*,* forgive me for the expression! Those Tsvaygnboyms, and Lieberman's daughter. It's unheard of – but such a piece of luck for them!" The women's words cast a shadow over Rochl's day. At the same time, she remembered that Dovid still hadn't appeared. Her main reason for coming out was the hope that she would meet him; otherwise, she told herself, she'd rather have gone to bed. It was now three or four days since they'd seen or heard anything of him, despite the fact that she had searched everywhere for him. God knows what had happened to him. And the atmosphere at home was worse than the fires of hell.

"Yes indeed, Frau Berman, better people than the Tsvaygnboyms wouldn't be ashamed of such a stroke of luck!"

"Yes indeed," sighed mothers of grown-up sons: "Well, may they only have good fortune!" They shook their heads with their newly coiffeured wigs, and, forgetting that they were walking in the crowded festive streets, had to scatter like hens when drunken lads, pushing their way through the crowds, elbowed and shoved them.

A filthy-looking boy grabbed Rochl round the waist. She nearly died of shock when he kissed her on the lips. "Pfui! Pfui!" She tried to spit out the taste of beer and pork, which the boy had left in her mouth. "Brrr!" Rochl shivered, and couldn't understand why, just at that moment, the image of that Hungarian rogue, Shapiro, flashed into her mind.

Chapter 3

In Somersstraat, above a second-hand bicycle shop, a Gentile woman in a blonde wig sat all day, scratching her bald head with a skewer, showering curses on the "idiots" on the second floor, a young Jewish couple, who came from the same Polish *shtetl** as the Bermans.

The two of them had come separately to Antwerp, and for very different reasons. The young man, Leybesh Bruckner, who back in the old country had been a brush-maker by trade, was a tall, healthy, brawny fellow, with straggly, fair hair like a Gentile, and clear, grey-ish-blue eyes and a freckled face. Back in the *shtetl*, the other Jews had not been very keen on him. No matter how affably he smiled at them, there was always someone who crossed the road in order to avoid him. They didn't answer his "Good morning", because they knew that the police had an eye on him. They didn't exactly know why. They did know, however, that it was simpler not to have anything to do with him.

"Did you hear that they arrested 'the prophet' yesterday?" other Jews would joke to each other: "he's a no-hoper, a real troublemaker."

"Of course I heard it," others would answer, adding sympathetically: "It's a shame for his mother. That poor widow, she stands all day on her swollen feet, burns her face at the oven, drags herself to the market to sell her biscuits, just so that her worthless lout of a son can eat his fill, and use up her hard-earned groschen. I sometimes think old Meyer Aaron has it better than his wife, may she have long life!"

"Ach! He wasn't much better, may he forgive me for saying so. He let his wife slave away and all he did, so they say, was to sit reading worldly books. He made his son into a worker, and instead of study-ing the *Talmud*,* he only read the Bible with him. A fine son he made of him. What do you think?"

"And poor Feyge-Tsirl mourns that son of hers, each time they take him to prison, as if he were dead. That's a mother for you."

43

"She suffers more than he does. He comes back hale and hearty; there's a devil in him."

"But all the same, our children should be protected from him," said the fathers and mothers, not realising that their own children were already on the same path, for they were already Leybesh's disciples.

Reb Elyohu Kornhendler,* the richest Jew in the *shtetl,* took the matter more seriously than anyone else. "Mark my words," he warned, pointing with his forefinger and making a fist of the other four: "It's a true saying that Satan doesn't only call at the other man's door. That scoundrel will spread his influence, God protect us! It's a *mitzvah,* a good deed, to denounce him. Let them send him to Siberia, once and for all. If they don't, it'll affect us all. I'll denounce him myself. And if I speak to the police, it'll be to everyone's advantage - it'll be a *mitzvah!*"

"As if Jews didn't have enough troubles," all the Jews in the *shtibl**agreed. Every one of them was glad that it was Reb Elyohu Kornhendler, and not he, who would be going to the police.

And certainly Reb Elyohu Kornhendler did carry out the task thoroughly, but it backfired on him. His own daughter, Gitele, a beautiful girl of marriageable age, also considered herself a bit of a socialist, even though she had not managed to plough her way through all of Karl Marx; she just couldn't make sense of him, even though she had a good brain. Nor could she get to grips with the various manifestos which she tried to read in bed at night; mostly she returned them to Leybesh unread. She was, however, a frequent visitor to Feyge-Tsirl's kitchen. She really loved its cosiness, the free and easy relationship between the comrades, and the songs they sang while drinking glasses of weak tea. Every evening, they covered the kitchen window with a torn old quilt, in order to muffle the sound of the discussions and singing. The boys and girls called each other "du"*, and were just like one big family. Gitele particularly liked the way they shared books, cigarettes, food, and especially the warmth of their emotions. Though Feyge-Tsirl did not take part in their activities, she did not prevent them, but she often warned Gitele, the rich man's daughter, that it would be better for her not to come.

"It's not right for you," she would say. "These are poor people's children; let them do all these stupid things. But what are you doing here? If your father gets to know of it he'll be furious, and I'll be lucky to get out alive."

Gitele knew that this environment was not suitable for a Jewish girl of good family, and that in any case she was in danger of being caught, but what exactly was meant by "caught", she wasn't quite sure. One evening, however, she heard her father tell her mother during supper that the next day, with God's help, they would be rid of the scoundrel (she knew very well who that was), and only then did she realise that the whole business was actually dangerous. This attracted her even more to the kitchen, and she rushed out in the middle of supper, went to Leybesh and told him, word for word, what her father had said.

"Your father's a fool," joked Leybesh but nevertheless, the same evening he climbed out through the kitchen window and fled to Warsaw, and from there, to Antwerp.

Then a tragedy struck Gitele's family. Her mother suddenly became ill, and very soon was "snatched away" - as the old women who supplied her with chickens and fish, put it. Gitele wandered round the elegant, empty rooms, which now seemed cold and lonely. She missed her mother very much. She began longing for the warmth of the evenings spent among her comrades in the poor little kitchen, and, gradually, she became convinced she was in love with Leybesh. Lying in bed at night, she would suddenly burst out crying for her dead mother, but she knew it was really Leybesh she was longing for. The cool silk of her thick feather quilt, and the fine, smooth linen of her sheets and pillows, made her shiver. She felt the only place for her was that kitchen with its blackened, crumbling walls and the bright faces of the young comrades, for whom working towards a better life was a kind of religion. It filled them with enough warmth and love, to melt stone. Karl Marx was their deity, and Leybesh, their simple, naive leader, was also a kind of God-like figure.

And the ironic name - "the prophet" - which the townsfolk had given him, became very dear to her. She felt it suited Leybesh. He never got any work as a brush-maker, nor was he temperamentally suited to that kind of work. He always went around empty-handed, and his eyes were full of spirituality, like those of a holy man.

Gitele's sufferings now increased. First, she missed her mother, who with her big apron and even bigger, authoritative voice had filled all the rooms of the house with her presence. Now a cold wind blew through the elegant house, and Gitele could find no shelter from it. Second, Reb Elyohu Kornhendler decided that a Jew should not be without a wife. Evil temptations lurked round every corner, his house was empty, his daughter wandered around the rooms like a stranger, money disappeared far more rapidly than when his wife, God rest her soul, was alive, and at night in bed, he lay awake for hours on end. Strange thoughts went through his head that wouldn't be driven out, so that he couldn't sleep. So he went to see the *rebbe*, who told him he should get married again.

Gitele really hated her stepmother. She could not bear her taking her mother's place in the household, and every time she heard a butcher or fish-seller calling her stepmother "Madame Kornhendler", Gitele put her hands over her ears. It broke her heart to see her father's new wife putting on her mother's jewellery. On her neck, the pearls looked to Gitele like scalding hot teardrops. Her father had even bought new trinkets for his wife, rings and bracelets, and he kept caressing her and flirting with her.

Gitele and her stepmother argued frequently. Once, after a particularly serious quarrel, Gitele decided to put an end to the situation. She simply couldn't stand any more. Her father felt the same. He listened to his new wife's complaints about Gitele. In a flood of words and tears she told him that his daughter begrudged her, her position, and that she was saying things like "Oh mother, why did you do it? Why did you let a stranger, an enemy, become the mistress in your house?"

"I'll go away," his new wife whimpered. "I'm scared of your dead wife. I don't want to stay here." As she spoke, gasping for breath, she shook her earrings, flashed the diamonds on her fat fingers, played with the pearls on her plump, white neck and sobbed: "Elyohu, I'm scared." And to heighten the effect, she started to take off her jewellery. Reb Elyohu Kornhendler was shocked and white with rage. He grabbed his wife by the arms:

"No!" he shouted hoarsely, "It's *your* jewellery, I gave it to you. You are to wear it in good health for the rest of your life."

He said quietly to his daughter: "If this doesn't please you, you are welcome to leave."

After weeping all night, Gitele decided to leave everything in her stepmother's hands, and at dawn, when even the servants were still asleep, she got up, packed a satchel with her own pieces of jewellery: the necklaces, bracelets and rings which her father and mother, and various aunts and uncles used to give her every birthday. She also took twenty roubles of her own money, and set out for Antwerp, to join Leybesh.

Having been spoiled by her mother, Gitele went first to a fine hotel and enjoyed the good life, until she suddenly realised she had pawned almost all her jewellery. When she told Leybesh she hated the rich, and swore by her dead mother that she would never have anything more to do with her father and only felt close to Leybesh, he was dismayed. What on earth was he to do with her? He was almost starving. He did not have much faith in her hatred of the rich. But she was here and that was that. So he gave her his bed and slept on the floor. Gradually they bought one or two cheap pieces of furniture together, and before he knew it, they became lovers.

Chapter 4

Leybesh was now a diamond cutter, but he never had any work and spent whole days wandering about with nothing to do, just as he had in the *shtetl*. There was always something wrong with his work; sometimes he cut the stones in the wrong way, sometimes he cut away too much, and yet worse bunglers than he, managed to keep their jobs. The bosses just did not take to Leybesh. They sensed that he was no friend of theirs. And he had another "virtue": he refused to curry favour, or give in, when the boss criticised him unjustly, and was determined to prove he was right. In the end the boss gave in to Leybesh, but at the same time gave him the news that unfortunately there was no work at the moment - perhaps another time. But the next time, the boss still didn't have any work for him. So Leybesh simply had to tighten his belt. It didn't bother him too much because he was used to it. A day with nothing to eat was quite normal, and, indeed, he was really rather surprised on the odd occasion when he was able to fill his stomach and not feel the familiar gnawing pangs of hunger. It was only after she arrived that he felt bad about these things.

When the Bermans learned that Reb Elyohu Kornhendler's daughter was in Antwerp, Berman began to enquire about her at the Bourse and at the Club. Rochl looked out for her in the Zoological Garden and the department stores, until one day she was absolutely delighted when she bumped into her on Pelikaanstraat.

"You look just like your mother!" she said.

"May she rest in peace," said Gitele.

Rochl was shocked to hear of her death. She asked Gitele all the details and invited her to their house.

And that was how Dovid Berman became a constant visitor at the Bruckners. He gradually got used to the dark rooms, and a meal taken at the wobbly table with the worn oilcloth seemed like a banquet. At first the food had stuck in his throat, and he had chewed very gingerly, fearing that he was going to swallow something distasteful, but this soon changed. He stopped looking round all the time for a serviette, when he realised, that in Gitele's household, such a thing did not exist. He saw that everything was in fact very clean, and it was only because the bits and pieces of second-hand furniture were old and worn, that everything looked so shabby. He gradually grew to love their poor home, and a warm feeling flooded over him as soon as he stepped across the threshold, a warmth which soothed him and filled him with contentment. So he kept coming.

For days at a time he would sit around their house, avidly following Gitele's every movement, as she bustled about. He watched her as she rolled her sleeves above her elbows and started washing the clothes. This excited him. He found her thin, white, fragile-looking arms, strangely attractive. Dovid had seen many half-naked women, on the beaches in the summer or at winter balls, with smooth, white, plump, powdered arms, but none of these had attracted him like the trembling of the skin of Gitele's arms when she was at the sink. With her woman's intuition, Gitele soon sensed this, and started blushing coyly, and smiling with pleasure. Her heart began to dance. Sometimes she found herself singing as she worked, and her blonde plaits, the only inheritance left from her old home, became silkier and glossier. She started brushing her hair more often than usual, and the plaits swung forward over her narrow shoulders, almost covering her small breasts, which moved gently, as she bent over the washing.

As this unspoken closeness developed between the two young people, Leybesh became more and more of a hindrance. Gitele no longer saw in him the deep-thinking person, whose poverty had ennobled him in her eyes, increasing the mystery surrounding him. Now she regarded him as nothing more than an irresponsible fool, a pauper and good-for-nothing, who could not even comprehend what a miserable state they were in. And it was into the arms of this man that she had flown!

Dovid came almost every day. Even though he was in a constant state of worry and agitation, and was bored to death with his life, he always managed to be clean-shaven and well turned out. He was always bare-headed, and dressed in a well-tailored suit; his gold pince-nez perched on his rather long nose. His face was smooth and of a dark complexion, his nails beautifully manicured. He wore gleaming white spats on his expensive shoes. His shirt was of the finest silk, with a wide black bow, like the Flemish actors wore. Moreover, he was an intellectual, a former student, and he possessed two season tickets, one for the Flemish opera and one for the French. Often, he carried a volume of Spinoza or Darwin around with him. And his eyes: deep, dark eyes which started smiling the moment they crossed Gitele's threshold. His sadness disappeared the moment he saw her. And Gitele's feelings overwhelmed her; she was helpless when he touched her. And so they became lovers, and she gave birth to a little girl.

Leybesh noticed that Gitele's face would light up and her eyes shine the moment Dovid came in, but this didn't surprise him. He said to himself that it was only natural, since they both came from affluent families and were both here in his poor dwelling by chance: the one from curiosity and a whim, the other because of indolence and bad luck. They recognised each other, for after all they were both of the same lineage! All the same, Leybesh did feel rather hurt, and he began to suspect that he himself was becoming fonder of Gitele than before. But he drove away these gloomy notions. In any case, he had no time for pointless thoughts like these, which occasionally creep into a person's head when he is feeling anxious.

He had already formed a "circle" in Antwerp. He was trying to set up a union, first of all getting together a library of socialist literature from Switzerland. It was easy to make propaganda here. No one bothered about it, and he already had a place where the comrades could meet. More than a year earlier, he had rented a room above a little synagogue. It still made him laugh when he remembered how he had got hold of this room. One Thursday evening, he had been walking along Kievitstraat. As he was passing one house, he heard an old woman shrieking at the top of her voice. Beside her, stood a man in a grimy, greenish frock coat with a darned collar and frayed cuffs, wearing a greasy skullcap on his head. He was waving a big, red handkerchief in the air like a sword, and screeching even more loudly than the woman.

"I'm telling you once and for all: never on a Thursday!"

Leybesh was curious about this strange couple, and he tried to find out what was going on from someone in the crowd, but nobody gave him a proper answer. They just stood there, joking and laughing. Eventually someone enlightened him:

"You see, the poor old woman really has to work her guts out for a crust of bread. She says prayers for the whole town, poor soul, if someone pays her to do it. She isn't a *shnorrer* and she's grateful to God when she gets work and doesn't have to beg. She goes up to the room above the synagogue there, and prays as fervently as if she were praying for herself. When she has a good season, she works really hard and doesn't have to go begging round the houses – she doesn't *want* to live on charity. Sometimes, a mean woman who doesn't want to pay comes along and says her own prayers, but this doesn't worry her, even though it takes the bread out of her mouth. But she really has a hard time when nobody in the town is seriously ill and requiring her prayers. She has to live, so in that case she goes round the Jewish restaurants, trying to sell shoelaces or chocolate, and from time to time someone gives her some money out of charity. She isn't a bad woman."

"So why is she screaming? And what does the man want?" asked Leybesh, still puzzled.

"Well, recently he's got into the habit of locking up the synagogue on a Thursday and doesn't let the poor woman go up there. The rest of the week, he says, is all right, but not on a Thursday. It's a real shame," said Leybesh's informant, a pale, rather sickly looking woman, who spoke in a soft, emotional voice.

At last, the old woman buttoned up her grubby old overcoat, straightened her wig, which had gone askew, and, dragging her fat shapeless body, went wobbling off along the pavement, still cursing and sobbing. The crowd dispersed, and the old man wiped his sweating face with his dirty pocket handkerchief. Leybesh had an idea. He took the old man aside, and asked if *he* could have the little room on a Thursday.

At first, the man looked at him suspiciously, fingered his greasy whiskers and went into the courtyard, to light a memorial candle* in the synagogue. But when Leybesh fixed his serious eyes on him and said, "Sir, I mean business," the man looked at him again and said "Not here: come into the synagogue!"

There Leybesh found out that the man had rented out this room to some young people who met there every Thursday; for what reason, the man didn't know. Leybesh offered two francs a week more, and so began his attempt to spread socialism in Antwerp.

Every Thursday, Leybesh dragged along a heavy suitcase full of literature, which he distributed among the few young men and women who gathered there, and on Friday he would cart the suitcase back home. In the little room, they chatted, smoked, debated, and even sometimes held a party for a male or female comrade, who had stopped in Antwerp, on their way to America.

Leybesh worked very hard. He didn't have an easy time of it, because most of the young people who came to Antwerp were young Hassidim who were fleeing to avoid being called up to the army, and knew that Antwerp was a town with many religious Jews. Leybesh realised that there was no point in trying to influence any of them. They had been old men from the day they were born, with rigid ideas, which they had inherited from their fathers, grandfathers and great-grandfathers. After work, people like them would sit studying all evening in all kinds of little *shtiblekh*. They say you can't make bricks without straw, but Leybesh was an optimist, and didn't let himself be daunted. His friends joked that even if he had no friends at all, he would still form a union consisting of one.

So he tried to find a way of organising the Jewish workers in Antwerp. He endeavoured to make contact with the leaders of the non-Jewish union to discuss with them the degeneracy of the bosses and the oppression of the Jewish worker: every parasite persecuted and exploited him, crushed and humiliated him, maligned him as a fawning sycophant, and saw to it that he lost his body as well as his soul. Afterwards, when everything had been sucked out of him like a flower after a bee has visited it, the persecutor did not even give him what the bee gives the flower. No, the boss would then simply exchange him for a younger worker, very often the worker's own son. Leybesh tried to explain all this to the secretary of the union.

While he was speaking from the depths of his heart, depicting with great earnestness the life of the Jewish worker, the secretary was leaning back in his swivel chair, smoking a fine cigar, listening intently, smiling graciously behind his blond moustache. He didn't interrupt Leybesh, but let him carry on till he had said all he wanted to. When Leybesh had finished, the secretary gave him a cigar and told him in a very friendly tone that unfortunately it was not possible for him to admit a Jew to the union. Leybesh asked why not, but, like a true diplomat, the secretary apologised, saying that unfortunately he was not able to divulge the reason. But Leybesh was not deterred. He thought that if he could just manage to express himself better to this idiotic secretary he would be able to show him that, of course, it was possible to admit Jews to the union. This was a civilised country, and it must be possible to get the better of asinine, self-satisfied secretaries. It was just a question of determination. So Leybesh decided to start learning Flemish properly, because without being fluent in the language of the country it was impossible to achieve anything. Very often, even while he was deep in thoughts about his work, an image floated into his mind, Leybesh didn't quite understand why, of Gitele and Dovid, together in his room, on the second floor.

Of all the Antwerp diamond merchants, Berman was the greatest expert in persecuting workers, especially Leybesh. He had no respect for manual workers, regarding them with even more contempt than he did the small-time diamond traders, who bustled around the exchange. The traders were, at least, trying to better themselves.

In the beginning, when Gitele had just arrived in Antwerp, and was still going around dressed in a manner that was appropriate for a daughter of Kornhendler's, with the necklaces, rings and brooches which so impressed Berman (even though all day he was up to his elbows in diamonds), he still had respect for her. But the moment he heard she was living with Leybesh, this changed to contempt. The prestige she had brought with her from the old country simply disappeared, like the sun behind a cloud. He soon stopped giving Leybesh any work, pretending that he wanted him to send Gitele.

"Send your wife to me. It's a shame that you should have to waste your time." And when Berman found that Leybesh did start sending his wife, and that she wasn't even embarrassed about it any more, because the hunger was gnawing so strongly, and she had to produce milk for the baby, he started looking for excuses. He got into a rage with her, regarding her as a *shnorrer*, completely ignoring the fact that she was a rich man's daughter.

"No, unfortunately, I have just allocated the last piece of work. What a shame, if you had only come an hour earlier." Berman always had an excuse, and not only did he not give her any work, but he poured salt in her wounds, by continually asking her about her father, how he was and what he had written to her.

"Ach, he was always my best friend."

Eventually Gitele was fed up with this game; her blood boiled and one day she slammed the door of Berman's office. From then on they became even poorer.

Leybesh took to going out a lot, and Gitele certainly did not grumble about this. No matter how late he came home, she didn't say a cross word to him, because Dovid had got into the habit of bringing supper with him, which they ate together. And after the meal, when Gitele began feeding the baby, Dovid was in seventh heaven. He would have been happy to sit there for hours, watching the baby sucking, grabbing her mother's breast with her tiny hand, squeezing it so hard with her little fingers that Gitele had to bite her lip. He saw how the little mite held onto the breast with all her strength, as if she was afraid that it was going to be taken away again. The baby sucked greedily, the tiny veins standing out clearly on her temples as if someone had embroidered a blue lacy design there. Dovid was filled with joy when he saw Gitele's blue eyes smiling with motherly tenderness as she looked down at the baby, delighted that her milk had not dried up, and that she was still able to feed her. And Dovid began to regard these two creatures as his little family, and Leybesh as a rival, or, at the very least, as an unwelcome guest who disturbed their intimate closeness in their warm little home.

Leybesh sensed the truth and yet didn't see the situation completely. Whenever Dovid had one of his quarrels with his father, it was Leybesh who suggested that he should stay with them until the storm blew over.

On one such occasion, the third night he had stayed at the Bruckners', just before the *kermis*, things came to a crisis for Dovid. "How is all this going to end?" he asked himself, but could not find an answer. There was no question of going back home. He had left, after such a serious quarrel, that both his mother and Jeannette had been in tears. He only had the clothes he stood up in, and it was several days since he had had anything at all to eat. The few francs he had possessed had been used up; he had spent them on Gitele, convincing her that he had eaten during the day at a friend's house, and so forth. She saw through this, but, seeing the pleading in his eyes, she realised that she should accept it, and not ask any questions. So she ate the food, although it stuck in her throat, and said nothing.

Now it was night. Dovid was lying on the shabby bed, unable to sleep. It was too hot and too bright; through the torn blind, strips of light shone onto the floor, the table, and onto his bed. Apart from this, he could not help imagining that Gitele was whispering secrets to Leyesh in the bedroom.

And while he was lying there, listening, Leybesh, tall and broad shouldered, came into the kitchen in his underpants, with bare feet and tousled hair, and an unhealthy pallor on his face. He was walking on tiptoe, so as not to waken the guest. Dovid stirred and wanted to ask something, not really knowing what.

"Shhhh! Go to sleep! Sorry for disturbing you." Leybesh waved his hand and moved towards the gas stove.

"What is it?" asked Dovid.

"Nothing at all, really. But who was it who said it's hard to be a Jew? I say: it's hard to be a *father*."

Leybesh lit the stove. Dovid saw a blue flame and heard the hissing of the gas. Leybesh was heating up a little water for the baby, who had a tummy ache. And it was Leybesh who was standing there, barefoot and half-naked, dealing with it.

Dovid was overcome by shame and started sweating. The baby began crying and he heard Gitele talking to her:

"Shhh! Shhh! Don't cry, my darling!"

A dull numbness came over Dovid. The shame he felt about his behaviour towards his friend, whom he was betraying so despicably, overwhelmed him. He felt so mean and worthless that he wished the ground would open up and swallow him. One more minute, he thought, and he would spring out of bed and scream out loud into the night:

55

"Look at him standing there, the idiot, letting himself be made a fool of!"

He took refuge in spiteful cruelty. "But why does he not see what's going on? Why is he so blind? Why does he put up with it?"

" Go back to sleep. Don't worry about it," said Leybesh.

Dovid's anguished thoughts were screaming inside him and he was bathed in sweat: "It's hard to be a father, but even harder to be a filthy, treacherous, cowardly good-for-nothing." The child screamed even more loudly, and Dovid was filled with pity for the baby and a strange anger towards Gitele. She had no right to betray Leybesh in this way. When this flashed through his mind, he took fright at his own thoughts, and felt a terrible choking tightness inside.

Leybesh went back into the bedroom. Gitele comforted the baby and Dovid heard her talking to Leybesh. Dovid looked into his own soul and, covering himself with the patched quilt, he burst into tears like a child.

Chapter 5

At dawn, Dovid left the house, taking care not to wake anyone up. Like a thief, he very quietly stole down the steps from the narrow corridor, and closed the door behind him, silently. His inner torments had left him exhausted; he was hungry, and had a bad headache, but his body felt light. Walking in the poor street in his elegant clothes, he looked like a drunken actor who had lost his way and wandered into this district from some night club or other.

The street was sunk in restful sleep. The shabby houses with their closed, wooden shutters were already bathed in bright, pure, almost silvery sunlight. Behind the narrow, dirty shop windows, lay goods for sale, in untidy heaps. Cats were dozing on doorsteps. Today, there weren't any bins, full of refuse, beside the gutters. These were usually placed there, by the housewives and shopkeepers, to be taken away by the dustmen. Their absence, made the impoverished district, look a little more festive.

The arrival of the milkman brought a bit of life into the sleepy street. His cart, decorated with gleaming brass and filled with milk cans, rattled merrily in the emptiness of the street. He stopped at every door, driving the cats from the doorsteps, leaving a can of milk and calling out his familiar "*Melkboer!*"* He swiftly worked his way right down Somersstraat, hurrying, because he wanted to be finished early, so he could enjoy the holiday.

"*Dag menieër!*" said the milkman to Dovid, as if he had known him for years. "It looks as if we'll have a good *kermis*, don't you think? It's nice weather, eh, *menieër?*"

"Yes indeed, it looks like it." Dovid glanced up at the clear sky and hurried away from the street.

He started walking in the direction of Borgerhout.* Some women were standing around. They had already scrubbed the pavement and the ground floors of their houses, cleaned the brass doorknockers and poured enough pails of water to put out a fire. They also wanted to get finished early and enjoy the holiday. Dovid repeatedly raised his hat in response to the "*dag menieërs*" from unknown housewives.

"Hallo!" Someone was stretching out a soft warm hand to Dovid, who was delighted when he saw who it was.

"Jules! What are you doing in the street so early?"

"What do you mean? It's the *kermis* today!"

"So why are you in such a hurry?"

"Why are *you* in such a hurry?" retorted Jules Tsvaygnboym, immediately feeling a bit embarrassed by the familiar tone he was adopting. He was speaking to Dovid as if he were his equal, as if something had changed in their relationship, and this disturbed him.

"No, I really mean it," continued Jules. "Can one actually sleep on a day like this? Something draws you out of bed and into the streets. What a glorious day it is! Perhap ..." Jules was about to ask Dovid something, but hesitated. He pondered a little, glanced at Dovid, and seeing that the latter looked like a ghost, he ventured to make his suggestion: "Perhaps we could even celebrate the *kermis* together?"

Dovid had no intention of celebrating any kind of festival today, even though he did so every year. He framed his "no", but Jules was already walking along beside him, chatting, telling stories, and even infecting Dovid with his laughter. So they walked back into the town together.

The wagons from the villages had begun arriving, and the streets were already full of young people. The bright sunshine and the mixture of girlish laughter and good-humoured oaths aroused in Dovid a genuine desire to celebrate the holiday. He forgot about the night, and said: "Fine! Let's celebrate!" and Jules was delighted. "But first we must eat something," said Jules, thinking, as usual, of his stomach.

Dovid remembered that he hadn't a single centime to his name. He, too, desperately needed to eat, but didn't want Jules to know about his predicament.

"What do you think, Dovid?" said Jules. "The thing is, I ate hardly any breakfast before I came out. I just grabbed whatever I could find. At home they're all sleeping like the dead." Jules chattered on. "And what about you, Dovid, have you already had breakfast?"

"No, actually, I haven't eaten a thing. But to tell you the truth, I haven't a single centime on me. I just came out for a walk and forgot to bring my wallet." Dovid blustered in his embarrassment.

"I'll pay, that doesn't matter at all."

"No, not at all, tomorrow I'll give you back what I owe you." And they went into a restaurant.

"Hey, over here, *garçon*," Jules called with cheerful assurance. It seemed to Dovid that Jules was addressing the waiter too arrogantly. He felt annoyed, as if he had been in the waiter's place.

The waiter, however, was not offended. Indeed, he appeared immediately, in response to the call, a short, fattish man with a flushed face, gleaming, fair hair and wearing a black frockcoat, with a white napkin over his arm. He bowed and said: "*Menieër?*"

Jules looked at his watch: "Look, it's ten o'clock already, how time flies! It's no wonder I'm dying of hunger. Should we order sole?"

"Yes, that's fine," said Dovid, who was dying to see food on the table, no matter what it was.

The waiter came with two good portions of fish. After they had finished, Jules wiped his greasy lips and discussed with Dovid the fact that it was permitted to eat sole; it wasn't meat, so it was *kosher.* Dovid agreed that sole was *kosher.* Jules rubbed his cheeks and said casually:

"What do you think about my brother?"

"What are you talking about?"

"What do you mean? Have you not heard? Bernard has got engaged, and he's getting a hundred thousand francs, what's more, *and* a watch, with diamonds the size of hazelnuts."

"I don't know anything about it," said Dovid, who knew only too well. Bernard's engagement had already caused him enough problems.

"Have you really heard nothing? Everyone is talking about it, I tell you. Diamonds the size of hazelnuts, that's not to be sneezed at! It's Lieberman's daughter he's engaged to."

"And what do you think about it?" asked Dovid.

"What should I think? If you make your bed, you have to lie on it; if he has consented, then I certainly wish him luck. With the greatest

59

pleasure!" and Jules's corpulent body shook with mirth: "Ha-ha-ha! If you make your bed, you have to lie on it!"

Jules paid the bill, joking and laughing. Having drunk a fair number of glasses of beer so early in the morning, he was a little tipsy, and he took Dovid's arm as affectionately, as if he were a girlfriend. They walked off towards the Sheldt in companionable silence.

The broad river sparkled merrily in the sunshine, dancing playfully around the little boats, full of passengers, colour and singing. Everything was in constant movement. Passengers were disembarking and new ones embarking, to sail to Sint-Anneke.* Workers, warmed by the sun and eager for the bright outdoors, the fresh air, the green trees and birdsong, stood in long queues waiting for a tiny space in one of the boats. They whiled away the time by singing folksongs, making jokes, and telling off their children. And the waves were swelling, flowing into each other, one swallowing another and then spitting them out again. Seagulls flew overhead with outspread wings, clamouring for food. The boats cut through the golden sunshine. Rays of sunshine flowed over the boats and the people with a warm caress, which raised their spirits.

From the distance, Sint-Anneke was a huge expanse of colourful movement. Girls were cavorting on the grassy meadow, and kissing and embracing their boyfriends. Their arms round each other, they were free to romance under the open sky, before the whole world, before the singing birds, which were flying from tree to tree and hopping from branch to branch. The birds were imitating the young people in the meadow, kissing each other, eating crumbs of bread from the outstretched hands of children, and generally enjoying the holiday. Men were kissing and cuddling their wives, as if for the first time. Little children were running around the meadow, getting under people's feet, and throwing themselves on their parents, giggling madly because they had caught mummy and daddy doing something naughty.

Dovid and Jules had just got off the boat, and before Dovid had time to turn round, he found himself being pulled down onto the damp grass by the shore. He stood up and tried to apologise to the blonde girl, who was lying face down on the grass, giggling. But before he could say anything, the girl caught hold of his right leg and pulled him down to her, so that again he was lying on the grass beside her.

"God save us!" she shrieked and started shaking with laughter. Jules saw what was going on and flung his fat body down on the grass, almost crushing the friend of the girl, who was lying beside her. As if they had already arranged it, all four got up and went off for a walk in the field like old friends. They found nicknames for each other: Zhaneke, Maneke, anything which occurred to them, what did it matter? As long as they were having fun. Dovid threw himself into the holiday mood with savage fervour. He forgot all the problems which his father had heaped on him. He forgot that he didn't have a single centime in his pocket. He even forgot the searing pain he had felt the previous night, and all his anger.

When the sun began to set, the Sheldt was suffused with red, and the little waves looked like flames dancing on the water. Couples with children had begun gathering up their empty baskets, jugs, bottles and pots, which had held milk and food. The sky darkened, but it was still full of colour: red, purple, rose-pink, copper, with streaks of dark blue. Tired children were carried on their fathers' shoulders. The young people were still singing lingering melodies with tired voices. Dovid, Jules and the two girls were already back in the town. Ravenously hungry, they went into a restaurant, sat down at a wet table, littered with empty beer bottles and discarded cigarette ends stubbed out on plates, and waited for the exhausted waitress to come and serve them. She didn't come at once. Like a hunted animal she was running from table to table, and still couldn't satisfy anyone. Everyone was clamouring to be served, getting cross, complaining. Only these four had plenty of time. The girls shrieked with laughter at Jules' jokes, and Dovid hummed a song. When the waitress did finally appear, Jules ordered such a sumptuous supper that even he was satisfied.

They looked around the town and, not seeing any other Jews around, they started kissing and cuddling the girls and, after arranging to meet again, they set out for home. A delicious tiredness flooded through the limbs of the two sinners. "Are you drunk, Dovid?" laughed Jules, who could hardly stand upright.

The two friends wandered through the narrow streets of old Antwerp, where the poor people had come out into the street in honour of the holiday.

All year long, these dark, crooked streets are empty and desolate, and the silence tells dismal tales. In the taverns, girls sit all day long, behind pieces of looped-back curtain, smoking cheap cigarettes, knitting, and keeping a lookout for possible clients. But if a sailor does happen to come past, he is usually penniless. His worn, blue, linen trousers, sunken cheeks and dull eyes bear witness to his poverty. His eyes light up briefly when he sees the girls, but they don't even interrupt their work for him. The sailor lowers his eyes and the girls realise he is ashamed. He can't even afford to come in and drink a glass of beer with them, which would give them a chance to escape, briefly, from their constant vigil behind the looped-back curtain. Sometimes, a girl will take pity on one of these sailors, but, mostly, she curses both him and his poverty.

In the evenings, things become more cheerful here. The curtains are drawn back, and a greenish light pours out, illuminating the black uneven stones of the pavements, which are so narrow that people can only walk one abreast. On Sundays, there is more going on during the daytime too. And if there is a holiday, especially the *kermis*, then there's a real celebration. The notices in the windows, advertising "room to rent", are superfluous because there isn't a single inch of space to rent. The serving girls have their hands full. From all sides people try to attract them to their table: "Here, miss, over here!"

Today it had been especially lively. From early morning the sun had shone brightly into the attics and cellars, not allowing anyone to sleep. The excursions to Sint-Anneke had begun earlier than usual, and people had poured from the narrow, crooked alleyways, which run into each other. Now, returned from Sint-Anneke, they all made for the taverns, crowding the streets, weaving around drunkenly, in a swirling mass of life; not like human beings with individual self-consciousness. The poor toiling dockworkers poured out into the street, like free citizens, to celebrate their annual *kermis*. Even the tiny patches of sky visible above the rooftops seemed prisoners like themselves. Just as those people still looked dirty after they had taken a bath, so the sky here always looked dark, even on the clearest nights, even on this bright night of the *kermis*.

But was anyone looking at the sky? Old and young were dancing, kissing, embracing and weeping, drunkenly. There were good-natured curses, people pushing each other off the pavements, joking, and neighing like horses. Women were trying to outdo the men and each other with jokes and quips, children were tripping people up and getting slaps, which they accepted philosophically and then carried on prancing around. Children with less stamina were falling asleep on doorsteps or in the middle of the street, running the danger of being trampled by their own drunken mother. Some of the good-natured joking developed into bad feeling, and quarrels broke out; from time to time, a normally quiet respectable worker, was led off to spend the night in the police cells, accompanied by drunken shouts, wails from his wife and curses for the policeman who took him. But after a while they forgot all about it and began singing a mixture of the bawdiest ditties and the most beautiful folksongs.

And so they celebrated the *kermis*: the poor man in his fashion and the better class of people in theirs. Both filled the pockets of the innkeepers and made the serving girls' life a misery. The town stank of pork fat and all kinds of shellfish, eels, fried potatoes, malt vinegar and sweat.

Dovid made his way out of the drunken crowd. At least he had managed to forget the quarrels with his father and, humming a festive song, he went back to his father's house, threw himself into bed fully clothed, and, a moment later, he was snoring like a real drunk.

Chapter 6

After Rochl had left with her daughter, Berman had a little nap with his head on the table, as he usually did. He woke up thinking that about ten minutes must have passed, only to find that he had been sitting there for hours. He felt strangely lonely. Stretching and yawning, he looked round the room. Not finding anyone to get angry with, he went into the kitchen to make himself a glass of tea. Despite the heat, a chill went through his body. It didn't feel like summer at all.

When he crossed the threshold and saw Jacques eating a large plateful of potatoes, he was really pleased.

"When did you come in?"

Jacques was startled. He put his hand on his heart and swore: "Papa, I promise you that I came in at lunchtime. That's the honest truth. You can ask Mama." With his spoonful of potato halfway to his mouth, Jacques kept on protesting: "I promise... honestly..."

"All right, all right, I believe you, you little rascal. Go on, eat!"

Jacques didn't need much persuasion. He had been running about all over the town and was ravenously hungry.

The gleaming copper kettle was singing comfortingly. Berman prepared his tea and turned off the gas. He took a glass down from the shelf, wiped it, held it at arm's length and looked at it against the light of the sunny window, just like he did with diamonds when he wanted to see their true brilliance. He poured himself a glass of tea. By this time, Jacques was eating his stewed fruit.

"Jacques, don't go out again. You'll come with me to the synagogue for the evening prayers, do you hear?"

Jacques nearly choked on his stewed fruit. Go to the synagogue on carnival day?! He had been gobbling down his potatoes while they were still burning hot, so that he could rush back out, and now this! He tried to protest, but Berman wouldn't listen. He took his tea into the dining room, leaving Jacques in despair in the kitchen. Jacques started writing with his finger on the windowpane, and thinking out arguments to use with his father:

"*Please*, Papa. May I never come back home again if you make me come to synagogue with you. All the other boys are outside today." But Berman felt that everyone had deserted him today and finding Jacques at home was some kind of miracle. He would not be moved by Jacques' pleading. The cold in Berman's bones had not been dissipated by the hot tea.

"Maybe, God forbid, Dovid has committed suicide." Berman shuddered, as this thought suddenly passed through his mind. "No! Not that! Not that!" a voice inside him kept repeating. He held the glass of tea in his hands, trying to warm himself a little. If Dovid came back now, this instant, he would not say anything bad to him. But this very thought brought his anger back again, and he sipped the tea and groaned as if he were in pain. Towards evening he went to the synagogue, taking Jacques with him.

In the synagogue there was certainly something to talk about today; the name of Tsvaygnboym was on everyone's lips.

Tall young men with thin, red, blond or black beards, dressed in black or dark grey coats and striped trousers, some with a pince-nez on their thin noses, their hats pushed back on their heads, were crowding round Tsvaygnboym, nodding absent-mindedly, with greedy smiles on their lips, shaking his hand and wishing him *mazl tov.*[*] What they all really wanted to ask him was that he should think of them when, God willing, he received the dowry. Some of them did actually ask, others bit back the words, putting it off till the next day. There were some men with broad beards, whose laughing eyes with their myriad creases and wrinkles only concealed their desperation. Their hats were twisted and so were their heads, from so much worrying over buying and selling diamonds, and managing to provide for *Shabbes.*[*]

Even now, after such a stroke of luck, Tsvaygnboym's eyes had not lost their permanent worried expression. He saw that not a single shred of his beard would be left, and so he started plucking it himself, in order to save it from strangers' hands. But the Jews were resourceful, and since the beard was not available, buttons and lapels were also a possibility. One man almost plucked out his own beard, which was rather scrawny to begin with. He sucked his sunken cheeks into his toothless mouth, and pleaded with Tsvaygnboym, with so much anguish in his forced smile, that Tsvaygnboym's heart bled for him. He recognised the situation he himself had been in only the day before, and he made up his mind to help this man, if the engagement actually did take place, and the dowry materialised.

"Do I need to tell you," the old man continued in an urgent tone, "that the value of diamonds is rising from minute to minute? I think you know this better than I. So I'm advising you, as a true friend, you should invest in diamonds now. Nowadays, when you buy a batch of stones, you've really got something in your hands. And you know that I, thank God, have access to the most important firms. They all know me and they daren't ignore me. They're well aware that I have numerous mouths to feed. *Ach! ach! ach!*" The man looked up at the ceiling, apparently seeking the One who could help, but seemed unwilling to do so: the Lord of the Universe.

"I won't, God forbid, forget anyone!" Tsvaygnboym reassured the crowd, just as you would try to placate a robber, so that he will spare your life.

When he saw Berman, he went to greet him.

In the town Berman was regarded as an extremely wealthy man. Tsvaygnboym told him the news about the engagement, and invited him very respectfully to come to the signing of the contract.

"Good evening, Herr Tsvaygnboym!" said Berman with a smile on his face. "I had indeed heard the news. Well, let it be with *mazl.*"

"He's already hobnobbing with the rich," muttered Tsvaygnboym's new friends, begrudging him this honour.

"Well, let him hobnob," interrupted one young man. "I wouldn't mind having the fifty or even twenty thousand, which he thinks he'll get, and won't." The young man was being moderate and taking eighty thousand francs off the promised amount of the dowry. "You know Lieberman's tricks. He did the same thing with his first daughter: promised a hundred thousand and actually gave ten. And, of course, the son-in-law was too ashamed to admit what an idiot he had been, and the fools in the Bourse believed he had got the dowry and were happy to give him credit. Well, anyway, at least it gave people something to talk about. And since he duped the first one, he's certainly going to do the same with this pauper. Lieberman will give him a hundred thousand plagues instead of francs."

"That's to say, he'll give him his daughter," laughed the young men.

"Believe me, that swarthy-looking man there," they said, pointing at Berman, "has more money in his breast pocket than Lieberman has in the world. He's all talk, is Lieberman. He really thinks you can fool everyone."

"Well, he's right too," a plump, clean-shaven man with a smiling, red face and round, black, owlish eyes, said gleefully.

Berman finished congratulating Tsvaygnboym, wished the bridegroom *mazl tov* as well, and stopped to chat with various people. He spoke little, but he heard a lot, and what he heard pleased him very much.

"Well! A hundred thousand, eh?! So that's how he does business, the rogue!"

And the smaller the dowry was reported to be, the more his anger against Dovid abated.

He accompanied Tsvaygnboym home. They chatted about business, and he asked casually about every detail of the dowry, and whether it had already been paid. He wasn't asking, God forbid, just out of nosiness, but purely as a friend. A hundred thousand francs, said Berman, is a good sum, and he looked Tsvaygnboym in the eye, dying for him to deny the amount. But Tsvaygnboym just agreed that it was a good sum.

"Thank the Lord, may His name be praised, I have nothing to grumble at, God forbid!" Tsvaygnboym continued, and Berman consoled himself with the thought that the man was a gullible fool, a real loser. You could persuade him that a bundle of straw was a plate of noodles.

When he got home, Berman's first question was about Dovid. "Have you heard anything?" he asked anxiously. "God save and protect us, I hope nothing's happened!"

"He's back! I don't know where he's been, but when I came back I found him sleeping in his clothes. Poor boy, he looks absolutely exhausted. Gedaliah, please go easy on him, you've got to go easy on your own child."

Berman became impatient. He had been worried sick, and here she was going on at him, the stupid woman.

"Go easy on him? I'll go easy on him, all right!"

But supper was more cheerful than usual. Berman made a pretence of being in a good mood. In fact he was relieved that Dovid had not, God forbid, done anything to dishonour his name. In truth he had been really worried about him. It seemed that he wasn't destined to have joy of his son. Well, so be it. The Lord, may His Name be praised, would probably give him joy of the other two children. He stole a glance at Jeannette. "She's a wonderful girl, *ken eynore*.* I must protect her like a precious diamond." But all the same, there was still something weighing on his heart, filling him with melancholy. He realised, that during supper, he had not yet given anyone an order, or lost his temper with anyone.

So he turned his attention to Jacques. "Jacques, go to bed." As usual, Jacques tried to bargain:

"Please, Papa, please, Mama, just a little while ..!"

But it was no use. After he had said the grace after the meal, Berman took Jacques by the ear, and personally took him off to the bedroom, which he shared with Dovid. Berman looked at Dovid's bed, wanting to reassure himself that Dovid really was back home. Rochl, feeling very tired, went into her bedroom, not even clearing up after the meal. Berman himself put away the prayer book, which Jacques had left lying on the table. He took a religious book off the bookshelf, tried to read it, but the words wouldn't make sense.

"Hm! Even ten thousand francs is a fortune for that pauper! Ten thousand! Ten thousand! These words danced on the page. But he became uneasy once more. "But perhaps it actually *was* a hundred thousand? Who knows?" He had been slaving all his life to earn this much, he had had a rough time of it, and now a loser like this who couldn't hold a candle to him, was to become his equal. Certainly Lieberman's daughter was no oil painting; to be honest, she was rather ugly. Apart from all this, Berman's father intended to pay them a visit. He said he wanted to see his grandchildren. Oh dear! What would he think of them?

Berman took a letter out of his pocket and read it over and over again. His father wrote that Berman's brother was, thank God, in perfect health, and he himself was feeling a lot better, so since the brother had taken over the shop after his mother's death, the well-off townsfolk had collected money for his journey, and he intended, God willing, to come to Antwerp, to visit his son. He had heard that Antwerp was, praise God, a Jewish city and that Gedaliah kept, thank God, a Jewish home. And he knew that Gedaliah would, with God's help, receive him with honour, because he had always been dutiful to his father. How well he had looked after him during the two years that he had lain in bed - it shouldn't happen to a Jew! So they would, God willing, see each other soon. And so on.

Berman put the letter away again, and tried to read his book. But it was as if the events of the day were printed on the page, and the words would not hang together.

"Huh! Grandchildren! Such a loser... ten thousand!"

Berman realised that he was struggling to no avail, so he put the book back in its place, and recited *krishme*,* pacing about the room as he prayed.

Chapter 7

Berman got up at daybreak as usual. The house was dark and quiet. The whole household was still asleep. Every day it was the same routine: as soon as he heard the milkman's cry and the muffled rattle of the can on the doorstep, he got dressed.

The maid was dozing on the iron bed in her little room. She rubbed her sticky eyes and hoped that a miracle might occur: that the master would sleep in because of the holiday the day before, and that she wouldn't hear the hated clatter of the wooden roller blind in the dining room being pulled up, announcing that she had to get up because he wanted a glass of *bavarke*, his favourite sweetened milk drink. She was dead tired after the celebrations and had a great desire to turn over to face the wall and carry on sleeping for hours.

But, just as he did every morning, Berman pulled up the roller blinds, intimating to Anneke that for *him* there had been no holiday yesterday. She gritted her strong white teeth and cursed under her breath: "*Godverdoeme*! God damn him!" Then she got out of bed, shivering with cold, though it was the middle of summer.

Berman went past her room, and out of the corner of his eye he caught a glimpse of her, barefoot, with her apron in one hand, while with the other she stifled a yawn, which was bursting out of her like a scream. He smiled and pretended not to see her standing there. Berman never had relationships with the maidservants, because afterwards they would prattle about it, which would not suit him at all: that's all one needed in Antwerp. He was not like Shapiro: all Antwerp gossiped about him, but it didn't bother him in the least. Shapiro had a bad reputation as a man of loose morals and, indeed, if he hadn't been such a good businessman that people needed his services, no right-thinking person would have stopped to speak to him in the street.

"Hmm, she's certainly not unattractive! A *shikse*,* but even so..."

He smiled and went into the kitchen to perform the ritual washing of his hands.

Berman inspected the silver tray to see that all was as it should be: that the spoon was there and the glass of *bavarke* of the right consistency. With a nod he allowed Anneke to go. He was putting sugar in his drink, when, without knowing why, he called Anneke back, looked at her, pondered as if he were trying to remember something, and then sent her away again.

"*Godverdoeme!*" muttered Anneke again, picking up the cat which was rubbing itself against her. She could have told the cat a lot of things, but instead she just kissed his little nose. She put him down, gave him a kick and said: "Scram!"

After breakfast Berman distributed some parcels of diamonds, and received finished work, but there wasn't a great deal to do. The workshops had been at a standstill the day before, and because of the holiday the cutters had not yet finished the work. The polishers hadn't arrived either.

Berman went off to the Bourse, but no trading was going on there. In the big hall, with its massive gleaming pillars, there was hardly anyone to be seen. The few dealers around, who had not gone away, were unwrapping their parcels of diamonds. The stones caught Berman's eye with their flashing colours of white, red and blue. The dealers showed each other the bargains they had bought and then wrapped them up again. The Club was empty too and only the *Shenkl*, where the small traders dealt, was full of life. Bearded young men with worried expressions ran around like scalded cats, stopped at tables, showed each other tiny, rose-cut diamonds, about a hundred to the carat, or rough diamonds, which looked like little pieces of greyish washing soda. They weighed them on small scales, wrapped them up again, talked and gestured with their hands, and swore by their wives and children. They tried to make deals, found they couldn't get the price they wanted, closed their cases and ran to the next table.

An elderly man was sitting beside the window, poking with his tweezers in a large heap of *bakvuils*, which looked like loose tobacco, searching for little diamonds. He raised his red eyes and looked at Berman, smoothed his grey beard reflectively, as if he was trying to remember something. "Hmmm ..." he said, "It's him! The black dog." Then he went on prodding around with his tweezers. Jules, his face red and shining as usual, was sitting directly opposite the old man. He was weighing grey diamond powder on a pair of scales, and wrapping it up in a paper packet, singing under his breath:

"On Sunday to Sint-Anneke I go,
Siiiint-Aaaa-ne-ke!"

A small, crooked young man with a melancholy look and nervous, watery eyes, stood beside him:

"If you please, hurry up a little, Herr Tsvaygnboym! It is almost lunchtime, and I haven't managed to get anything done yet. I told you there wouldn't be enough diamond powder. I certainly wasn't trying to rob you. I've had to run back in the middle of my work, and now I'm wasting time, for nothing," said the young man, justifiably upset.

But Jules, having seen Berman coming in, stopped singing and got up, taking the diamond powder with him. He stretched out his dimpled hand to Berman, and went as red as a beetroot. The young man with watery eyes just stood there, his hands raised in amazement and indignation: "Damn that bastard! Here I am, rushing around like a madman and desperate to get away. He could at least have given me the diamond powder *before* he went off to fawn around that black rogue." The poor creature was so agitated that he started coughing, and his dark face and little, black beard, seemed to shrink. It was almost midday, when the polishing machine would come to a standstill.

But the polisher need not have got so agitated, because Berman did not even give Jules his hand, but merely asked him hastily how his father was and then turned away arrogantly, while Jules stood there with his hand outstretched. Embarrassed, he returned to his table. A desire to prove that he really was the boss over the workers surged up in him, and he shouted at the polisher: "Just see that the stones turn out well! Do you hear me?!"

"Yes, yes," muttered the young man and hurried out of the room.

Berman looked around and saw that there was no one left to stop and chat to except the nobodies and paupers who were ten-a-penny. Nevertheless he answered the "good morning" greetings of the small dealers and brokers on his way out. He remembered that he had to go and see Shapiro; yesterday the Hungarian rogue had said he had some goods, so it was worth having a look.

"How dare he come to my house? The bastard, the scoundrel!" Shapiro's jibes of the day before had started to gnaw at Berman. His rage was rekindled when he remembered how Shapiro had deliberately riled him so that he had nearly had an apoplectic fit. He was tempted not to go to him, just to show him that he, Berman, was not someone to be treated lightly. But on the other hand, what else could he do? He had to go, for the sake of business. Shapiro had said "I've got fine goods," and he was a man you couldn't trifle with. It would be better for him to go to Shapiro than for the latter to come to him, even though Shapiro was just a broker and he, Berman, a diamond merchant. Shapiro never had any difficulty in selling his goods. They were usually already sold before he actually had them in his hands. He had devilish cunning. He had access to the most prestigious firms and the finest stones, so that if you wanted to get hold of high-quality goods and make a profit, you couldn't afford to quarrel with Shapiro. He looked like a rogue but you could absolutely rely on his word. He never cheated, never "lost" any diamonds, or exchanged good stones for rubbish. He was honesty personified in his business dealings, and it was an honour to do business with him. No one could become a respected merchant without going through Shapiro.

Glancing at his gold watch, Berman saw it was too early to go to Shapiro's house, so he walked more slowly and took a detour round the side streets. It was better to be on the late side than too early.

He thought about Jules: "Huh! He's become a fine gentleman, that impertinent so-and-so, just to add to my troubles. Hmm ... I bet he just works with tiny stones, a thousand to the carat!" He smiled contemptuously, though it did irk him that Jules had held out his hand to him. "These *shnorrers* now think they're our equals. How can he be so presumptuous? Just because his older brother has made an advantageous match, he thinks he can become a successful dealer, and who knows, he might well succeed. *And* they're trying to drag the father out of the dirt as well." No one had been as sorely tried by God as he had, thought Berman, full of self-pity.

And so, bemoaning his fate, he arrived at Shapiro's house. Shapiro was sitting at a highly polished mahogany table covered with a thick sheet of bevelled glass.

"Ah! Herr Berman!" Both their faces were beaming and they kept shaking hands as if they would never let go.

"Please, do sit down, Herr Berman!" Shapiro pulled out a chair for his guest, just as Berman had done the day before, and sat down at the head of the table. Berman saw his reflection in the mirror-like surface of the table, and, looking up at the ceiling, noticed how fine it was. The chandelier was genuine crystal, the carpet beneath their feet was soft and thick, covering the whole of the floor. It was plain blue, without a single flower motif on it. And the walls were beautifully papered, the gold strips at the edges harmonising so tastefully with the blue – magnificent!

"What this rogue has managed to achieve! He's just a broker, and I am the diamond merchant. How is it possible? There is so little furniture and yet it all looks so sumptuous!"

"Lenchen!" Shapiro called out to his wife.

Madame Shapiro emerged, as if she had been hiding, from behind a heavy, dark blue, velvet-covered door near the window. She greeted Berman, giving him her hand. She had dull, round eyes, set far apart. A watery smile did not enliven her lethargic expression. Berman looked at her for a long time. "Hmm ... I think she's even more repulsive than before," he thought to himself. In her well-cut skirt, heavy crêpe de Chine blouse and beautifully coiffeured wig, all of which had obviously cost a great deal of money, she looked like a great lump of wood wrapped up in silk.

Madame Shapiro excused herself, went into the kitchen and came back, accompanied by a tall slender girl of about eighteen who wore a starched blue dress with a tiny tulle apron, with a white cap on her shining, blonde hair. The girl carried a glass plate full of fruit, and her dazzling smile and large, blue, childlike eyes contrasted favourably with Madame Shapiro's appearance.

"Don't wait to be invited, Herr Berman!" said Madame Shapiro, and Shapiro himself filled two glasses with sparkling liqueur from a fine cut-glass carafe. They clinked their glasses and emptied them.

"You can go now," said Shapiro, sending the girl back to the kitchen, devouring her with his eyes as if she had been honey cake. Berman could not understand how Madame Shapiro tolerated such a beautiful Gentile maidservant, when she herself was so ugly. It was no secret in the town that Shapiro picked the servant girls, and that only after he had given his approval did his wife start to negotiate about wages and so forth; a few ducats more or less were not the deciding factor here. "My God, what a hypocrite!" thought Berman. "The way the rat calls her 'Lenchen', so affectionately, thinking he's deceiving everyone." Wiping his moustache, he said aloud: "Now, let's see what you've got for me."

From his breast pocket Shapiro took out, and unwrapped, a parcel of diamonds. They flashed red, blue, yellow, green. "What do you think of that? Fine goods, eh?"

The diamonds in Madame Shapiro's ears seemed to respond, lighting up in fiery colours as if they recognised old friends. The two men spoke for a long time, gesturing, one with his large brown hands, the other with his plump white ones, until at last they shook hands on the deal and started chatting about this and that: politics, the past.

Berman said goodbye to Shapiro, almost forgetting to give his hand to Madame Shapiro. But she pushed her bejewelled hand into his:

"*Auf Wiedersehen*, Herr Berman! Please give your wife my kind regards." Madame Shapiro's large, dull, black eyes, her nose, even her cheeks seemed to laugh and cry together when she spoke. Berman promised he would not forget, thinking that it was not surprising Shapiro was such a womaniser. Rochl suddenly came into his mind, dressed in her finest clothes, as she looked when she was going to a wedding or a *bar mitzvah.** The image of her filled him with pleasure.

He wondered how old Madame Shapiro was. It was hard to assess. She could be anything between thirty and fifty. And Shapiro was still quite a young man. He must have married her for the dowry.

The women who gathered in the zoological garden on summer afternoons gossiped a great deal about the Shapiros and discussed Madame Shapiro's habit of sitting at her window for days at a time. She would gaze into the street to pass the time. She didn't come to the zoological garden because she was embarrassed; she knew very well that people realised the expensive clothes and jewellery which her husband draped round her did not signify deep love on his part, but rather his desire to make her into a living advertisement of his wealth. She had even heard the women denigrating her, and she wept not only with her eyes, but with her nose, cheeks, mouth, even the curls of her wig.

On the way home, Berman thought about the bargain he had just bought. In his mind he went through all the richest merchants in the Bourse to decide on the most suitable purchaser, but they had all gone away on holiday. Still, the stones wouldn't spoil. Thank God, that was a good purchase. Shapiro certainly was clever, damn him!

It suddenly occurred to Berman that once again he had not followed his doctor's orders to take a daily walk for his blood circulation. When you are always so busy, you forget all about your health! So not having anything particular to do until lunch, he set out on his walk for the first time in three months.

The streets and lanes of Zurenborg* had all been swept clean. The brass knockers of the white and yellow doors were gleaming, and the windowpanes shone. Figures of women, children and angels danced on the lace curtains. But the streets were absolutely empty. Berman strode through all of Zurenborg until he came to Borgerhout. The pungent smell of fresh, warm wax, which permanently hung over Borgerhout, poured out of the candle factory. Berman found it impossible to continue his walk here. He covered his nose with his hand and turned back into the city.

The afternoon activities had already begun. The department stores were full of women looking for bargains. Some had gone to the zoological garden for a cup of coffee and a gossip. The pavements were blocked by prams. They were pushed by women with cheerful faces and pointed, red noses. Their white hands sparkled with diamonds. Little white bonnets decorated with Brussels lace and blue or pink ribbons were visible in the prams. The sleeping children, covered in silk and lace were cuddling their dolls.

But there were also worn, grey-faced mothers pushing shabby prams with grubby children who were either sucking dirty pieces of rubber or sticking their hands into their mouths. These children had thin faces and sallow skin.

Berman pushed his way through the crowds. An elderly Jew was

76

tottering along beside a plump middle-aged man who was clean-shaven and wore a light, grey suit. The two were arguing. The old man saw Berman, raised his crumpled hat and greeted him. He was like Madame Shapiro, his eyes and cheeks seemed to be laughing and crying at the same time. The wrinkles round his eyes deepened as he spoke, his bluish lips became moist. In his efforts to gain the upper hand over the corpulent gentleman, he was working himself up into a frenzy. But the latter just kept smiling with an indifference which maddened the old man.

"You certainly won't regret it! Old Tsimerman always lets me have goods at a lower price than the others. I've already been lucky with him, and he knows that I am an experienced broker, not a crook!" said the old man eagerly.

"But I don't *need* small stones," said the merchant, making an impatient gesture. The old man's face fell.

In the middle of the street, pale young men with wispy beards and older men with long thick ones were riding on tricycles. Their sallow faces told sad tales. Their beards brushed the baskets full of fish, bread and meat, which these former diamond traders and other poor people were delivering to rich houses where parsimonious housewives lived, who were quite prepared to go into the shops, pick over the goods and haggle for ages. They were not prepared, however, to carry the purchases home themselves. The errand boys with long beards had to deliver the goods, while nostalgically remembering the time when they had arrived in Antwerp with their dowry in their pockets, full of hopes of becoming rich. But having no talent, they were soon fleeced in the Bourse or at the Club. And now this was how they made their livelihood. Some were in business for themselves and pushed flat carts with dogs harnessed to them, which they had bought in the *Vogelmarkt.* They had to push the carts to help the dogs pull the load, and they dragged themselves around the poor Jewish lanes which looked as crooked and exhausted as the peddlers themselves. They called out their miserable wares as if they were chanting from the *Gemara.*

It always amused Berman to see these hopeless cases with their dog carts. But he didn't, God forbid, laugh at them! For who can tell what tomorrow will bring.

Chapter 8

The table was neatly laid at the Bermans'. The silver cutlery gleamed and there were dishes with all kinds of *kugel* and delicious conserves. Siphons of soda water sparkled, and the red medicine which Berman took after meals was awaiting him. Anneke was still wandering about with a yellow duster in her hand, making a show of looking for dust, which was nowhere to be found in this venerable and luxurious dining room.

Dovid came down from his bedroom in his slippers and dressing gown. His hair was tousled and his face looked yellowish and puffy with sleep. Anneke grabbed her duster and made for the door, but Dovid called her back and pulled her to him. Blushing, Anneke broke free then rushed to the door. Jeannette came down from her bedroom wrapped in a long, blue, silk dressing gown trimmed with white fur, and wearing high-heeled slippers. Her hair was wet and her dainty little ears were rosy. She ran to Dovid, sat down beside him on the wide velvet sofa and started kissing him like a lover.

"Oh, you're here, Dovid!" Then she prattled on: "Listen, Dovid, this week I read an amazing novel. You won't believe what happens in it! You'll go mad!"

"You certainly are mad!" said her mother, suddenly appearing at the door. "I can't imagine what she finds in those books. She doesn't even want to eat her breakfast!"

"Oh, Mama, if you could read you'd know what I mean. Dovid, you really must read it. It's extraordinary!"

"But you say that about every book you read."

"That's because they've all got something special about them. Oh! Dovid!" She hugged him hard.

"Aha, I see my sister has gone off her head!" Dovid retreated to the corner of the sofa.

"Look, Dovid, this is the way she danced!"

"The way *who* danced?"

"You'll see how the dance goes!"

Jeannette positioned herself in front of the mirror, lifted a corner of her dressing gown between her fingers and started dancing, slow and stately at first, then gradually building up to an ecstatic pitch, spinning round faster and faster, like a whirlwind. Suddenly she kicked off her slippers and raised one leg in the air, showing her blue silk underwear and her bare, brown legs. Dovid, reclining in the corner of the sofa, languidly followed her every movement, with the critical air of a connoisseur.

When Berman opened the door to the dining room, a flash of blue silk darted in front of his eyes, and he stopped dead. Jeannette was still dancing, spinning wildly then dancing with a more measured pace. She finally came to rest with both feet together, like a ballerina on the stopper of a perfume bottle. Berman just stood staring, rooted to the spot, hardly comprehending at first that this was his own daughter dancing. Jeannette was tired and sat down beside her brother on the sofa. When Dovid saw his father, however, he immediately stole off back to his bedroom.

"That's how she danced," Jeannette kept repeating, not noticing that Dovid was no longer there.

"Who danced?" asked Berman, puzzled.

"Oh, Papa dearest, I thought you were Dovid!"

"But *who* danced?"

"Oh, it was in my book. I have a French novel in which a girl dances because she's in love! You should read it."

"I can't be bothered with your foolishness! I don't know what you're talking about! Rochl, let's eat. I'm starving."

Rochl looked at Dovid's empty place and sighed: "Where will it all end?"

In the afternoon Jacques showed an elderly man into the Bermans' dining room, making use of the opportunity to slip out of the house. The old man was obviously expecting a cool reception. "I was just passing and said to myself: 'Well, surely they won't *eat* me.'"

Berman looked at him and replied with a cynical smile: "Well, I certainly have no intention of *eating* you – what a thought – ugh!"

Pretending not to notice the sarcasm, the old man approached the table.

"What is it you want?" Berman said quickly.

"Well... ehm... joking apart..." The old man took out his snuff box. "Joking apart..." He tapped all four sides of his snuff box to loosen the snuff. "As someone once said: 'There's no harm in trying', so I thought, 'Well, perhaps', after all, it was quite a dowry. But in fact, it really wasn't a suitable match for your son, was it? I realise that now."

"So what are you gabbling about then? One thing or the other: if it wasn't a match for us, why have you come to bother me now?"

"And what a joke! I thought to myself: she certainly is no spring chicken, but on the other hand – such a huge fortune! However, the moment I learned that the hundred thousand had shrunk to ten thousand, I took my hat out of the ring!"

"But didn't you have *two* different hats in the ring at the same time?"

"Who said that? God forbid!" said the man, with a start.

"I know you very well. As soon as you realised that I wasn't willing to sell my son to that old hag, not even for ten million francs, you went off to *them*. I'm very well aware that you were trying to play one of us off against the other. So what is it you want now?"

The old man pretended he didn't know what Berman was talking about. He sat down at the table, stuffed snuff up both nostrils, took a large red handkerchief out of the pocket of his long coat with the sheepskin collar which he wore both summer and winter, wiped his angular face, grasped his pointed, grey beard with both hands and sneezed loudly.

Berman moved away to the far end of the table; he had to sneeze as well.

"Listen, Herr Berman! You know very well that no one in Antwerp has ever got married without me. No one has ever slipped through my fingers, except perhaps where there's some question of being in love. But even then they have to come to me in the end."

"So what exactly is it you want from me? A kiss on the cheek? All right. Come closer and I'll give you a kiss." Berman laughed and stood up as a sign to the old man that he should leave. But the latter remained seated, until Berman simply said: "Reb Beynish, I have to go out. I simply don't have time for you just now."

Reb Beynish stood up, gave Berman his hand, and said: "Don't worry! Something suitable will come along, God willing. Then we'll have a drink of vodka together, that's for sure. Heh! heh! heh!" and off he went.

Reb Beynish was not lying. He made matches for all of Antwerp, and it was his habit to negotiate the same match with various families at once. Thus he almost always had success, because if it didn't please one family, then it did please a second one, a third, a fourth, a fifth. He had come to Antwerp as a young man, and hadn't let the grass grow under his feet: the very same evening he arrived he started matchmaking. Usually he snapped up young men from the Hassidic *shtiblekh*. They had come from Poland or Russia in order to avoid military service. If one of these young men did not have any relatives in Antwerp, he usually had a letter from his *rebbe* to a Hassid who lived in the town. The young men from Galicia did tend to have relatives in Antwerp. Therefore Reb Beynish caught them in the street, in the synagogue, in the *shtibl* or at home. Among all the worshippers he was always the first to greet a newly arrived young man, ask him in great detail who he was, where he came from, what he did for a living and so on. Even if the young man was a silent type, or a slippery customer, or simply someone who did not like talking about himself, Reb Beynish always managed to prise everything out of him. It was impossible to hide anything from him, and when he had found out all he wanted to know, he started talking to the young man about making a match.

"You say you're not ready to get married? Always the same old tune! Heh! heh! heh! You're just teasing me, that's what you're doing. It's always the same! But never mind, you'll soon be ready, you'll soon be ready! After all, what are you going to achieve here? Nothing at all! You'll soon use up the few roubles you possess, and even if it's a few hundred roubles, does it make any difference? So, you'll learn to be a diamond cutter. Well, yes, that's a respectable trade," and Beynish tapped his bone snuff-box to loosen the snuff. "A new livelihood. It may be a fine livelihood, but not for a Jew. Certainly if you were, God forbid, a *goy*,* you could join the union, and you'd earn enough for your bread. Not just for bread, you could get drunk too on your wages, you could roll around in the dirt, heh! heh! But because you are, thank God, a Jew, and not a *goy*, God forbid, you'll have to work a good few years for nothing. In fact, why do I say 'for nothing'? You'll actually have to *pay* a few hundred roubles to be taught the trade. And do you think you'll be taught properly? Not on your life! *Half*-taught, that's what you'll be. And apart from that, they'll certainly not let *you* get your hands on a parcel of diamonds, because there are masses of cutters and polishers around who haven't a crust of bread to put in their mouths, and they're all running round after the bosses, trying to get hold of a couple of stones. If you don't kiss the boss, you know where, then, I'm sorry to say, you'll just be sent packing. What will you do then? I ask you, eh?" Then Reb Beynish takes a pinch of snuff and holds it between his fingers until the young man starts sneezing:

"Atchoo! Atchoo!"

"Bless you! So you're sneezing at my honest words? May all Jews have the benefit of such sincere advice. I tell you, they're all cut-throats out there. They're just looking for a sucker who doesn't understand their tricks yet. And, at the end of your so-called training, you'll still have to pay off your machine, which'll be rusting in the corner. And even if you do get hold of a few stones, you'll make a mess of them. For how could you know how to cut them? And then you certainly won't get any more. At home they'll get tired of supporting you and sending you money, because it's a real burden, do you understand me? When I see a young man like you in a synagogue or *shtibl*, it tears my heart out," sighs Beynish, making sure that the young man can't get a word in edgeways. He continues his monologue at breakneck speed, without pausing for breath. "If you follow my advice you will bless the day you met me. I've got a girl for you. She's not a girl, she's a jewel! And from a fine family! What am I talking about? From an *exceptionally prestigious* family! You will get a wonderful dowry and a furnished apartment. Your father-in-law will take you into the business and make a merchant or a broker of you - that's not bad either. We should all be as lucky as Shapiro who is better off than many of the great merchants! I tell you, if a broker has a good brain, then it's an excellent livelihood. You don't have to put your own money into it, but you certainly can take plenty out of it.

"What does a broker do, you ask? He mediates between diamond merchants. It's simple: you're a merchant and I'm a merchant. I have a parcel of diamonds I want to sell. The broker runs round the offices, the *Shenkl*, the Club, the Fortunia, and even the Bourse, until he catches a merchant - you, for example - and you just happen to need exactly the goods which he has for sale. You buy them, and the broker gets his percentage. Now what do you think, isn't that a good job? You don't have to invest anything in the business except your brains, and many brokers become rich. But, suddenly, on a normal working day, there is a huge commotion among the merchants. The town is buzzing with excitement. What's happened? Someone has lost diamonds again. So what does that mean? It means nothing at all. It means that the broker who was entrusted with some merchandise, has ostensibly "lost" it, or has been robbed. You know very well that it is just a trumped up tale, but what can you do, if he doesn't have it? Do you think he'll be put in jail? Or won't be able to show his face in the marketplace? You would be wrong. On the contrary, in a few weeks' time he'll be given even more merchandise than before. Because those who aren't afraid to "lose" merchandise, also know how to sell very well and always get the true price, whereas those who never "lose" are considered to be mediocre, and no one wants to have any dealings with them. Apart from Shapiro, you don't know him yet, how could you? But everyone knows him. He is a rich man, who, they say, never loses stones. And yet he goes round decked out in gold. He has his own way of doing things, they say, and no one knows what it is, but he is as rich as Croesus, and who was it who arranged his marriage? To whom does he owe everything? To me! And his wife, she's a really virtuous woman, a good soul!

"Follow my advice and you'll do well in the world. You'll have a home, a wife, a family, and you'll never be lonely. You'll never have to roam around. You can at least look at her! Someone once said 'Looking is not marrying.' If she pleases you, then that's fine, and if she doesn't, well, we'll find another one who will please you."

Reb Beynish goes on talking and talking, squeezing the young man against the wall in the corner of the synagogue, pressing against him with his heavy, bony body in the black coat with the sheepskin collar which he wears summer and winter, and doesn't release him until the young man sees, whether he wants to or not, the logic of Beynish's argument: that taking a look at her is not the same as marrying her. And the result is that for nine out of ten of them a match is arranged and he dances at their weddings in his black coat with the sheepskin collar, which smells of sweat, snuff and mould. Sometimes it happens that he doesn't succeed at the first attempt, in which case he goes to the young man's relatives and teaches them a little of his logic. He convinces them by all manner of veiled hints, even, if necessary, in a very rusty Flemish that it would be greatly to *their* advantage if the young man got married and had a place of his own.

It happens very frequently that a young man passes through on the way to America. Even though he is only in Antwerp for a few days, Reb Beynish manages to catch him and arrange a marriage for him. Usually Beynish himself doesn't know who he means when he praises the prospective bride as "a jewel of a girl", because he has a long list of names inscribed in his notebook, which he can't possibly know off by heart. His thick greasy little notebook is worth millions – who knows the total value of the dowries he carries around in his pocket? It's not until a young man agrees that taking a look does not amount to marriage that Beynish has recourse to his notebook.

Now, after his visit to Berman, Beynish was in a really bad mood: was this the way he deserved to be treated? "Is it possible? He simply threw me out! What a bastard!" Beynish just couldn't get over it. "I try to make a match on his behalf, to marry that good-for-nothing into a fine family, with a wonderful dowry, and not only does he not thank me for all the efforts I've made to no avail, but he gets into a rage with me. Well, all the same, it's not easy for him. God help a father who has such an empty vessel for a son, such a godless, dishonest wastrel. Berman will have to sort it out for himself."

With these thoughts Beynish made his way home, striding through the streets of Antwerp in his greasy coat. That afternoon he didn't even put his nose into the *shtibl* to see whether a new prospective bridegroom had turned up.

Chapter 9

When he arrived back from the synagogue, Berman was met by Rochl. She was wrapped in a dark shawl, her eyes red with weeping, and her wig uncombed.

"What's the matter?" asked Berman, shocked.

"Gedaliah, something terrible has happened! I told you that you should go easy on your children. Now what will people think of us? Antwerp will certainly have something to gossip about now. Our enemies were just waiting for this, may their tongues dry up!"

Berman stared at her, frowning with his heavy eyebrows. He did not understand what she was talking about, but he wondered where Rochl had suddenly found such a flow of oratory. Normally she couldn't string two words together.

"What's happened? Tell me now!"

Rochl sobbed loudly. "Dovid is going to be a simple manual worker! He is going to train as a diamond polisher. He says there's no point in trying to dissuade him. Oh my God, this is all I need!"

Berman burst out laughing.

"For God's sake, you almost gave me a heart attack. What I have to put up with from this fool and her son!"

He sat down at the head of the table, demanded his supper, and continued: "Don't worry, that lazy slob will never make it as a manual worker. Just let him try and he'll find out what it's like to have to earn your daily bread. My father didn't support me, so I had to learn the hard way. But Dovid's as likely to become a worker as I am to become a priest! What a thought! Dovid, a worker! He lies in his stinking bed till four in the afternoon, then he dresses himself up at my expense, parades around doing nothing for the rest of the day, and if you say a word, his answer is to run away from home, and his dear mama has to run around the town searching for him." Berman seemed to have already forgotten his own earlier anxiety about his son. "Bah, I know what he's up to. He's just trying to scare us."

But Dovid was very much in earnest. He had decided to put an end to his way of life once and for all. He was sick of the scenes with his father, and of lying in bed all day, simply in order to make the time pass. He had had enough of trailing aimlessly round the streets of Antwerp, feeling totally superfluous in society, a figure of ridicule to himself and everyone else.

And though his evenings with Gitele had been wonderful, had he not paid for them with his self-respect? Skulking around like a thief and a coward, not having the courage to say to Leybesh: "I love your wife and she loves me, and I am going to take her and the child - *my* child - to live with me." In fact he was worse than a coward, because he had no means of supporting her. He was a hopeless failure, that's what he was.

But it couldn't go on like this. If he couldn't trade in the Bourse, he had to find some other way of making a living. So he decided to learn a trade, which wasn't such a terrible thing. A worker is a human being too, after all. He'd be able to set up his own home, and even if it was very modest, he would be with Gitele and his child.

He went to tell Gitele of his decision, expecting her to be delighted. But instead, Gitele looked at him with a half-sad, half-ironic expression, made an impatient gesture and said dismissively: "Another of your great ideas."

Dovid had pictured her embracing and kissing him, weeping with joy and telling him that his honest, genuine love was more precious to her than jewels. She would promise that as soon as he was in a position to keep them, she would go and live openly with him as his wife. This would put an end to their ambiguous situation. Instead of that, she mocked him, declared that he wasn't fit to be a worker, and advised him against taking this step. "Listen, Dovid," she said, "Manual work is the last thing you should do. It isn't for you, and you'll just get humiliated for no good reason. And in any case, what will you achieve? Let's say you do get work, you'll still remain a pauper for the rest of your life. You can see what the situation is in this house. Working for someone else is like working for the devil."

Just as Dovid had not anticipated that his mother would mourn him as if he had died, he had not expected Gitele to react like this. To hell with them all! Living like this was worse than anything. He was going mad. A man had to do something. So he approached Rosenkrantz, a well-known factory owner, and told him that he wanted to learn polishing. He said he wanted to become expert in all areas of the diamond business. The owner didn't really believe him, but asked no questions; if he wanted to learn the trade, let him get on with it.

When Dovid went into the factory, accompanied by the boss, fifty astonished workers turned to stare, their eyes popping out of their heads.

"Eh, what's Berman's brat doing here? And at nine o'clock in the morning?"

"He must have fallen out of bed!" muttered a fair-haired lad to an older, bald-headed man with a wrinkled face.

"Look, Rosenkrantz is demonstrating the scaife to him." The workers' curiosity increased. "Oh my God, perhaps his daddy's going to take over the workshop."

"Well, what's it matter? Do you think you'd get a worse deal?" said another, gesturing at the boss.

"You bet! Compared to *him*, ours is an angel."

"Oh yes, sure, an angel with wings!"

"A pure and saintly soul! If his saintliness migrated into a dog it would start frothing at the mouth!"

"Shhh! He's coming over with him."

The boss approached the man with the bald head. "Now, Berman, Kupershteyn will show you what's what, and if you apply yourself, you'll get good training in my workshop. Don't you agree, Kupershteyn? Only good polishers go out of here, and if you've been trained with me, that's a recommendation in itself. Eh, Kupershteyn?" and he slapped Kupershteyn so heartily on the back that the latter nearly fell off his stool.

Kupershteyn's bald head became pink, and his eyes reddened. He muttered something inaudible, but the expression on his wrinkled face said "Go to hell!"

Dovid sat down on one of the high stools, which were scuffed and blackened with age. The boss himself brought him an overall, and when Dovid put it on, he suddenly felt as if Rosenkrantz was somehow deliberately humiliating him. He was overcome by such a feeling of depression that it was all he could do not to burst into tears. When he looked at the overall it seemed as if it was guilty for the strange mess he was in, and that if he didn't have to wear this, it wouldn't be so demeaning to work in a workshop. He couldn't concentrate on anything the old man with the bad-tempered wrinkled face was telling him. All he was aware of was the bald head, which looked like a skull, and himself in a prison uniform. And why were they all craning their heads round and staring at him? What were they looking at?

He looked himself up and down and realised it was probably because he had forgotten to take off his white spats. One of the apprentices sniggered, others said "Shhh!" and Dovid felt keenly the absurdity of his situation. If only he hadn't put on that overall! His ears were burning, and he felt confused and embarrassed. He sat at the scaife, the wheel turned, and the whole workshop spun round with it.

The workers, in their dirty, often torn overalls followed the revolving wheels with their experienced eyes. They spun round faster than the layman's eye could see, and all Dovid saw was a circular blur of gleaming metal. On the wheels, diamonds of all sizes and colours were being polished: single cuts, small stones with only eight facets, as well as large, valuable full cuts with fifty-seven facets.

Kupershteyn was an old and trusted polisher, who never took the loupe* away from his eye, nor his eye off the stone he was working on, in case it disappeared. Very large precious stones were entrusted to him, which he guarded with his life.

Dovid sat and watched. No one said a word to him, and Kupershteyn, his teacher, paid Dovid no attention at all. At last Dovid asked: "What should I do?" "Just watch!" was the answer.

Dovid realised that all he was allowed to do was to look and look again. As soon as one facet was finished, the stone was taken off the disc, which then began flying round again at dizzying speed, like magic. A worker took the diamond off the dop, melted the lead on the little blue gas flame which, like the flames of hell, never went out, put the stone back on the dop and another facet was polished. The workers clustered round the scaife even though they didn't have a great deal to do. Looking was the most important activity. They all looked grubby, as if they worked in a coal mine instead of polishing diamonds to glitter on the necks, arms and breasts of leisured ladies and gentlemen. Even Dovid's hands were grimy, and, under his beautifully manicured fingernails, a layer of dirt built up; this was the black diamond powder mixed with oil, which clung to the skin as soon as one went near it.

Old Kupershteyn took off his overall to go home for lunch, and Dovid saw with surprise that all the workers, as if at a given signal, got up, grabbed an overcoat or a scarf and eagerly made for the exit, as if they hadn't seen the outside world for years.

Dovid had felt so forlorn that he was positively delighted when the old man suddenly seemed a little friendlier, asking him whether he had brought his lunch with him. "No," said Dovid.

"I've brought mine!" shouted someone else.

"Hope it chokes you!" muttered the old man, and went out without even saying goodbye, leaving Dovid totally bewildered. "What a strange bunch," he thought. "Not an ounce of common courtesy."

The street seemed brighter than usual to him, and he felt as if everyone was staring at him. And, indeed, someone was walking behind him, discussing him at the top of his voice. "What do you think of that fool? I thought I'd die laughing. Imagine coming to the workshop in a pair of white spats!"

"He must be a bit touched, eh? Who is he anyway?"

"Who is he? Berman's son, of course!"

"*What?*"

"Yes, did you not realise?"

"What, is he short of money?"

"No, he's short of a brain!"

"Ha, ha, ha! Our boss is right when he says "You can't have money *and* brains!"

"Ha, ha! Too right!"

The sweat broke out on Dovid's forehead and he was seized by a helpless rage towards the workers.

When Rochl saw him coming home for lunch with a grimy face, she clasped her hands to her stomach, like a goose flapping its wings when it sees something threatening. She begged him not to be offended, but asked him not to appear in this state in front of Anneke.

When Dovid looked in the full-length mirror, he was shocked at what he saw. He looked black, his hair was tousled and even though he hadn't done any real work yet, the strange exhaustion he felt showed in his eyes. He was tired out from just being at the workshop. He flung himself down on the big velvet sofa and Rochl brought in a basin of warm, scented water and a large white towel, after which she gave him his lunch.

"Dovid!" exclaimed Rochl, "For my sake, *please* don't persist in this."

"And what about the millions of workers who slave away their whole lives, in strenuous work like diamond polishing, and still they thank God that they have work, eh, Mama?" Dovid was really putting this question to himself.

"It's different for them, they're used to it. I myself ..."

But she stopped herself just in time, realising that it was better that Dovid should not know that she used to be a cook, and that she was the daughter of a carpenter. May her children not know about such a life, she murmured quietly, to God.

After a few days the work had become so unbearable to Dovid that he thought it would be better to go and break stones in a quarry, rather than work as a diamond polisher. He got along well enough with the bearded Jews in the workshop, with skullcaps on their pale brows, who would sing a Hassidic melody while working with the stones. They were also there because they had no other choice, and Dovid felt that they understood what he was going through. So although they were amused by him, they behaved politely towards him, with the odd good-natured jibe. But it was the common young men whose fathers were tailors or cobblers, for whom it was an honour to work in a polishing workshop, who made Dovid's life a misery with their vulgar laughter over the incident with the spats, which they would not let him forget. They were so arrogant, and their language! That old man with the bald head who looked like a criminal, he would only speak to

Dovid if he absolutely had to, and his stubborn silence got on Dovid's nerves. Above all, he couldn't bear feeling dozens of eyes on his back, knowing that they were full of contempt. This hurt him much more than the fact of having to stand around and watch the entire time. He felt like an absolute idiot, and the overall was the worst thing of all.

One morning the boss came into the workshop elegantly dressed, his hair combed and his face flushed after his ample breakfast. He called the foreman to him and conferred with him for a long time, giving him orders, discussing the matter, then thinking about it, then giving more orders. After this he left to attend to his business affairs and didn't notice Dovid. In fact he had completely forgotten about him. He just noticed there was a trainee watching how it was done, which was fine. This really annoyed Dovid. The boss had not even come over to address a few words to him. And yet it was only a week ago that they had meet on the Keyserlei, greeted each other like equals, and although Rosenkrantz was considerably older than Dovid, he had been happy for Dovid to pay the bill, he had smoked a good few of Dovid's cigarettes, and now, he didn't even know him. Dovid forgot that he was now only a simple worker, and felt tremendous resentment towards Rosenkrantz.

No, he wasn't going to carry on working there. He would show him, the bastard, that he, Dovid, could afford to stop if he wished. He would make fun of Rosenkrantz the next time he met him, he'd tell him that he was a fool to have thought that he, Dovid Berman, was really going to become a worker. His mother had been right.

"Look at the way he got himself all dressed up today. He just put on his best suit to provoke and humiliate me, and he deliberately raised his voice when he was lording it over the foreman. He was bellowing so that I would hear, and yet he refused to notice or recognise me."

Dovid was in such a fury that he suddenly pulled off the blue overall, threw it on the ground, and left the workshop without saying goodbye to anyone.

The next morning Rochl was so pleased when she saw Dovid was lying in bed without any intention of getting dressed to go to work, that she joyfully carried up his breakfast to him.

The men from the workshop stared in amazement when they saw Dovid sauntering around the streets in the middle of the working day.

"What, has he given up already?" they all asked, open-mouthed.

"Why are you asking me? Ask him." Dovid's mentor shook his bald head and took another stone off the disc.

"Well, what did you imagine?" said the foreman, a stout young man with a red beard. "Did you really think that Berman's son would sit here forever polishing stones with the likes of you? Did you think he had nothing better to do? He was just making fun of you, and you fools just let yourselves be taken in." He spoke with smug satisfaction and his eyes shone as if he had been dealt a hand with three aces in a card game in Hershl's Restaurant.

Each of the workers felt that Dovid had made a fool of him personally. They had believed he was serious and even been quite pleased he was working with them - when in fact that devil, that fawning cur, was just having a laugh at their expense.

"His father can afford to support his precious, aristocratic son. To hell with him! As for us, we're just the scum of the earth, we can't afford that luxury. Just imagine walking out of the workshop in the middle of the working day!"

"There's nothing you can do about it," a young disciple of Leybesh's said bitterly. "You have to cower here making sure that Rosenkrantz's diamonds don't, God forbid, run away, and that they end up looking magnificent, flashing and sparkling!" he continued, stirring up the workers and himself.

"Come on then, that's enough talking! Back to work!" interrupted the foreman.

They quietened down and the machines started up again, the wheels turning. The young Hassidim started humming their *rebbe*'s melody. The monotonous routine of examining the stones, and the continual hissing of the hot tweezers as they were dipped into cold water to harden the lead carried on, just as it did every day.

Chapter 10

When Berman next went into the Bourse, he saw that the other merchants were giving him strange looks. There was suspicion in their sharp eyes, and they spoke to him in a less respectful tone than they had previously.

"Ha, that scoundrel has obviously kept his word and gone off to bring shame on my name!" thought Berman. It was clear that they had already heard that Dovid was training as a diamond polisher; there was no doubt of that.

Horowitz stretched out his hand to Berman with a familiar and friendly air, as if they were equals now. "Well, it seems that neither of us is a millionaire, eh? But don't worry, we'll manage somehow!" Horowitz and the other merchants would never have dared to speak to him in such a tone before. He was acutely aware of the way they looked at him.

"Well, well, Antwerp certainly hasn't been sleeping," he thought to himself. "They're already assuming that I am bankrupt." So was this the way Dovid had repaid his father's kindness in turning a blind eye when he came back from the carnival in such a state?

Muttering and grumbling to himself, Berman left the Bourse and went along Provinciestraat. Trintshe, the fishmonger, a large Gentile woman, who almost filled the doorway of her shop, shouted a friendly greeting to him: "*Dag menieër*! Nice weather!" Berman looked up, suddenly filled with a feeling of warmth towards Shprintse,[*] as the Jews called her. She greeted him as she did every morning, without funny looks, not knowing, presumably, that Dovid had become a worker. Wanting to convince himself that he enjoyed the same respect as before, he went over to her and started examining the assortment of merchandise laid out on the large marble slab, unable to decide what he should buy. There were huge sole with white fins and even whiter bellies, little Dutch herring with silver scales and red eyes, fine broad bream with bloodshot eyes, speckled roach, mackerel with green backs and fat bellies, and a huge mound of little silvery fish, about a hundred to the kilo. Outside, on one side of the doorway, there was a big, square basin, in which black eels squirmed around, and on the other side stood a barrel of salted Dutch herring and a barrel of pickled cucumber. Berman didn't fancy any of these.

A large salmon, which lay apart from the other fish, had attracted Berman's eye. Its stomach was slit open, and its dark silvery scales were stained with blood. To Berman the salmon looked as aristocratic and haughty as he was, and he took pleasure in instructing Trintshe to wrap it up very carefully. She was surprised, for this was the first time that Berman had bought a salmon without asking if it was fresh and how much it cost, then offering half the price she had quoted him. She said nothing, however, but, as she always did, praised the fish as she was wrapping it up.

When she had the money in her hand, she drew his attention to a glass tank in which gleaming brown carp were swimming around with half of their scales floating in the greenish water. She asked him to be sure to tell his wife always to come early on Thursdays, because today she didn't have very many carp left.

Then the Gentile woman, knowing that the next day was the Jewish Sabbath, wished him "*Gut Shabbes!*" in Yiddish.

Berman glanced at the carp. On a bench beside the tank was a dish full of pink shrimps. He looked at them crawling around, one on top of the other, in a slow-moving mass. He thought of the unspeakable things they devoured, which made them so vigorous. Berman turned away from the squirming creatures and couldn't help spitting in disgust. He was really spitting out the sour taste he still had in his mouth from the Bourse. He started for home with the fish under his arm, thinking malevolent thoughts about his son.

Among a row of Jewish dairies and grocers' and butchers' shops with prominent, but crumbling, dirty, kosher signs, one bright shop window displayed a skinned pig with a red, bleeding snout. It held a bunch of parsley in its mouth. On a white marble slab various chunks of horse meat were laid out. On both sides of the shop door hung about two dozen rabbits with their fur still on. The fat, ruddy-complexioned, clean-shaven butcher was standing at the door of his shop in a white coat, whistling cheerfully. He greeted Berman as though the latter had been his best customer, also telling him the news that it was nice weather today. Berman agreed wholeheartedly with this, and walked on with his fish under his arm.

"So that wastrel has got the better of me! He's playing games with me, while I have to pinch my cheeks to bring some colour into them! I'll have to support that layabout for the rest of his life, feed and clothe him like a lord, while he spits in my face. That's all the thanks I will get for everything I've done for him."

When he got home, Berman threw the fish on the kitchen table and without even greeting Rochl, went into the dining room and sat down, tired and bad-tempered, to look through his private mail, which was waiting for him on the table. "All rubbish!" A young man has a new cutting machine, and since he hasn't been able to meet Berman in his office in Pelikaanstraat, and has had no reply to letters he has sent him, he is taking the liberty of writing to his home address. His letter is full of verses from the Bible and Talmud, and ends with *kol hatkhiles koshoys* – every beginning is difficult.

"Just asking for favours! Just rubbish!"

When Rochl came into the room to ask what he wanted done with the salmon and whether he would like a glass of tea, he shouted at her "Tell me, you! Where is your darling layabout son, eh? Don't shrug your shoulders; you know very well where he is working, eh?"

Berman's eyes glittered and seemed to be popping out of their sockets. Rochl shrank back in alarm, imagining that any minute now they would spring out and roll around the carpet.

"What do you mean, shrug my shoulders? Who says Dovid is working somewhere? He's still lying in bed!"

"Ha! Did he think better of it, then?" wondered Berman and edged open the door of Dovid's bedroom. Yes, there he was lying on his back with rumpled hair and a thick book in his hands. He didn't notice his father peering in.

"So that's how it is? I wonder what happened. Did they mock him, or give him funny looks? I bet they're rejoicing at his failure. I wonder what went through his mind. A strange affair."

He turned on Rochl angrily. "Why are you standing there like an idiot? Get me a glass of tea!"

"Sons like him should be drowned at birth," muttered Berman, making the blessing over his glass of tea.

Chapter 11

That evening Berman didn't go to the synagogue, even though he should have said Kaddish* for his mother. Instead he said the evening prayers at home. He lit the crystal chandelier, although it was still light outside.

When he had finished praying he lay down on the sofa and tried to take a nap, but he was too agitated. His thoughts raced around in confusion. People actually thought that *he*, Berman, the respected, well-established diamond dealer, was bankrupt? How many enemies he had! How delighted they were to think that he had gone to the wall! But who were his enemies? And who had gone to the wall? Dovid had not actually gone on to be a diamond polisher after all, even though he had made a show of threatening to do so. It was all that stupid woman's fault. As usual Berman made Rochl the butt of his rage, even though he was not absolutely sure what exactly he was angry about.

A knock at the door interrupted his tangled thoughts. He sat up, and Anneke, not waiting for his "*Entrez!*" opened the door a crack, expecting him to tell her to bring in the tea. But Berman just rubbed his eyes and yawned.

While Anneke was wiping the glass for his tea, someone knocked at the front door, hammering like mad on the brass knocker, and Anneke ran to open it, her dishtowel still clutched in her hand. "*Godverdoeme*, what's the rush?" Anneke thought it was one of the errand boys with the long beards.

Instead of an errand boy, a Flemish porter stood there. He was dressed in a faded, dirty blue, torn linen uniform, and had a cap with a badge. He looked very fed up.

"Does *Menieër* Berman live here or not?"

"Yes, he does."

"That's his father!" The porter pointed at an old, bent Jew in a threadbare gaberdine and muddy boots with a torn, velvet cap on his head. The porter carried two patched suitcases over the threshold and said something to the old man, from which he understood that he was to enter as well.

Anneke, not listening to the porter's words, saw a beggar standing there, one of the many hundreds who pestered her, and for whom she always had the same answer ready: "There's no one at home." She kept on repeating it, but when the old man didn't understand a word and just stood there smiling with half-closed eyes, she lost her temper:

"Can't I get rid of the likes of you? Look at the mud you're going to bring into the house. Can't you at least wipe your feet?" She addressed the old man disrespectfully by the familiar "*du*", pointing at the brown doormat.

"Why are you yelling at him?" interrupted the porter. "He's *Menieër* Berman's father."

Anneke laughed. "You're off your head!"

"Here, read this, and you'll see." And he handed her a scrap of paper. "A Jew at the station gave it to me. Hurry up, Miss, and tell *Menieër* Berman that he's got to pay me. The old man has no Belgian money."

Anneke hesitated, but finally knocked on Berman's door and announced quietly, in an almost guilty tone, that some old man had arrived.

"He says he's your father! I told him there's no one at home. But he's just standing there, and won't go away. And the porter says it's true." Anneke's face flushed fiery red.

Berman felt a surge of shame.

"Can it really be my father?" he thought. "Has he actually come?"

"You can go!" he said angrily to Anneke, as if it had been her fault that he had not answered his father's letter and made sure that the old man had arrived more appropriately dressed.

He went out into the hall, paid the porter, and ordered the maid to carry the cases into the room. A sudden strange feeling of warmth flooded over him, even though a few moments earlier the news of his father's arrival had upset him. He embraced the shabby, crumpled old man, kissing him over and over again.

"*Sholem aleichem*, father! Welcome!"

"*Aleichem sholem, aleichem sholem*, my son!" The old man was trembling with emotion. He kissed his son on both cheeks, and murmured away to himself, praising the Lord of the Universe and blessing his son.

"Sit down, father." Berman tried to make his father sit at the head of the table, but the old man protested: "God forbid! God forbid!"

His dim old eyes began to shine, and a gentle smile crept over his good-natured face, spreading into all the folds and wrinkles, into his broad, grey beard. The smile expressed the joy he felt that his son, by offering him the place at the head of the table, was fulfilling the commandment to honour his father. He looked round the room.

"What opulence, *ken eynore*!"

And his son wanted *him*, an old, sick man, to sit at the head of the table? And to think that he had agonised over the decision whether to come or not, especially as his son had not answered his letter. And yet it was obvious that his son was, thank God, an honourable Jew. He had, God be praised, a proper beard, just like his other son back home. "*Oy*! Have we not a good father in heaven! Not a hair of my son's head has been harmed, God forbid. Though he does look like a count, *ken eynore*!"

"Why don't you sit down, father?" Berman had prepared another place of honour at the table for his father, opposite him.

His father wiped the seat with a trembling hand, wanting to protect it from his travel-stained coat. He sat down slowly, not quite knowing how to behave. Berman went into the kitchen and told the maid to make tea. She was not to bring it in, though, simply to knock on the door, and he would take it from her. After that she was free to go away if she wanted to. She wouldn't be needed any more that day.

Anneke skipped for joy with the tray in her hands, nearly spilling the tea, such a piece of luck didn't happen every day. "Strange folk, those Jews!" she thought in amazement.

The old man felt ashamed of his clothing. He simply hadn't expected such affluence. He looked so poor, and his son was dressed like a king. He should have changed. But then he remembered that he had changed, that this was in fact his best gaberdine for *Shabbes*. It was a miracle that he had changed, but why did his best gaberdine look so shabby? At home, he thought, it still looked like a perfectly decent garment.

Rochl came in with Jeannette. All day they had been looking round the department stores, searching for bargains for the approaching High Holidays.*

"Oh, Papa! We've bought some material. It was a wonderful bargain! I found it, dear Papa." In her usual way she flung herself in jubilation on her father and started to kiss his bushy beard. Berman's father started back in amazement. Jeannette was chattering about their bargains and didn't even notice that there was someone else sitting at the table.

The old man was absolutely aghast. Could that be his granddaughter? The one his son praised so highly in his letters, calling her a sweet child, saying that he thought the world of her? That was impossible! You could see quite clearly that she was *not* a nice Jewish girl; although she was speaking Yiddish. But there were strange words mixed in with it, so that you could hardly understand what she was saying. Perhaps it was German she was speaking? But why was his son letting her kiss him in such an unrestrained way and what did she mean by "*goeie koop*" and "*charmant*"?*

Jeannette did indeed pepper her Yiddish with Flemish and French and a good bit of German. Rochl was surprised that Anneke wasn't in the kitchen. She noticed the poor, dusty old man sitting there as if in a trance, and was astonished. Since she had known Berman, she could not remember him ever inviting anyone who looked like that to their table! Who on earth could it be? Berman was kissing his daughter, and some old *shnorrer* (God forgive her for saying it!) was sitting there, drinking tea.

Suddenly Jeannette sprang back with a squeal as if she had been stung:

"Oh look, Papa, what's that?"

She was holding her hand on her heart to show what a fright she had got, and had called her grandfather "what".

"Jeannette, be quiet and stop playing your foolish tricks! Sit down and you will hear. And you, come here too," he ordered Rochl. "Do you know who this is?" Berman smiled with pleasure to think what a surprise his wife and daughter were about to have. The fact that his daughter had called his father "what" somehow made him feel closer to the old man.

The old man went red from the top of his head, which was hidden under his worn skullcap, to the tips of his toes.

"This is my father. Do you not recognise him, Rochl? And he's your grandfather, sweetheart, do you hear me? Your grandfather."

"You know, father," he said, turning to the old man, "in this foreign country children grow up as savages!"

"Of course I recognise my father-in-law, may he remain in good health!" exclaimed Rochl. "How could I not recognise him? How are you, father-in-law? It's a good few years since we last met." Rochl had forgotten that the last time they had met he had not yet become her father-in-law. "Shall I bring in something to eat, or would father-in-law like to get washed first?" Then Rochl looked at Berman and reddened. Had she perhaps insulted his father by this question?

But Berman was quite happy, agreeing that he should go and have a wash. In any case they would have to change his clothes, he thought, so that at least Dovid and Jacques wouldn't see his father in garments like these.

"Certainly, that would be the correct thing to do," said the old man to his daughter-in-law, looking at his son with the helplessness of a small child. He got up with difficulty from his chair. Only now did Berman realise that his father was still half-paralysed. He had difficulty walking and his right arm hung down uselessly. Berman was overwhelmed by pity and recollections of the sadness of the past, which plunged him into a melancholy mood. He took his father by the left arm, and led him to the bathroom, like a little child.

The old man had difficulty getting into the bathtub. Berman soaped and washed him, rubbing the soft sponge over the weary, old body. The old man groaned with pleasure: his own son was standing there in his shirtsleeves washing him, like a bathing attendant. That fine beard of his was dipping in the water and getting wet, and how dignified his son looked with his square, silk skullcap!

After the bath, Berman dressed his father in clean underwear and a black suit, which Rochl had found in his plentiful wardrobe. When he combed his father's beard, Berman almost started weeping, as his memories drew him back to the little Polish *shtetl* of his childhood, which now felt completely alien to him.

He brought his father back into the dining room.

"Do you remember, Gedaliah, how you used to comb my beard and give me water when I was in bed? Do you remember? That's why God, may His Name be praised, has granted you success, *ken eynore.* He will continue to multiply His blessings to you."

"Amen!" said Berman out loud.

"Amen" said the old man softly and earnestly.

Rochl had set the table with good things to eat, and she lit all the branches of the candelabrum. The silver and fine food looked even more attractive in the shining light. The festive atmosphere did not, however, delight Berman's heart as it was filled with a gnawing, bitter-sweet emotion. Strange thoughts came into his head which he could not drive away, and he felt that today he was not the same person as usual. His father realised that his arrival had awakened a great many memories in his son, and he knew that he was pleased to see him, for Berman kept passing him more and more things to eat, as did his daughter-in-law. He was seeing many of these foods for the first time, and some of them, he was sure, were forbidden to him. These tomatoes, for example, looked to him like some kind of fruit that wasn't kosher, and he was surprised to see his son eating them. He wanted to ask him about it, but couldn't bring himself to do so.

"Eat, father!"

"Father-in-law, you should eat!" urged Rochl.

"It's good for you," insisted Berman encouragingly.

He himself ate only for appearance's sake.

Dovid came home. In the street he had already heard the news, and Berman was pleased that his son had come to greet his grandfather. "I'm really glad you've come, Dovid," said Berman, trying to bring the tension between them to an end. "Father, this is Dovid."

"*Sholem aleichem,* grandfather," said Dovid, genuinely pleased to see the old man, to whom he took an immediate liking. "He seems to be a real, pious Jew," thought Dovid, looking eagerly at the food, for it was a long time since he had eaten at such a fine, festive table. He washed himself and recited aloud "Lift up your hands in the sanctuary, and bless the Lord."*

Jacques rushed into the dining room. "Papa, they say my grandfather has come!" He ran up to the table with such speed that he didn't even see the old man.

"Now, now, and what do you say to your grandfather?"

Jacques blushed. "*Sholem aleichem*, grandfather."

"*Aleichem sholem, aleichem sholem*, my child," replied the old man, kissing Jacques on both his smooth olive-skinned cheeks, so that Jacques got his beard full in the face.

"Jeannette, this is no time to read. Put your book away and come to the table. That's it!"

"Lovely children, *ken eynore*! And you can see that they are Jewish children, praise be to God." The old man expressed his pleasure warmly.

"Well, what else would they be? Of course they are Jewish children!" said Berman, glancing swiftly at Dovid. "Hmm ... of course they are real Jews."

After the meal the family talked until late into the night. They couldn't persuade the old man to go to bed and get some rest. Every time it was suggested, he made a dismissive gesture with his good hand, saying that he would be happy to sit all night long chatting with his children and grandchildren. All evening he kept looking round the room and giving thanks to the Lord of the universe. "Praise be to God, blessed be He, that He has allowed me to live to see this. Yes, may the Lord above be praised for His grace."

When they finally did go to bed, Berman couldn't get to sleep at all. He was remembering being a child in the tiny *shtetl*. He saw it in front of his eyes, clear and vivid. His mother, who had died just a few months earlier, had been a bitter, bad-tempered, and tearful woman. She had grumbled and groaned as she dragged herself round the cramped house, bemoaning her fate and bearing a grudge against her sick husband because he wouldn't take her advice and give up being a *shochet* * in order to become a shopkeeper. Her father had given her a dowry of five hundred roubles, and anyone else would have opened a draper's shop on the market. But since he had to be a *shochet* of all things, as well as being a *mohel* * and the leader of the prayers in the synagogue, he could at least have become a *shochet* in a big town like anyone else would have done. Instead he had lived all his life in this godforsaken place where she and the children were dying of hunger. All he did was slaughter and father children. Slaughter? It was her and the children that he slaughtered, not the animals! And where were the animals anyway? He thanked God when there was the occasional calf or sterile cow to slaughter. Even a hen appeared only rarely, unless someone was ill or giving birth in the *shtetl*. Ech! *Shtetl?* It was nothing but a village, a dump. And she was going to die here and her children as well and not a living soul would know or care. And he just refused to admit their troubles to anyone. Instead of screaming, "Help! We're dying of hunger," he just answered, "Thanks be to the Lord, may His Name be praised, for everything," if someone did actually once in a while ask him how things were.

And so she would go on, regurgitating the same words over and over again, thousands of times. The children knew this litany off by heart and knew which sentence would come next. She never listened to her own grumbling. The children were really sorry for their poor sick father, who was being worn down by her constant complaining.

Now a dark period of his childhood assailed Berman. He remembered how one day his father felt pains in his right arm, and told his wife that he was frightened to carry on slaughtering in case, God forbid, he made a mistake and didn't slaughter the animal according to the Law. Then one morning he suddenly sat down on the edge of his bed, put his hand to his heart and burst out: "I feel ill!"

That morning had etched itself deeply on Berman's young mind. His mother had come running up with a bucket of water and poured it on the unconscious man, pinching him and emitting such strange cries that the whole *shtetl* came to see what the matter was. After this, his father did not leave his bed. Some men of the village laid him in bed and covered him with the heavy quilt, even though it was very hot outside. The rabbi came to visit him, and shook his head so that all the cream-coloured lambs' tails on his hat bobbed around. He told the men that he had suspected for a long time that there was something wrong with the shochet's right arm, because once, when the shochet had handed him the knife to inspect, the right hand seemed to have been shaking. Even then he should not have been carrying out the slaughtering.

"But may the Lord forgive him and grant him a complete and speedy recovery!" And the rabbi cast his rheumy eyes to the grimy ceiling. At that moment Berman was seized by such a hatred of the rabbi that he wished he would collapse on the spot, just like his father.

Then the rabbi said to his mother, without even turning to look at her, that their Father in Heaven would probably not forsake them, and Chaim Yoysef's wife should not lose her faith, and everything would be all right. He went away, leaving Berman's mother sobbing and weeping, and his father with a paralysed arm.

Afterwards, however, the rabbi travelled round the forests and collected a hundred roubles from the forestry officials. This enabled Berman's mother to open a little drapery shop. The *shtetl* employed a new *shochet*, but imposed a tax on him of ten percent for each cow and five percent for a calf. From then on Berman's mother was very busy: although no customers appeared, she sat all day in the shop, and the twelve-year-old Gedaliah had to look after his two little brothers and his one-year-old sister, who screamed all the time.

Berman's father lay in bed for eight years. His arm and one side were paralysed. He would say that God, Blessed be His Name, had kept his left arm healthy for his *tefillin.** And so he lay, summer and winter, under the grubby quilt. His broad beard became grey and tangled. Beside his bed stood a little three-legged table, wobbling precariously, so that the various bottles, pillboxes and nonsensical cures, which women and even Gentiles had supplied, and which were about as much use as cupping a corpse, were in constant danger of falling on the floor. As well as this, the children used to deposit bits of leftover stale bread there, and unwashed bowls, cups, and glasses stood on the table. Flies buzzed and crawled around; wandering freely and impudently over Berman's father's yellowed face. The old man put up with this until it became too much of a nuisance, when he tried to flap them away with his good hand.

He lay on his back with his beard over the quilt, studying a religious book. When food was brought to him, he dipped his hand in the clay dish of water, which stood on a stool beside his bed, said the blessing before food, and ate.

His wife had no time for him. Either she was busy in the shop with a customer, or she had gone to the neighbouring *shtetl* to buy a few goods, and there was no one to give him his food, so he just buried his kind, wrinkled face deeper into his book and forgot that he was hungry.

How clearly Berman could visualise his mother; her shrivelled face, criss-crossed by hundreds of blackened wrinkles, looked like dark, ploughed up, earth. She wore a threadbare, satin bonnet on her head, its ragged lace framing her face. A few forlorn plums dangled there. The bare wires of their stems were visible, where grapes and all kinds of other decorations had once adorned it.

Berman shivered. Another dark morning from his past came to him, the worst moment of his childhood. This was the morning when he got up and went out into the street, and for the first time heard the children calling his mother "witch". They ran away and it seemed to him that even the adults had abandoned him.

He remembered how, despite the fact that his mother really did love his father, was faithful to him, and wept over his sad fate, she had moments where she couldn't help attacking him, scolding and cursing him. When this fit came over her, all she could do was to scream and shout. Her shrieking could be heard all over the *shtetl*; children and adults stopped at the window, and the children shouted through the window "*mekhasheyfa lo takhaye*, thou shalt not suffer a witch to live."* The adults got angry with the children but among themselves they said that "something" was screaming out of her, and that one fine day she might put an end to him, God forbid, with her shrieking and the evil spirit, which was staring out of her black eyes. Sometimes she would carry on screaming, cursing herself, her husband, her children, her customers and the *young* shochet's wife, who, in fact, was about ten years older than her, until she had no more strength left. Only then did she sit down on a chair, lean her head against its back, and go to sleep like a child.

After these scenes she would go round for several days in silence, not saying a word to anyone, not even to the children, and the house was so eerily, terrifyingly quiet that it was worse than when she was screaming.

It was the new *shochet's* wife who had first called her a witch. She was a fat, smiling woman with goitre. The people in the *shtetl* didn't hate her, but she hated them. She could not forgive them for taking ten percent of her husband's meagre earnings for the previous slaughterer.

"My husband", she would complain, "creeps around in all weathers, in deep mud." And here she would put her hand up to her neck to show the depth of the mud he had to wade through. "He creeps about all the time, searching to see if there could possibly be an animal to slaughter somewhere or other. He never sleeps in the same place twice, and he gets dirty and miserable sleeping on planks in peasants' kitchens, just so that the countess there can prepare her *Shabbes*. Every Thursday morning, I haven't even had time to pour away the washing water, and there he is already, that brat, come for the money. And the impudence of it: he rushes in as if it were his own house, whining: 'Mother says you owe her half a rouble this week.' I owe her, indeed! She just puts the money into her business. She spies on me, so that she knows *exactly* what I owe her!"

Because of her terrible rage against the "countess" she spread it around that she was a witch. How well Berman remembered that summer night, when they had sat all day in the hot, dusty shop, hoping in vain for customers. Not a single customer had as much as stuck her nose into the shop, even though it was a propitious time: the harvest was in, so that the farmers were not very busy and had got money from the sale of grain, vegetables, wagonloads of hay, and cows which had stopped giving milk and were being sold to save pasture. In groups of three and four the women wandered past her shop, all dressed up in hand-woven skirts, with flowery headscarves on their freshly washed hair and necklaces of red glass beads round their necks. They carried their new boots and walked on their bare, toil-toughened feet around the hot dusty village. Laughing and chatting they passed her and went into the shop directly opposite. All the shops were packed except hers, which was completely empty. Apart from all this, the sick man had had a bad day. He had been groaning all day long, and, as if to spite her, the baby did not stop crying. About a dozen millstones lay on her chest, pressing and squeezing. She was so tense that she felt she would burst, her head ached and she was so depressed that she couldn't even scream.

So that evening, after putting the children to bed, she went out into the meadow and walked straight towards the river, without knowing why. She certainly wasn't thinking of suicide, in fact she had never heard of such a thing. She simply was drawn to the cool water, desperate to get away from her house, from her sick husband, from other people, and most of all from herself. She sat down on the riverbank, stared at the darkness, murmuring.

Just at that moment the new *shochet* was coming home from a distant village, feeling very pleased with himself, with two roubles in one pocket and a nice portion of lungs and liver in the other. He saw the former *shochet's* wife sitting by the river, deep in thought, holding her head with its patched bonnet in both her shrivelled hands. She looked like a child who had fallen asleep by the river in the middle of its play. The *shochet* got a shock: a Jewish woman all alone at night by the river? He told his wife about it, and the next morning the *shtetl* was buzzing with the news that the former *shochet's* wife was a witch, and that at night when everyone was asleep, she would go down to the river to cast her spells.

Women spat and wished bad dreams on her. The men-folk, however, were angry with them, calling the women "stupid cows". Some of them were even of the opinion that the new *shochet's* wife's evil tongue should be silenced, and that to make amends for the sin of defaming the good name of a Jewish woman, she and her husband should pay an additional five percent slaughtering tax. They ordered their wives not to listen to these ridiculous stories. But despite their efforts, the nickname remained, and the children of the *shtetl* avoided the house. When they were sent on errands, they deliberately made a detour round various streets in order to avoid going past the shop, just like they used to do when they had to pass the hut of an old woman who lived at the edge of the town. When little Gedaliah appeared and wanted to play with the children, they scattered like hens.

Someone only had to say "There he is!" for the crowd to flee. Humiliated, sad and bitter, the child would go back to his shabby house which smelt of mice, mould and medicaments.

For as long as the inhabitants could remember, Berman's father, Reb Chaim Yoysef, had been able to remove the spell of an evil eye from people. Everyone knew that if he pronounced the words to remove the evil-eye, an affected person would recover on the spot. Berman's mother used to fly into a rage if children came to have the evil eye removed, screaming at them that they shouldn't come bothering a sick man:

"It'll be the end of him! Every time he removes the spell, he's ill afterwards. It saps his strength."

But Reb Chaim Yoysef would gesture with his good hand, say "It doesn't matter," ponder, and pronounce:

"Yes, it was the evil eye" or "No, it wasn't the evil eye."

Now that the children refused to go there, she missed them. If a child did come to have the evil eye removed, she was delighted as if he had been a customer.

Twelve-year-old Gedaliah became a hermit. At this young age he had already begun to hate: first of all the new *shochet's* wife, then the children and finally people in general. So he sat at home, helped his mother, went on errands, and when the mess in the house became so bad that it literally wasn't possible to move, he would wash dishes, sweep out the room, put a basin of clean water at his father's bed, sit down by the bedside and slowly, dipping the comb in the water, comb out Chaim Yoysef's beard. The hairs which came out he laid, for his father's sake, between the pages of a sacred book. He did not love his mother very much, but he loved his father deeply.

"Father, when I am grown-up I'll deal in all sorts of things and get very rich and when I have a lot of money, I'll give it all to you. You'll get well again and we'll move away from here to a big city. I'll get so rich that we'll be able to move to the biggest city in the world, to Warsaw, that's where we'll go!"

He was not telling his father stories simply to entertain him, but believed absolutely in what he said. His faith in the power he would have when he was older and his certainty that he would be rich were

109

so strong that the chaos in the neglected house, the polluted air, full of the smell of the sick man's sweat, of dirt and medicaments, didn't have any effect on him. In his imagination he didn't live in this room but somewhere far, far away, in big cities and beautiful rich palaces. His dear, sick, half-dead father did not lie under a grubby quilt, but sat on a red, velvet chair, like the rich man of the *shtetl*, reading a sacred book. But even then he saw his mother as she really was, in her torn bonnet, in her dusty, little shop, and heard her screaming. He was unable to draw her into his fantasy world.

And that is how he pictured her now, in the darkness of the night, as he lay under his pure white sheets, in his richly decorated bedroom, where everything shone and glowed. The strips of light, coming in through the gaps in the curtains, fell on the blue, deep-pile carpet, and on his bed. All this brightness made his poor mother appear even more dark and dingy in his memory.

He remembered the morning when a large, covered wagon drew up at their shop. It was lined with hay covered with a patched sheet. Pillows and a quilt were carried out. They, too, were patched but freshly laundered. Then some of the men of the *shtetl* carried out Berman's father and laid him in the wagon. They carried him slowly, as if they were scared he might break. The *shtetl* gathered round their house, as if for a funeral. The rabbi himself stood beside the wagon, shook the lambs' tails on his hat, gave his father some advice, which no one heard. A smile spread over his father's sallow face which Berman would never forget. His mother, sitting in the wagon, looked so tiny, huddled in her black coat with her black bonnet; she contrasted strangely with the white all round her. And so they took Berman's father off to the hospital in Warsaw. Berman recalled that he had been jealous of his mother, and even of his father, because they were going off to the big city.

Then his mother came back on her own, and they worked together in the shop. She felt a lot better from then on. The children and adults were sorry for them both and were friendly towards them.

"Poor thing! Without her husband. What a terrible thing!" The women sighed and started buying from them.

The sighs of pity made Berman resent the women even more. But worst of all he hated being a poor boy and he fantasised all the more about the things he would do when he was grown-up.

His father was much better when he came back home. He didn't need to lie in bed all the time, but could sit in an armchair. Berman's little sister died of scarlet fever. His mother wept and wept and then stopped.

When Berman turned twenty he went to the nearby town, and with a small amount of money, which he had managed to save up, he bought a ticket for Antwerp. He paid no heed to his mother's reproaches that he was leaving her alone with his invalid father and the little children, who were, in fact, no longer little children.

"Mother, there's no point in crying. It's time I started looking for a proper livelihood. And in any case I'll soon be called up to the army, so, please, that's enough!"

He packed his good Shabbes gaberdine and his tefillin bag and with these riches he set off one rainy evening and arrived in Antwerp.

As soon as he stepped over the threshold of the station restaurant, an old woman with a stupid face and a mouth full of gold teeth started to try to make a match for him. Berman said he wasn't interested, but the old woman wasn't put off by his reply. "You'll soon be interested," she said, speaking German to him. "When you see the bride! You'll certainly be interested! And if you make enquiries about her, you'll find out that she is my own niece, and *then* you'll certainly be interested!" The old woman seemed to think that to be a niece of hers was a particular honour.

"Perhaps I can have a bowl of barley soup?" asked Berman, who was ravenously hungry.

"Of course, with the greatest of pleasure." The old woman opened a door and called: "Rosa, a plate of barley soup!"

Berman was astonished when he saw that the old woman's niece was none other than the daughter of Yankl Eli, the carpenter in his *shtetl*. His mother used to send him there as a little boy to collect wood shavings and bits of wood left over from the coffins which the carpenter was making. Yankl the carpenter's daughter Rochl! She recognised him too. "What are you doing here?" she asked stiffly in German and blushed to the roots of her hair.

"And what are *you* doing here?" Berman spoke familiarly to her in homely Yiddish, not yet having absorbed any "foreign manners".

Berman had been attracted to Rochl for a long time, ever since they were children, in fact. He was always very ashamed to carry off the sack of wood shavings in front of her, as if, God forbid, he had been some peasant. But both his desire to see Rochl, as well as his love of sitting around in the coffins, daydreaming about leaving home, made him obey his mother and go for the wood shavings.

Rochl's father used to say to him that you shouldn't sit in a coffin, because it could bring about your death, but Berman didn't believe him: he knew that adults always like telling little boys that they "shouldn't do" things. So he used to answer that you couldn't die because of that, and carried on sitting there.

Rochl's father was a stout, good-natured man with a fleshy face which always looked tired from the hard work he did. His eyes were blue and childlike, his nose round and shiny, and he had a broad, thick, tobacco-coloured beard, which always had wood shavings sticking in it. He used to say "you shouldn't ..." and then just carried on planing his coffins, forgetting Berman's existence. Then Berman used to lure Rochl into the coffin too, and they would drive around in his "carriage".

When he was older and stopped coming for the wood shavings, he really longed to go back to their house, though he didn't realise what it was that attracted him to it. There wasn't really much to pine for, in fact. There was no furniture in the big square room apart from two beds, a table and a few chairs. On the long carpenter's table there was almost always a child's coffin, painted pale yellow, the lid decorated with a large brass or tin cross. On the grey floor, which was covered with heaps of sawdust, wood shavings, square bits of wood and little scraps of white and yellow tin, there were always adult coffins standing around; some were painted, some still unpainted, some adorned and some still bare. They told tales of measles, chickenpox and scarlet fever epidemics in the villages, of children with stomachs swollen from hunger, of sombre funerals on dark wintry days, of black horses on the white snow, of the stifled weeping of peasant women and the lowered heads of their menfolk.

In this sea of curly wood shavings, Rochl's bad-tempered step-mother shuffled about, either grumbling and complaining under her breath about the houseful of girls who were idly lounging around, or actually quarrelling with them, so that the *shtetl* would gather to see the spectacle. Rochl's father the carpenter did not intervene between his wife and his daughters. On those occasions his plane would move faster and faster, working at breakneck speed, as if Death itself was driving him and demanding the coffin from him.

More than once Berman walked past the carpenter's house, hoping that by chance he might see Rochl coming out. But it didn't happen, because she had already gone off to live with her aunt in Antwerp. This aunt, who tried to marry her off to every boy who crossed the threshold of the restaurant, didn't dream she would have this piece of luck.

Berman did well. He soon learned all that was necessary, and became a broker. His sharp instinct for the business soon won him the trust of the diamond merchants, who recognised his ability. They sent him around with parcels of diamonds, and he soon learned to speak German, mixed with Flemish and Hebrew, like all the respected Antwerp merchants. He started making money. He loved Rochl, who was very beautiful, and because of her he always ate in the same restaurant, until one fine morning he took her away from her aunt's pots and pans, married her and set her up in her own kitchen, so that she should cook good meals, as only she could, for him, instead of for the general public.

After they were married Rochl proved to him how much she esteemed him for this, as she continued to do throughout their marriage.

Chapter 12

Berman got up late with a dull headache, and Anneke poured him a good warm bath. He got out of the bathtub feeling refreshed, put on his crimson satin dressing gown. It had black flowers and a broad silken girdle with two thick multicoloured tassels, which swayed in time to his movements, giving dignity and rhythm to his gait.

His father was seated at the dining room table reading one of his sacred books. Berman smiled with satisfaction. Reb Chaim Yoysef was already quite a different person. Last night he had looked like an old beggar, but now, sitting there, he was a dignified old Jew. His velvet skullcap looked so homely on him, the yellowness had almost disappeared from his beard, and a gentle, childlike smile hovered on his wrinkled face. He was bent over his book, swaying back and forward, like an obedient child who has been given a picture book to look at.

The old man realised someone was looking at him, and raised his eyes. The sight of his tall, broad-shouldered son in his satin dressing gown, with his long, neatly combed, black beard, in which a few silvery hairs gleamed, gave him a feeling of awe and respect. Here, he felt, stood a person of high status, and he even tried to stand up in order to greet him.

"Did you sleep well, father? Have you already had some tea? Would you like to go to a *shtibl*?"

"Oh yes indeed, I certainly would!"

Berman took his father, who was a Gerer Hassid,* to the *shtibl*. He wanted his father to have his own place there, and was anxious to show him that he was able to get that for him too. But in the shtibl Berman was not shown the same degree of respect as in his synagogue. Young and old addressed him with the familiar "*du*", as if they had been bosom friends all their lives. One man, wearing a grubby green frock coat, which reached to the very heels of his boots, poked his long snuff-stained nose right into Berman's face, and, being deaf, bellowed into Berman's ear that he should pay for some vodka because the shtibl had a guest. He seemed to think that the guest was the shtibl's, not Berman's. Everyone heard the remark and started demanding vodka.

Berman prayed, said Kaddish for his mother, paid for a generous amount of vodka, and, following his father's wishes, left him in the shtibl.

"You know the way home, father?"

"It's all right, don't worry, you can go, we'll show him the way."

After Berman left, the Hassidim started asking the guest where he came from and why he had come. They were really delighted that he was there. He had brought with him a flavour of the "*alte heym*" which they missed greatly.

Some old Jews sat and studied at a long, scratched wooden table spotted all over with wax, instead of praying with the rest of the congregation. One of them was a thin, bloodless man with skin like faded parchment, a red translucent nose and a long, scraggy beard. He recognised Chaim Yoysef. He placed a handkerchief full of holes on the open *Gemara* which he was studying and addressed him:

"Do you not remember me, Chaim Yoysef?" He immediately answered his own question: "I see you don't! I'm not surprised. It's been a good few years. Don't you remember? It was when the old man died, blessed be his memory."

"You mean the *Sfas Emes*?"* asked Chaim Yoysef, addressing him by the formal "*ir*".

"Who else would I mean? But why are you speaking to me so formally? You do seem to have completely forgotten me. Do you not remember Leybele Strotsker?" said the man, giving the name away himself.

"Ah!" exclaimed Reb Chaim Yoysef, greeting him warmly, and gazing with great respect at this man with the cadaverous head, which shook like a dry willow branch when he spoke. He smiled all the time, sometimes rather tearfully, like a child who has been hurt by something, and sometimes as if he were delighted that fate had chosen to cast *him* into this city of diamonds, where the Evil One can seduce anyone he likes, except him, Leybele Strotsker.

115

"Yes, now I remember you! Of course I do! Who could forget Reb Leybele Strotsker?" Reb Chaim Yoysef spoke with great respect to this skeletal figure dressed in rags. "Have you been living here for long?" He again spoke formally, absolutely unable to call his former friend "du".

"Ten years!"

"For ten years?" echoed Reb Chaim Yoysef, at a loss for words. He was full of amazement and pity that the great scholar and righteous man should be in such a state. "Ten years!" he repeated, as if the important thing was his having lived there for that length of time.

The next morning at breakfast, Reb Chaim Yoysef asked his son why the community allowed a great man like Reb Leybele Strotsker to live in that state. Berman told him Reb Leybele had a son in Antwerp who was a very rich man, but he was not pious, did not keep *Shabbes*, and his father refused to take a single penny from him. Indeed he would not accept help from anybody. At first this had caused the community great distress, but gradually they had got used to it and didn't bother about it any more. And in fact the Hassidim suspected him of secretly being one of their rabbinical opponents, because it wasn't the way of the Hassidim to refuse charity. Berman smiled at this and carried on:

"So after the death of the *Sfas Emes*, Reb Leybele stopped going to the Rebbe's court, it's no secret that he doesn't think much of the present one."

Reb Chaim Yoysef thought about this but his only reaction was to mutter into his beard: "Hmm! Hmm!" He didn't think much of the present one either.

Dovid came in, freshly washed and shaved, having got up early in honour of his grandfather. The old man smiled at his grandson, but looked at his clean-shaven chin, which still had a dark shadow because of the blackness of his hair. The old man was greatly displeased that his grandson had shaved his beard off, God preserve us! He was dying to ask his son how he could permit Dovid to do such a thing, but he didn't dare.

No, he didn't have Reb Leybele's strength of character.

Chapter 13

Berman saw Dovid once more lounging on the sofa in his silk dressing gown, yawning. But instead of telling him off, he regarded it as a miracle. Dovid would certainly never have gained entry to the Bourse, had he carried on working as a diamond polisher. That thought horrified Berman. "The bastards would have refused to show me their best merchandise." Good friends would have pitied him, and his enemies would have rejoiced.

"Oh well, it could be worse. He could, God forbid, have married a *shikse*. When all's said and done, he's made his bed, so he'll have to lie on it. I can always give him food and clothing. Nevertheless, it hurts when a father has to watch his grown-up son lolling around and not doing anything. What will become of him? He'll end up being a *shnorrer*." Berman knew the taste of poverty. But, as the saying goes: "You can lead a horse to water but you can't make him drink." He had given Dovid money, introduced him to the Bourse and shown him the ropes. And when the good-for-nothing made a mess of it all, he had tried, despite everything, to make an advantageous match for him. Marriage would have forced Dovid to work at diamond dealing. He would have got acquainted with the business and become a respectable family man. Berman felt he had done all he could as a father.

Mulling all this over as he changed to go to his office, he felt a sense of relief because at least he had a clear conscience. He gave Rochl money, instructing her not to give too much to Dovid, in case he was tempted to do something stupid: "Do you understand? You're to see to it!" Rochl made it obvious she had no idea how to deal with the situation.

"You don't understand? What a genius!" Berman gave a condescending smile and walked out.

In the town they said this had been the worst summer for trade they could ever remember - business was completely dead.

For days at a time the diamond cleavers, cutters and polishers wandered around in their best clothes, which by now had turned into their everyday clothes, looking up into the empty sky as if they expected that some movement would come from there. Perhaps the obstinate diamond merchants from America, India and elsewhere would wake up from their aristocratic sleep, descend on Antwerp and put an end to the long fallow period, which was dragging as slowly as the seven days of mourning after a death. The machines all had their covers on, but the women sighed and dressed up in their best clothes, to hide their poverty.

Shopkeepers had long since stopped selling on credit to ordinary people, and women didn't dare to go into the shops without money in their hands. Only the diamond merchants' wives were still buying on credit. The shopkeepers suppressed their rage against the rich women and vented it on the poor. And the rich women just kept on taking. The shopkeepers feared it would be dangerous to stop giving to them, since they would lose important customers as well as the money which they were owed. So instead they argued amongst themselves, quarrelled with their wives and cursed each other and their own children. The errand boys with the long beards were weak with hunger, and the small diamond dealers simply could not hold out till a better season came. So they sold their diamonds at a loss. Brokers wandered round the streets with despair in their eyes, with empty pockets and empty hearts.

All this time Berman had kept on buying, and giving out work. He bought for cash, and paid the workers their due. Other workers were jealous of Berman's people and were dying to get work from him, but Berman refused to act unscrupulously and change his workers. If a man worked for him, he should carry on doing so.

The anteroom of the office with the frosted glass door was crowded. About two dozen cutters and polishers were waiting with the parcels of stones they had brought, their hearts pounding and their faces expressing surprise and foreboding.

"What can have happened? He's never been as late coming to the office as this!"

"Perhaps he hasn't any work for us today and so he's taking his time! He won't miss the few francs at the end of the week. He'll have enough to pay his rent, that's for sure!"

"Rent? *Rent-shment*! Are you trying to tell us that's not his own house?"

"It could be his grave for all I care!"

"So why should he be bothered to come today if he doesn't want to? He's not going to lose any sleep over us!"

"Shhh, he's coming!"

"He's coming?!" they all exclaimed with one voice and then fell silent.

They needn't have worried. Berman told his secretary to hang up his coat, just as he did every day. He combed his beard with his fingers, straightened the square silk skullcap on his head, smoked a cigar, then puffed on his pipe. He sat down at his large mahogany desk with its green baize top which was covered with account books and papers. On one side of the desk stood a large gold-framed photograph of Jeannette in an old-fashioned crinoline. The skirt was a little on the short side and the wide, old-fashioned, pleated pantaloons edged with fine Brussels lace peeped out from underneath it. Her hair was smooth and her plaits were wound round her delicate little head. She had a gracious smile with just a touch of coquettishness. The photograph had been taken before she went to a masked ball in aid of the charity hospital, at which she took part in a dance entertainment with young amateurs from the rich orthodox community. Berman looked at the photograph and beamed. Even his beard seemed to smile too.

"What a beauty she is, *ken eynore*!"

He instructed his secretary to open the correspondence, looked through it, and then told her which ones to answer and which to ignore. Then, at last, he remembered the people who had been waiting outside for hours, and he smiled. The scene in the corridor, though he witnessed it every day, never failed to amuse him. The way they all sprang about, competing to be the first to wish him "good morning!" If they had any sense they would concentrate on their work instead. Then they wouldn't make so many mistakes, he thought.

"Well, call them in!" he said.

He started re-reading a letter he had already read so that he did not have to look at the people while they were coming in. Finally he called out: "Friedman!"

When he had finished with the poor, long-suffering workers, he gave the secretary a multitude of tasks to perform before he came back, and went to the Bourse.

In the big, pillared hall the portly diamond merchants were strolling about. They would spy a fellow dealer, greet him, and stop to chat, giving the impression of not being there to do business, but just to ask each other how things were. At other times, when business was flourishing, the dealers would go round asking each other what was for sale. They would sit down at a table, or, if it was business which had to be done in private, leave the Bourse and drop into a nearby restaurant for a glass of tea. Now, however, there was more talk than action. Berman sat down at a table where a ruddy-cheeked, heavily-built merchant was poking with his tweezers in a little heap of diamonds. His shiny nose looked so soft that a touch would squash it, and both his nose and his fat cheeks were criss-crossed by a network of little red veins. As he moved them around, the diamonds he had just purchased changed colour from red to blue, white, fiery orange, translucent green, and back to blue. A huge diamond adorned the little finger of his podgy white hand, glittering along with the purchased stones.

As he peered through the loupe, this American dealer hummed an English song, the latest hit in the vaudeville theatre. Berman took up one of the stranger's stones and looked at it, while the latter kept on poking around as if these were not costly diamonds but bits of glass he didn't care about.

"And when she smiiiled, my love" sang the dealer, enjoying both the song and the stones, which he had just bought for his firm in New York. They were a real bargain.

"Pity they're dark cape, don't you think?" asked Berman.

"Dark cape? How on earth can you call them dark cape?" retorted the American, addressing Berman by the familiar "du" as he did with everyone, young or old.

"Well what would *you* call them then?"

At this point the good-natured American began to lose his equanimity. His face turned even redder, so that it looked as if he had been scalded.

"It's none of your business. They're not for sale anyway!"

"What, are you going to pickle them?" Berman joked.

"They're already sold, you see."

"Well, they're yellow nonetheless." Berman paid no heed to the dealer's story that they were already sold. "Or are you trying to tell me they're blue-white?"

The American completely lost his temper: "I'd define them as silver cape. Anyway, they're not for sale. You mind your own business!"

"To hell with him!" said Berman to a merchant at a nearby table, where he stopped, even though he had no business to do there. "Yankee Doodle is raging. I think he'll burst a blood vessel!"

The other merchant laughed: "Yes, he doesn't look in very good shape!"

Berman sat down at a table by the window, which had just become free, took out a few parcels and started examining them. He put back some stones, and examined others again just for show.

"Hmm, these have turned out well."

Very soon some dealers and brokers had gathered round Berman's table.

"Top silver?" one of them suggested.

"Is that all you think of them?" countered Berman.

"They could be dark cape for all I care. I'm not buying today in any case."

Berman laughed. "If I had a parcel of blue-white you'd soon snap it up!"

"I've just seen some blue-white. Tsvaygnboym has some. He's got really fine goods. You know, that man's doing excellent business. They say he hasn't even got his hands on the dowry yet, and already everyone trusts him."

"I'm really pleased to hear it! I wish him well," said Berman, trying to smile, to the amusement of the other dealers. "He can pretend all he likes, but he's as jealous as hell," they said to each other.

A pale young man with a pointed nose and small, deep-set eyes burst into the room, looking as if he were about to faint. "Have you heard the news? The Dutch guilder has fallen!" he exclaimed. "What?!" the dealers exclaimed. "How is that possible?!"

"Here you are! Look!" And he spread a Flemish newspaper out on the table and pointed at the page with his thin forefinger.

Then he raised both hands in the air and brushed the newspaper with them as if he was trying to wipe out the freshly printed news. Someone else brought in a paper.

"Look, here it is, read it! You see, the guilder has fallen; there's panic in the stock exchange!"

"And I have only guilders! Not a single franc." The young man was shaking and looked as if he were about to collapse; he had forgotten that speaking the truth in the Diamond Bourse was more dangerous than only having guilders.

Soon half the people in the Bourse were crowding round Berman's table, grabbing the afternoon paper, reading it, their heads lowered, their eyes devouring the tiny lines of print. Berman packed up his diamonds, and smiled to himself. Out loud he said: "Others may be better looking, but I'm the clever one."

The crowd fell on Berman's words thirstily; all eyes were peering at him intently, anxiously waiting, as if the whole business depended on what he had to say about it; as if the guilder would rise or fall even further on Berman's say-so. Berman smiled wisely and said: "Last week I predicted that the guilder would fall."

The merchants all stood there, feeling that they had been made fools of.

"Is that all he has to say about it?"

Most of them went out into the street, where it was impossible to walk on the pavement. There were little knots of people everywhere: big dealers, little dealers, and even insignificant characters who had no guilders, no francs, no money of any kind, but who were also highly agitated. Flemish and Dutch merchants who were not normally seen in this street mingled with groups of Jewish merchants, talking frenetically, enquiring, consulting each other.

"Listen to what I say!" said Berman in a firm voice. Despite their disappointment at his earlier remarks, they all listened to him. "Let's stop getting so excited and let's not block the pavement, so that other people can get through." Berman had become public-spirited for a moment. "Let's stop trading for a day or two to see how things develop. It's possible this is just some kind of speculation and you are all getting into a state unnecessarily. We'll know in a couple of days. If the guilder really has fallen, then we'll just have to adapt. And if it is a case of speculation on the stock exchange, we'll get to know about it."

"That's right!" said some of the merchants of a calmer, more reflective disposition. Others were panicking and didn't want to go home. They just hung about the streets.

Berman, for his part, went home to eat. He had no guilders and did not see that there was anything to concern him. So he enjoyed his glass of tea with Rochl's home-baked biscuits.

The next day it turned out that the news in the paper was the invention of some cheap journalist or other, who had no other news from Holland to fill the columns of the paper, so he invented this story to spice up the edition. The dealers were ashamed to look each other in the eyes. Why had it not occurred to them that a telephone call to Holland would have revealed the truth within a few minutes?

"What did I tell you?" said Berman triumphantly, as always. And as always, he congratulated himself on being a person of a calm, reflective disposition.

So once again he sat at a table, surrounded by dealers. People were apparently talking about everything and anything except business: they were discussing the city, or politics, making jokes and telling stories about mutual acquaintances. Then, as if it were just an afterthought, one of them would produce a parcel of stones. The rest would examine it. Someone else would take out a parcel. There would be a fiery flash, and then another pair of eyes would flash like the diamonds. A blue gleam, a trembling drop of water - and then there was a bargaining, a resolution, a shaking of hands and an exchange of "*mazl un brokhe!*"

And as Berman sat there peering through the loupe, concentrating hard on someone's stone, a woman in a black suit came into the Bourse. Her wide-brimmed hat was pulled down over her light-blue eyes so that one saw little of her well-nourished, clear-skinned face. Her plump neck and the skin revealed by the deep décolleté of her crêpe de Chine blouse were white and attractively feminine.

She approached the table and the dealers started to pass remarks about her, some in a subtle fashion, while others, openly vulgar, made ambiguous jokes and shook with mirth. The woman ignored them. She took out a parcel from her large, black handbag and handed it to Berman. He opened it and was taken with the fine sparkling stones, but immediately said that they were not for him. The woman said something, which only Berman heard; she leant over so close to him that he felt her warm breath. Everyone else strained to hear, but to no avail.

"Very well then," said Berman, "if you insist, please come up to my office."

This meant: "That's a different matter. I may be willing to buy stolen goods, but not here."

The woman shut her handbag, inclined her head and started leaving.

"Show us what you've got!" a dealer shouted after her. The others burst out laughing, though the dealer had meant it quite seriously and wanted to see her goods. But she pretended not to hear.

"What do you think of Gretchen? She's certainly putting on weight. We'll soon have to extend the walls of the Bourse."

"If we just knock down the pillars she'll get in all right," joked the dealers.

They continued to laugh, in their coarse, cynical fashion.

"She's a determined woman, and what a head she's got on her shoulders! They say that when her husband was alive, he sought her advice about business, and didn't make a move without her!"

Berman stood up, wandered about the Bourse for a while, exchanged a word here, a look there, and then he left and went straight back up to his office, nearby. The woman was already waiting for him. Berman sent his secretary off with a note to Rochl about his father's bed, even though he knew very well that Rochl couldn't read. She would have to wait till he got home to read the note to her. The secretary skipped gleefully down the stairs two steps at a time, thinking to herself, "I can take half an hour off!"

The woman brought her chair closer to the table.

"Herr Berman, you remember the blond *goy* who robbed the till and stole diamonds, and brought dishonour to the Bourse? You remember how poor Rosenbaum shot himself?"

"Yes indeed," said Berman, looking at her eagerly and enquiringly.

"The *goy* has been arrested, but the whereabouts of the goods are unknown, and the money has disappeared without trace."

Berman pretended not to hear.

"How many stones to the carat?"

"To the carat? You mean how many carats to the stone! I'm talking about stones of five and eight carats, blue-white!"

"We'll soon see if that's true!"

"Very well, take a look."

Berman put his loupe to his eye and examined the stones, trying to hide the excitement he felt just looking at them.

"You've got black ones too?" He laid the stones on one side as if they didn't interest him at all.

"Black ones too, certainly."

The stones flashed black, red, green with a silver shimmer. Then red again. Berman gave an involuntary shiver. One seldom saw anything as good as that.

"He certainly knew what to steal, that damned *goy*."

The woman was watching Berman's every move. She saw the impression the diamonds made on him. She knew this little game only too well.

The two of them haggled for a long time. The woman stood her ground and would not reduce the price by a centime. She know that Berman would pay, because he realised that he stood to earn a fortune. At last he said:

"Leave the goods here, and I will give you a definite decision in a few hours' time."

The woman counted the stones once more, gave Berman her soft white hand, inclined her head slightly and left. Her face was flushed as if she had drunk a large vodka, her eyes were shining and she had the sensuous beauty of a woman after making love, rather than doing business. She regarded the goods as sold. Berman would not be able to resist such a purchase.

Berman was rubbing his hands: Praise be to God! This was a wonderful piece of business. Then he remembered his father at home and gave a pious sigh.

"There'll have to be a trip to London. I can't keep this merchandise in my possession for very long," he thought. He decided that the next morning he would quiz the woman, who had suggested London, to find out exactly what the office in London was like. How did she know that the goods could be sold there? Had she herself sold stones there? And so on ... He wouldn't go to London himself; Shapiro could go instead. He was younger and more active than Berman, and why shouldn't he also profit from this? Berman was now feeling generous. He telephoned Shapiro at his office.

"Come here quickly, please! A very important matter!"

When his secretary came back, Berman told her she could go to the cinema. "There's nothing more to do today, but come early tomorrow morning. There'll be a lot of correspondence."

"Thank you, I certainly will."

This time the girl flew down the stairs three at a time, singing: "*Ooolala, in het park van de nachtegaal ...*"

Shapiro, who never touched stolen goods or "lost" parcels, arrived at Berman's office. "That fellow will end up in prison one day, long beard and all. He's worried sick already, and yet he can't resist," he thought to himself and smiled when he saw the stones, which he immediately recognised. The woman had already shown them to him.

"Hmm ... you know my principle, Herr Berman. Hmm ... these goods are not for me."

Berman, confused and angered by Shapiro's response, was about to make a harsh riposte to him, but he swallowed it, even though it stuck in his throat. It was, after all, typical of Shapiro. He gave one of his sly smiles, which always made Berman nervous. This meant that he had already seen these stones and knew what kind of merchandise they were. So Berman just had to bite his tongue and be silent. Nevertheless, he was angry.

"You see how the bastards lose things! We'll have to be careful that

126

they don't lose parcels of ours one day." He was just searching for things to say, just so that he didn't have to look at Shapiro's little smile.

Berman straightened up, but he felt a great tiredness in his aching limbs. It was always the same after he had struck a good bargain, but this time he felt as if someone had beaten him up instead.

"Damn it all, that Shapiro's just play-acting, striking a pose. He, Shapiro, wouldn't do such a thing, God forbid! What a thought! He, the respectable citizen. Bah! The cut-throat, more like ... the ... the ...." Berman couldn't find the right words to describe Shapiro. His mind went blank. He grew angry with himself.

"What an idiot I am! Did I really have to phone *him,* that saintly character, that Hungarian rogue! I think he's just trying to pull a fast one."

"Listen to me, Herr Berman," said Shapiro, who could read Berman's thoughts, "I advise you as a good friend: don't get involved with that Gretchen. Don't jeopardise your good name through dubious deals like this. She even informed me of an office in London where I would be able to dispose of the goods. Ha ha! The way she called the thief "the blond *goy*" as if she herself were Jewish. You remember, Herr Berman, how poor old Rosenbaum, may his soul rest in peace, shot himself on account of those two bloody Germans?"

Berman's eyes had a glassy stare and he felt a shiver running through him. He was sitting hunched up with his hands tucked into the sleeves of his jacket, fighting a hard battle with himself. It was very, very difficult to relinquish diamonds like these. They danced before his eyes, filling the room, and flashing round the walls; their orange, white, red and yellow fire made his senses reel.

"Herr Berman, withstand this temptation and you will be grateful to me."

Berman gave a start: had he been asleep? How long had he been dozing? And Shapiro was still there? What was happening?

"You are right, Herr Shapiro!" Berman stretched and felt a sudden sense of relief, as if a heavy burden had rolled off his shoulders.

"That Gretchen will get what she deserves; mark my words, Herr Berman."

The two men carried on talking for a long time. After Shapiro had

left, however, Berman looked at the diamonds again, and the temptation was just too strong ….

Gretchen was sitting in a first class compartment; both hands buried
in the sleeves of her loose travelling coat, thinking about her visit to
the dirty office above a private pawnbroker's shop. The owner, a Gentile with red hair, a pinched, red face and steely-grey eyes, was one of
five partners. Gretchen had gone into the front shop by mistake,
where the owner was standing behind the counter examining a pair of
sheets, grey from frequent washing, which a tall, gaunt woman in a
patched, velvet coat, with a man's cap on her head, was trying to
pawn.

"Mr Brown! On my word of honour, I only bought them a month
ago," she assured him, seeing that he was not too keen. "Only a month
ago," she insisted pleadingly, her watery blue eyes becoming even
more despairing. And the curlers and hairpins in her thin, colourless
hair bobbed about.

Mr Brown laughed. He had a drunken look in his eyes, cracked
jokes and roared with laughter, and the other ragged women with
their strained, lined faces, who were standing waiting in a queue,
roared with laughter too.

"Oh, isn't he a scream!" they all chuckled, showing their prominent front teeth, hoping thereby to find favour in Mr Brown's eyes.

"But in which century was that?" laughed Mr Brown, enjoying
his new joke, and he flung the tall woman a few pennies across the
counter.

The women started feeling their own packages, running their
crooked, bony fingers over the bits and pieces of clothing they had
brought in to be pawned, and their urge to laugh suddenly disappeared.

"Did you see what he gave her! He's gone mad!" they whispered
to each other. "I won't be able to manage till Friday on that, it won't
even be enough to provide dry bread, and the kids have such ap-
petites!"

"It's the same with me. It's a disaster!"

Seeing Gretchen come into the shop, a thin man with a greenish face and cunning, grey eyes abandoned a package he was examining, and without saying a word came out from behind the counter, took Gretchen up to the first floor, showed her the door of the office, and, still without speaking, went down the crumbling stairs again. It was here that Gretchen had disposed of the goods.

Chapter 14

When Jacques came home from school with his schoolbag on his shoulders, Berman told him to go to *cheder** immediately; he knew everything and if Jacques tried to get out of it again, he would get what was coming to him that evening. And Berman told him that on no account should he forget to take his grandfather to the *shtibl*. Then he went off to take a nap.

Jacques set out with his grandfather. On the way he met some friends and when one of them whistled to him, Jacques changed direction and turned into Leeuwerikstraat, taking his grandfather into the wrong *shtibl* by mistake.

"There it is!" And Jacques disappeared like a streak of lighting. Before the old man had a chance to look round, Jacques was with his pals and Reb Chaim Yoysef had no one to speak to.

"Oh well, it is a holy place too," he thought. He took out his *Gemara*, found the page where he had stopped reading and sat down to study.

But the Jews all laid their pocket handkerchiefs on their books and started asking where he had come from, whom he was visiting and how long he was staying.

"Oh! Berman? Well, if you're visiting a son like that, then it certainly is a good thing to sit quietly studying. It is good to walk on foot beside a heavy wagon; don't you think so, Reb Itshe?

"Yes indeed!" answered Reb Itshe, who was the *dayan,* the judge in the religious court. His rabbinical clothes hung too loosely on his small, bony frame. He went up very close to Reb Chaim Yoysef, and peered at him with his little black eyes, then, unable to think of anything else to say, he went back to his *Gemara*. One tall thin man, however, wouldn't let the *dayan* study. "Do you think he will be able to stay long at his son's house, eh, Reb Itshe?" he asked him.

Reb Itshe didn't reply but carried on rocking over his open book like a child.

"The reason I say that," carried on the man, who seemed to like the sound of his own voice, "is that when a good old-fashioned Jew from the old homeland comes over, and is not used to the customs here, it's really difficult, especially ... well, anyway, may the Almighty stand by you."

"Well there certainly are things I don't approve of," admitted Reb Chaim Yoysef, who didn't understand what the speaker had meant by his "especially". "I mean, my son is, thank God, an observant Jew, but my grandson has removed his beard. It's very distasteful to me. Admittedly my daughter-in-law says that he removes it with some kind of powder, and certainly that is permitted under the law. Indeed one reads that the sages were explicitly commanded to remove their beards in honour of every Jewish festival. But Jews in the Diaspora should not do it. That's the problem with being in a foreign country. At home, in Poland, a decent young man would never touch his beard. God forbid! But what can one do? And apart from that, they go around dressed like *goyim*. Even I am going around like that now."

"Oh well, if that's the worst thing that happens! He's just playing at being a *goy*. For our kind of people this isn't a real homeland," opined the previous speaker. "God be praised, my children are observant, thank God."

Reb Itshe smiled. "His sons have convinced him, the fool, that their beards don't grow!"

"What do you mean?" asked Reb Chaim Yoysef, bewildered.

Reb Itshe was about to explain, thought better of it, said nothing more and started swaying over his open *Gemara* again. When a woman came in to ask advice about a fowl, he folded down the page, closed the book, felt around in the intestines, licked the liver a few times, and pronounced that it was *kosher*. He was so delighted he was able to give this judgement, and did not have to condemn it, that he did not go back to his studying, but listened to the conversation instead.

The loquacious man was still talking. "Hmm, from what you say, the law of the Gentiles rules in your son's house! Thank God, I have better luck. My sons, God be praised, don't have any beards. At first I was really upset about it, but now, God be praised, I am really pleased. I see that the Almighty knows better than I what is for our good. For what if they had started shaving their beards, and then perhaps, God forbid, had completely left the right path. God preserve us, the things that can happen here!"

"What do you mean?" Old Reb Chaim Yoysef still didn't really understand, but the man didn't let him ponder long:

"You're surprised, eh? Well, you're not the only one. No one believes me. But my sons told me themselves."

Reb Chaim Yoysef, finally getting the point, gave a little smile and stuck his nose back into his *Gemara*.

"What a fool!" he thought, wanting to resume his study, but the other man would not let him do so.

"You know, if you had asked my advice before you set out, you wouldn't have come to Antwerp. It is Sodom and Gomorrah. Here, if you can't flatter, lie, swindle and steal, you can't make a living. Good Jews come here, poor creatures, and they think: 'Antwerp is a Jewish city, they deal in diamonds here, there'll certainly be no problem making a livelihood here.' They think they will get really rich and so they invest their few roubles, and who is it that gets rich? The absolute good-for-nothings! That's what this city's like!" He ended his diatribe with a heavy sigh.

"God forbid!" exclaimed Berman's father. "It's blasphemy to speak badly of a whole group of Jews. On the contrary, I have heard that there are many honest Jews, who honour the *Torah*[*] and who sit here and study, just like at home. And after all, you know the saying: 'a people without bread, is without *Torah*.' At home Jews can't get a livelihood, may it never happen to you, and they're in such a state that they can't even concentrate on looking at a sacred book."

"Is that what you've been told? Well, I can tell you a different story. You see that man who is just going out? That's Reb Mordecai Danziger. In the space of six months he lost about ten thousand roubles. And his wife, a woman from an illustrious family, had to take in shirts to sew. And now in their old age, when their children are grown up and have begun to support them, so that they could have expected to have a little peace and leisure, they have a new worry. Their children, God preserve us, have departed from the true path. I've heard

132

that they even go to the opera on *Shabbes*."

"What's 'opera'?"

"Oh, I don't know, it's a kind of thee-ay-ter. The son reads secular books and even non-Jewish books. He hasn't put his nose into a *shtibl* for years. It's even rumoured that he doesn't bind on his *tefillin*. I'm sure that can't be true. But still, all the rest is shocking enough. And you'll meet many decent pious Jews here who are toiling away, trying to do business, running around the Diamond Club. A stranger, seeing them, would think that they are achieving something, but that's not so. They're running around the offices, wearing out their shoe leather and going home with nothing at all. And it's the same thing with the workers: more often than not they go away empty-handed. You see, it's all right for the *goyim*. If a Gentile deals in diamonds, he is a rich man, because no poor Gentile would think of going into business. But a Jew, as you well know, has no other choice, so he has to hold on by his fingernails. Take someone like Reb Leybele Poltaver, for example. A fine person, a great scholar, used to be a rich man in the old homeland, and what has happened to him? Ruined, in an instant. Now his wife has opened a dairy business and she's not doing well at all. As I say, Sodom and Gomorrah." The man spoke with a mixture of anger and pity: he was sorry for those who had done badly, like himself. But he was also full of enmity towards those who had done well, no matter how honest they were. His motto was, if someone was doing well, he was probably a swindler.

Reb Itshe made a dismissive gesture, blew his nose loudly and said with irritation:

"That's absolute nonsense! I have lived in Antwerp for many years now and I know that there are good, pious Jews here, who keep the Law, and many real scholars of the *Talmud*, who are very rich men. So it's not just the good-for-nothings who get rich. The truth is that God helps the man who is destined to succeed. And if someone, sadly, is *not* destined to succeed, even if he's the cleverest swindler in the world, it will not help him one jot. It's the same in Antwerp as all over the world. If it is God's will, then honest men will make a livelihood, and if, sadly, it is not His will, then their lives, God preserve us, are bitter as death. But to give a bad name to a whole city? Probably there *are* some swindlers among us; that's very sad, and the whole community suffers because of them. If a Jew steals, then the Gentiles say that *all* Jews are thieves - but for you, an honest Jew, to suggest such a thing? It's a terrible calumny, which harms us all!"

Reb Itshe had got really worked up, and his Adam's apple was moving up and down like a big plum in his scrawny throat. He could hardly breathe and his hair was sticking to his head with sweat.

"And apart from anything else, how can anyone rely on the word of a man who has convinced himself that his sons don't have beards?"

"Don't worry, I'm used to people saying things like that!" said the man, gesturing with his hand, which was shaking uncontrollably. An anguished smile appeared on his dark face, spreading into his unhappy eyes. "I've already said that no one will believe me."

Berman's father felt a great affinity with Reb Itshe and the warmth he felt towards him seemed to lift a weight off his heart.

Suddenly a new voice was heard: "Listen, everyone! This man is absolutely right. I'm not talking about his sons and their beards, that doesn't interest me." Everyone looked round. "Let him think that, if it gives him pleasure." It was Leybesh speaking. He was sitting in the *shtibl* waiting for the beadle to come with the key to the synagogue. "He's absolutely right. All rich men are thieves, because business itself is theft. Therefore the man who loses because he is not a good businessman - he's *not* a thief! And the one who succeeds - he *is*! It's quite simple: profit is theft, and the profiteer will do everything in the world to make a profit. He'll stop at nothing. Theft, murder, everything is kosher. And that's not just in Antwerp, but all over the world. And there's no difference between Jews, Gentiles, mythical monsters, or whatever."

The three conversationalists looked round: "Ha? Who's that? Is it a madman or something?"

They didn't know Leybesh, were surprised by his intervention, and didn't understand what he was talking about. Where had he sprung from? What on earth was he getting at?

All three stared in amazement and huddled closer together as if to protect each other from this man who seemed like some kind of disturbing hallucination. And so they made up their quarrel.

In the evening rich Jews came into the *shtibl*, with fine beards and frock coats, some of them with longer jackets: a compromise between God and Europe. Many of them were dressed entirely in European clothes, with gold watches on thick chains dangling over rotund stomachs, and diamond rings on their middle and little fingers. There were also Jews with dirty jackets and coats mouldy with age, their beards poor and unkempt. Young men came in too, diamond cutters, polishers and cleavers, who had come to the *shtibl* after work to pray and study. Though these lads wore European clothes and straw hats, they looked even more unworldly and pale than *yeshiva* boys.* They sat down at the long tables and waited round the open *Gemara* until their *rebbe*, a man with a rabbinical hat and an intelligent face, had finished chatting with some diamond dealers. They were talking about blue-white diamonds, about big and little stones, offering each other a pinch of snuff and being offered a cigar in return. After all this, the Talmudic lesson which the *rebbe* gave them every evening could begin.

The worshippers went home. The young men at the long tables swayed piously over the open *Gemara*. The *rebbe* with the intelligent face stood swaying back and forward, intoning:

"And Rashi* says ...."

Chapter 15

Dovid had seen nothing of Gitele and the baby for over two months. He hung around Somersstraat, but she never appeared. Sometimes he got angry. He decided Gitele hadn't really loved him. She had just wanted to get her hands on his father's money, and when she saw that he wasn't likely to get any of it, she didn't need him any more.

But what was he to do? He could find no peace, and pined for Gitele and his baby. He even missed Leybesh, at the same time both hating him and feeling shame for his own behaviour towards him. In his imagination he saw the tall figure of Leybesh standing there barefoot and dishevelled in the small dark kitchen, with that kind smile on his face, saying to him: "Go back to sleep. Don't worry about it," with such infinite goodness in his blue eyes. And he, Dovid, lying there in Leybesh's bed in that poor kitchen, enjoying Leybesh's hospitality. He felt like a worm.

No, he certainly couldn't go back there, and yet his longing grew stronger all the time, and he could find no solution. He sat for days on his parents' velvet sofa, unwashed and unkempt, in his blue satin dressing gown and slippers. He smoked constantly, filling the elegant dining room with thick smoke. He thought and thought but found no answer. If only he had some funds, he could make a new start in business.

After a long inner battle he at last suggested to his mother she should pawn her jewellery. It cost him a great deal to make himself ask her such a thing, but Rochl told him she only wore imitation jewellery made out of cut glass, the kind used for display purposes in jewellery exhibitions, and her real diamonds were in a safe in the Bourse. Dovid couldn't believe his ears. His mother didn't even have any real jewellery to wear! But he knew she would never tell him a lie, and he had to believe her.

There was no point in speaking to his father. Dovid had already lost ten thousand francs' worth of business, and knew that his father would not give him another chance, or another centime. So he sat on the sofa and counted the flowers on the carpet, though he already knew how many there were: every flower, every piece of silver on the sideboard, and every candle on the candelabrum. When it got too claustrophobic he went on one of the tedious walks he knew so well, or sat in the park trying to read, though he absorbed nothing at all. More often he just sat staring at the people around him. There was a young woman with a pram coming into the park. She asked Dovid if the place beside him on the bench was free, and sat down. A chubby, little, fair-haired girl about two years old sat in the pram, playing with a yellow, velvet teddy bear. She was tormenting it, pulling its nose, poking its beady eyes with her forefinger, chatting to it, throwing it out of the pram and demanding that her mother pick it up again. The mother began to get impatient, and warned the little girl that she would not pick the teddy bear up again.

A dog ran up, stopped by the pram and looked up at the child with its black, moist eyes, its floppy ears quivering with excitement. It wagged its tail and barked at the teddy bear. The child bent out of the pram, nearly falling out, waved the bear in the dog's face and started chuckling. The child's laughter rang out like little silver bells. The dog shot off with the bear like an arrow from a bow, but brought it back. The woman chased the dog away and the child burst into tears.

Dovid's heart was aching. His longing for Gitele and their baby was so strong that he felt like embracing and kissing the woman, her little girl, and the dog - all at once. The woman stood up and went off into the park with her pram. Dovid got up too and walked off, not knowing where he was going.

He walked about the streets, not even bothering to look around. Nothing had changed: the streets and people were the same as a year ago, or even ten years ago. Trintshe the fishmonger had the same broad smile on her greasy face as always. He tried to avoid Somersstraat but suddenly found himself there, right opposite Gitele's window.

The woman with the blonde wig sat knitting a vest, and greeted

137

him with a mocking smile on her thin lips. Dovid sprang back as if he had been stung by a bee. He didn't answer her "*dag menieër*", but turned angrily on his heel and walked on.

A horse harnessed to a high cart full of manure stopped with a whinny, shook its mane and started walking on again, its clumsy hooves fringed with dirty tufts of hair. Dovid stared after the man sitting on the box smoking a pipe and apparently dozing, and really envied him: a man doing a day's work.

He was already far from the Jewish district, and as he walked, he thought out the plan which he had been carrying around in his head for a few days. He was scared to put it into action, because he didn't want to act foolishly again and let people find out his situation.

He turned into Cogels-Oyslei,* a beautiful wide street. The front gardens were all laid out differently from each other, with a variety of colourful flowers. He felt the street was like a poem, in which all the different individual words fused together in one melodious, harmonious rhythm.

The streetlamps were being lit. The lamplighter carried his long stick from lamppost to lamppost, even though the sun still shone on the flowerbeds. The man went down the street whistling a little melody, and the green gaslight mingled with the remnants of daylight, creating a bluish twilight. Here, thought Dovid, he could live with Gitele and their child, if he managed to make a success of his life ... yes, he would put all his failures behind him! He had to try once again, or else he would go mad.

Suddenly he thought of his grandfather. *He* was really driving David mad. "When you have to look at a corpse with a frozen smile on its dead face sitting there rocking back and forward all day long, is it any wonder that I have to leave the house?" Dovid thought to himself, with a sudden surge of rage.

He turned back into the town. An old school friend of Dovid's, with whom he used to play sometimes, in their free time, lived on Pelikaanstraat, and Dovid went up the steps to his house. This friend was now a diamond cleaver with a very good reputation. The biggest and most expensive stones were given to him to split, and he did it really expertly.

Why was Dovid scared? His friend could only say no. But Dovid's heart was pounding in case he was making a fool of himself again. He threw open the door, not even pausing to knock, because he knew that if he hesitated for an instant, he would just run back down the steps.

His friend stared in amazement at Dovid. He was delighted to seem him, but could hardly believe that Dovid Berman was actually paying *him* a visit. "Ahh! Who's this I see?" He stretched out a thin, freckled hand to him. "You are an unexpected guest. Do sit down. Please excuse the state of the place. When I'm working, I can't avoid it. It's a real pigsty!"

"No, no, don't worry, it doesn't matter at all: a productive mess is a good thing!" Dovid babbled in his embarrassment.

"And one's hands get pretty filthy too," continued the young man apologetically.

Dovid sat down on the chair, which his friend had wiped for him. The young man hovered around awkwardly for a moment or two, and then took up the diamond again, which looked like a piece of dirty washing soda, speaking to Dovid as he examined it: "If it didn't have so many imperfections it would be a real find!" He was about to cleave the rough diamond, but he had first to weigh up the possibilities: where and how to split it, in order to obtain the biggest and purest diamonds. "If one could find a pure stone of this size," he said, "which didn't need to be split, it would be worth a fortune."

"Really? Then diamond cleavers wouldn't be needed at all," said Dovid, encouraged to hear that such pure stones were very seldom found.

The young man brushed back his thick locks of red hair with his hand, straightened his skullcap, and explained to Dovid: "You see that little black speck? Like an island in the middle of water."

"You're right!" said Dovid, peering intently at the diamond.

"We have to get rid of that dirty little island so that only the pure water remains."

So saying, the diamond cleaver made a groove in the stone with another diamond, right on the black spot, after which he split the stone with one sharp blow.

"I'll have to split it further," he said. "What a shame! A giant like this and all we'll end up with are tiny little stones." The young man regretted this, even though the stone didn't belong to him.

Two other young lads worked there. They were cleaving small stones. They also looked, made a groove, gave a sharp blow. They glanced at the guest, obviously envious of him, and greatly impressed by his expensive clothing.

Dovid's friend talked to him, trying in a roundabout way to find out the reason for Dovid's unexpected visit. But Dovid sat there rooted to the spot, chatted about this and that and couldn't find an appropriate way to broach the subject he had come to discuss. He felt faint, and broke out in a sweat. How could he suddenly tell this former school friend about his problems? He and his friend had pursued totally different paths when they left school: the friend had started working, and he, Dovid, the rich man's son, had gone to the high school to carry on studying. He remembered how envious his friend had been at that time, because he was more intelligent than Dovid, and really wanted to study; how could Dovid tell him that now, years later, he had come to beg him to teach him how to cleave diamonds? The friend would look at him as if he were mad. So Dovid was at a loss what to do. If only the two other lads hadn't been there, looking him up and down, from his head to his white spats, very obviously envying him and expressing their admiration to each other in a joking, ironic way. Dovid felt frustration welling up inside him.

Suddenly his friend looked at the fiery red window, illuminated by the evening sun. He stood up and said to the other two:

"Time to say *mayrev!* You probably haven't prayed yet either?" he asked Dovid.

"Eh? Prayed? Ehm ... no ... not yet."

"Then we'll pray together!"

The little room huddled into the approaching darkness. The window flamed even more brightly and particles of light from the setting sun made patches on the floor, but the corners of the room were engulfed in shadow.

When they had finished praying, the three workers tidied the room very quickly, and then all four went down the steps. Dovid walked along with his friend, and finally told him about his plan.

"But that's not for you! What on earth made you think of that? What an idea! And why would *you* need to do that?" His friend simply could not and would not understand him. "If one wants to be a merchant, does one have to learn the mechanics of diamond cleaving? No, of course not! That wouldn't occur to anyone else. If you're a merchant, you can deal in diamonds without all that. Did your father, for instance, learn how to be a cleaver? Take it from me, it's not necessary, so forget all about it. You'd pay a thousand francs for the apprenticeship, and waste several years of your life. If I had your money, I wouldn't sit up in that workshop for a single day. Even the smallest dealer has more chance than the best worker. I myself am starting to buy and sell in a modest way. I want to be done with this work. What an idea, a healthy man climbing into a sickbed!"

Dovid found no words to answer him.

"So that's no good either. I'm obviously a hopeless failure. I might as well go and jump in the Scheldt."

Chapter 16

The High Holidays* were approaching, and Berman's mood became more sombre. This period heralded the end of the summer and the coming of winter, which Berman dreaded because he always suffered terribly from bronchitis. Apart from this he always got rather depressed during this period. He greeted the High Holidays with a mixture of fear, respect, and joy, but the time leading up to them was very difficult for him. At night, all sorts of thoughts would race around in his head, preventing him sleeping. On nights like those, when everything was dark and silent, he would lie there, mulling over his life.

The stolen diamonds would often creep into his mind; they seemed to stick in his throat and choke him, until he felt such nausea that he wanted to wake Rochl and tell her the whole story. He would prove to her that actually he hadn't done anything wrong. Rochl was lying in the other bed, breathing rhythmically, and dreaming innocent dreams, not suspecting that Berman was lying awake for hours trying to justify his actions. But no matter how hard he tried, the Authority before which he was trying to justify himself kept rejecting his arguments, and pushing the same thoughts back into his head until Berman started sweating all over his body and burst out in a fit of coughing. Then Rochl would wake up and fetch a glass of orange juice for her husband. Before Berman had finished drinking it, she would be snoring gently again in the other bed.

If he had a night like this at any other time of the year, he would ask her to come into his bed and help him to get to sleep. But such a thing was not permissible so near the solemn festival.

So Berman just lay there wrestling with his conscience. After all, what should he have done? If he hadn't purchased them, someone else would have. Non-Jews might even have bought them. Would it have been better to let them fall into Gentile hands? What would the

Gentile do with the money? Get a better dog, buy a new cross to adorn his church, or else go and get drunk. And in any case, did he, Berman, buy *only* dubious merchandise? No, every year he bought thousands of francs' worth of honest merchandise, and he always paid the full price for rough diamonds, according to all the regulations of the London syndicate. And apart from anything else: for whom did he provide a livelihood? For Jews. Didn't about a hundred Jews: dealers, brokers, polishers, cutters and cleavers, live off his business? *He* didn't give the work to Gentiles, God forbid, like many Jewish merchants did, even though they had to pay a higher price. His principle was that one Jew had to help another, especially as Jews were cheaper anyway, and didn't bother with unions. Why was he tormenting himself? So he tried to drive away these troublesome thoughts, but they wouldn't leave him. He spat, turned his face to the wall, but still couldn't get to sleep.

Apart from all these other worries, he had now taken responsibility for his father; he had taken him out of poverty and wanted to keep him in a manner that was fitting, so that he too could benefit from all that God had bestowed on his son, and enjoy his old age. After all, we pray that God should preserve us into old age. Then Berman sighed deeply, as the thought of Dovid came into his mind. Who can tell how children will treat one in one's old age?" he thought, and tears of self-pity welled up in his eyes. Immediately he felt much calmer; it was as if the tears had cleansed him from the sin of buying the stones, and, at peace with himself once again, he fell asleep.

In the morning he got up refreshed, went to the Bourse and carried on with the usual wheeling and dealing, but the sleepless nights and the dark thoughts and the inner battles did not cease.

During the two days before *Rosh Hashana*, when other merchants were busy getting jewellery out of the safe and managing to do a last little bit of business before the festival, Berman was already sitting at home by the warm stove, looking at the New Year cards. No matter how warm it was outside, the stove was already lit in the Bermans' house. He was deciding who ought to receive a big gold card and who should get a smaller, silver card; and who, finally, should only receive a white card decorated with a tiny, purple flower.

This was a task which Berman enjoyed. He would choose the cards, smile, take a sip from his red glass of tea, and forget that night was coming on. He loved the unaccustomed leisure, and to enjoy it all the more, he would say to Rochl:

"And those idiots are even now pulling the jewels out of their safes."

Rochl sighed, but when Berman looked at her she put on a cheerful air, agreeing:

"Yes, what fools! In the synagogue, all packed together; what do they need their jewellery for?"

At the Bermans, everything had to be absolutely ready some time before *Rosh Hashana*. Since Berman had nothing much to do, he liked to take a walk around the streets of the Jewish district on the eve of the festival. He closed his office around midday, smiling at the workers as he paid out what he owed them, even expressing his gratitude. He wished them a happy and prosperous New Year, accepted with great pleasure the stream of good wishes from them, and set off on his walk.

He started out at the first stone arch of the long railway bridge, which divided Antwerp into two parts. One part had the atmosphere of the big city, with brightly lit streets, large, colourful shops and department stores, and garish advertisements in neon lights. There were theatres, cinemas, wide boulevards, cafés and everything which belongs in a big city. In the other part, where the Jewish district was situated, it was crowded, poor, and had a very intimate atmosphere. It was here that Berman took his walk, glancing first of all at the big railway station clock and checking the time with his own massive gold watch, which made him smile with satisfaction: "Accurate to the second!" It was a fine watch, which he had had for about twenty years.

He crossed Pelikaanstraat, and at once he was in the heart of the bustling *Rosh Hashana* preparations. Jews with sombre faces were dragging cartloads of tasty foods and orchards of fruit round the streets.

"Fruits to greet the New Year, come and get them, ladies!" The vendors were yelling and the colours of the fruits shouted even more loudly. The shaggy dogs were exhausted; today they had run all over Antwerp pulling huge loads. The women were only making a show of

144

haggling, as their minds were already on the joyful festival, and the spirit of *Rosh Hashana* was reflected in their faces.

In the dusty shop windows there were still mounds of plaited bread and poultry for sale. The hens, hanging upside down with their bluish skin, blackened blood and closed eyes, looked miserable, like blind people full of self-pity. The poor women who prodded these hens were hardly any less miserable, having had to wait till the very last moment to see if their husbands or sons would bring home some meagre wages.

Because of customers like these, even the hairdressers had to work right up until the festival was about to begin. In the previous weeks they had already worked their fingers to the bone, fashioning all sorts of waves and curls and ringlets in the wigs of rich ladies. But even now, after weeks of hard work, these poor, tired fingers, which had been eagerly waiting for *Rosh Hashana*, were still not allowed to rest. They could be seen through the shop windows, listlessly curling the last bits of hair on the wooden heads, preparing the poor women's wigs.

When Berman saw all this, he felt an urge to raise his hands to heaven and give praise to God who had lifted him out of this wretched state of poverty. Then, once again, the thought of Dovid came into his head.

It was the eve of *Rosh Hashana*. Berman was dressed from head to toe in new clothes. He had even bought himself a splendid new prayer shawl with black stripes and long tasselled fringes. His new top hat was tall and shining. He was waiting for his father for whom he had also had new clothes made, despite Rochl's objection that he already had lots of good frock coats in his wardrobe which could easily have been shortened. No, his father had to have a fine new outfit. Berman had helped his father to dress, to ease his stiff old body into the new clothes. He was certain that the Almighty would repay him with interest for this good deed, and he felt a glow of satisfaction.

But the old man spoiled his pleasure slightly. It embarrassed him to wear a top hat, and he begged his son to let him wear his velvet skullcap as he always did. In the end, however, he gave in and put on the top hat, but for the first time since he had arrived in Antwerp he regretted having come to stay with his son. Nevertheless he forgave him, since he didn't want to bear him any grudge on *Rosh Hashana*.

Dovid's white spats shone whiter than ever. Both his grandfather and father blessed him, as if he had still been a little boy. It was the same every year. Rochl blushed as she made the blessing over the candles, and her glass jewellery sparkled. But there was a tear in her eye: she felt cheated and ashamed, as if she were betraying the candles at this holy festival, because their pure flame was being reflected in false diamonds.

Jacques couldn't prise himself away from the mirror. He was so pleased with himself in his new clothes that he couldn't wait to see the other boys in the synagogue and find out who had the finest outfit, though he already felt sure it would be his. He stood admiring himself like a girl, until Jeannette pushed him away as if he were just some obstacle in her way. Wearing her grey fur coat, she filled the whole mirror. She put cream and rouge on her face, twirled in front of the mirror and twirled again. Everyone was waiting for her. They were in a hurry to get to the synagogue, but Jeannette wouldn't stop admiring herself in the mirror. Rochl put on her fur coat as well, even though the weather was still warm and humid.

All of Antwerp was going to synagogue. The little streets of the Jewish district were full of people. The great synagogue, where Berman worshipped had a huge ornate interior. It seemed as if a special exhibition of diamonds, tiepins, cufflinks and rings was taking place. The men had dressed up just as much as the women. In the women's section a huge sea of diamonds sparkled and flashed in the sunlight.

In the streets of the Jewish district, the sound of the *shofar*, the ram's horn blown on *Rosh Hashana*, still echoed around. During the following ten days of repentance, Jews prepared themselves for *Yom Kippur*, the awesome day of judgement in which their sins of the past year would be counted. They went around with lowered heads, piety written on their faces. During that period Berman went to the Bourse and his office, where he treated his workers with kindness.

As for Dovid, he slept even later than usual. The eve of *Rosh*

Hashana, when he had let his father bless him, still lingered in his mind and rose up before his eyes, seeming to mock him. It was even more upsetting than usual. He spat, full of shame and disgust at himself: why had he not taken the silk prayer shawl with the blue stripes which his father had given him, wound it around his father's neck and strangled him? That would have put an end to it all! Dovid was horrified by his own thoughts. He got up and went out into the street. It was the day before *Yom Kippur*. As usual, Dovid tried to prevent himself going to Somersstraat, but found himself there in the end, thinking as always about Gitele, but finding no solution to his problems. Suddenly, there she was, coming towards him, dressed in a new coat and hat. She looked quite different, with fuller cheeks, clear skin, and shining, happy eyes, which did not look so huge as they had when her face was thin and pinched. He had never seen her looking like this before. She smiled cheerfully at him and gave him her soft, warm hand. Dovid trembled: he wanted to hold her hand and never let go. He was scared that he would put his arms round her in the middle of Somersstraat and start kissing her passionately. But something stabbed at his heart.

"Why are you out in the street so early?" he stammered, looking at her with desire.

Gitele laughed. She realised that Dovid was jealous of her new clothes and her happy new appearance.

"Why are you laughing?" Dovid gave her an angry look, not knowing himself why he felt annoyed. He didn't realise that he was upset to see that Gitele could dress herself smartly and look good without him.

"I see you're surprised, so I'll tell you what's happened. Leybesh is working for an employer, and he's earning. He already knows how to polish a stone perfectly."

Dovid felt the blood rushing to his head.

"How ... how ... I mean ... where have you left the baby?"

Gitele laughed again, which made Dovid want to scream at the top of his voice: "*Stop* laughing; it gets on my nerves!" but instead he just repeated: "Where is the baby?"

"I've pawned her!" she answered, angry with him for looking at her accusingly, as if she were a bad mother who had neglected her child. And Dovid, who hadn't seen the baby for two months, had suddenly become her protector!

Dovid saw the ludicrous nature of his position and calmed down. Changing his tone, he asked:

"May I ask who he is working for?" as if it made any difference to him who Leybesh's employer was.

"For Rubin!"

"Do you mean Rubin the philosopher?"

"Yes, he comes up to my elegant residence; he has become a great pal of Leybesh's and gives him as much work as he wants. But I must get home because Leybesh has to go out and he won't have anywhere to leave the baby. I just came out to get some shopping. You know how Leybesh has a feast with his disciples every *Yom Kippur.*[*] To tell you the truth, I'm not very keen on this ...."

Dovid didn't wait to hear any more; he spun round on his heel and ran away like a scalded cat. Gitele wanted to say something else to calm him down, but he had already disappeared.

"So that's how it is, she has to run home to her beloved Leybesh." As if to torment himself deliberately, Dovid misinterpreted the sense of her words. "So, Leybesh is now the father of her child, and she leaves her with him, so that she can go and buy food for a *Yom Kippur* feast, even though she disapproves of it. Well!"

He strode home swiftly, his head feeling empty and dull. When he arrived he looked round the room, and was surprised to see everyone looking perfectly calm and busily occupied; it didn't occur to any of them that something terrible had happened. On the contrary, they were bustling around even more than usual. Mother was helping Anneke to pluck white hens in the kitchen,[*] Jacques was absorbed in carving something with his penknife. Jeannette was reading, Anneke, her hands covered in blood, was plucking the birds and quietly singing a little song. It didn't seem to worry her that these hens, which were still warm, were the same ones she had heard half an hour earlier clucking and squawking, and that she had seen them lying dead on the cold stones of the slaughterhouse, bathed in their own blood – that same blood which was now all over her hands. She sang: "Her sweetheart is an idiot ..." and kept sweeping up the feathers, which were fluttering all round the kitchen. When Dovid's mother saw him standing in the doorway staring as if he were in a trance, she called out to him: "Oh Dovid, I'm glad you're here. The cockerel has been lying tied up, poor creature, since this morning." She told him to take it and perform the atonement ceremony,* so that she could have it slaughtered.

Dovid looked round and woke out of the state of paralysis which his jealousy, rage and sense of his own failure had inflicted on him. In his anguish he burst out into unnatural, spasmodic laughter, and his eyes filled with tears. Rochl was shocked: had her son suddenly gone mad?

Leybesh had been doing well recently. One of his previous disciples had a brother, Rubin, who was an adherent of the Haskalah, the Jewish Enlightenment movement; he knew Hebrew but no Yiddish, he had a miniature picture of Dr Herzl instead of a diamond in his gold signet ring, and he wore a soft black cap and gold pince-nez. He liked Leybesh and hoped to make a Zionist of him, and so he gave him work. He often came up to Leybesh's place to try to convince him.

"I tell you, socialism is an abstract idea, and Marxism an abstract theory!" This was his favourite argument. "It's a fairy tale without a proper ending. Your best proof of this is the French Revolution. And another thing, what happened to the revolution of 1905, eh?"

But when Leybesh remained implacable, the boss took it philosophically and they remained good friends. He realised that Leybesh was an educated man with his own ideas. Eventually, he believed, Leybesh would realise that he had been misguided. But what about his own brother, Leybesh's disciple? How had *he* got involved with all this?

"You, with your bird brain, you want to save the world, do you?" Rubin reproached his brother. "You'd do better to sort out that tangle of wool inside your own head first!"

The young man took his brother's words to heart. In any case, he really hadn't understood a word of Leybesh's teachings. He used to fall asleep during the "sermons", and when he woke with a start he would see all the comrades smiling at him. The boys and girls would ask questions during a discussion and Leybesh would hear them out with great seriousness, making notes with a pencil on a scrap of paper, after which he would answer everyone's question in order. This young man was amazed at this and envied Leybesh and the comrades for being able to understand such things. He loved Leybesh for not making any difference between him and the other comrades, treating them all alike. But still, Karl Marx was too hard a nut for him to crack, and so he decided Rubin was right: one can be a good socialist even if one is not a wage slave. He took his brother's advice, got married and received a large dowry, then became a diamond merchant and did very well.

So Leybesh was working for this young man's brother. He would bring the completed work back to his employer and then sit chatting with him until late into the night, and the boss was so delighted that Leybesh almost always lost to him at chess, that he would sometimes stand him a bottle of wine. So this *Yom Kippur*, Leybesh was able to have a real banquet.

Outside, the sun was pouring down on a sea of top hats worn by Jews, rich and poor: the wealthy diamond merchants as well as the grocers, peddlers and even poorer people. Even the errand boys with the grey beards wore top hats today.

They were all going to synagogue, the women in fur coats, sweating within an inch of their lives, men with bellies on which dangled gold chains and watches as big as turnips, and others with worn-out frock coats and split top hats, together with their work-weary wives in their best clothes, hiding their poverty as best they could. The town streamed into the synagogue.

You would have thought that Antwerp ended here, and that the lively, vibrant city on the other side of the bridge had disappeared. It was as if the entire city were observing this awesome day. Only the trains clattered across the bridge in their normal everyday routine, puffing and whinnying out their long, echoing whistle which desecrated the solemnity of the day.

There was a merry atmosphere at Leybesh's. The two little rooms were packed with the male and female comrades, the "irreligious" girls were busy cooking and frying, and not allowing Gitele to do any of the work. They knew that Gitele did not approve of this business. She believed one could be non-religious, and, indeed, she herself did not believe in anything, but nevertheless, cooking on *Yom Kippur* seemed to her to be overstepping the mark. The girls worked like mad to get everything done, singing revolutionary songs, catching a remark from a comrade in the other room, giving a riposte, laughing. And soon they were all sitting round the table.

Leybesh, taking a cigarette out of the large box which he had set out on the table for the guests, started heaping abuse on Antwerp and its Jews:

"You know what, comrades? In the old homeland I still had a grain of respect for the pious Jews. I could see their stupidity and prejudice, but nevertheless their absolute faith did sometimes move me. Faith has beauty! We believe that too because, after all, make no mistake: when we read Marx, although we have to agree that his mathematical calculations are absolutely correct, just like two times two equals four, and that although this decaying economic order is bound to collapse of its own accord, it's still our holy duty to *help* to hasten its destruction as much as we can; we mustn't wait until that decayed building does collapse and bury too many victims underneath, or let too many good human beings get TB from its damp, unhealthy walls.

"Nevertheless ..." and Leybesh took a new cigarette, since the first one had burnt itself out in the corner of his mouth, "... nevertheless, we would have lost the courage to carry on if we had stopped having *faith* that a better tomorrow will come. Mathematical calculations alone wouldn't be enough to keep our disgust at so much nauseating hypocrisy and baseness alive, wouldn't keep us constantly *aware* of the filth through which we have to wade. Only faith holds us together. And that's why I say that I used to have a little spark of sympathy in my heart for the Jew who truly believed. Naturally I pitied him for his blindness, but I didn't despise him in the way I despise these ones here. When I see them going into the synagogue to repent, while at the same time they're sinning, even on their way there: carrying their jealousy, hatred, snobbery, vanity with them in a word, everything that they'll soon be beating their diamond-encrusted hearts over, it makes me want to spit in their fat faces, so that they'd drown in that one huge gob of spittle!"

The comrades all agreed absolutely with Leybesh. Even Gitele was persuaded of the case he was making, and felt that she had never fully appreciated how clever he was.

"Where do the diamonds come from?" asked a girl who had just arrived in Antwerp from a *shtetl* in Poland.

Leybesh took another cigarette. He knew the history of diamonds better than many of the big dealers, who handled hundreds of thousands, even millions of francs' worth of diamonds every year. "Till the end of the nineteenth century they came from India, but now a great many of them come from South Africa. Diamonds were discovered in South Africa by chance. A child was playing with a little stone, and a certain Dr. Otterstone happened to see it and realised that this wasn't just any old stone, but a diamond. So they started digging, and now it's our black brothers who are digging out diamonds, making others rich and dying of hunger themselves. They work in dreadful conditions and when they finish after a gruelling day's work, they are stripped naked and searched everywhere, even in their ears, to see whether they have, God forbid, hidden a stone to keep for themselves. They have the right to work for others, to be worked to the point of exhaustion, and illness, but they haven't the right to have enough to eat. And it doesn't seem to occur to anyone that this is an absurd injustice. No one bothers about poor white people, so is it likely that anyone will care about poor blacks?"

"Who owns all the diamonds after they're mined?" asked the same girl.

"An organisation called the De Beers Company. They control all the main mines in South Africa, which are in Kimberley."

Gitele was amazed. This was the first time that she had heard Leybesh talking about diamonds, and he seemed to know all about them. She remembered that she had once asked Dovid, and he hadn't had a clue, despite the fact that *he* had gone to high school. And who knows what school Leybesh had attended? Dovid had said that his father didn't know anything about diamonds either. However he *did* know how to make money from them. When Gitele thought about this, her respect for Leybesh wavered slightly.

In the afternoon, Leybesh led the band of comrades to the House of the Inquisition, which for him was a sacred ritual every *Yom Kippur*. The grey fortress* had stood in Antwerp for hundreds of years, from the time when Antwerp was just an insignificant township. The Jesuits later made the castle into the headquarters of the Inquisition, and it still stands there like a dirty stain on the city. The thick walls are as white as chalk in places, and as black as coal in others, or as black as the air inside its cellars. The narrow windows are black slits which seem encrusted with the dried blood of the tortured victims. Leybesh and his comrades made their way to this fortress.

When Leybesh opened the arched wrought iron door, and they bent their heads and went inside, a skinny little old man greeted them, smiling with his toothless mouth and his dim, blue eyes under their bushy eyebrows. He had a yellow, pitted face, like old parchment, with a pointed, trembling chin. He found some candles and, counting the visitors and the candles very carefully, gave each one a lit candle, said: "All right, quick march!" and laughed foolishly.

Led by Leybesh, they made their way, in procession, to the dark, narrow hole from which some steps led down to the cellars. It was so dark that they couldn't see each other, only the melancholy little flames twisting and turning like the sharp, dusty, grey steps, which seemed have sad stories to tell. Trembling, black silhouettes danced on the dark walls. The girl who had just come to Antwerp let out a scream and dropped her candle. Leybesh, expecting this, had been walking beside her the whole time. Now he took her arm and calmed her: "Don't be scared, comrade! There's nothing to be frightened of. If only people were as scared of the real evil in our world."

The girl appeared to calm down, and even managed a weak, tremulous smile.

Leybesh relit her candle, but she shuddered and categorically refused to hold it. She huddled up to Leybesh like a child and stared wide-eyed and terrified at the horrible instruments of cruelty, which were now revealed. Leybesh explained them to her: "Look, that's how they broke people's fingers. And with those bits of rusty iron they

153

broke people's arms. People whom they should have revered, people who were great free spirits!"

Leybesh showed her an innocent-looking machine which was standing in a corner.

"Human beings were locked into that and forced to stand motionless until they died. And that's the axe ...."

"That's enough, comrade, please! I don't want to see any more! I can't bear it!"

Leybesh felt her violent trembling and decided not to show her any more. "All right, but I just want to show you one more thing. You see how the walls are covered in scratch marks, so that there is not a bit of empty space? If you come back another time to read them, you'll see that they date from hundreds of years back; they are dates, names, pleas, curses and prayers, which the torture victims scraped on the walls, as well as recent dates scratched by tourists. All of them read as a curse against the Jesuits who perpetrated such crimes, allegedly in the name of the true religion, torturing human beings to death in the eternal, holy battle for supremacy. This is the way they interpreted Jesus' teaching, that if a man strikes you on one cheek, you should turn the other one to him."

The girl listened, and every word that Leybesh said was a new *Torah* to her; she had never heard anyone talk about such things in her provincial *shtetl*. She had become more used to the darkness now.

When they got back up to the surface, the watchman was in the middle of his meal, munching with his toothless jaws and smiling in his good-natured but simple way. "Good day, *menieër*." He greeted them politely, remembering the generous tip Leybesh had given him the previous year.

Outside, opposite this House of the Inquisition flowed the broad, serene, shining River Scheldt. They all gasped with relief and the girl from Poland positively squealed with joy: "Ohhh, how lovely!"

"Now comrades, let's go down to the river", said someone, and they all wandered slowly to the banks of the Scheldt.

The sun was just about to set, and here and there, little patches of blood red, gold, silver and violet were reflected in the water. "I've never seen such a beautiful river," cried the girl with delight. This pleased Leybesh and he talked about the river with pride:

"I love the Scheldt because of its breadth - I love everything which is broad."

"Except women," joked one of the comrades.

Leybesh laughed heartily.

All along the Scheldt, almost at the very edge, lay boats of every size and colour. A flag fluttered on each one, telling the world which country they came from. One large ship, which took up a huge berth, came from Hamburg. One boat stood out from the others in its luxury and its gleaming, pristine whiteness. Some of the crew were airing and cleaning the cabins. The doors of the first class cabins were open, and their mirrors, velvet furnishings and nickel plated fittings caught everyone's eye. The ship was empty because the passengers had gone into Antwerp to see all the essential tourist attractions.

"Perhaps some of them are in the Inquisition House" said someone.

"And some in the synagogues!" laughed Leybesh.

"*Lehavdil,* God forgive the comparison,"* said the provincial girl automatically and then blushed to the roots of her hair.

On the quay there was a long row of warehouses which received merchandise from all over the world. An elderly Flemish man in a pair of stiff, shiny trousers and a torn, dirty, blue jacket was carrying a huge chest on his shoulders, almost collapsing under its weight. He had a thin, lined face covered with sweat, with a sharp nose and red, protruding eyes. It looked as if he could collapse at any minute and the heavy chest would fall on top of him and crush him to death. But the man was obviously used to the work and he deposited his heavy burden in its correct place, wiped away the sweat with a greasy rag, rolled himself a cigarette and started out again to collect another chest.

The skinny, stooped porters darted back and forth over the rails, their loaded, green barrows making a deafening metallic clatter, which almost drowned out the din of the porters themselves, who were shouting to each other. The cranes continuously deposited one lot of merchandise and lifted another; it seemed as if the exchange of goods was going on all by itself.

The volume of merchandise was huge, and all this hullabaloo was going on as if it were a normal working day, even though many of the owners of the businesses had been spending the day in synagogues. The comrades walked almost the length of the Scheldt, and it was only when the sun had completely disappeared in the west and the tall electric lamps were lit, sprinkling the rippling water with fragments of gold, leaving other parts dark blue or black, and a galaxy of stars twinkled in the water, only then did the little band of comrades go back home.

The Jews had already gone home from the synagogue. Their souls were emptied of their sins and their faces were drained of blood; and they had little packages under their arms containing their prayer books, prayer shawls, and smelling salts. They expressed their relief that the fast was at an end, that it was the evening after and not the evening before *Yom Kippur*. They all wished each other a good year; even the poorest of them shook hands then hurried home to break their fast.

Chapter 17

From the beginning of the month of *Kheshvan*,* fine rain fell incessantly. It dripped on everything with a monotonous rhythm, so that the city looked dull and shabby. Heavy clouds, like lumps of dirty cotton wool covered the sky, and the leaden mass seemed to press down on the earth. Instead of the usual winter cold, the damp crept over people's bodies like worms, penetrating their bones and choking their throats.

As a result, Berman's health was worse than usual that winter, and he constantly had to protect himself against chills. He paced around the brightly lit, well-heated rooms of his house, wearing his red velvet dressing gown, reproaching the Almighty for punishing him with ill-health while allowing all sorts of paupers, losers and other nonentities to wander round the streets, haggling and selling their wares. They went into restaurants with trays of chocolate, matches, cigarettes, buttons and socks. They went around half-naked in all weathers, but it didn't seem to do them any harm. Even if they caught colds, they might cough a little but suffered no ill-effects. Whereas the moment he, Berman, caught the slightest chill, the doctor insisted that he stayed in the house, warning him that it could get very serious, because the bronchitis could weaken his heart. Who wouldn't be scared of that? So, poor Berman stayed at home, fretting. He would rather be out there earning money, and instead the office had been closed for over a month. That, of course, was not an insurmountable problem, because the workers came to his house to collect work from him, and he could sell from home as well, since his brokers knew where he lived. The real problem was buying new goods.

You had to be on the spot in order to buy. There were always plenty of people competing for a bargain. You had to look into the other merchant's eyes, and interpret a look or gesture of his which indicated that he had something to sell. Then you had to be astute, greet

157

the other in a friendly fashion, ask after his health and his wife's health, ask him why he hadn't been around, take his arm as good friends do, and saunter out of the Bourse together for a cup of coffee in a back street somewhere. Only then would the real negotiations begin.

Instead, Berman was sitting at home. No one, he realised, was going to bring merchandise to his house. The diamond merchants were not working for the good of their souls and wouldn't think of coming to help a sick man; you'll only get food if you manage to get to the trough. He sighed and raged and stormed, and Rochl shrank from him, wishing she could transform herself into a cooking pot to avoid attracting his attention. He needed her constantly, however. One moment he was too warm in his quilted dressing gown, the next moment he was too cold in his velvet one. Then he had to take his medicine. Either the fire in the hearth was blazing too fiercely, or it was too low and needed stoking. One minute he was coughing and choking, then he was starving hungry, or he was simply angry and had no one to vent his rage on, except Rochl. There was no point in her trying to hide or pretend she hadn't heard his call. The house became a living hell for her.

On top of all this, the old man had taken to his bed, and stayed there all winter. At least he lay there quietly, and as long as he could put on his *tefillin* and pray, he needed nothing else. If someone gave him something to eat, he ate it, and if not, he didn't. But food was always available and Berman himself would come and bind on the *tefillin* for him. So the old man felt fine and wanted for nothing; that's what he said if one of the family happened to come in to see how he was getting on.

Dovid was at a loose end all winter. He listened to his father's tales of woe about the financial losses from the bronchitis, to his mother's timid little sighs, and to his sister bragging about her successes with all the charity dances she performed in aid of various schools and hospitals for the poor. He watched his grandfather's face becoming yellower and his fixed smile more and more like *rigor mortis*. Dovid did not know what to do with himself.

He told himself that his attitude towards Gitele was absurd and that he was doing her a great injustice. What had she done, apart from buy a few new clothes, improve her standard of living and in general look better, which any woman would do if she had the wherewithal? He knew he should root out the horrible rancour and suspicion he harboured against her, and not let them grow; otherwise they would poison his blood. But it was too late: the poison had already entered into him, so that day or night he could find no peace of mind, and, gradually, he found himself turning against Gitele, and even against his own child.

Sometimes, however, when he was aimlessly walking round the streets in order to escape from the atmosphere at home, his feet would lead him to their house, and his longing would reawaken. Seeing their shadows through the curtains, he recognised Leybesh's tall silhouette with the tousled hair, saw Gitele's small form appearing and disappearing. He heard the faint sounds of the baby crying and someone singing to her. In those moments his longing to catch a glimpse of the child became unbearable. Using all his willpower, he would tear himself away. On those evenings Dovid did not go home, but found his way, not to his usual haunts, but to the cabarets, where he would drink the night away with Jules. In their new intimacy, Dovid didn't care who paid the bills.

His scandalous behaviour was soon the talk of Antwerp. No one was particularly interested in Jules but Dovid was a juicy topic of conversation: everyone was keen to gossip about Berman's son. Rochl began hearing snippets and was devastated to realise that her son was at the centre of scandal. Even worse, it was just at this point that the servant girl, Anneke began to get yellowish blotches on her face. She often felt nauseous and had to run to the kitchen sink. Rochl realised very quickly that she was pregnant.

"What's this, Anneke?" she asked, pointing at Anneke's belly. Anneke flushed but immediately retorted: "Nothing!"

"What do you mean: 'nothing'?" persisted Rochl. Anneke burst into tears, then calmed down, blew her nose, wiped her eyes and told Rochl that she already had two other children and that the father had promised that this time he would marry her. "My dad says that if he doesn't, he's going to kill him."

Rochl was not unduly surprised. In her experience Anneke's situation was not uncommon among the Flemish people.

"And who looks after the children?" she asked.

"My mother of course," replied Anneke, obviously surprised by the question. She carried on washing the dishes as if nothing had happened.

"My God, what a way to live, they breed like rabbits. God forgive me for the thought." Naturally Rochl dismissed her servant, but rumours were already circulating in the town.

"Is it true that Madame Berman has sent her servant girl away?"

"No! Really?"

"Well, are you surprised? With a son like that in the house?" the women whispered to each other, even though Anneke had never breathed a word of accusation against Dovid. She knew who the father of her child was, and that he, a young man who worked in a coalmine in Charleroi, would not be able to keep her and she would have to carry on working, but she didn't mind that. Far worse than this, was dealing with her father. When he came home drunk he beat not only her, but also her mother and the children. Anneke told people that when he was sober he was really good-natured, played with the children, kneeling down on the floor and letting them ride on him. "They can do whatever they want with me!" he would laugh.

He looked really comical, and he was tickled pink when his wife pretended to be angry with him, calling him "old fool". But it was a disaster when he got drunk. Then he would punch Anneke's mother in the stomach, and threaten to throw the children out of the window. Once he had actually almost done it, and who could tell whether he wouldn't really murder them all, some day?

"And you're no better than your mother!" he bawled at his daughter. "By the time she was twenty-two she had four children and no husband, and here's her daughter just about to have her third. You women deserve what's coming to you ..." and, saying that, he spat in her mother's face.

Rochl went round for days with lowered head and a shawl round her shoulders, wiping her eyes and hiding so that Berman wouldn't see her crying. Eventually she decided to speak frankly to him:

"It makes it all the more painful when you think how much we have cherished our child, our Dovid."

"'Our child'? He's a worthless child! A loser, a lazy slob and an enemy to his own father! He's *your* child! It's a wonder you're not still suckling him!" Berman's bitter laughter brought on a fit of coughing, which started deep in his chest, mounted to a paroxysm and wouldn't stop. Rochl went and fetched his medicine. "Here you are. Take this."

One cold, bright, frosty day Berman got up early to get a breath of fresh air while the sun was still shining. Rochl handed him all the warm jackets he demanded, brushed the fluff off his overcoat, wrapped the woollen scarf round his neck and accompanied him to the door, glad he would be out of her way for a while. After he was gone she opened all the windows to let some air into the rooms and get rid of the smell of the medicines, exclaiming, with a great sense of freedom: "Ahhh! Thank God!"

The Bourse was more lively in winter than it was in summer, because the merchants were all back in town. The electric lights shone brightly. There was a warm, friendly atmosphere, and a homely, familiar din. It was as if the diamonds sparkled more colourfully than before, and the merchants were even more absorbed than usual in their trading. Berman concluded as much business with as many merchants as he could, and then went off to the Fortunia. Not knowing whether he would have another opportunity like this in the near future, he wanted to pack as much into the day as possible.

The long hall of the Fortunia was full of smoke, which mingled with the steam from the countless glasses of tea being sipped at the tables. The floor was damp and a layer of wet mud was spread through the centre of the room, from the door right up to the counter at the other end. The merchants were sitting in groups around the small tables. Some were playing chess or dominoes, while others were exchanging jokes. About twenty people were crowded round one particular table, engaged in a serious game of cards. In the centre of the room some young men were playing billiards. The white balls rolled swiftly and merrily around the green surface, and the players were so absorbed in the game that one would have thought they had come here purely to watch the white balls, and that there was nothing further from their minds than trading in diamonds.

One young man with a small, black beard, a sharp nose and alert, attractive, black eyes (the kind which make girls fall hopelessly in love) stood watching with great interest to see who would win the game. Catching sight of Berman, he came over to him and stretched out both his fine, white, rather feminine hands to him: "Ah, how *are* you, Herr Berman? We haven't seen you here for *such* a long time. God willing, you're feeling better?"

"Yes indeed, much better, thank God! And how are you, Herr Tsvaygnboym?" Berman managed to call the young shrimp "Herr."

They sat down at a table, and Berman, remembering that he was still not well, ordered a glass of warm milk. As he sipped it, he interrogated the young man like an investigating judge. He wanted to know how he was doing and how married life suited him. He was particularly interested in whether Tsvaygnboym was already finding his feet in the business, whether he intended to trade in rough diamonds like his father-in-law, or in polished stones, and whether perhaps he intended to go into manufacturing jewellery. Berman asked how much he had received as a dowry. He was *not* asking out of idle curiosity, God forbid, but because he felt a genuine friendship towards the young man, and was also a close friend of his father-in-law, as Tsvaygnboym knew. And that's why he asked.

But the young man gave nothing away, simply replying that he himself didn't yet know exactly what he intended. His father-in-law was doing well, thank God, and as for the dowry, he had nothing to do with all that, it was entirely between his father and father-in-law.

The more Berman asked, the less he found out, so eventually he took his leave of the young man and angrily went to sit at another table. These paupers, these Tsvagnboyms, knew what was in their best interest; that was for sure. His idiot son on the other hand ....

Merchants came to greet him from all sides, good friends who wanted to know how Berman was, expressing their pleasure that he was back in business, and trying to sell him parcels of diamonds. Berman greeted and responded to each one, had a look here, a sniff there, peered through the loupe, poked around with the tweezers, and took out some parcels of his own. He opened up one and shook it to make the diamonds glitter. They sparkled like dewdrops in the sunshine when they are shaken off a leaf.

Berman did good business both here and in the Bourse, and around three o'clock he wrapped his scarf round his neck, buttoned up his long overcoat to the neck, and went home while it was still daylight. He didn't have many days as good as that for the remainder of the winter.

Chapter 18

Winter gave way to spring; then the sun became hotter and spring turned into summer. Berman was back in the Bourse doing good business, always being the first to spot fine merchandise. He was constantly in the company of clever young men in well-cut suits who wore large diamond rings on their middle and little fingers; both he and the young men glittered like cats' eyes on dark March nights.

His office on Pelikaanstraat was open and once more the workers smiled at the frosted glass door of his Holy of Holies. The normal routine was resumed. In fact, Berman was doing better than before, and was just beginning to recoup the losses he had suffered during the winter, when as luck would have it, some prince or other in Serbia had to go and get himself assassinated. Because of this prince, whose accursed name Berman had never heard of before, a wretched war broke out and put a stop to everything! Business ground to a halt, the Bourse was empty, and all anybody talked about was the war.

"It's a serious matter, you know, an Austrian prince! Austria isn't going to take that lying down, why should they?"

"I knew straight away that Austria wouldn't take that lying down! You can't play games with Austria!"

Berman couldn't have cared less whether Austria was going to take this lying down or not. All he was concerned about was that his business was being ruined. No one was buying or selling. No one knew what to do and everyone was scared to buy, for it was obvious that the value of the goods was going to fall. Who would be interested in buying diamonds when war was raging? Some merchants thought the opposite: that this was the very time they should be preparing diamonds for sale. That would be a prudent move, they argued, because in wartime the supply of rough diamonds from Africa was going to dry up, and when rough stones were in short supply, the price would rise, and anyone who had polished diamonds to sell would make a pile of money.

So they talked and talked, expressing their opinions and giving advice to all and sundry, but no one really knew what the best course of action was. No foreign merchants came, and those who were already in Antwerp rushed to get home as soon as possible, especially the Americans, who were the best buyers. Work stopped and trade came to a standstill; it was an absolute catastrophe.

Once again Berman wandered around his house in a state of agitation. The machines in the diamond cutters' houses were again standing as still as corpses, covered over with a bit of curtain or an apron, their inactivity seeming to mock their masters, the workers, robbing them of their livelihood and sucking their lifeblood. But the workers could do nothing about it. *Their* greatest worry wasn't whether or not they should buy diamonds, but whether or not the baker was going to allow them to buy a loaf of bread on credit. They hoped, even though it was obvious that no one would sell bread on credit in wartime.

So even before the actual outbreak of war, people were going around in a dark and troubled state of mind. As soon as they read the first rumours in the newspapers about the imminence of war, they started taking everything they possessed to the pawnbroker.

The streets were full of people. Crowds of people were everywhere. All the inhabitants of Leeuwerikstraat had come out of their houses and were milling around in the street. They were gesticulating, shaking their beards, airing their own theories and dismissing the ideas of others. Galician Jews* were giving strategic advice to the Austrians and Germans, and putting paid to the enemy with a wave of the hand or a frown. This annoyed the Russian and Polish Jews, who started shouting and bawling: "In God's name, whoever heard of such a thing! These enemies of the state are allowed to stand in the middle of the street, peeping out from under their black hats and giving 'advice' to the Germans."

At this the Galician Jews, with an air of intellectual superiority, pushed their hats back on their heads so that their foreheads were uncovered and their side-locks emerged from behind their ears. They plucked at their own and other people's beards, lapels and buttons with their white hands. In squeaky effeminate voices they tried to vanquish the enemy, waging war in the middle of Leeuwerikstraat with the Russian and Polish Jews. So the Russian, Polish and even Lithuanian Jews forgot for a moment that they were all supposed to hate each other like the plague and made a united front to drive back the impudent Galicians. They mocked the Galician "heroes" who were rejoicing prematurely and boasting of German superiority.

Even Hassidim, who went to the court of the same *rebbe*, and normally ate the remnants at the same *rebbe*'s table and trembled together at the door of his study, divided into two camps and waged war on each other day and night in their synagogues and prayer houses. In the end the beefy Russian Jews refused to have any dealings at all with Jews from the enemy camp. If a Galician "arse-licker" happened to be holding a newspaper which was just off the press, so that you could still smell the ink, a Russian Jew would ostentatiously reread his old newspaper (which in any case was usually only about two hours old), ignoring the new one, in order not to come into any kind of contact with the "enemy".

Women didn't even get round to combing their wigs because they were so busy helping their menfolk in the war against "the swinish Russian" or the accursed German. Mixed marriages were a terrible problem; if a Galician woman had a Russian husband, or vice versa, she would suffer double pain, on account of both her husband and her country. Even children were drawn into the battles.

This wasn't just happening in Leeuwerikstraat. All of Antwerp had taken to the streets. This year the Flemish people couldn't celebrate their annual carnival, but nevertheless the sun was shining, generously flooding over everything and pouring out heaps of gold, as if war had never been heard of. The broad pavements on the Keyserlei were packed. The uniforms of officers and soldiers created splashes of colour, and their wearers drank and flirted with women. Countless flags fluttered majestically from windows and balconies, shouting out the national colours wherever you turned. It was a sea of yellow, red and black. The newspaper boys shouted out the latest news.

Flemish and Jewish housewives hurried round the shops in order to provide themselves with foodstuffs for the "four-week war." The diamond cleavers, cutters and polishers wandered around, dressed in their best clothes, and stood in front of the Bourse, talking politics, trying to guess how long the war would last. It was only from their faces that one could tell the merchants from the workers. And the sun carried on pouring out her festive light, soothing and warming everyone and shining on friends and enemies, bosses and workers, adults and children. She did not care one bit that human beings were going mad with worry, that workers had put on their festive clothes to hide their far from festive spirits. It was a matter of complete indifference to her that the merchants could not decide whether or not to buy diamonds. She even shone on the silent machines.

Berman alone stayed at home.

"Four weeks!" he said, jabbing with his finger at his Flemish newspaper, though he wasn't very competent in the language. "*They* think they know that it'll last for four weeks. Huh! If you get into a war, who can tell when it will end!"

The streets got more and more crowded, with groups of people talking everywhere. At last even Berman, anxious to hear what they were saying in the Bourse, went out into the street. He stopped and listened to one of the groups which had congregated there.

"Fools!" he thought, turning away from them. "Squabbling about their countries, these paupers, one defending Efroim-Yossel's kingdom,* the other the Tsar's, idiots that they are! They'll see, Franz Josef and Nicholas II will soon give them a means of earning their livelihood ...."

"What do you think of this terrible business?" A young man addressed Berman. He had yellow, parchment-like skin, short, crooked legs and wore a cotton jacket, green with age, which was mended here and there with white thread. He stretched out a clammy hand to Berman.

Berman snatched his hand away impatiently leaving the young man's hand suspended in midair, and consoled him with a mocking, disdainful smile: "You have nothing to worry about. *You're* hardly likely to be sent to the front line."

It was Berman's smile more than his words which upset the young man; he tweaked the left side of his spectacles where the lens was cracked, and saw two Bermans. He glared angrily at them both and retorted:

"You can never tell who will survive and who will not." Berman, unnerved, stepped back.

"Damn him, that rat; that pathetic, consumptive weakling, opening his trap and spilling out such rubbish! He's already coughed up most of his lungs and yet he's worrying about the war! Let him go to hell!"

Berman went away, shaken by the young man's doom-laden words. The latter was, on the other hand, very pleased with himself that he had managed to unnerve Berman. "I really gave him something to think about," he thought as he wandered off, his greenish jacket and the uppers of his worn boots shining in the sunlight.

Berman looked after him, and sent one final curse after him: "I hope he dies like a dog!"

It had been a strange day. Still not completely recovered from this exchange, he walked on, in an agitated frame of mind, to the Bourse. On the way he was stopped by another young man of about thirty years of age, who held out a large angular, rather grubby hand to him and asked the same question:

"What do you think of this terrible business?"

Berman was suddenly scared. He felt as if the other young man's hand lay in his and those doom-laden words, "You can never tell who will survive and who will not", were haunting him. He snatched his hand away as if he didn't know this young man, who, not noticing Berman's strange reactions, continued speaking: "I've just come from the Bourse. It's a catastrophe, an absolute tragedy. They say that the Germans are just across the border, and today or tomorrow they'll be here, damn them to hell! What do you feel about it, Herr Berman?"

Berman felt as if all the spineless characters were swooping on him today, and he wanted to shout out: "What are you trembling for, you fool?" but, since it was one of his brokers standing there, he swallowed the harsh words, finding it difficult to hide his own fear.

"What am I saying?" continued the young man. "Who *wouldn't* be worried about it? And to make matters worse, my wife's expecting. We're already eating into our savings."

These last words especially made an impact on Berman. When you start living off your capital it flows away like water, as he well knew. He was about to tell the young man that he agreed with him, but the latter didn't let him get a word in edgeways. He was constantly touching a deep furrow in his left cheek. It was surrounded by little lines and puckered skin, and his left eye, which looked like a glass eye, was sunk deep in its socket above his cheekbone.

"Do you see this?" he said, pointing to his disfigurement without any embarrassment. "Do you see it? It cost me a fortune in money and pain. I risked my life so that I wouldn't have to go and serve in the Tsarist army. A Jew, I said to myself, should not serve the Tsar. Instead of respect, all you get is humiliation. You have to do the hardest and dirtiest work, they beat you, stuff pork into your mouth whether you want to eat it or not, and mock you. These fools, these dunderheads, who haven't as much brains in their entire bodies as the stupidest Jew has in his little finger, mock you. My brother served in the Russian army, and that was enough for me. When I came to Antwerp I saw it was different here and that if you serve here it's just for ten months and apart from that, you're a citizen, and they treat you like a human being among equals. Why did I start telling you all this? Oh yes, I wanted to say that I'm not scared on my own behalf, because they'll not send me to the front line, my Russian experience has already seen to that, but nevertheless it is a terrible tragedy. Do you know what it feels like to start eating into your savings? I tell you, it's a really terrible thing."

When Berman arrived home, the door was locked and there was not a living soul in the house to open it for him. For the first time in his life he had forgotten to take his keys with him.

"Damn them all!" he said. "Those fools and idiots! What are they thinking of? Hell and damnation!"

Cursing and swearing he went off again, and wandered into a park for perhaps the first time in his life. He sat down on a bench, leaning on his walking stick like an old man, and basked in the warm sun. He suddenly felt utterly alone, as if he had been driven away from his own home. "Hmm, eating into your savings, a terrible thing!" he thought, remembering the young man's words.

The park was flooded with light and fine, white threads were floating in the air and attaching themselves to the trees. Spiders spun their square, finely woven webs between the bushes. The grass was dry and burned brown by the sun which had been blazing for weeks. Flocks of birds were whirling around in the air, twittering as if they knew there was some kind of danger hanging over their heads. Here and there, soldiers and their girls were walking arm-in-arm, holding on to each other full of longing, whispering secret words of love, pensive and anxious, and then parting. Apart from them the park was empty and forlorn.

Berman went back home to see if anyone had returned. Rochl came to meet him with a cheerful expression on her face:

"Gedaliah, we have visitors!"

"Visitors? Who?"

"Gitele and her husband!"

"Oh, for God's sake!" muttered Berman crossly as he exchanged his hat for his silk skullcap. "Could they not have found a better time to come paying social calls?"

But he entered the dining room with a broad smile.

"Whom do I see here? A guest! Welcome!" He didn't see Leybesh until the latter stretched out his hand "Oh, I didn't notice. You're there too. Well, sit down!" The expression on Berman's face reminded Leybesh of the days when Berman told him to sit and wait, only to give him the news that he didn't have any work for him that day.

"I knew that I'd find them eventually," said Rochl, very pleased with herself. "I was just walking along the street, looking for Dovid. I was thinking that it isn't a good idea for a healthy young man like him to attract too much attention just at the moment. And then, whom do I see, but Gitele! And all this time, that naughty girl hasn't even come to see how we're getting on. It must be a year and a half since we've seen each other - fine *landslayt** you are!"

She carried on chattering: "And what do you think of the baby? She's already a proper little lady, *ken eynore!*" Rochl lifted her out of the shabby pram which stood in the corridor and brought her in to show Berman. She was a skinny, sleepy little creature dressed in a worn, woollen dress and her knickers were damp.

Gitele was sweating with embarrassment, which Rochl didn't no-

170

tice at all. She pressed a biscuit into the child's hand and carried on chatting to her: "We're quite a young lady now, mmm?"

The child had a very serious air. She took her grubby finger, which very frequently had to make do in place of food, out of her mouth. Her dark, melancholy eyes looked large in her tiny face and told of hunger. Rochl took her hand with the biscuit in it and guided it to the child's mouth, but she started to cry.

"Shh! Shhh! Oh, I see you've really been spoiled, mmm? Now shhh! Sweetheart!"

Leybesh took the child, who calmed down in his arms and started nibbling the biscuit.

The maid brought in tea, and Gitele nearly died of shame when she saw that the maid was better dressed than she was.

"What a pity the children aren't here, especially Dovid. He'd be so pleased to see you. If he knew you were here, he'd come running back immediately." Rochl carried on talking, not dreaming that every word she said about Dovid pierced Gitele's heart and made her burn with shame.

"What do you think of the terrible business?" said Gitele, trying to deflect Rochl from this topic. She glanced at Leybesh and felt furious with him: "For God's sake, I wish he would stop eating. He just carries on munching and munching. It's *really* embarrassing," she thought.

As if Leybesh had read her thoughts, he nonchalantly took another pear from the dish and started peeling it. He ate it with relish, all the while counting the silvery beads on Rochl's blue silk dress and thinking that she fitted perfectly into the ambience of this bright, cheerful dining room.

Gitele moved nearer to the table, trying to hide herself behind it, not knowing where to look and wishing she could disappear. Rochl kept on talking, and every word was directed at her. The silver on the sideboard, like its owners, exuded affluence and respectability, just like the silver on the sideboard in her father's house, and it seemed to Gitele that it was looking down on her, smiling scornfully as if to say: "What's going on here, in *our* dining room?"

"Yes, it's a terrible thing!" Berman finally replied to Gitele, after deliberating and drumming with his forefinger on the tablecloth for a long time. Gitele, meantime, had forgotten what she had asked him. "Yes indeed, it certainly is. Human beings are always searching for something new. They get tired of the eternal struggle for a crust of bread. If they *do* have a livelihood, even if they are rich and have sampled all the delights of the world, they become jaded, feel bored and empty, and sometimes even long for a little hardship to spice up their lives. The way horseradish makes meat tastier and the juicier the meat, the more horseradish one craves. And so you prepare a huge pot of horseradish so that your eyes are stinging from it. And when you've tried the bitterness, you don't want to admit it's too sharp, and so you avert your face and wipe your eyes and smile at your companions at the table and urge them to sample it too. You assure them that it is good for them, and they persuade others, because they don't want to admit it's too sharp. Instead they just bite their lips until they bleed. That's war. Do you understand what I'm saying?" And Berman stirred his tea reflectively. He had forgotten his worry about eating into his capital, because he felt so pleased with his own oratory.

Glancing at Gitele he saw that she understood very well what he was talking about. "A fine young woman!" he thought. "What a shame she has thrown herself away!"

Leybesh gulped his tea, bit into some honey cake and thought that for once Berman was talking almost like a human being. And it was many years since he had eaten such good honey cake.

When Leybesh and Gitele were leaving they met Dovid on the doorstep. Gitele was covered with confusion. Her shoulders trembled and her face turned as white as chalk, then fiery red. Her desire to see Dovid had made her put up very little resistance to Rochl, who, she presumed, had invited them in to bring some life into the house during this trying time. Why in God's name could she not have taken control of the situation? She felt humiliated, and lowered her eyes but glanced surreptitiously at Dovid. She could not help wanting to see what effect her presence was having on him, and to get an impression of how well he was managing without her. Instead of feeling reproachful, her eyes suddenly filled with fear when she looked at him. Dovid was bent over like an old man, and his face was a waxy yellow.

172

She wanted to ask him what had happened, but she couldn't speak.

Dovid broke the silence.

"I have just signed up for the army," he blurted out.

"What?!"

"What have you done, Dovid?" said Leybesh, equally horrified.

"It's the best solution," said Dovid hastily and disappeared quickly into the house. He went straight up to his own room and locked the door, speaking to nobody. "She did go pale all the same," he thought. "Perhaps that means that there's still a spark of something there. But this is the best solution." He felt very, very tired.

Leybesh eventually broke the awkward silence between himself and Gitele: "If it wasn't an imperialist war, I would sign up too! I really can't understand why Dovid feels he has to take part in this mess. Someone who is living in such luxury, why does he have to quarrel with that fine father of his? As far as I can see, Dovid doesn't have any kind of ideals, so what's preventing him from following in his father's footsteps and living like all the other parasites? Perhaps it's true that he is not suited to business, but that doesn't mean he has to throw himself into this conflagration. It's a real shame for his mother, who obviously really loves him. She's a nice woman and it will kill her. I just wish my boss's only son would do the same; all these stinking bourgeois should taste hardship for once!" Leybesh went on in this way to Gitele. She wasn't listening to a single word and gave Leybesh a look filled with so much hatred that he didn't open his mouth again.

Leybesh's boss had realised that he had no influence on Leybesh. He was getting nowhere in trying to make a Zionist out of him. Leybesh would carry on believing that Karl Marx's teachings were the only truth. Furthermore he finally realised that Leybesh was the better chess player, but that he didn't take it seriously, and always let the boss win. This made the boss wild. He considered himself to be a great intellectual. He knew the exact dates of Moses Mendelssohn's birth and death, all about his friendship with Lessing, and why and when the Jews of Holland had persecuted and finally excommunicated Baruch Spinoza from their community. He knew when the Zionist movement began, and could recount the history of the Lovers of Zion movement. He was a man who carried Herzl's picture in his signet ring instead of a diamond and this nobody - *his* library was worth more money than Leybesh had ever seen - this *good-for-nothing* was trying to make a fool of him? Leybesh obviously thought that he was some kind of simple ignoramus, just a diamond merchant whose sole aim was to make money, while *he*, Leybesh, had studied Karl Marx. Who was this Marx anyway and what importance did he have after all? Thus Leybesh's boss had a quarrel with Karl Marx and stopped giving work to Leybesh. Then in the Bourse, the Fortunia, the Club, or even in the *Shenkl,* whenever the subject of socialism came up, which it did almost every day, he casually mentioned that a plague had come to Antwerp and its name was Bruckner, a man who led pious young people astray, led our sons and daughters off the straight and narrow with a new *Torah*, Karl Marx's *Torah*.

"It will all end with our children forsaking Judaism, mark my words." He wagged the finger on which he carried Herzl's picture instead of a diamond.

The merchants took him seriously and from then on didn't give Leybesh a single diamond to polish.

After Leybesh and Gitele had left, Berman lost his temper with Rochl. He raged and stormed at her:

"I just want to know, you stupid fool; who asked you to invite that devil into my house? That's the last thing I need, for people to find out about it! One good-for-nothing attracts another; God damn you, you stupid cow!"

Dovid heard his father's shouting from his room, but he felt total indifference. What did he care about Leybesh now? He couldn't even summon up any real pity for his mother.

Chapter 19

Once again, Berman got up the next morning with a headache. He had slept badly and had been plagued by bad dreams. He had been beating up the tubercular young man with the doom-laden words, and had started shouting out in his sleep. Rochl had just got to sleep at that point, and she jumped out of bed in fright. She woke him up and pulled away his hand which was clutching his own chest.

"What's the matter, Gedaliah? Why are you shouting?"

Berman stared at her with a frightened look as if he didn't recognise her, rubbed his eyes, and as his dream gradually came back to him, he spat:

"Damn him, I hope he dies like a dog!"

He got dressed and went into the kitchen, pulled up the wooden shutters with their familiar clatter, and asked for his drink of warm sweet milk. Putting on his prayer shawl and *tefillin*, he got ready to say the morning prayers.

Rochl's heart was heavy and she felt weak. She could not stop thinking about Gitele and her baby.

"How dreadful! What awful poverty! That poor little mite; suffering from hunger, so early in her little life. If Gitele's mother came back from the grave and saw how her daughter was living, she would die all over again. That father of hers is a pig!" Rochl was shocked by her own words, which she had shouted out loud.

At breakfast, as Berman was putting sugar in his coffee, Dovid began twisting and turning on his chair, not taking his eyes off his mother while he sipped his coffee. He opened and closed his mouth once or twice, wanting to say something but not knowing where to start. How would his mother react? He knew very well what she would do: she would tear off her wig and sob. That's what he feared. He couldn't stand tears.

His own eyes were moist, and he tried to speak but couldn't find the words. His tongue stuck to the roof of his mouth. Berman noticed his discomfiture.

"He needs money again, the wretch!" He'd give him a plague instead of money; that was for sure. If you eat into your capital, it flows away like water....

In the middle of these gloomy thoughts, he heard, or perhaps he imagined, Dovid calling him "Papa" like he used to do when he was a little boy. Yes, Dovid was talking to him, but Berman couldn't understand what he was saying. Why was he repeating: "Papa, Papa...?"

Finally Dovid blurted out: "I've joined the army!"

Was it night-time? Was Berman still dreaming?

"*What* did you say?"

"I said that I've signed up for the army."

"Are you mad? Is this some kind of silly joke?"

"I am not mad and it isn't a joke. I have to report for duty tomorrow."

Berman's eyes looked as if their pupils were going to burst out, leaving two black holes in the middle of the whites, which were bloodshot from his sleepless night.

Rochl did not tear off her wig, nor did she sob, she simply said "I don't feel well," then slid off her chair and lay on the soft blue carpet, like a corpse. Father and son worked together for the first time in years, lifting up the unconscious woman, putting some brandy to her lips and rubbing her with vinegar. When she came to, they carried her into the bedroom and put her to bed.

Jeannette stood there shrieking in her silk nightdress. The servant girl brought a hot water bottle. Jacques was the only one who didn't lose his head, but ran to get the doctor. Rochl suddenly remembered what had happened and started weeping uncontrollably.

"Dovid, what have I done to deserve this? What do you want of me that I haven't given you?"

Deeply concerned, old Chaim Yoysef had come into her bedroom and tried to comfort her.

"Don't weep, daughter, with God's help we'll find a solution. We won't let Dovid fall into the hands of the *goyim*. With God's help!"

Berman sat on a pink basket chair with his head in his hands. He looked as if he were in mourning. Dovid was sitting on his mother's bed, wiping the tears from her eyes and stroking her cheeks as if she were a child.

"Don't worry, mother. We have to defend the country. Someone has to go!" He tried in vain to convince her that the step he had taken was right.

Chapter 20

In the city, the scent of war was in the air.

German and Austrian citizens were ordered to leave the city within twenty-four hours, but this edict didn't apply to many Gentiles, apart from a few rich hotel owners, and it was the Jews, as always, who packed their bags and left. Yesterday's confident German and Austrian patriots now took all their worldly possessions, their tearful wives and bewildered, sleepy children, and crept to the railway station, with bowed heads. The streets in the Jewish district were empty and abandoned, with lowered blinds and locked doors. In among them, like the living in a graveyard, the odd Russian or Polish Jewish family remained.

At the Bermans' the atmosphere was frighteningly still. For days at a time the shutters remained open, and Berman sat reading prayer books. Jeannette, who couldn't stand the gloomy atmosphere at home, went to stay with a friend. She couldn't bear to watch her mother endlessly wandering about the house, hunched up and wrapped in a shawl, wringing her hands and weeping as if she were bereaved.

Flemish families on the other hand were different. When their sons had to say goodbye to their parents, relatives, dogs and cats, the family accepted the situation as if it were the most natural thing in the world. Some fathers even envied their sons, regretting they themselves were unable to go and defend the fatherland, but then they had a fatherland to defend.

"Ah, we'd teach them a lesson, those damned Germans!" muttered old men into their grey whiskers.

In front of the door of a shabby house stood a group of men puffing clouds of smoke from their clay pipes, talking agitatedly, with excited smiles and with rage in their voices. Now and then they spat into their leathery palms and looked at their hands.

"We're not scared of *them*! There's no such thing as a small, helpless nation!" exclaimed a fair-haired young man, slapping his thigh with his iron fist, his eyes gleaming with an unnatural brightness.

"We'll show them" spat out a toothless old Flemish man, wearing a pair of brown, striped, velvet trousers. "I don't know what to do with myself," he went on angrily. For the last few days his life had been turned upside down. For over forty years he had set out every morning with his wagonload of clay, smoking his pipe and serenely contemplating his big Belgian horse with its bushy mane and large hooves clip-clopping along. It knew the way, when to stop and when to carry on. Now the man was hanging about with nothing to do, while the horse stood in its stable eating him out of house and home, and not even earning its keep.

"They're never satisfied, those damned Germans, and they think we are all afraid of them," said someone else.

"Afraid? *Godverdoeme!* Who's afraid of them. Do you see this hand? It's itching to get at them" said the fair-haired young man, scratching his palm. Everyone laughed.

"There's no such thing as a small, helpless nation" repeated another. "If a nation is determined, ha! ... if a nation is ready to go through fire and water to defend its land ...!"

"To protect our homes," cried a woman and burst into tears.

"We'll show him, that bastard of a Kaiser!" The flaxen-haired young man went on, showing his white teeth as he grimaced. We'll give them "*Deutschland über alles*"!

"It should be 'Deutschland *unter* alles'" shouted a few voices and everybody laughed again.

"Long live King Albert!" exclaimed someone, and everyone joined in: "Long live King Albert!"

"Do you see these arms of mine?" A small man with a straw-coloured moustache pushed up his right shirtsleeve, revealing an arm with a mass of thick, greenish veins.

"I'll put bullets into those Germans just like I hammer the nails into shoes. If they'd only let me, they'd find there's no such thing as 'too old'." shouted another voice in the crowd. "Who wouldn't give his last drop of blood for our country? Who wouldn't leave everything, even his wife and child and all his possessions? I ask you."

"Don't forget to mention the cow and the calf, you couldn't take them into battle either," laughed a passing milkman who continued on his way with his little cart full of brass-trimmed milk cans. "All for the fatherland!" His words resonated against the big milk churn, leaving an echo behind him.

"You see, he thinks I'm right" said the shoemaker, not realising that the milkman had spoken with an ironic smile on his face, and he became even more passionate: "Long live Belgium!"

"Long live Belgium!" they all shouted.

"Belgium and our King!" the shoemaker went on with wild excitement.

"*Godverdoeme*! Are you all off your heads? What are you getting so worked up about?" A fat, red-faced shopkeeper appeared on the doorstep of his fine butcher's shop. He wiped his hands clean of the pork fat which was dripping off them, fixed the crowd with his burning eyes and laughed bitterly. "Our lives and all our possessions are in danger and they are whooping with joy!"

"Aha! He's afraid for his possessions" said the shoemaker, glaring angrily at him "*That's* the problem with *him*!"

"Oh, they've all gone mad!" the shopkeeper muttered and went back into his shop.

The milkman's wife, whom the shopkeeper had just served, came out of the shop with a full basket of goods, which she had just purchased to help to see her through the "four-week war". She stopped and listened to their conversation.

"You should stop talking when you don't know what you're talking about," she said. "They're clever and powerful. What are we compared to them? We're just worms. They'll squash us underfoot." From the way she took the part of the Germans, it seemed as if she had forgotten that she was Belgian, that her husband was a naturalised Belgian and that she had Belgian children. "You're going to pit your strength against Germany, are you? What a joke!" she said, and went off.

"She's German, you know, and so's her husband! You're all just sheep, not soldiers at all! What great heroes you are!" mocked a woman, sparks flying from her eyes. "You should have torn her apart

180

like a herring, that's what you should have done! She's a traitor!"

The people looked at each other. "God damn it! We should have broken her bones!"

"We should have done her in" said the shoemaker, hoarse with savage rage and burning with desire to do just that.

The merchants came into the Bourse, had a little look, a little sniff around, and went away, for there was nothing to do, and the emptiness of the place drove them home again. The deserted *Shenkl* was worse than the Bourse. There were no black hats, no small-scale dealers with red cheeks and white, feminine hands, weighing their insignificant "goods" adeptly on little scales. They were no longer poking skilfully into piles of diamond waste with their tiny tweezers, tying up their little finds beautifully and shaking diamond powder into white paper parcels with tissue paper lining.

They had been disdained when they had been there but they were missed now they were gone. If they had been there now it wouldn't have seemed so deserted, and the atmosphere in the *Shenkl* wouldn't have been so dismal for those who came in: there would, at least, have been something going on. The Russian and Polish Jews had been sorry for those other Jews when they had seen them leaving with their wives and children, with hanging heads and stifled weeping, leaving the homes, which, by working hard, they had managed to make into cosy nests. Jews who remained had tears in their eyes; at that time they didn't think about the fact that these people came from enemy countries; they saw Jews being driven out, not knowing where they would end up. They felt great sympathy for their plight.

Berman went to the *Shenkl* just to have a look. Even though he knew that no business was going on, he wandered around from one place to another, just to get out of the house. He felt bad at home and even worse when he was out. He was scared of meeting people; he felt that they were pointing the finger at him and judging him: "What kind of father is he? He's driven his own son away into the arms of death."

He didn't know what to do with himself, and sat down at a table where some Jews were carrying on a military campaign on a scruffy chessboard, trying to capture strategic positions from each other. This made Berman really cross:

"You're just like children! Is that all you can think about?"

The others were surprised and embarrassed, and Berman didn't know what had come over him.

"What? Is the war over already, that you're *not* thinking about it?" laughed one of the men. "I hope the real war is over so soon!"

"It will be, it will be!" someone else reassured him. "A war like this can't last for long, certainly no more than four weeks."

"I think so too," put in a young man. "If it does, the world will come to an end. You can't play games with a war like that. Am I not right, Reb Elye?" He turned to a self-important man who had been giving advice on strategy, deferring to him as if he were a great expert in matters of warfare.

"God forbid!" pronounced Reb Elye after a moment's deliberation. "Stuff and nonsense! It won't even last four weeks, I promise you that!"

The Germans, however, paid no attention to Reb Elye's promise, and drew ever nearer to the city.

Among the Belgian aircraft which had been buzzing in everyone's ears for days, more and more enemy planes began to appear, flying wildly around Antwerp's peaceful sky. Quite unexpectedly, in the middle of the day, people had to leave everything and creep into the cellars. It was even worse, though, when they had to crawl out of their warm beds in the middle of the night.

One night Berman wasn't feeling well. He had finished reciting the evening prayers, had gone to bed early, and had only just fallen asleep. He was in the middle of a vivid dream, when suddenly the alarm sounded, and everyone had to go into the cellar. Berman stood there in a state of shock, holding his trousers. He looked around as if he were a stranger in his own house, then shuddered suddenly and raced downstairs. He had time to see a dark mass of people in the corridor, who had been out in the street when the alarm sounded and had knocked on every door they had passed. They were standing in his corridor like lost sheep, and seeing Berman rushing past with slippers on his bare feet and his trousers in his hand, they all darted after him. Rochl was wailing:

"Where will my son hide?"

The people in the cellar tried to console her:

"Believe me, there are forests there where you can escape from the shooting. And if, God forbid, it's not possible to escape, then hiding is not going to do any good. And anyway, do you think you're the only mother? Even if he hadn't signed up, he'd have had to go now in any case. They're all going: Gentiles, Jews, young and old. You're not the only one to be affected by the war, Madame Berman."

"Great sorrows bring their own consolation," said someone else comfortingly.

Berman was sitting on a cushion in the corner of the cellar. His nose was pinched and pallid, and he had put his fingers in his ears so that he would not hear the rumbling of the "destroyers" above the rooftops.

Suddenly the house shook, and they all thought they were going to be buried in the dark cellar full of spiders' webs, in which the only light was a tiny flame from a paraffin lamp which the servant girl had placed in the furthest corner so that it would not shine out too brightly. The light flickered and the shadows on the walls started madly fluttering and dancing about, filling the people with horror. An old woman kept going "Ssshhhh!" even though nobody had said a word. Then, crash! A house collapsed nearby. Berman sprang up, then slumped back down again.

Afterwards, when with great difficulty they had helped old Reb Chaim Yoysef back up the steps, and laid him on a bench in the kitchen to sleep, Berman calmed down again, but the old woman absolutely refused to go back home. She sat down beside the big stove, warmed her frozen hands, and kept on going "Ssshhhh!"

This drove Berman mad. "Go home! Do what I say: go home!" he shouted in a very ungentlemanly fashion at the confused old woman.

"Go home and recite a Psalm or two!" joked Jacques, for whom the business of creeping into the cellar was great fun.

The alarms became more frequent and the visits to the cellar tedious. People's fear, however, increased and their mood became more depressed. The rich diamond merchants had gradually left the town, locking their doors behind them and taking with them as many assets as they were allowed. Some had gone to Amsterdam and others to England. It was mainly the poor people and shopkeepers who were left. It was not so easy for the latter to take their merchandise with them, and so they stood for days at a time at their shop doors, not even unpacking their bundles of woollen undershirts, towels and underclothes. They stared at the sky and soon were able to recognise an enemy aeroplane at first sight, whereupon they locked up their shops and were the first to get into the cellars.

Most of the houses had closed shutters. The highly polished doors of elegant houses were locked. The city emptied as the panic intensified. Life got more monotonous, and those who were left became ever more dispirited. Berman alone made no move to go. He was existing on pills and all sorts of medicines, and a proliferation of white hairs had invaded his beard. He slept badly, fearing death, starting at every noise, constantly sleeping in his clothes. There were long periods when he could not take a bath in case an air raid started; all this exasperated him, but he stayed nevertheless.

"There's no other way, one has to just sit it out! Building up a home and a business is difficult, destroying it all is easy," said Berman to himself. And his great fear of death and love of life could not outweigh his determination to hold on to everything he had achieved with so much effort.

Rochl had no desire to leave either. It seemed to her that here in Antwerp she was nearer her son, and if she went away she would be abandoning him and subjecting him to even greater dangers.

But early one morning, when the Bermans had just got to sleep after a night during which their beds had been shaking and seemed to be lifting off the floor, a policeman knocked on the door of the bedroom where they all now slept together, mumbled something indistinctly and hurried off down the stairs again. The policeman was overworked that morning. Like a Jewish beadle going round to waken everyone in the *shtetl* to come and recite the prayers of penitence, the policeman proceeded from house to house, hurriedly ordering the sleepy people to leave the town.

Berman rubbed his eyes, not having understood a word. Had

someone denounced him about the business of the little "bargains" he had purchased, or was the policeman really a spy? In wartime anything was possible. His normally dark complexion had turned a waxy colour, and his eyes were red-rimmed from lack of sleep.

"*What* did he say?"

Rochl didn't know either. Her teeth were chattering with fear.

"Perhaps we've been robbed?" suggested Jeannette.

Berman's face lit up. He actually prayed to God that there would be such a simple explanation. But soon a neighbour knocked on their door:

"Hurry, Herr Berman, don't waste a moment!"

Berman looked out of the window and saw people fleeing to the railway station. They were streaming from all directions, carrying packs and babies and leading older children by the hand. The Bermans swiftly packed a few necessities and by the time they were ready to leave, the town was abandoned. There was a throng of people at the railway station.

The city stood empty and deserted, as if in mourning, veiled in smoke and gloom. Occasionally the sky was lit up by rockets, flaring up and then sinking back into the smoky darkness.

Because of the old man, the Bermans made slow progress along the streets, and it seemed to them that they would never reach the station. Suddenly the thunder of exploding cannon lifted people off their feet and Berman's father had to quicken his pace to keep up with everyone else.

They managed to get onto the last train, which took a whole night to get from Antwerp to Holland. The peasants left the villages on foot. The city was already cut off. Berman and his family were the last to squeeze into a carriage, where the people were packed in like sardines, standing, sitting or lying on top of one another. The closed, black curtains created an oppressive muffled silence which caught in the throat and depressed the spirit. Even children did not cry. They looked around and like the grownups, they forced themselves not to burst into tears.

Chapter 21

Dawn was the colour of blood. Early morning sunshine flooded the cottages in the little villages, shining on blue and white checked tablecloths, crockery, and healthy, early-rising Dutch peasants. Their breakfast of freshly baked bread, delicious yellow butter, real Dutch cheese and steaming jugs of cocoa was laid out on the long tables, calling temptingly to them.

The sun illuminated the dark carriages with the same generous silvery light, stealing in through the cracks, caressing and warming the crumpled travellers. It stroked the children's faces, creeping into their dimples and making them smile, even conjuring up a spark in Berman's black eyes. It didn't spare the glass of the carriage windows and the black curtains, which had been drawn back; the sunlight made both look even grubbier.

Berman stood at the door of the carriage. The train was now travelling at normal speed, and he saw brown, white and dappled cows and grey sheep lying on harvested fields. Horses with glossy coats were grazing on the fresh grass and the farmers in their wide linen trousers, wooden, snub-nosed clogs and wide straw hats were already working in the fields, bringing in the abundant grain harvest. They looked at the trains, which streamed endlessly past on their journey from Belgium, packed with people who the day before had been affluent citizens and were now paupers.

Peasant women were going out into the fields. They wore deep-brimmed bonnets on their freshly washed hair, and pleated skirts of woven linen with close-fitting bodices which revealed the fine lines of sturdy female limbs and firm, full breasts straining against the stiff fabric. Many had children with them, whom they would suckle and lay to sleep in hammocks or even in the fragrant grass. All were going to spend the day in healthy, productive work under a free and peaceful sky. The sun shone down on the scene, warming both the fields

186

and the people.

Some had been in the fields since very early in the morning, digging potatoes. The spades gleamed as they came out of the black earth, catching the sunlight, before burying themselves again. Others were making hay and stacking it, or cutting the ripe corn. The women laid the corn to dry on the bare, newly harvested fields. The golden sun poured out its abundant warmth, drying the crops and blessing the peaceful, harmonious labour. Everywhere on the train's route, windmills reminded the exhausted refugees that they were in Holland, a free country which always maintained its neutrality.

Berman breathed deeply through the open windows of the carriage, drawing in as much of the early morning air as he could. He almost felt happy, until he remembered his possessions in Antwerp, and then the fields disappeared, and the sky became cloudy and overcast, shrouded in deep gloom.

The train stopped in Rotterdam. The dishevelled passengers, their faces yellow and exhausted after a night cramped up in the stuffy carriages, woke up, yawned loudly and tried unsuccessfully to find space to stretch their stiff, painful limbs. Some attempted to stand up and get out of the carriages, but could not get past the solid wall of bodies. An old man, still half asleep, didn't know where he was and, rubbing his sticky eyes, he cried out:

"Is this another pogrom? Jews, let's bar the doors!"

His wife and a few neighbours managed with great difficulty to calm him down. He stared at all the people, not recognising them, and unwilling to believe that it was "nothing at all", that they had fled because of the war. Eventually he remembered, rubbed his eyes again, shut his toothless mouth and fell silent.

"What a life! Wars, pogroms ..." someone else started to philosophise. Gradually people managed to get out of the train, and on the platforms there were scenes of confusion, as people's luggage got mixed up and they shouted and argued. But soon representatives of the Jewish charity organisations arrived. The very sight of these officials with their civilised appearance: placid, well-dressed and well-groomed, reassured the bewildered fugitives a little. They were packed into omnibuses and driven off to some unknown destination.

Then they got off the buses and were placed at tables, where numbers were stuck on their luggage. The men were shown where they could go and pray. Berman was not happy with the arrangements. How could he sit and eat with people like *that* at one long bare wooden table?

"Why on earth did you have to wait until the last minute? I *told* you this was going to happen," complained Jeannette. "You see what kind of people these are? Paupers and *shnorrers*, the lot of them. No one like us at all!"

Berman didn't answer her. "That'll do as a breakfast for them, but not for me," he said, pushing the plate of bread and butter away.

A young lady in white overalls with a string of real pearls round her neck and a polite smile on her thin red lips came up to Berman, putting on a more dazzling smile which revealed her small white teeth. She could see by his fine, well groomed beard he must be a "better class of person". She started apologising:

"You must excuse us! We have had so many people do deal with quite unexpectedly. It has been absolutely impossible! But I shall report it." The young lady, a voluntary worker who herself came from an affluent family, understood the situation, and reported it to the secretary, a fair-haired young man wearing spectacles with thick, brightly polished lenses. He told her to serve the Bermans separately: "We'll see. Perhaps he is a better sort of person, or perhaps he's just one of that kind that we know very well …."

"He *is* a better class of person. You can see that by his smart clothing."

Some of the refugees were discussing their new situation. Others sat silently. Poor people, who had been longing to leave Antwerp but hadn't been able to afford the fare, were loudly lamenting the fine houses they had left behind and describing how they had been impoverished by the war. Those who really had wealth and possessions entered into their fantasy and started believing what they were telling them.

"And you know what?" boasted an old Jew who had made his living by selling a little chocolate round the restaurants, "for my business alone I wouldn't take a thousand francs."

"That's because nobody would give you a thousand francs for it!" joked someone else.

"And I suppose you are a millionaire yourself?"

"Well, I'm not boasting."

"Because you haven't anything to boast about." Everyone laughed.

Berman wandered round the streets of Rotterdam on his own, angry with the world. If only they had been set down in Amsterdam, he could have gone into the Bourse and had a look to see what was going on. "Everything is going to the dogs!" he thought, forgetting that if he wished, he *could* go to Amsterdam and have a look at things. "When you are living off your capital you might as well go and bury yourself alive. When you eat into your savings, they just trickle away like water." These words kept running through his mind, and suddenly his childhood home flashed before him; he remembered all the ugliness which went with poverty. He saw himself as if he had been his father, lying helplessly in bed under the grubby coverlet, and the rabbi swaying over him with the lambs' tails bobbing around on his shabby hat.

He was roused from his reverie by a lot of shouting, and felt immensely relieved that for the moment he was still the affluent Gedaliah Berman who had fled the danger of the war.

The shouting came from a group of people standing at the edge of a canal, talking loudly and agitatedly, and evidently angry with a small boy who was standing there. Berman approached them.

The boy had been playing with some of his friends at the water's edge, sailing paper boats and trying to catch fish. Suddenly he lost his balance and was floundering around in the water. He surfaced, grabbed hold of the rope of a barge which was moored at the edge, lost his grip and was about to go under again.

A fisherman with a ruddy complexion, who was carrying his catch of shellfish and frogs, handed the sack to someone, jumped into a boat and fished out the young rascal. He brought him back to the bank to a storm of applause from the onlookers. He sat the boy down on a stone, dripping wet, and spoke sternly to all the boys:

"I'm going to keep him sitting in my house for a whole day! And I'll let the lot of you drown if you don't get away from the edge of the canal! One day there'll be a real accident!"

"Where's the policeman?" wondered the onlookers, getting themselves worked up in sympathy with the fisherman. "Oh, he'll arrive when he's not needed any more. *Godverdoeme!*" said the fisherman crossly, drawing on his clay pipe and exhaling clouds of smoke through his nose.

In the end he wrapped the little boy in his own sheepskin jacket and, with his bag over one arm and carrying the child in the other, he took him home.

Berman stopped and, in his broken Flemish, asked someone what was going on. A fair-skinned Dutch lad with a long, shiny nose, wearing wooden clogs, told him that a little boy had drowned.

"*Almost* drowned, you mean!" a voice from the crowd corrected him. Berman went on his way. "What a stupid lot they are," he thought "not even knowing exactly what happened. But this town - nothing but water wherever you turn. It's a wonder they don't all drown. The town's a river - nothing but water and refugees. Whoever heard of *goyim* wasting their time wandering about with nothing to do, staring all day into the water? Of course, for all the lazy fools from Antwerp, this is the high life. The war's a blessing in disguise for them. They've got enough to eat, so they're just strolling around with their hands in their pockets, as if the world belonged to them. If they had left everything behind, as I had to, the results of years of toil, it wouldn't be such a joyful holiday for them!" Thus Berman, who seemed to have forgotten that he himself was also just "strolling around", vented his spleen on the people who filled the streets of Rotterdam. In reality, they were full of the quiet desperation of people who have nothing left to lose.

He stopped by a stall and bought a herring fillet, ate it, licked his lips, and went back to the lodgings. He lay down on the mattress which now served as his bed, and tried to make up his mind which option would be better, to go to Amsterdam, or to England. How on earth could one make that decision? Who could tell which would be the better choice?

One morning the fair-haired young man polished his spectacles with particular thoroughness, positioned them very carefully on his fleshy nose, assumed an extremely serious expression and came into the big hall where the refugees were sitting round the tables, drinking cocoa from dented tin mugs. He tried to speak in a deep voice, but it came out with a squeak, which spoiled the whole effect.

"Nobody is to leave the building today!" he announced and without further explanation he retreated into his office again. The refugees were anxious to question him about this, but they couldn't get to him. He had put the chain on the door and wouldn't let anyone in.

So they had no choice but to sit around playing chess and trying to guess where they were going to be taken. Some guessed it would be London; others thought that they would all be spread around Holland. But no one knew, and, as their feelings of bewilderment grew, they started fighting over a knight or a pawn, taking out their uneasiness and anger on each other. Berman was most displeased with the situation: that a young ruffian should order *him* to sit and wait, without giving him any explanation! How dare a scabby boy be so insolent to *him*, Berman? So he stood up, combed his beard with his fingers and knocked on the door of the office.

When the young man saw through the window that it was Berman, he came out:

"*Mein Herr?*"

"I should like to ask," said Berman, also speaking German, "the reason for this."

"Oh certainly, sir, of course," answered the young man respectfully: "I have received an instruction that this evening all the Jewish refugees are to travel on to London."

"So! *Danke!*"

Berman was pleased that they were going to London. Fate seemed to have made the right decision, and he felt quite satisfied. He had managed to bring some fine goods with him and had no doubt that he would be able to do business there.

"What? So we're actually going to London? Why didn't he tell us?"

"Why should he tell *you?*" laughed Berman.

The people made angry objections to the young man, when he

191

came out into the hall that evening with a thick cigar between his fat, red lips to announce that they were leaving in an hour:

"But they say that we'll soon be able to go back home. How long can the war last? So what's the point in dragging us all the way to London?"

"Ask the Germans that, not me!" he answered, and left the room.

The refugees got into a terrible state of agitation.

"Who would have expected this catastrophe?!" "They've really sold us down the river." "We're sitting here like cats in a sack. We're not little children, after all!" "They think they can do just what they like with us!"

The refugees raged and stormed, but nevertheless stayed where they were and didn't try to leave the building. Jews who used to push little carts, sell knick-knacks in restaurants, or slave away in shops which didn't even provide a livelihood, were jubilant, but even so, they joined in the protests volubly, not wanting to advertise their poverty by remaining silent. The young people, who were always keen to travel, were more delighted than anyone.

During the night they were led away like sheep. Women were weeping for the homes they were leaving behind, even though they had already left them by coming to Holland.

The ship was dark, and the bunks, which were stacked on top of each other, were just hard planks of grey wood. The only lighting consisted of a few dim lamps. The people sat or lay silently, with their mouths pressed firmly shut, in an attempt to control their nausea. Now and then someone couldn't cope and vomited all over the person underneath. A few girls got together and started singing, joking, making fun of the older people who were groaning and moaning and vomiting, all in an attempt to make themselves look brave. But, in the middle of it, they too were overcome and threw up.

The voyage lasted through the night. Berman, suffering from terrible stomach cramps, lay there clutching his belly, with a wet cloth wrapped round his head, inhaling from a bottle of smelling salts.

Berman's father whispered softly. Rochl was weeping with muffled sobs. She was imagining heaps of slaughtered corpses without arms and legs, and among them was Dovid, lying in a pool of blood and mud, dead on the field of battle, with no one to cover his wounds or to bury him. And *she* was travelling away from him, far away to England, leaving him lying there dead. The more she tried to drive away these terrible thoughts and shocking images, the more they crept into her mind, assuming ever more dreadful forms, and England seemed to her a million miles distant from her son; the greater the distance between him and her, the greater the danger for him. She sobbed loudly.

Meanwhile Berman was preoccupied with his own problems. The stomach ache and nausea prevented him from getting to sleep. He didn't want to sleep in any case, because he wanted to keep his eye on the merchandise he had brought with him.

And so the ship slowly made its way through the rough, black sea; the sky was cloudy and a cold rain was falling, in contrast to the warm, bright weather in Holland.

Chapter 22

The Bermans stood slightly apart from the other refugees, their suitcases at their feet, in the strange, huge railway station. Berman was carrying a large silk umbrella which he had bought in Rotterdam, having heard that it rains all the time in London. He was feeling extremely impatient. What a dreadful noise! What chaos! There were people milling around everywhere, and the cries of the newspaper boys nearly drove him mad. Names of racehorses and the latest headlines about the war were echoing from one end of the station to the other. Berman tried to stop up his ears, but the cries managed to penetrate, deafening him:

"All the winners! All the winners!" "German aeroplane brought down!" "Eight people burnt to death!" "Murder case verdict!" "Murderer sentenced to death!"

The refugees all stood in the enormous railway station listening to these strange foreign words echoing in their ears with a dull, rattling sound, like beans being thrown on a metal surface. The terrible tumult and the huge size of the place angered Berman, and he was indignant that he was being kept waiting for such a long time. As usual he took his frustration out on Rochl.

"This isn't a railway station, it's a madhouse," he grumbled ill-temperedly to her.

Tall, phlegmatic Englishmen constantly entered and left the station. They wore grey coats and mildly surprised, tight-lipped expressions on their clean-shaven faces. They glanced surreptitiously at the refugees as if they were a collection of small-town relatives who had come to attend the wedding of some rich London cousin, who had been too busy to come and collect them, or had simply forgotten all about them.

Two Englishwomen walked past. They wore sporty, grey suits and their neatly coiffured heads were crowned by broad-brimmed felt hats. Their mannish shoes, gloves and suitcases were all of good quality brown leather. As they passed they shook their heads and quietly expressed their sympathy with Berman, who stood apart from everyone else:

"Poor man. Isn't it a shame!"

"He looks like a gentleman."

"Yes, indeed," agreed the other.

"He looks different from the rest."

"Yes, indeed," agreed the other.

"So this is London!" said Berman loudly with a grimace, as if he had understood what they were saying.

"He seems to be a fine chap," said the older woman, glancing at Berman with her steely grey eyes.

"Yes, indeed," agreed the other.

They both walked off, the mother with her grey bun, the daughter with her blonde one.

At last some Jews arrived to meet the refugees. They appeared to be well-nourished, and wore gold watches dangling over their stomachs and Star of David tiepins in their cravats. They were all carrying umbrellas. A tall young man, the under-secretary of an institution wrinkled his sharp, crooked nose and muttered something to himself. His keen eyes darted around. The secretary with the flaxen hair from Rotterdam stepped forward to meet him, and smiles, sweet as honey, beamed from both their faces. Two hands, one white and plump, the other brown and lean, pressed each other heartily, holding on as if they never wanted to let go.

The London secretary twitched his nose and called out to the crowd in general:

"Follow me!"

The refugees looked at each other: "What does he mean?"

"What does he mean? He means we should follow him!"

"How can we be his followers if he's not dead yet!" joked some witty individual, but all the refugees felt despondent and nobody was in the mood to laugh. They followed meekly after the London "cousins", who had remembered to collect them after all.

Outside the station, buses were waiting for them. Once again the refugees were packed in together, some sitting, some standing, being driven off again to an unknown destination.

By standing apart from all the others, Berman managed to achieve what he desired from the under-secretary: respect. The latter reserved two benches in the bus especially for the Berman family, made sure that they were not squashed, and quizzed the Rotterdam under-secretary about Berman.

"Who is that man over there?" he asked, pointing at Berman's broad back.

"Oh, that man? He is a better class of person." With this he had divulged all the information he had about Berman to his London colleague.

The refugees were taken to the Eastern Hotel. This was an old Jewish institution, whose very walls seemed impregnated with the troubles of Jewish immigrants, and saturated with Jewish tears. Its dismal, redbrick walls rose up from its massive, grubby foundations; it was blackened by the dust, of many arid summers and the smoky, black fogs of many winters.

No one could say who was more amazed at the new type of immigrants who had just arrived, the ancient walls of the hotel or the hotel porter. They were not so dirty, dejected and exhausted as the thousands and thousands who had stayed there on previous occasions. These immigrants were dressed more respectably and what they saw with their astonished eyes caused sardonic smiles rather than tears, to steal across their faces.

"Is *this* our place of refuge?" these immigrants seemed to be thinking, smiling dismissively, like people who know their prison sentence will only last for one day.

Soon the London assistant secretary began to go up and down the benches at a leisurely pace taking down people's names, occupations and Antwerp addresses.

"A polisher? All right!"

"What kind of cutter? ladies' or gentlemen's?"

"What do you mean?"

"Well, are you a cutter of women's or men's clothes?"

"We're not *tailors'* cutters! We're diamond cutters!" The Antwerp workers regarded his assumption as blasphemy against their craft, and gave him contemptuous smiles and condescending looks.

The assistant secretary, however, was not impressed by their mention of diamonds, and he called out in a loud voice:

"Be seated round the tables."

His loud, harsh voice, his piercing eyes and the solemn, almost fierce expression on his face intimidated the refugees so much that they began to look more like those other immigrants with whom the secretary normally dealt.

Berman alone was completely unabashed. When the secretary came up to him, Berman didn't wait to be interrogated, but instead started to interrogate the secretary.

"Tell me, my good man," he said, smiling sarcastically, "for what reason are you wandering around with *two* pencils?"

The secretary, who was not accustomed to being questioned, looked at Berman's face and was so taken aback that he lost his power of speech, just when he was supposed to be noting all Berman's personal details in his little book!

"I ... I ... ehm ... I wanted to ask, I mean ..." he stuttered: "Eh, what is your name please? You understand, I must give it to the authorities, I mean ...."

"Oh, I see, that is what you wish to do! Excellent! And of course for that reason you need *two* pencils. I understand perfectly: the one behind your ear is the reserve pencil. Well, my name is ...." Berman finally decided to stop teasing the young man.

Once they had got rid of this self-important official, the Jews felt more at ease and some lively discussion got under way.

"What do you think of this welcome?! You know, those Germans wouldn't have eaten us, believe me," asserted an Austrian Jew who had Russian papers. "They're actually fine people."

"Well, just you go back to your 'fine people' then!" retorted a woman from Odessa who had a deep mannish voice: "Even when I was still in my mother's womb I hated those pigs of Germans. All my life I've managed to avoid having anything to do with them. When I came across them in Berlin, on my way to Antwerp, I nearly died. Such stiff, pompous brutes, with murderous eyes: that's your 'fine people' for you. You can see what a fine mess they have made of a great country like Belgium, where people are accustomed to live and let live."

"Well in my view they *are* fine people and they'll be here before you know where you are, I can assure you of that!" blustered the Austrian Jew.

"Bite your tongue off for saying such a thing! We should denounce him; he's obviously a German sympathiser." Everyone was now in a rage and it looked as if a new war was about to break out between the Galician Jew and the rest of the refugees.

A small woman wearing a stiff white apron like a nurse, with a dark lively face and a large black bun on top of her head, waved a bundle of keys and, with her nose in the air, called out imperiously:

"Sit down at the tables and be quiet!"

The young man, who had returned to the room, repeated it after her like a good mimic.

"Sshhh! Quieten down!" the woman repeated. No one paid much attention to the man, but the little woman looked like someone who was used to her orders being obeyed.

The people all sat down, but there still wasn't complete silence. Here and there someone spoke, a young man whistled, a girl quietly imitated the "nurse", and everyone laughed. The woman saw that she was dealing here with a quite different type of immigrant; she pursed her lips and fell silent.

Berman had no intention of staying there. He planned to go out to Hatton Garden to have a look around. However, there was no harm in waiting for a couple of days. For one thing it was better that the merchants in Hatton Garden shouldn't get to know that he had been one of the last to flee Antwerp, together with all these paupers. And apart from that, he had heard that rich diamond merchants were not kept here, but provided with proper accommodation and paid subsistence money.

And so it turned out. The organisation found out who was who, and divided the refugees into two groups: the common people were sent to the Palmolive Hotel, where they were provided with the basic necessities, and the "better-class" refugees were sent to the Central Hotel.

Chapter 23

The Palmolive Hotel was packed with refugees. Every time a new family was sent there, the tiny area which the inhabitants called their accommodation became even smaller. The folds of the flowered curtains on metal rods which closed off the living areas were bunched closer together, and everyone became uneasy. "We soon won't have any space to sit down at all!" they complained.

It was exclusively workers who were living there. The men went out to work every morning. Diamond cutters and polishers learnt within a couple of weeks to be tailors' pressers* or to operate sewing machines. Their meagre wages contributed to the costs of living in the hotel. And their wages were indeed meagre. The bosses didn't pay much, because they believed that the refugees were getting their subsistence free, and so they exploited them. Someone whose abilities qualified him to earn two pounds a week was paid less than one pound. No matter how efficiently and quickly they did the work, the bosses insisted that they weren't yet properly trained and still had to learn the trade.

The refugees got used to working hard for very little money, and to living behind curtains instead of walls. If you took the curtain away, they were totally exposed to a hostile world. However, a good number of new English citizens did emerge from behind the flowery curtains, and the Anglo-Jewish charity workers who looked after the refugees were honoured with the role of *sandek*, holding baby boys during circumcision ceremonies. They paid for this honour with presents for the babies, who were greatly loved and cherished, especially in a time of war. The parents very quickly realised that because of the children they themselves were treated with more respect, and they applied themselves diligently to fulfilling this objective!

Everything settled down and their lives were going reasonably smoothly, apart from the problems caused by a few revolutionary "troublemakers", as the members of the committee called those who voiced the justified objection that they were having to contribute to their living costs, while the rich diamond merchants, who earned nuggets of gold, were living like lords in the Central Hotel, and not paying a penny. Why did Mr Brown stand at the exit every morning stopping every worker and making him inscribe his name in a list, so that he would not be able to get out of paying a shilling or two of his earnings? Why, on the other hand, did no one control the movements of the diamond merchants at the Central Hotel? It was simply because they did not need to go out until about eleven o'clock and at that time no one, it was assumed, goes to work.

Because of those "revolutionaries", animosity flared up in the hotel. No matter how much Mr Seltzer, a naturalised Englishman who wore a big, shiny top hat even on weekdays, tried to reason with them, arguing that all people are not equal and cannot expect to live in the same way, he was unable to convince them or to quell the jealousy, which was increasing all the time between the two camps, the Central Hotel and the Palmolive Hotel. Every time a refugee went to visit friends or relatives in the Central Hotel, he would come back with stories that made people's eyes pop out.

"My cousin lives there. You should see the rooms, the furniture, the mirrors, the marble walls, the porter at the entrance!"

Hearing descriptions like this, people's imaginations started to run away with them and they fantasised and painted such pictures for themselves that they were eaten up with desire, these "common people", and tears of frustration came into their eyes. It got to the point that if someone had a relative in the Central Hotel, he would bask in the reflected glory and refuse to come out from behind his curtains, not wanting to mix with the *hoi polloi*.

But the members of the committee found a way of dealing with the revolutionaries. They gave a stern warning, threatening that they would evict them and take no further responsibility, leaving them without any support. So the revolutionaries quietened down and suffered in silence.

One young man, who was a member of the committee, was able to pour oil on troubled waters and repair the damage, which had been caused to relations between the committee and the refugees. This Mr Greenberg, who was in his early thirties, devoted his time - and he had a great deal of time to spare - to the inhabitants of the Palmolive Hotel. He knew everyone by name, knew their history and their aspirations, their problems and joys, and he treated them very well. He remembered all the children's birthdays and always gave them little presents. The children adored him, as did the women. He would appear in the yard, with a friendly smile and a shiny top hat perched on his pomaded hair. He wore an English suit of good quality and dazzling white spats over expensive shoes. He only had to wave a yellow chamois leather glove and the children would run from all the corners of the hotel and swarm round him, like bees round a honey pot. They spoke English to him, learning the language before the adults had time to turn round. The children knew this would make a good impression on Mr Greenberg, so they really made an effort. Mr Greenberg took his time and waited till the clamour had died down before he said casually, to no one in particular: "Whose birthday is it today?"

It was apparently *everybody*'s birthday, but they couldn't pull the wool over Mr Greenberg's eyes, and he had a good look round and was able to see who was lying and who was telling the truth. He put a beautifully manicured finger to his nose, assumed a stern expression and warned them: "I don't want to hear any lies! Anyone who tells lies won't get any sweets for three months. And in any case, I *know* who it is," he went on, taking a psychological approach. "Come here, Miss Blum!" He picked out one little girl and gave her a bar of Nestlé's chocolate. "It's *your* birthday, isn't it?"

The children realised that he really did know, so they stopped lying to him and began pestering their mothers: "Mama, when's my birthday, when's my birthday?"

The mothers scolded and smacked them but couldn't put them off, so they made up the dates of their birthdays and grumbled to each other: "This is impossible! He's really spoiling our children!" But though they went through the motions of complaining, in fact they idolised him so much that their husbands began to be jealous.

The situation in the Central Hotel was very different. When they had started looking for another place to accommodate the increasing numbers of refugees pouring in from Holland, it transpired that it was impossible to find anywhere suitable, apart from this elegant hotel, which had formerly belonged to an elderly German Jew. The owner had left England because of the war, and the government allocated this hotel to the refugees. The rich English Jews took on the work and in the course of a few weeks they had created an institution which was a model of philanthropic effort. They could hold their heads up high before the English government, which was providing for the Christian refugees.

The refugees who were being accommodated were impressed by their surroundings:

"Have you seen the dining room? Amazing! Mirrors and marble everywhere!"

"Yes, but it's not costing them anything! They just took it over from that German."

"Serves the old *yecke** right! Ha, ha, ha!"

"We'll live like Kaisers here!"

"What a shame that Kaiser Wilhelm can't be here!"

"Yes, he'd really have had a great time!" one young refugee quipped.

"'Rejoice, oh young man, in thy youth!'* What naiveté!" retorted the Galician Jew with the Russian papers, who was enraged at their jibes. "Just you wait, he *will* be coming here, Kaiser Wilhelm, *and* Franz Josef, he'll be here too, you'll see! The war's not over yet!"

Everyone started shouting:

"Throw him out!" "Let's denounce him!" "Yes, that would be a *mitzvah*." "Just leave him be, he'll betray himself out of his own mouth, the fool! He won't be able to keep his mouth shut."

"Go on then, do it, am I stopping you? Denounce me if you like! You can all go to hell - I've got papers, ha, ha, ha!"

An elderly man was beside himself with rage: "I'll go and denounce him myself!"

"No, Reb Mordecai, don't soil your mouth! He's not worth it! These Galician patriots; Kaiser Efroim-Yossel's their *rebbe*."

"Well, at least we've got proper leaders. Who are your *rebbes*? Those bloody Russians! Just wait; you'll all be subjects of Franz Josef in the end!"

There was a tremendous tumult:

"He's insulting Jews. He's an atheist! Throw him out!"

Thus it almost came to a punch-up on the very first day those fortunate refugees spent in the Central Hotel. But the feud between the Galician and the Russian Jews soon abated. They couldn't get enough of admiring the opulence and luxury of the place, the gleaming mirrors, the marble and the crystal chandeliers. The next morning however, some of the older men were tut-tutting discontentedly. They had to sleep under fustian blankets and almost froze to death. Despite the magnificence of the marble, it certainly did not keep them warm.

Soon there was something in the air which was impossible to define and yet was enough to overshadow the mirrors and marble, and make the refugees forget that there were such things in the hotel. It began to have the smell of an institution. This odour rose up from the cellars and penetrated as far as the sixth floor, right into the bedrooms. Apart from this, the women were unwilling to be confined in the kitchen all day, peeling potatoes and washing dishes. So tensions started emerging between the providers and those provided for.

Despite all this, the people in this hotel were, on the whole, fairly well-off. They had separate bedrooms, and larger families were allocated two or even three rooms. The children were catered for by an English nurse with a scrubbed face and flat, straw-coloured hair. She wore a large, white, starched, respectable cap and a light blue, pleated dress with a stiff, round, white collar which cut into her neck, and gave her a double chin. She went round distributing portions of rice pudding, milk and other good things, which made the adults' mouths water. But this righteous nurse tried to make the adults understand that she had her orders: it was only for the children.

She absolutely could not comprehend that some people could not speak English, and that the women, who were trying to persuade her to give them a little of the food for themselves, simply did not understand what she was saying to them. The women, on the other hand, couldn't understand how this nurse, who had such a naive look in her eyes, could possibly differentiate between one word and the next, since she gabbled all the words in one breath, and they all sounded the same in any case. And yet these Anglo-Jewish philanthropists understood her very well. They shared jokes with her when she was talking with them, and she laughed with them, obviously very pleased with herself.

"It seems as if this English is a real language after all!" said the women to each other.

Once she started shouting, put on her straw hat and seemed to be about to leave for ever. The women were shocked, but one of the female voluntary helpers talked her round, and in the end she started smiling again, said it was "all right", and was soon busy at the serving table, baffling the women with her strange chattering.

Even stranger than this nurse was the "old maid" with the large, horsey teeth, a hat permanently on her head and huge spectacles on her nose, who was employed down in the cellar, entrusted with distributing bundles of clothes to the refugees.

When the women, who till recently had been the mistresses of affluent households, heard that clothes were being distributed, they descended on the cellar like locusts. The old maid, poor thing, had a really hard time of it, and she scolded the uncivilised women who were besieging her, desperate to get their hands on a few underclothes, or a pair of shoes, or a winter coat, or all of those things. But she was loath to give away such expensive clothes, which, ten or fifteen years ago, had been worn by real ladies, women of the highest rank in society. It vexed her that common people, refugees at that, should wear these things, so she could not bring herself to do her duty even though these clothes had not cost her anything. Thus the cellar became another battleground.

"Can't you see, Miss Jacobs," said a woman pleadingly to the old maid: "I've been waiting for hours and you're letting people in who have just this minute come down, and giving them the best things, just because they are dressed in fur coats. They don't even need the clothes; they'll not catch cold in any case. But I'm going round in my summer jacket, and I'm freezing!"

"And I suffer from rheumatics. This damp cellar is making me ill," complained an elderly woman, her teeth chattering. "Because they're wearing diamond rings you give them the best clothes as well, and us poor people get nothing," she said, justifiably upset.

"That's just it, if you don't have any luck, it would be better not have been born," another woman mused.

"*I* had to leave all my good clothes behind," explained someone, thinking this might help her.

But the old maid knew who had actually left possessions behind and who had had nothing to leave. Sometimes she simply lost patience and gave so many things to the first person who came in that the recipient could hardly carry the load. This was not any kind of solution either.

"God forgive me for saying so, but the *shnorrers* have all the luck! She won't give anything to me though I've asked her six times. You have to be able to whinge and plead, and I just can't do that!" said a skinny old woman, sucking in her sallow cheeks and chewing her blue lips, which were split and dried up.

"Well, what have you lost by it?" retorted a fat woman with a wobbling, wrinkled, double chin and grey whiskers.

While they were arguing among themselves, a lady came out of the room, which was the goal of all their aspirations; she was dressed in a beautiful fur coat and carried under her arm a neat parcel, wrapped in brown paper. The parcel was tied with a new piece of string, as if it had been bought in a shop.

"Just look how she's packed it up for her! I won't tell you where I'd like to pack all of them up and send them." exploded another woman, cursing all the women in fur coats.

"Why are you in awe of them?" protested the old woman with the grey whiskers: "Tell them straight, the wealthy *shnorrers*, that they should be ashamed of themselves, coming down here in their fancy coats and flashing those diamonds, scrounging and still thinking they're better than us."

"Don't you realise, they've actually come to make a contribution!" laughed a young man who was coming out of the room.

"Eh? What are you doing here? Why were you not queuing for

205

men's clothes?" asked the women in surprise.

"My wife is ill and I came to get a coat for her. You obviously could have done with my assistance too."

"God bless him, he's right," gushed the old woman with the whiskers. "The man certainly has brains."

"Oho, he's certainly courageous!" laughed the women, and the muffled echo of their laughter reverberated through the cold, damp corridor of the dark cellar.

The old woman finally lost her temper, decided to act and simply knocked on the door of the room. The old maid came out and peered around in the darkness, blinking her red eyes.

"Who had the temerity to... ?"

"I did" said the old woman, looking her straight in the eye.

"Listen, my good woman, I must serve these ladies first. They've been waiting far too long as it is."

"That's a lie! We've been waiting much longer! You're giving *them* all the best things, and spending time wrapping them up in brown paper. *We* will..."

The old maid was frightened. After all, she was on her own and there was an entire mob of them. And she couldn't rely on the stupid boy who helped her to pack up the parcels. He would just stand there staring with his bovine eyes and by the time he grasped what he had to do, they would have beaten her up. She started hurriedly making excuses:

"It's not my fault, I'm only following orders. And you know the saying, 'If you have much, you'll get much more. If you have little, you'll lose the little that you had before.'"

"Yes, but why should it be like that?" protested the women, unwilling to accept this idea.

But the spinster had fled back into her room, taking with her one of those who were to get much more.

Scenes like these were an everyday occurrence in the hotel, and people got used to them. The only person who could not get accustomed to such upsets was Frau Zederbaum, the lady president of the Committee, a tall, thin woman with a decidedly Jewish nose, wide-open blue eyes that made her look naive, and a lugubrious expression.

206

She wore a prickly, black straw hat which nearly hid her long angular face. Frau Zederbaum, who had originally come from Galicia, and had married a naturalised Englishman, was a millionairess, but the only luxury she permitted herself was an expensive black ostrich feather which she wore both winter and summer. She did many charitable works and was very active in all the philanthropic institutions.

A knocking on the table which made the walls tremble announced to the refugees that Madame Zederbaum had arrived and was about to preach a sermon to the effect that she had yet again discovered some heinous crime which had been committed in the hotel. She inevitably chose to give these homilies just when the refugees were sitting at the tables having their lunch. She would stand on a little square of red velvet which acted as a sort of podium, separating her from the "poor people". She would speak as follows, her attempt to speak Yiddish coming out as slightly garbled German:

"*Mein geehrte Damen un Herren*! I am really sorry to disturb you in the middle of your lunch, but I can no longer keep silent about the following matter. Once again I have actually found a dirty milk pan simply thrown away in the corridor. All the inquiries made by our respected supervisor have not succeeded in identifying once and for all who is so shamelessly discarding cooking utensils, just because they have got burnt. It is absolutely shocking! Therefore, ladies and gentlemen, we are forced to hold all the inhabitants of the hotel responsible and penalise everyone. We shall have to cease giving out milk and also coal for the bedroom fires, so that there will be no possibility of milk pans being burned."

To reinforce the impact of her words, Madame Zederbaum produced the pan, wrapped in newspaper, which the supervisor, who had presided over this lecture, ceremoniously handed her. She unwrapped it, and held it up, so that everyone could see it.

The refugees sat with their spoons halfway to their mouths, apparently listening with great seriousness, and trying with all their might not to burst into gales of laughter. The long, skinny lady left her podium and went walking about the tables as if nothing had happened, enquiring about the meal: "I'm sure your lunch is delicious?"

Jacques left his table and followed her, imitating her walk, and asked in a quiet, refined voice: "I'm sure your lunch is disgusting?"

The people burst out laughing and Madame Zederbaum shook her black feather, and nervously left without saying another word. The refugees, after their moment of mirth, sat there in gloomy silence. She had ruined their appetite. The truth was that this enforced idleness had made the women so lazy that they couldn't be bothered to wash a single pot.

Madame Zederbaum wouldn't have interfered in such matters if it hadn't been that the "potato king" - so the women maintained - had needlessly shoved the dirty pans, which were already the talk of the Central Hotel, under her nose.

This potato king had a thick, flaming red beard and a neatly trimmed and pomaded moustache, and his nose was as round as the King Edward potatoes which he peeled from morning to night. He really worked hard, the king, and the three deep furrows on his low forehead became even deeper and wider as he worked.

His wife, the queen, looked so like her husband, that if it hadn't been for the fact that she wore women's clothes, no one could have told them apart. She also had a little red beard, smaller than his, naturally.

This couple had come from Belgium with all the other refugees. No one knew why they had been picked to help in the kitchen, peeling the potatoes, which were cooked every day. Nor did anyone know who had crowned them with their royal titles. The refugees liked the nicknames, which certainly suited the couple very well. However, what happened? After he had inherited his kingdom, the kitchen, the king began to act like a despot: stern and uncontrollable, never asking for or listening to advice from anyone. A veritable Nicholas the Third.*

The other refugees rebelled, and every lunch time, a new Civil War broke out. They suspected the potato king of not putting all the available meat and potatoes into the soup, so that the soup was thin and didn't satisfy their hunger. So they demanded double helpings. The king did not deign to answer them. He did give out double helpings, but only to certain people, who had found favour in the king's eyes, namely, the rich people. No lunchtime passed, therefore, without screaming and shouting, but it was like talking to the wall.

In the end, someone would pluck up enough courage to go to the office and put the matter in the hands of the authorities, the philanthropists, so that they should judge it. The "telltale", as the ladies and gentlemen of the institution called him, would, however, come out of the office looking crestfallen, and after these episodes the king would reign even more despotically than before. When the people saw that they were not going to have any effect on the king, they began to squabble among themselves and take their anger out on each other.

Berman did not like the hotel at all. The mirrors and marble did not excite him in the least. He wrinkled his nose and declared to all and sundry that this was no place for him.

Madame Zederbaum made a gesture with her delicate white hand, as if to say: "*Ach*, you'll soon get used to it!"

But when she saw that her promise to put more furniture in his rooms on the first floor, to install an easy chair on the balcony and even a gas stove in the bedroom, hardly impressed him at all, she realised that she was dealing here with a better class of person, which impressed her considerably.

"*Ach so*, Herr Berman, we shall see what we can do. I shall raise the topic at the next meeting and you will find you can rely on me. You will in all probability get a private flat."

Berman decided to humour her and stay for a few more days.

"He is a very nice man," she said to Mr Green, her assistant.

"Yes, one can see that straight away" agreed Mr Green.

The potato king had already heard of Berman when they were both still in Antwerp. With a doglike instinct he sensed that Madame Zederbaum thought highly of Berman, and he immediately allocated him a double helping.

One morning when Berman came down to lunch there was a great turmoil going on. A woman about fifty-years-old was making a fuss, shouting at a thin woman some twenty years younger, who had squeezed herself in at the head of the long table where the cream of the Antwerp Jews sat. These were stout men with long beards, fat stomachs and even fatter wives. The young woman, who had a child on her knee, was weeping, and, at the same time, trying ineffectually to dry her eyes, with a rather grubby pocket handkerchief.

The older woman's bosom was heaving under her silk blouse, diamond earrings dangled from her bluish, elongated ear lobes, the whiskers on her chin were trembling, and her thick lips were purple with rage and flecked with spittle.

"The insolence of it! Scrawny little fool! She has the cheek to think she is my equal! Thank God everyone else from Antwerp knows who I am! How dare she come and sit at this table, the *shnorrer*. No sooner is a little bit of soup doled out than she sticks out her dirty hands and grabs it. She doesn't even know that anyone who grabs gets their fingers smacked, the skinny little idiot!"

The young woman was sobbing, not understanding why the woman was shouting at her. She tried to ask the people at the table what she had done wrong, but she was so upset that she could hardly speak. Some of them thought it was funny and just laughed at her, others were asking the indignant woman to stop shouting, everyone else was busy with their own concerns, and no one answered her.

Berman looked at the older woman and recognised her as the wife of a rich merchant with whom he did business. He glanced at the young woman. "What on earth is a woman like her doing at this table?" he thought, and then he realised, with horror, that it was Gitele. He asked someone else what had happened, and found out immediately, for *he* had no difficulty in getting an answer, that a second helping of soup had been set out for this woman. Gitele, who hadn't yet had any, had assumed it was for her, and had put her hand out. This had made the other woman apoplectic, and she had started screeching at Gitele.

To make matters worse, the potato king came out of the kitchen and started bellowing at Gitele:

"Shut up, will you! You'd think someone was murdering you. Stop scrubbing at your eyes. The committee doesn't like scenes like this. If you carry on like this Madame Zederbaum will come in and when she sees what trouble you're causing she'll send you to the Palmolive, where you'll have something to cry about!"

Berman was very tempted to tell the potato king that Gitele was in fact the daughter of a rich man in Poland, but he decided that it was better to know nothing and not to get mixed up in the whole business. He gestured to Rochl, who understood what he meant and also said nothing. But she refused the double helping which she was offered, and old Reb Chaim Yoysef sank his head so low that his beard touched the table. He sighed heavily and almost choked on the bread which he had softened by putting it in his soup. He said quietly to Rochl, whose eyes were brimming with tears: "This is what we've come to, daughter."

Not only did the potato king have his favourites, but the people themselves had formed cliques. As if by magic, each table was occupied exclusively by people of the same type. At one table sat people who filled their day - before, during and after the meals - with discussion of higher matters. Shakespeare was never absent from this table for one moment, and Bernard Shaw, Ibsen, Heine, Goethe, Homer, Rembrandt and Michelangelo all occupied places of honour there. The intellectuals at this table were experts in everything, sculpture, music, literature. And, of course, they discussed all these matters in loud voices.

The rest of the eaters, even the bearded men at the top table, and their wives with the silk blouses, began to listen in to these conversations, not understanding a word but with a feeling of respect for the people at that table.

The potato king inclined his hairy ear to them and listened intently to find out what those snotty-nosed intellectuals were jabbering about. Hearing them constantly pronouncing names, which he had never heard of, neither in Antwerp, nor in London, nor even in Galicia, he started to ask around and when he found out that it was books they were discussing, he shook his big head and asked:

"So why do people discuss books? Books are for reading! Not for messing up your brain. Ach, what fools!" He decided on the spot that *they* would certainly not get double helpings.

"A crowd of lazy good-for-nothings, that's all they are!" he said to his wife, but nevertheless he put their food in front of them without banging it down on the table.

He sat Gitele at that table, and she became even more dejected. When the group saw a young woman with a child at their table, they completely ignored her. So she looked for another table, and sat down at a table with poor women whose husbands, even here, were going out to work in order to be able to contribute something towards the bill. These women helped in the kitchen with the washing up – they couldn't afford to throw away dirty saucepans. They sat all day in the women's room, sewing pillowcases and sheets for the hotel bedrooms. At this table everyone welcomed Gitele's child, petting her, and telling Gitele stories about what lovely homes they came from; although their husbands were simple workers, they had kept nice kitchens with steel fittings, sideboards, and even gramophones.

Here Gitele felt at home, and yet, not really at home.

Chapter 24

One morning Berman dressed himself like a bridegroom in his smartest clothes in order to make his first visit to Hatton Garden. He paid particular attention to his beard, plucking out all the grey hairs which had appeared during the last few months, after which he combed, brushed and smoothed it, and divided it neatly into two halves. Then he put on his best frock coat with the silk lapels and a deep cut in the back, his fine, woollen overcoat with its velvet collar, his brown leather gloves, and took the black, silk umbrella which he had bought in Rotterdam. Altogether, he looked like a Jewish banker.

In a leisurely fashion, he came down the broad, marble stairs of the hotel and walked along the wide corridor. He paused on the long mat, which lay in a recessed oblong of concrete at the entrance. He was greeted by Mr Green:

"Good morning Mr Berman! Going out in weather like this?"

"When needs must," said Berman, with a stern smile, and went out into the street.

The streets were shrouded in thick, black fog and even though it was not raining, Berman's face was soon damp. The sky was not visible; the grey layer which hung so low that it seemed as if any minute your head would touch it, did not look like sky at all. The wet tarmac gleamed black and cold.

"Brrr!" Despite his thick warm clothes, a cold shiver went right through Berman, into his very bones. He hesitated near the broad door of the hotel. Should he carry on or not? To go back would be bad luck, but he was afraid of going on.

The tall buildings of the city and the dense traffic on the streets were both enveloped in the thick blackness. The streetlamps looked like the tiny flames of penny candles suspended here and there in the fog. The muffled clatter of heavy goods carts, the jangling of trams, and the warning shouts of conductors and carters, rang out dully through the thick air. The traffic was a dense mass, stretching all along the street; it stirred, moved on, and then was immediately tangled up again. The pedestrians on the pavements kept close to the walls.

Berman spread out his arms like black wings in an attempt to avoid bumping into other people. After walking along for a few yards he was completely disorientated. At the edge of the pavement some workers were mending sewage pipes. The paving stones, which had been removed, were heaped at the edge of the road. The long trench was marked out by little, red lamps, and big torches swinging in the fog, illuminated a small stretch of the road. An old man sat in a little wooden hut, warming himself at a brazier. The coals glowed in the midst of the fog. The workers stood around leaning on their spades, smoking pipes and chatting about the weather, as if it were something new. A few of them were surreptitiously warming themselves at the brazier. The foreman, who should have been seeing to it that the workers weren't slacking, was chatting and laughing with them. The trench could wait. But finally one of them felt that it wasn't right, and they really should get on with some work, so he jumped into the trench and started shovelling out earth. The others carried on chatting, but didn't stand in his way: "If you want to work, you're welcome to get on with it!"

For a good while Berman crept gingerly along the walls of the buildings, feeling his way in the gloom until he came to the corner, where several streets met. A tall policeman raised his white-gloved hand, which looked dirty in the fog. A mass of pedestrians seemed to emerge from nowhere, and suddenly rushed across the road.

Berman jumped on a tram, which was dripping with moisture inside. The green light could hardly penetrate the bluish steam in the air. The passengers and the benches both looked damp, and wet, dirty tram tickets were lying about the black, slimy floor. Berman could hardly breathe.

The conductor called out his familiar "Tickets, please!", and told each and every passenger the news that the fog was terrible. The passengers admitted that he was right: "Terrible!"

At last, Berman reached his destination.

A grubby, square building, with unpainted walls, blackened slates, a window splashed with mud to more than half its height, and a crumbling, dirty, wet "kosher" sign: this café served as the Bourse.* Berman couldn't believe his eyes:

"Is that all it is?" Why had he bothered to dress up smartly? However, soon he saw that the whole of Antwerp was here. All the merchants were known to him. They had exchanged their Antwerp frock coats for English clothes, but business was just as lively as in the Bourse in Antwerp. They were sitting round long tables covered with black oilcloth, poking around in little heaps of diamonds as they had done at home. As usual, the colours of the diamonds were flashing and changing: blue, red, green, gold, brilliant white. They glowed and burned, fascinating the eye, but the merchants hardly even looked at the spectacle. They were examining the diamonds for fractures, and feeling completely at home, as if they had been born and bred here.

For a moment Berman was disconcerted, feeling that he looked like a clown, out of place in these clothes. Oh well, it was easy enough to change his frock coat for English clothing, and if this was where he was to try and earn a franc or two from now on, then so be it, as long as it was possible to do business.

The London merchants were drinking tea with milk, which looked like coffee. They spoke English with a Yiddish word here and there, and as well as diamonds, they showed each other gold, platinum and strings of pearls. Minor dealers and brokers who did not have entry to the Antwerp Bourse mingled here with the important merchants.

"They've done well for themselves," thought Berman. He resented the fact that the war had brought them advancement.

At a table by the window sat a young man, poking among big mounds of diamonds rather than small heaps. "Is this what Hatton Garden's like? Hmm!" said Berman to himself.

"He's doing great business, that youngster," said a merchant, joining Berman at the table where he had sat down.

"Long may he continue!"

"He's still wet behind the ears, and yet they say he's extremely rich. Do you know him?" asked the merchant.

"Who doesn't know him? He's Lieberman's older son-in-law, Kuper."

"Oh, I see, now I understand. He comes, I believe, from Antwerp,"

"He comes from Antwerp, he comes from London; he's here, there and everywhere. He grows! They say that he's even going to overtake his father-in-law. Yes indeed!" said Berman, sighing, and looking over at the young man.

An elderly man with yellowish eyes came and stood by Berman's table, coughed, put his hand to his hollow chest and asked Berman if he had a few carats, for he had a customer. But before Berman had time to reply the old man went off again as if he had just asked for the sake of asking and didn't have a customer for the "few carats" at all.

"He's not interested after all, then! How do you like my customers?" laughed Berman.

The merchant waved his hand dismissively:

"Ach! He's not worth bothering about. There are a lot of people like him, just trying to persuade themselves that they're doing business. And look over there," he continued, "at the way those little brokers are swarming round Kuper like flies, and he gives them goods; he really is a good-natured young fellow, I must say."

"Hmm, well, goodness like that would make a dog rabid!" laughed Berman.

The young man was shaking his head, tossing back his thick fair hair, which kept falling over his red face. He glanced around with his blue eyes, before poking around again with his tweezers, pretending not to see the crowd of eagerly peering brokers who were swallowing up his heaps of diamonds with their greedy eyes.

"I got notink!" He thought by speaking in broken English he could drive them away, but the brokers pretended not to hear him.

"Herr Kuper, I give you my word, I have a customer waiting. I desperately need a few carats."

"Is that my fault? There are other merchants sitting here - why don't you go over to *him*?" he said, pointing at Berman and laughing.

"Some hope! He'd rather kick the bucket than help someone to earn an honest penny."

The waitress brought a glass of coffee and put it on the table. The young man pulled her to him and pinched her, whereupon the girl tore herself away with an expletive and hurried off to another table.

"Well," continued Kuper: "Tell me, do you think I can't conduct my own business? I don't need any brokers!"

"Already he's doing without brokers!" said the other brokers with sad resignation.

"You can rely on him, he knows what he's doing, he's a clever one," opined a middle-aged broker, pulling at his pointed beard and winking at the young man as if to say: "Those idiots don't understand you, but *I* do!"

"Here you are then!" said Kuper suddenly, distributing parcels of diamonds. "But see that you get the full price for them. And that's all the goods I'm giving out today. Diamonds are rising in value just now, so I'm losing money on every bit of goods I dispose of."

The brokers weren't listening any more, but were all going out into the thick fog. They started scribbling in their notebooks at the door and then rushed off to the various merchants' offices.

"In Antwerp, the Bourse shuts at three o'clock during the winter," Berman told the London merchant.

"Very nice!" laughed the merchant. "If we only operated during daylight hours here, we'd do no diamond trade at all; it's always night in London!"

The waitress brought two glasses of tea with lemon and Berman sipped his, never taking his eyes off Kuper.

A Galician Jew with a venerable grey beard came over. He was an ex-broker who had never had any success and now constantly hung around Hatton Garden.

"Listen, Herr Berman. I tell you, it's absolute stupidity, the way they are holding onto their diamonds. It's wartime after all, who's going to buy diamonds, eh? Who's thinking about diamonds at the moment? They have persuaded themselves that diamonds are rising in value and they're holding onto them. Take my advice and get rid of all the goods you have. Later you'll be glad you listened to me. Those idiots are going to lose their shirts!"

Berman laughed.

"If I had his money, I'd go mad," continued the old man, point-

217

ing to Kuper. "He's just a baby, and yet he thinks he knows it all and won't listen to a single word of advice from an older person."

"Well, carry on! What's stopping you from giving him some of your good advice?" said Berman, teasing. He stood up and went over to Kuper, with the old man following him.

"How are you, Herr Kuper. Doing a lot of business, are you?"

"So-so."

"You've brought the goods?"

"Yes and no."

"What do you mean by that?"

"I mean that I really have no desire to sell them. Diamonds are rising in value!"

"Stuff and nonsense! Don't let yourself get taken in by this madness which has suddenly infected them all. They're all going to come a cropper. Who's going to be interested in diamonds in wartime?" retorted Berman, making use of the old man's argument.

Kuper shot him a poisonous look at him and did not answer.

"So, have you got them or not?"

"I have them, but I'll only sell them according to our agreement, as I told you. And there's another thing."

"What's that?"

"I want Reb Mordecai to earn something too. You know what I mean."

The old man's yellowed cheeks glowed with pleasure: was he actually going to earn some money that day after all?

Berman acted as if he hadn't heard. Kuper took a parcel from his breast pocket and shook out about a dozen stones onto the black oilcloth. Their flashing colours lit up the room as if the sun had suddenly come out.

"Are they clean?" asked Berman, just for something to say, trying to hide the impression the stones made on him.

Kuper did not answer.

Berman had already seen the goods the day before at Kuper's house, where he had examined every stone. Nevertheless he put the loupe to his eye and started peering at them again. Without a word he took out his chequebook and wrote Kuper a cheque.

"That won't do!" said Kuper angrily, giving him back the cheque. Berman frowned, worrying that Kuper might change his mind and the whole deal would fall through. He was a moody young man. Berman started tugging at his own beard and stopped when it started hurting.

"Why have you put them back in your pocket? I've given you the amount you asked for! Why are you not shaking hands on the deal with the usual '*mazl un brokhe*?'"

"I already told you yesterday, and today once again, that I want five pounds for Reb Mordecai."

Berman growled like a lion in pain. If it hadn't been that diamonds were indeed rising in value every day, he'd have taught that insolent young devil a lesson. But what could he do? He didn't see stones of this quality every day and he couldn't possibly let them slip through his fingers.

"The devil knows where he gets hold of these goods! The best diamonds seem to fall into his hands. And he supports a gang of brokers that he needs like a hole in the head. He throws money right and left, and yet he's as rich as Croesus. It's always the same, God helps the rogues."

Reb Mordecai had started to lose hope. "That black dog Berman has never helped anyone to earn a franc. Nothing's going to come of this. If he bought them, I might get something. I can't understand why Kuper is haggling with him. I'd be happy with three pounds, or even two would come in very handy," thought the old man, gradually lowering his expectations.

But nothing swayed Kuper: neither Berman's objection that he was buying the goods directly from Kuper and couldn't see what Reb Mordecai had to do with it, since he had played absolutely no role in the transaction, nor the old man's silent prayer that Kuper should become more tractable.

"I'm not moving an inch from our agreement." Kuper started examining a heap of rough diamonds and smiled with double satisfaction. It gave him great pleasure to have Berman pleading with him. But he was even more delighted that the waitress kept hovering round his table, and each time, when he gave her a pinch, she complained that he didn't behave like a gentleman. He paid no attention to Berman, who finally wrote out another cheque and handed it to Kuper. The latter saw that Berman would have liked to stuff the cheque down his throat, and this filled him with glee.

"Here you are, Reb Mordecai, five pounds for you." He handed the old man five crisp, green banknotes and Reb Mordecai couldn't believe his eyes.

"Well, Kuper, you certainly are an accomplished merchant, there's no denying that" said Berman, complimenting Kuper so that the latter should not think that he had impoverished him. But he couldn't bear to look at Reb Mordecai's trembling hand.

"You see, Reb Mordecai? That's the way to get blood out of a stone!" said Kuper, laughing.

"For this you should be rewarded with blessings and success wherever life may lead you!" exclaimed the old man, trembling with emotion.

Berman shook the diamonds out again, put the loupe to his eye, even though this was totally unnecessary, and turned them over and over. Each stone gleamed and sparkled with changing colours in the electric light. Berman gazed into their brightness. Like a loving mother looking into the eyes of her only child, and rejoicing in their purity, he peered into the diamonds for the hundredth time, revelling in his stones and finding it difficult to pack them away from view. He moved them around with the tweezers, though these diamonds were big enough to hold without them. He could hardly prevent himself laughing aloud with delight.

"Wonderful goods!"

He would soon squash Kuper, without any difficulty! That one was more interested in girls than business. To sell goods of this quality at this time, when diamonds were appreciating in value? Even though he had his father-in-law behind him, he was nothing but a rotten charlatan, not a real merchant. Berman took malicious pleasure in these thoughts, avenging himself for the injury and humiliation that Kuper had caused him. He ordered a steak.

The delicious aroma of the brown gravy whetted his appetite. Berman tucked his beard into the big white napkin, and, dipping his bread in the meaty juices and the sharp horseradish, wallowed in the pleasure of it.

"Ah, who's this? Whom do I see here?" It was Shapiro. He sat down beside Berman like an old friend, shaking his hand over and over again. Berman was pleased as well.

"Have you been in England long?" asked Berman.

"Yes indeed, I came as soon as war broke out."

"So what's new? Are you doing good business?"

"What else should I be doing, writing the texts for *mezuzahs?** And you?"

"So-so! This is the first time I have been to Hatton Garden, so how could I have managed to do business yet? I see that everyone dresses like an Englishman here," said Berman, looking at Shapiro's new suit.

"When in Rome ..." Shapiro was pleased that Berman had noticed his new clothing.

Another man came and sat down with them. "Ah, Herr Mandelboym!" said Shapiro. "Don't speak German here; it's better not to."

Mandelboym took off his hat, and the white skin of his bald head gleamed. His ears stuck out, and he had glittering deep-set eyes, white, fleshy cheeks and thick red lips. He looked more like a piglet than a human being.

Berman concentrated on his steak and pretended not to notice Mandelboym, whom he had always considered to be an obnoxious person.

"So how are you, Herr Berman?" asked Mandelboym, ignoring Berman's obvious dislike of him. It really didn't matter much to him whether people liked him or not.

"And you?" asked Berman, not raising his eyes from his plate.

"I'm *alright*" replied Mandelboym who was already mixing English in with his Yiddish speech, "except that you can't get anything decent to eat here. I like to eat noodles at lunchtime, and you'd think I'd be able to get them with *my* money, wouldn't you? If I can't have noodles, then my *dinner*'s not my *dinner*. The meat isn't meat and the fish isn't fish. 'You'll just have to eat something else,' says that snooty waitress - I hope the worms devour her! If I hadn't had to meet a mer-

221

chant here, I certainly wouldn't have stuck my nose into this dungheap!" Having worked himself up into a rage, Mandelboym put his hat back on his head and went away again without even saying goodbye.

"Let him go to hell," laughed Berman. "Him and his dinners!"

"*And* you and your non-existent business deals!" said Kuper, who had suddenly appeared at their table. He had been ready to go home when he was seized by a desire to bait Berman once more. Shapiro gave a little laugh, and Kuper said goodbye to Berman and left.

"We should go too," said Berman, seeing the dense, dark grey swirls of fog seeping in through every crack. When Shapiro opened the door, a thick, black mass enveloped them, making their eyes smart and their noses sting. They went out into the street and the cold cut right through them. They linked arms like an old married couple, and, shivering, they went off into the darkness to find a taxi.

Chapter 25

Gitele lay on the iron bed in the small "servant's" room on the sixth floor of the hotel for days on end, tormenting herself.

Why did Dovid go away without even saying goodbye to her or to their child, on a journey from which he might very well not come back? What had she done to deserve this? She kept asking herself the same questions and could not find any reason for what had happened between them. Had he simply wanted to free himself from her? Perhaps he didn't love her any more. But in her heart she knew he did, so why had she done this?

As she went over it in her mind, she could still feel his every touch and caress, and saw him looking at her with infinite love in his dark eyes. She felt such warmth flooding over her that she could hardly breathe. At the same time she was deeply troubled. Why had she let him do whatever he wanted with her?

Gitele was filled with both shame and yearning. She felt burning hot. She knew that if Dovid came back now, she would not hesitate. She would go with him and make love to him. She would *want* everything to happen all over again.

What about Leybesh? What did she care about *him*? She hated Leybesh for the way he sometimes laughed at Dovid. Leybesh, she thought, was just a socialist without a heart. If only Dovid would come back, or at least write her a letter.

When she lay awake at night, feeling cold under the regulation brown fustian coverlet, the image of Dovid always appeared before her. They had been alone together in the shabby little room in Somersstraat and Dovid had lifted her up in his arms as if she had been a little child. She hadn't had the strength to resist, and, why should she try to deny it? She had not wanted to resist. She blushed as she remembered. She felt his fingers gently exploring her body. She had tried to speak, but Dovid had whispered "Don't say anything Gitele, hush my darling!" and he had covered her mouth with his sensuous lips, kissing her over and over again until she almost suffocated.

And now - not even a letter. She pressed her face into the hard pillow and wept with a mixture of shame and happiness at these memories.

There was the sound of crying from the little green cot: "Mama! Mama!"

She wanted to ask Leybesh to go and see what the child wanted, but seeing his bed still made up and empty, she shivered and got out of bed. The little girl was screaming:

"Papa! I want Papa to come home!"

Gitele gave her a drink, rocked the cot and sang her a lullaby, trembling with cold and emotion. She saw the child's dark eyes, Dovid's eyes, gradually closing, veiled by lashes which seemed thicker when she slept. She looked at her for a while and realised that when she grew up she would look just like Dovid's sister; she would be a beauty like Jeannette.

The little one was fast asleep again.

Gitele was tired and cold and couldn't see Dovid clearly any more. She tried to carry on reliving her memories, but now he appeared as if in a mist; she could see the child, but not Dovid. She thought about the way Leybesh often peered intently at his little daughter, and each time after doing so, he didn't come home for several days. Gitele didn't fall asleep until dawn.

When she started up out of this uneasy sleep, the first thing she noticed was that Leybesh's bed was still empty and hadn't been slept in. The child sat up, laughing merrily, threw off the few bits of bedclothes and called for her Papa to come and lift her up. Then she burst into tears: "Where is Papa?" She started stamping her little feet and howling: "I want Leybesh to come home!" Then, tickled at hearing herself call her Papa "Leybesh", she started giggling.

Leybesh was hardly ever in the hotel, because he was really busy. He knew all the London contacts. In fact, however, the London socialists weren't particularly taken with Leybesh - there were far more important big shots than him in London, and Leybesh's considerable knowledge of Karl Marx's Das Kapital didn't impress them very much at all.

He was soon sidelined and never given any important work to do. The way he flaunted his knowledge made them want to push him out. Any time he tried to make a point during a discussion, the chairman either didn't see Leybesh's raised hand, or else he tore up the note which Leybesh had sent over to him, and it was always some insignificant young lad who was given the floor, but never Leybesh.

So Leybesh gradually distanced himself from the work of these circles. Nevertheless, he was itching to do something. He tried, but failed, to create a circle of his own. Other comrades who also bore a grudge against the clique were keen to break with it and go with Leybesh, but somehow they never did.

Meanwhile, letters had started arriving in the hotel, all with the same contents: workers were required. Minor employers came in person to recruit them. Because of the war there was a great deal of work and a shortage of hands. These small-time tailors, shoemakers and cap makers who previously had existed on private work, using only their wives and children, now needed thirty or forty employees. Khaki uniforms, shoes, shirts and caps had to be made for the soldiers who were getting ready to go to the front. The employers had contracts with the government, but were unable to deliver the work on time. They were scratching their heads, unable to solve the problem.

Leybesh was the first to go off to work. He was as excited as a small child: for the first time in his life he was in demand and his work was needed. Soon, however, his joy abated, when he began to think about the fact that he was now participating in the "imperialist" war.

He observed the girls with their hair cut short, broad leather straps over their slim shoulders, wearing high, laced boots and short skirts, adjusting men's caps on their charming little heads and calling out with a triumphant gleam in their eyes: "Tickets, please!" They carried out the work as efficiently as if they had been used to it all their lives. This upset Leybesh. If only girls like these all over the world would devote their boundless energy to a different cause! If only they would open their bright eyes to the task of getting rid of the governments which were the cause of this pointless bloodbath, what a magnificent ideal they would be helping to realise. It annoyed him that they got such satisfaction from this work. Such bright eyes, and yet they were so blind!

But what about Leybesh himself? Wasn't he going into the workshop to press uniform trousers? Who knew whether some Dovid somewhere or other would die wearing a pair of trousers which had been carefully pressed by him? How many mothers, Jewish and Gentile, were dying a little every day in their anguish over their sons on the battlefield?

But the world took no notice at all of Leybesh's ideas. Everywhere, in the ammunition factories, on the trams and buses, even on the railways, women were working. More and more they were replacing the men who had gone to the front. They had forgotten that women were supposed to be delicate, and to pamper themselves. It wasn't only girls, but middle-aged women too who cut off their hair, put helmets on their womanly heads, donned blue uniforms, white gloves and clumsy, masculine shoes. Their weather-beaten faces took on a masculine appearance as they did guard duty or directed the traffic, as efficiently as male police officers did. They were doing their duty for king and country with energy and amazing patience. Even the Soho pickpockets and "corner boys" of Aldgate began to have respect for these forceful females. They stopped making suggestive remarks and laughing in the faces of the helmeted policewomen.

The women liked the work. They suddenly discovered that they were a force in the country, a force which would later have to be reckoned with, and they had no desire just to sit in workshops sewing trousers. Jewish girls discovered that there was a great demand for office workers. One can learn shorthand and typing in six months, so even the poorest of mothers saved their last ha'pennies,* and didn't send the girls into workshops when they left school at the age of fourteen; instead of making sweatshop workers out of them, they aspired to make them into office "ladies", working with their brains instead of their hands.

The workers were in clover: the employers treated them like kings. When the Jewish owners of tailoring workshops came to recruit workers among the refugees, they found out that this trade had been unheard of in Antwerp. There you could get all sorts of occupations: diamond cutters, polishers and cleavers, unimportant merchants and brokers, market traders, street traders, beggars - everything in the world except tailors and cap makers. But the Jewish employers were undaunted:

"We'll teach you! You'll see, it's not a bad business at all! Just come, it'll be all right! *Anyone* can be a presser! Even a baby can do it. Anyone can learn to operate a sewing machine. In a week's time you'll become expert machinists!"

To the girls they said:

"Even if the trousers are not absolutely perfect, does that mean the soldiers won't be able to wear them when they're lying in the trenches? Just come and work for me. It'll be all right!"

Leybesh was the first to volunteer. On the first Thursday the boss said to him:

"Why should you go back to the hotel? It's such a *shlep!* A little bit of food is neither here nor there for me; if I'm providing for ten, there's enough for eleven. Do they really give you good fresh food there? I see that you are a fine young man." The boss offered Leybesh a small room of his own, and Leybesh eagerly seized this opportunity. He wanted to put as much distance as possible between himself and the hotel, Gitele and the child.

That evening Leybesh put away his iron exactly at the moment when it was time to stop work, but the thin, dark-eyed young man who was in charge of him showed no sign of intending to stop. Furthermore, the boss was plucking his beard and asking beseechingly, with such pleading in his eyes, that they should do overtime.

"I don't work on *Shabbes*" he explained to Leybesh "So the time is short and I have to deliver early."

Leybesh hesitated. He was against working overtime on principle, and the *mitzvah* which he would be doing thereby, helping the boss to keep *Shabbes*, did not accord with his philosophy either. But the boss seemed to be such a decent man that he couldn't refuse him, and carried on working until far into the night.

Jack, Leybesh's instructor, banged his iron down, emitting clouds of cigarette smoke through his nostrils at the same time. He was angry

227

with Leybesh for not paying attention and making a mess of the trousers. Either he damped them too much or he ironed them completely dry.

The boss pretended not to hear, and hummed a Hassidic melody to stay awake. He told his oldest daughter Katy to go to bed. But Katy refused the privilege and insisted on working on with the men, glancing at Leybesh all the time she was sewing.

At long last they draped the work over the chairs and went to bed. In the morning, when Leybesh got up and dressed himself, still half-asleep, the boss was already standing with a candle in his hand knocking gently on one of the doors at the front of the house:

"Children, time to get up!" he called softly, in a slightly guilty tone. "It's getting on for seven o'clock."

"Aa-ll ri-i-ight!" From the other side of the door came a drowsy voice, accompanied by a loud yawn.

"Good morning! Why are you up so early?" The boss's wife, carrying a jug of milk, greeted Leybesh with a friendly air. "Did you ever hear anything so stupid? It's not six o'clock yet and he's waking the household. Strangers want to sleep a bit longer, but he won't let them. As if the children don't know his trick! They'll not get up for another hour anyway, so what does he carry on like this for? He's mad, that's all there is to it!" she exclaimed, crossly.

"What does a woman know about it?" the boss retorted. "I simply can't get it into her head that if I tell the truth, the children will turn over and at seven o'clock I'll have to go and wake them all over again! They'll say: 'It's cold, it's foggy, it's dark, let us sleep!'"

"'Let us sleep, let us sleep!'" said his wife imitating her husband and turning a kipper over in the pan.

"Would you like some breakfast?" she asked Leybesh, turning over another kipper.

Leybesh did indeed want something to eat, but the smell of the kippers took away his appetite.

"Well, certainly, I'll drink a glass of coffee if you have it and perhaps a roll."

"Why won't you have a kipper? They're nice! I should be so lucky as to eat them all the time! *My* kippers don't stink the house out, like the neighbour's. I swear the king himself could eat in my house!"

Soon a noise was heard in the corridor, the door opened and several girls tumbled in, one after the other.

"Hello! Not kippers *again?*" exclaimed a girl of about twenty, apparently the youngest.

"All right Sadie dear, tomorrow I'll make something else."

"Tomorrow you'll cook bloaters for a change!"* Sadie laughed, showing a mouthful of little white teeth, pointed like a puppy's.

When she noticed Leybesh she quietened down and sat down at the table. The other girls wandered about the room, looking for something, combing their hair and powdering their noses. Jack came in with his hair standing on end, wearing slippers, with his braces hanging down over his trousers, and his shirt unbuttoned, revealing his thick, black, chest hair.

"Good morning, Sadie!" he said, embracing the youngest daughter, who pushed him away with both hands; squealing with delight and scolding him at the same time:

"Go away, you dirty dog!"

The boy was about to start again, but he saw Leybesh and stopped.

When they had finished eating, the girls drank their tea standing up, shouted goodbye to the world in general, and hurriedly went off to catch the crowded bus or tram to get to their offices.

When they had all left, the old woman sat down to enjoy the peace and quiet. "Ah, thank God for that!" she sighed with relief.

Mr Marks, the boss, put out the lamp and the room was shrouded in darkness. Letting out a screech, his wife got up and lit the gas again. Wisps of fog tinged with a melancholy, greenish colour drifted round the room. Mr Marks combed his sparse beard and the few grey hairs which sprouted from the crown of his head, put on his prayer shawl and phylacteries, and started to pray.

The old woman laid the table, put out a pickled herring, a pickled cucumber and a brown loaf. Leybesh's mouth watered and he took a piece of herring.

"Ah, a real Jew from the old homeland!" said the boss with approval. Seeing Jack going out to get a packet of cigarettes, he continued: "Look at that savage, Jack! He won't even deign to try a piece of

229

herring. And what these children eat isn't to my taste at all. I wouldn't take a hundred kippers for a piece of pickled cucumber."

"Well, we've got to put up with them, we've no choice!" sighed his wife: "Since they're the providers, they're the bosses, can't you see that?"

Mr Marks frowned in embarrassment. He didn't want Leybesh to know that until a few weeks ago he had been living off his children. He made no further comment on that, however.

"This war's a miracle for us!" said the old woman, looking at her husband with disdain.

On Friday evening, Mr Marks invited Leybesh to go to the synagogue with him, and Leybesh accepted, because he had nowhere else to go. Mr Marks was delighted.

"Oh, it's wonderful to meet a real Jew from the old homeland! That Jack would never come to synagogue with m. He'd sell all the prayer houses in the world for a game of football!"

Mr Marks put on a shirt front and cuffs made of paper, found his top hat and off they went.

The synagogue was brightly illuminated by electric lights, and before the Holy Ark hung a velvet curtain which embroidered with real gold thread, which the president of the ladies' group had made herself. On the *bima*,* which looked like the stage of a theatre, stood the cantor, a fat red-faced man in a black frock coat with a starched, white shirtfront. His round, shiny collar looked like a raw bagel which has been simmering and is just about to be popped into the oven. Surrounded by his helpers he gave a speech to welcome the *Shabbes*.

The men of the congregation, who all turned their heads to greet the newcomers, looked more like blocks of wood, than normal Jews.

"Hello, Mr Marks!"

"Good *Shabbes*, good *Shabbes*," replied Mr Marks, smiling with satisfaction, and glancing at Leybesh as if to say "*Now* do you see who I am? Though I'm not well-off, they honour me here in the synagogue as if I was the finest master tailor."

"And who is the young man?" asked a stout man wearing a big gold Star of David on a thick chain. Not waiting for an answer, he went on:

"Aha, Mr Marks, I understand. *Mazl tov*, I congratulate you!",
and to Leybesh he said:

"You're all right with Mr Marks, young man. He is our *Torah*
reader, you know, and not everybody can do that. Well, I certainly
couldn't! Ha, ha, ha!" He laughed merrily at his own shortcomings.

Mr Marks opened his mouth to say something, but changed his
mind: they obviously thought ... but why not, it did no harm to let
them think ....

"That's our president. He's very wealthy, you know!" said Mr
Marks to Leybesh, basking in the reflected glory of the president's
affluence. "He has about twenty workshops. He used to be a simple
tailor, and he can still show his workers how to make a first-class coat."

Going home from the synagogue, Leybesh was amazed at what he
saw. Through the windows of crooked, impoverished little houses,
Shabbes peeked out with an embarrassed air. In the back rooms of the
tiny workshops two or even four brass candlesticks stood on tables
laid for the evening meal. The flames flickered shyly, watching as the
same hands, which an hour ago had covered the women's eyes while
they were saying the blessing for the candles, flew over the army
trousers and tunics, working away skilfully, making buttonholes,
sewing on buttons, pulling out basting threads. The men were sitting
at the machines sewing together chalked pieces of garments, and
pressers were lifting their irons, spitting on them to test the heat, then
banging them down on the finished clothes, so that the flames of the
Shabbes candles jumped and trembled, throwing shadows on the
grubby walls.

In one such room sat an old woman with a tiny, dark-skinned face,
all lines and wrinkles, wearing a black wig. She was playing with a
child. She pretended to touch the candle flame with her thin fingers
and then touched the child's neck with them, each time saying "tickle,
tickle!" The child laughed heartily, trying to imitate the old woman.
She was obviously trying to entertain her grandchild so that the parents could carry on working. The Jews coming home from the synagogue looked in at the work going on in the workshops and were
interested to find out how many employees their various acquaintances had working for them. Unlike Leybesh, who stared in amaze-

231

ment, they were not at all surprised at this activity.

"Why have the women lit candles?" he asked. "Are they religious?"

"Ha, ha! You're just like all the new immigrants! You think it's shocking to work on *Shabbes* with the candles lit? That's the way it is here! Did you see that old woman? When she came from Poland two years ago, she was so shocked that she wanted to run back home. She wept the whole time because people worked on *Shabbes*, and she wouldn't eat at her daughter's house, but now, as you see, she's got used to it all. You'll soon learn, Mr Bruckner, that in London it's very, very difficult to keep *Shabbes*!" concluded Mr Marks with a feeling of superiority.

After they had eaten, Mrs Marks shook out a pile of monkey nuts from a paper bag, put out a dish of oranges, bananas and grapes, and went up to bed, tired out. Mr Marks told Leybesh that he would have to go out again because the association of Jews from his *shtetl* met every Friday evening to study a portion of *Eyn Yankev*.* "And a member can't be an ignorant peasant," he said as he left.

Chapter 26

Berman was prospering. Not only had he been allocated an excellent flat and an allowance, but he was doing good business in Hatton Garden. His time was taken up with buying diamonds. He didn't concern himself with selling, relying on his brokers for that. There were always people keen to buy Berman's goods, because he was a genius at nosing out and snapping up the special bargains. Before other merchants realised that they were selling something for which there would be many eager buyers, Berman saw it in the twinkling of an eye. He would appear, make faces, wrinkle up his nose and ask offhandedly what the price was. Then he would burst out laughing and try to persuade the merchant that he couldn't be serious and was simply having a little joke.

And although the other merchants were also very astute, Berman managed to get the best goods at a low price. He always paid cash, and although the merchants realised that he only bought at knockdown prices, the temptation of his pounds sterling was too strong. They also knew that they had no need to lie awake at night worrying in case he went bankrupt, so they were happy to do business with him. It was also well known that Berman was willing to purchase goods that other merchants didn't want to have lying on their hands, and so it was to their advantage to stay in contact with him.

It was the same with the cutters and polishers he employed. He demanded first class work, but paid rock bottom wages, absolutely sucking the workers dry: no cutter or polisher could make a living by working for Berman, unless he was prepared to work fifteen hours a day. Nevertheless the workers, as in the Antwerp days, fought to be taken on by him, for the simple reason that there was no slack time with Berman, and he did not sack his workers. If a worker was good enough to satisfy Berman, he had a job for life. He never had anything to do with Gentile workers. He did not like their way of doing things nor their way of thinking. They couldn't make any decisions for themselves, but with every trivial issue they ran to consult the secretary of the union and never made a move without his say-so. And when that official made a pronouncement, the employers would burst with frustration as the Gentile workers demanded their rights! (The handful of Jews in the union were no better, however.) For these reasons Berman avoided Gentile workers like the plague. It was a mystery to him why so many Jewish workers were unemployed and desperate for a bit of work, and yet Jewish workshop owners were taking on Gentiles. As a Jew, Berman felt that he had a duty above all to help other Jews to earn their living. No, he decided, God would not punish him for this.

Now that he did not produce his own cut and polished diamonds, he had time to nose around, so he had bought plenty of goods for himself. Occasionally, the thought that perhaps the value of diamonds would indeed fall, crept into his mind, to torment him. He banished this niggling worry with the same decisiveness that he had shown in relation to many different issues where he had not shared the general opinion, but had turned out to be right in the end.

Berman had made one significant change in his life: he had begun to live more modestly, without his customary luxury. He left the three rooms of their flat as the committee had furnished them, without adding to or altering them. And because he had so much free time, and having time hanging heavy on his hands was torture to Berman, he began involving himself in household matters and checked up on every penny which Rochl spent.

Rochl was frequently ill and Berman, undaunted, did the cooking himself. The doctor said she had a weak heart, so she should not work and, especially, should not worry. So Berman bought himself a white smock and demonstrated that his cooking skills were just as good as his ability to trade in diamonds. After all, more than once, he had chopped up fish for his mother when she was busy in her shop. He knew exactly how much pepper, salt, sugar, and bitter almonds one should add. Fish, he had explained to Rochl, should be cooked for three hours, slowly, with not too much water and, most important, uncovered.

On Thursdays he prepared the chicken: he made it *kosher* and scalded it, examining it with the same attention as he devoted to his diamonds, making sure that not a single feather was left on it. He scraped the fish as well, feeling it all over with his hands to make sure that every single scale had been removed. He cut off the head and laid it in a deep bowl so that it couldn't jump out, letting the blood spill. If the head did start to jerk about in its own blood until all the life went out of it, or jumped out onto the floor and lay there dead, then he groaned over the little bit of blood in the same way that he groaned when he thought he had made a bad purchase in the Bourse.

When Jeannette saw the dead fish's head on the floor, she started shrieking, her eyes almost popping out of their sockets: "Papa, I'm going to die! Please don't touch it!"

Jacques, however, liked their new way of life. He had great fun chopping up orange boxes for firewood, and was thrilled to see his father busy in the kitchen, his white smock stained with blood. "Papa, you look just like a *shochet*!" Jeannette objected to this, saying: "Wrong again: he looks like a surgeon."

Berman got the same pleasure out of preparing for *Shabbes* as he had formerly from handing out parcels of diamonds in his office on Pelikaanstraat. Rochl, on the other hand, found it absolutely impossible to follow the doctor's advice not to worry, and of course she wasn't short of things to get agitated about. When she received a card from Dovid, with half the text blocked out by the censor, she got into a state, not believing Dovid's assurances that everything was all right. She wondered what the censor had obliterated. If the post was delayed, she also worried. Then she remembered that she was supposed not to worry, and this worried her all the more.

Furthermore, Jeannette had started behaving in a wholly improper fashion. Rochl was frightened that similar problems to those they had had with Dovid were starting all over again. Jeannette was growing up, and for days on end she didn't come home. Rochl was terrified that Berman would find out. She found the situation very worrying, Jeannette was a beautiful young girl, and she had a wilful and tempestuous nature. Rochl was also uneasy about taking the responsibility of concealing Jeannette's behaviour from Berman, even though her father-in-law had warned her against telling him anything:

"You know that he has a hot temper. With God's help everything will turn out all right. If you forbid her to go out, then she'll be even more determined. It's better to leave her alone. *I* never reined in my children and yet, thank God, they all turned out to be decent people. Take Gedaliah: is he not an honest Jew? Well, he has a bit of a blazing temper, but that's just his nature." With these words the old man tried to comfort his daughter-in-law, but he sighed nevertheless.

Rochl followed her father-in-law's advice and didn't say anything to Berman.

Often there were concerts in the Central Hotel, to which artistes gave their services free; some of them had considerable talent, some none at all - the organisers were not very choosy. Jeannette alone was chosen from amongst the refugees. This was such a huge surprise and honour for her that it almost turned her pretty head.

She bought a pair of wide trousers in striped green velvet, started to smoke cigarettes in a long amber cigarette holder, and wandered round the three rooms of their flat with her long hair loose and flowing over her shoulders, wearing dangling earrings in her dainty, little ears and about a dozen bracelets on her arms. She spoke to no one, but spent her time dancing and rehearsing her part. Her behaviour shocked Rochl.

"Perhaps, God forbid, she has gone mad?" she suggested fearfully to her father-in-law.

At one of these concerts Jeannette made the acquaintance of a young man, a violinist and writer, and fell head-over-heels in love with him. Even though he was the son of a rich factory owner, her lover never had a penny to his name. Before becoming an artist he had worked as a commercial traveller for his father, an Englishman and a Conservative, driving around all day in a big black automobile, supplying mineral water and other drinks to smart restaurants. At one point, however, he met a writer, a cunning person who, having discovered that the young man had literary talent, accepted a good lunch as payment for this insight, smoked the young man's cigarettes, drove around with him in his father's automobile to all the London nightclubs in order to gather material for the young commercial traveller, and the latter began to write.

When he had finished his first novel, the "new talent" abandoned the automobile in the big wet yard of his father's soft drinks factory and walked out of his job, leaving behind a huge pile of unsorted accounts, and went off to the literary café by the Thames. He sat down, stretched out his legs languidly in bohemian fashion and waited there for the writer who had "discovered" him.

This café stood in a lane where baked clay jugs were sold, from which "various pharaohs and kings had drunk mulled wine thousands of years ago". In every other shop window all manner of Egyptian, Roman and Greek gods were for sale. Chinese gods smiled down, revealing huge stomachs with protuberant navels; strings of beads, all of them hundreds of years old, were hanging there, and all sorts of other things lay in a chaotic jumble: stags, elephants, cats and dragons. There was a Madonna holding up the carved folds of her gown, a naked baby Jesus on her arm, and her round, maternal breasts exposed to view. She looked down on her son, a world of warm and holy love in her eyes. And beside her was the Messiah himself, already crucified this time, with congealed blood on his hands and feet. Wealthy factory owners ordered "classical masterpieces" in this lane, which were carved or painted in an attic studio and ready within a week. Artists strolled around in flannel trousers, with sandals on their bare feet, and wild, tousled hair.

The artists' café completed the scene. Jeannette's lover, the ex-commercial traveller, introduced her to it, and she became a frequent visitor and a close friend of the owner: a young woman with sallow cheeks, big, blue-grey eyes and messily painted lips. She wore a hundredweight of beads round her neck and long, dangling earrings swung about and brushed her cheeks as she served the customers. Her black, satin dress had a deep décolleté, revealing her naked back, the cleft between her breasts and various red scratch marks on her freezing body.

This woman was great friends with all the scribblers and failed artists who would sit there for days on end without buying anything, filling the café with smoke, literary trash, envy, scornful, malicious jibes and decadent behaviour. Jeannette got to know this motley group very well, and talked to them in various languages: a little English, a soupçon of French, and a smattering of German. The artists were not absolutely sure what to think of her. The men were all keen to give her a kiss. The old maids who also frequented the café, however, hated Jeannette like the plague. They constantly carried their yellowing, rejected manuscripts around with them, enveloped themselves in blue smoke, shooting out sparks of hatred and refusing to accept her as one of them. Whenever she tried to speak to them, they fixed her with a frozen gaze and a cold smile which revealed their large front teeth.

Ronald, Jeannette's lover, with a salesman's instinct for ingratiating himself, soon fitted in to the café society. He had a pleasant smile, was as elastic and malleable as a snake, and above all, the little bit of education he possessed stood him in good stead. He was soon the best of friends with this group of artists, even the few respected writers and theatre directors among them. He did not, however, have the slightest spark of talent. The novel he had written soon became a joke among the trashy writers and a tribulation for the real writers whom he had already bored to death with it. He had begun to realise that he had no ability, and wanted to go back to the factory, but his father was implacable. He was not prepared to forgive Ronald for not joining up like his other brothers and prove himself to be a good Englishman. He could have excelled as a soldier and brought honour to his parents. The two crimes together had put Ronald beyond the pale as far as his father was concerned. He wouldn't let his son over his threshold and refused to speak to him. Thus Ronald had no choice but to loiter round stage doors or sit for days on end in the café borrowing small sums of money from people, until at last he found a new means of making a living …. Girls began to fall in love with him, one after the other.

Now he hung around with Jeannette, who, as a result, soon got into financial straits, and started racking her brain to think how to get some money out of her father. This created a new problem for Rochl: she had to prevent Berman finding out about his daughter's way of life, and to silence Jeannette, so that she didn't blurt it out to him. So against her will, she gave her money. And Jeannette's financial needs increased from day to day: Ronald had to have good evening meals, theatre tickets and cigarettes. Rochl wept and counted out the money.

The couple strolled around the elegant Oxford Street and Piccadilly, mixing with the leisured rich, with strange, tall ladies and gentlemen who led little curly-haired dogs on leads, with Belgian and French refugees who had nothing to do with their time, with officers and soldiers who were waiting to be sent to the Front and were passing the time by dallying with women of dubious reputation.

Ronald kept nodding to passers-by, and then relating to Jeannette what important people they were:

"The man with the beard is the greatest living English sculptor. That one with the lady beside him is a Lord. And that man with the long hair and the velvet jacket is the famous writer, Pinkerton."

Jeannette was thrilled. She had become infatuated with Ronald and plundered her mother mercilessly.

She particularly liked walking along Oxford Street. She couldn't get enough of staring at the expensive shops, attracted by the satin evening dresses with long trains, white fur cloaks, hats, shoes, socks, gloves and various elegant trinkets which decorated the huge, shiny shop windows. She adored these sumptuous clothes and longed to take them home. She wanted to stroke them and put them on. But she didn't even have enough money to buy a new hat. Ronald took it all.

In the beginning, Ronald's mother had sent him an occasional cheque, but he simply took them without thanking her and asked for more as if it were his right. So she stopped sending him money, and instead tried to persuade her husband that it was wrong to drive out one's own child. She argued that they might still be proud of him in some other way. If he became a writer, for instance, they would have as much honour from that as from the sons who were officers at the Front.

Her heart ached. One day while she was arranging the flowers in the salon, she thought of Ronald. "Who knows if he even has enough money to buy himself his Sunday dinner?" she sighed. That afternoon, when she and her husband were sitting in their comfortable easy chairs beside the glowing fire, she tried to persuade him to take his son back into the business. Her husband laid the Bible down on his knees, took off his spectacles, looked at her with a hard-hearted expression in his clear eyes, moved his pipe into the corner of his mouth and muttered hoarsely between his clenched teeth:

"Never!"

The old lady sighed, and they both started looking at the Bible again, until the old man leaned his grey head back in his armchair and started snoring. Ronald's mother got up, touched her husband's shoulder and suggested in a mild voice: "Would you like to lie on your bed for a while, dear?"

That was the end of her attempt to intervene on behalf of her son, and it was Rochl who had to pay the price for her failure.

Chapter 27

The mood at the Bermans' was gloomy and subdued. In the evenings they sat around with nothing to do except keep warm round the black iron grate. Jacques and the old man went to bed early, Jacques because he was told to, and his grandfather because he was exhausted, though when he got to bed, he couldn't sleep. Only Berman and Rochl stayed up, she with her hands folded in her lap and he with a religious book on his knees, looking like a doddering old man. His heart was heavy. They were waiting and hoping that, for once Jeannette would come back home from the dancing. Both were terrified of what this gallivanting was leading to, but neither admitted this to the other. The experience with Dovid had taught Berman that it was better to stay silent.

Did this mean one had to stay silent even if one's heart was breaking? Yes, it did! So he carried on looking at the book, even though he was taking in nothing at all. The door was the focal point, to which his head turned at every little noise: the door and the clock.

Days and weeks and even months passed like this. Sometimes Berman couldn't take it any more and would lose control and start shouting. Then Jeannette would come running in, rush over to her father and put her hand over his mouth, kiss his beard and talk to him as if to a child:

"Is my little Papa cross then? Papa, dearest, *feh*, that's *naughty!*"

Then she would kiss her mother:

"Poor little mama! Is Papa a naughty boy then?"

Her silly antics made Berman want to laugh, but this feeling lasted only a moment or two, and then his laughter died on his lips. Somehow his daughter was different, her teasing and joking not as spontaneous as it had been in the Antwerp days. She looked more serious and older, a lot older. This ritual, of embracing and kissing, seemed somehow like a performance, as if she were pretending to be impetuous and carefree. He was sure she was hiding something, and he became very perturbed. He didn't smile and stroke his beard with delight as he used to do when his daughter kissed him. Rochl was almost demented with worry: "A young girl like that...."

One night when he was lying in bed, Berman decided that he couldn't let things go on this way. Perhaps, indeed, he *had* been too strict with Dovid and had driven him away. Perhaps, if only he had ... but he couldn't bear to think about that. However, because of that mistake, was he to allow a young girl to wander around all night in a city like London? Perhaps by being too soft he was doing her more harm than he had Dovid: "A young girl like that...."

One day he followed her. In Bloomsbury, opposite the British Museum, he saw her kissing and cuddling with a fair-haired young man, obviously a Gentile. Lying in bed that night he didn't shout at Rochl. For the first time in his life he discussed his fears with her and both of them desperately tried to find some way of separating her from this man. Finally Berman had an idea:

"Do you know what has just occurred to me? We'll get her married, that's what we'll do!" he said to Rochl, delighted with this solution. "You know Rubin?"

"You mean the old bachelor?"

"He's not as old as all that! Furthermore he's just inherited about fifty thousand pounds, and he already has a huge fortune of his own."

"Oh no, he's a really peculiar old man. He has no intention of getting married, and in any case, do you think for one minute that Jeannette would meekly accept him? If someone tried to suggest such a match to her, she'd scratch his eyes out! What an idea!"

"You never know. I'm telling you, Jeannette is perfectly able to appreciate the advantages of having a rich husband. We can at least try."

Rochl burst into tears. "How can we do that to her, in all conscience? She's just a child and he's old enough to be her grandfather!"

"What are you talking about, you stupid woman! Is the *goy* a better match then?"

"Please, Gedaliah, don't rub salt into my wounds. I agree that she mustn't see that man any more, but we can make a better match for a girl like Jeannette, even if we have to give a few thousand francs for a dowry. She doesn't have to take an old dodderer like him! Is she an old maid, is she ugly? You know very well that she's a beauty."

"I know that, but we will try to persuade her to take Rubin. What do you know about it anyway?"

When Jeannette found out from her grandfather that her parents knew whom she was going around with, she actually felt relieved. She had already been trying to find ways of getting rid of her lover. Her feelings had changed towards him and now she really loathed him. Apart from the fact that he was always sponging off her, he had recently started flirting with other girls who came into the café and would leave her sitting alone like a stray dog. Whenever she couldn't give him as much money as he demanded, he shouted at her like a cruel husband. He was vindictive and spiteful. Sometimes he secretly pinched her flesh to hurt her. And he was always threatening to go and make a scene at her parents' house. He didn't really intend to do this at all, but Jeannette believed him, and so she stayed with him, did what he wanted, and felt more and more trapped.

When her father spoke to her of the proposed match, therefore, he was amazed to find that she fell on his neck and sobbed so that he had to comfort her. She swore that she would never see Ronald again:

"You'll see, Papa, I'll stay at home every evening and never leave the house."

Encouraged by this, Berman got in touch with the matchmaker. One Thursday evening in the middle of the bustle of *Shabbes* preparations, when pots full of different foods were cooking on every flame and a comforting red glow shone through every crack in the stove, there was a knock on the door. Berman hastily threw off his white smock, smoothed his beard and called out: "Come in!"

By the time the matchmaker had crept down the few steps which led from the ground floor to their basement flat, Berman was sitting in the wooden chair at the head of the table, reading a religious book and wearing his elegant silk skullcap, which gave him a calm, dignified air.

"Good evening, Herr Berman! What a dark, dismal night. You could, God forbid, get murdered in the street! And these stupid houses have stairs everywhere. They may not have any sense, these English, but they've certainly got stairs. What strange people they are!" grumbled the matchmaker, finding fault with both the houses and the climate.

Berman drew up a chair for him at the table, but he preferred to sit beside the fire.

"Aahhh! It's nice and warm here in your house. In mine, you freeze; no matter how much coal you pour on the fire, the heat just escapes into the street. This is delightful!" Steam rose off the old man into the warm room. His beard and whiskers were wet and he wiped them with the palm of his stiff, old hand and sighed with pleasure.

"So, what have you to tell me, Reb Beynish?"

"Nothing much. He won't hear a word of it. I've already suggested lots of matches for him, but it's like talking to the wall. Do you know what he answered me when I asked him: 'And what about the commandment to be fruitful and multiply?' That he's wiser than the Lord of the Universe!"

But the next day the matchmaker came hurrying back as fast as his old legs would carry him, and even before he got round to unbuttoning his overcoat in order to warm himself at the fire, he blurted out with great satisfaction: "I've managed to persuade him to view the bride!"

"Hmmm! *Managed* to persuade him, eh? I don't believe a word of it! I would be willing to bet that he's so excited about the prospect of seeing her that he won't be able to sleep tonight!"

"Well … perhaps, what does it matter? The main thing is that on Sunday, God willing, he will go to Bournemouth. I've told him that your wife and daughter are staying there for the sake of your wife's health. That's what you wanted, isn't it?"

"Yes, yes, and …?"

"And, nothing! They'll have a look at each other! Neither of them knows what the other is doing in Bournemouth, and so if they like each other, well, it'll all end happily, heh, heh, heh!" The old man took a pinch of snuff from his bone snuffbox, sneezed, tapped the box to shake down the snuff, and offered it to Berman, who refused it politely. Old Reb Chaim Yoysef however, who was sitting there silently, stretched out his healthy hand for a pinch of snuff.

"Here you are, enjoy it in good health!"

"Atchoo, atchoo! Very fine snuff!"

"So the crux of the matter is," said Berman to Rochl, "that you and Jeannette will go to Bournemouth."

"And what about *Shabbes*? Has someone prepared it, then?" asked Rochl.

"What a fool! You can take fish and meat with you. They're very expensive there. Listen, Rochl, you'll have to make sure that Jeannette behaves properly and doesn't make faces or do anything silly. This fellow thinks a lot of himself, and certainly he has got something to boast about."

"Oh, my God!" Rochl laughed and sighed all at once.

Jacques, who had been listening to this, suddenly blurted out: "Well, he's such a youngster, time's on his side, isn't it?" Berman looked at him and was about to shout at him for interrupting when adults were talking, but the mockery in Jacques' intelligent, black eyes, and the bitterness and hatred in his smile, took him aback. He was embarrassed in front of his younger son. He noticed that on Jacques' upper lip there was the trace of a moustache, which intimated that he wasn't a child any more and had the right to interrupt when adults were talking. Berman had a premonition that Jacques' growing up was going cause yet more problems for him.

Jeannette was sitting in the spacious, comfortable lounge of the hotel. She was leaning back in the deep, plush sofa, stealthily smoking a cigarette, and from time to time surreptitiously glancing at the door and blowing out columns of smoke. She had rouged her full lips, which looked like two sweet, moist ripe cherries. Her hair swept down so smoothly from its centre parting that not a single hair escaped to tumble down over her rounded forehead.

A cheerful, bright fire burned in the hearth, the yellow and blue flames licked the coal, leaping and crackling merrily. The lights were reflected in a large, gilded mirror above the mantelpiece, which cast bright splashes onto the dark carpet, creating a festive atmosphere in the luxurious room. Velvet and silk cushions were scattered around on all the sofas and armchairs, and even in the corners of the room, and heavy curtains were drawn over the broad windows. Outside the noise of the sea could be heard. It was a cold day, and the hotel lounge seemed cosy and intimate by contrast.

Rochl appeared at the door of the room with an old man of about sixty, or so he looked to Jeannette. She swiftly stubbed her cigarette out in the ashtray, trying to guess who the man could be. Then she realised. "It's *him*, that old dotard!"

She wanted to burst out laughing: was *this* going to be her husband? "Oh God, whoever has money can get whatever he wants!" she thought.

Her hand went cold when he touched it, but she managed to say: "How do you do, Herr Rubin?"

"Not bad, but what do you think of the weather outside? It eats into your very bones!"

Jeannette invited him to sit down, pulling out a chair for him, but, as the matchmaker had in their house, Rubin sat down right beside the fire, warming his dried-up hands. He "aahhed" in satisfaction, in a cracked, old man's voice. Then, remembering that he had to act young, he broke into a friendly smile.

Jeannette laughed: "Are you cold, Herr Rubin?" He bit his lip and blamed the weather: "It's cold outside!" he repeated.

Not being able to burst into tears here, Jeannette just laughed to herself.

That morning she had walked to the poor part of the town and found a doctor's surgery. In the waiting room, the leather seats of the chairs were shiny and torn, and on a round table lay a pile of old magazines. The waiting room was empty, apart from a young woman wearing a tucked-up skirt, a thin woman, who looked as if she was depressed, and a boy sat beside her, of about twelve years, who had a red nose, greyish skin and the eyes of an old man. His hair was cut very short, almost shaved, except for a tuft of fair hair at the front.

Another patient came in: a small woman in black with a screaming child in a ramshackle pram. The child looked round the room fearfully and stopped crying, managing to control himself like a grownup.

The door of the doctor's consulting room opened and Jeannette was aware of a red face, a white coat and a strip of greenish light. The doctor ushered Jeannette in. After he had interviewed her he asked her to go behind a screen and he admitted the woman with the ten-year-old boy. "Yes, my lad?" he said to the boy, who looked at his mother. "He's coughing, Doctor," she said, "and he has a sharp pain in his left side."

"Well, get undressed, but be quick, for a doctor is a very busy man, my lad!"

The boy tried to get undressed, fumbling clumsily, and the doctor repeated: "Yes indeed, Mrs Brown, nowadays a doctor is a very busy man" for the benefit of the smart lady in the fur coat, by whose visit he felt honoured.

"Oh yes, I realise that," agreed Mrs Brown, nodding her head.

He put the stethoscope to the boy's chest, making him repeat "ninety-nine" again and again. The little boy stood half-naked, holding his trousers in his grubby hands, looking timidly at his mother and the doctor and trembling with cold. The doctor went into an anteroom and came back with a bottle of brown chicory water.

"Give him this three times a day, and come back in a few days' time!"

He took two shillings from her and came to examine Jeannette.

"There's nothing wrong with you, Madam, you're pregnant; that's all."

Jeannette's legs gave way and the doctor caught her in his arms.

"Sit down, Madam! Why are you so shocked?"

"I don't want to have a child! Suppose I wanted to get rid of it ... I mean ..." stammered Jeannette.

"No! I don't do that sort of thing. It's a criminal offence, Madam!"

Jeannette felt faint and everything went black before her eyes. The doctor laid her on the couch and gave her some drops. When she came to herself she started sobbing so violently that the doctor became anxious. But there were patients waiting, so he left her resting behind the screen and went back into his consulting room to carry out his duties.

Later he came back and put the stethoscope to her chest. "Better?" he asked.

Jeannette was still sobbing.

"Listen, Madam, that's not going to solve anything. You must see that he marries you!" said the doctor, who realised what the situation was. "Are you from these parts?"

"No!" sobbed Jeannette. She paid the doctor, who stroked her soft fur coat as he accompanied her out of his consulting room.

When Jeannette came back to the hotel, Rochl didn't know what to do with her daughter, who sat all day on the sofa in the corner of the room lost in thought, refusing to eat anything. She knew she had to control herself, which she did, like an older and more experienced person, like her father when he was negotiating over diamonds. Then she started laughing, and couldn't stop.

"Do you still feel still cold, Herr Rubin?"

"When I look at you, I feel warm!" said Rubin, rubbing his hands together, feeling pleased that he had managed to transform himself so cleverly from a frozen old man warming his cold bones at the fire, into a prospective bridegroom talking amorously to his fiancée.

"In that case I must come nearer, so that you can have a good look at me."

She stood up and, smoothing down the dress over her stomach as if she were brushing off crumbs, she came over to the fire and sat down beside Rubin. The bridegroom smiled with delight.

Jeannette was looking even more beautiful than usual that day. She had smoothed cream into her olive-skinned face, and had combed, stroked and caressed her hair as if it too had been weeping. In the light of the standard lamp with its green shade, she looked extraordinarily beautiful. Her anxiety gave her a serious expression and seemed to reveal more delicate traits in her young face.

"She's not just beautiful, she is clever as well," decided Rubin.

A tall waitress with a white cap on her fair hair announced that dinner was served. Rubin called her back and demanded she wipe over the chair again before he sat down, even though there wasn't a speck of dust to be seen on its gleaming surface. Jeannette herself tucked the napkin into Rubin's collar as if he were a child.

"You know, Fräulein Berman, the napkin is poking into my neck a little," he said coyly, like a flirtatious young man, in order to get Jeannette to come over to him again. She stood beside him once more and adjusted the napkin, touching his scrawny neck with her soft warm hand. Rubin started sweating with embarrassment and pleasure.

"*Ay*, what a girl! She's certainly worth getting married for!"

Having finished the grapefruit, which was bitter and tasteless, Rubin ate the main course, liver and onions, with great enjoyment and felt on top of the world. Through his thin cheeks one could see every little bit of bread being chewed, and his Adam's apple jumped around in his throat. His napkin kept falling from his collar, and now it lay on his knees. He never took his eyes off Jeannette. He felt his tired old blood coursing round in his veins, bathing him in a pleasurable warm glow. He observed how Jeannette held her knife and fork in her long, beautifully manicured fingers, and how elegantly she ate. "She's a real lady too," he thought.

It occurred to him that she was bound to laugh her head off at him and mock him mercilessly when she found out why he was here. But she was smiling at him so warmly, so charmingly, and yet there was an earnestness about her; he thought that she really must be in love with him. He glanced at himself in the mirror opposite: "Hmm! Why not?"

He saw his long face and fine white hair. He looked intelligent, which was not surprising: hadn't he read a great many books? What a lot of reading he did in the course of one of his sleepless nights! And of course that was visible in his face.

"My word, the little lady certainly has good taste. She knows what she wants!" And gradually he became more and more confident of his success.

When Berman arrived in Bournemouth in the middle of the week and began sounding out his daughter, he couldn't believe his own ears: "Rochl, it's going to be all right! Go and talk to her, strike while the iron's hot. He is certainly keen enough!"

Rochl wiped away a tear. "Gedaliah, think for a moment! She's just a child. He could be her grandfather!"

"What a heartless creature," she thought. "He's thanking God that his daughter did not lose her temper and make a huge scene as he had expected. That's all he's interested in." And she carried on bargaining with him.

Berman lost his temper: "Look, stop playing stupid tricks, trying to get round me by making eyes at me. Just go and talk sense to her, if you have any yourself, that is. If you don't, then she can just go off and marry the *goy*, do you hear? This fellow is an extremely wealthy man. So stop whining, you stupid cow!"

Rochl's legs were trembling. A young girl like her ... Berman was a brute. He was just using this *goy* as an excuse! Jeannette wasn't even seeing him, she had been sitting all day at home, and *he* was using this as an excuse to sell off his own child.

Rochl felt a strange pain in her heart. Somehow today Berman's brutal language had really stung her, even though she had got used to it over the years; apart from when they were in bed, she never heard a kind word from him. But somehow today it really hurt her.

"You go and talk to her yourself! Then it'll be your fault if she starts making a scene in a strange place! If you want to sell her, go and sell her yourself. What do you want of me?" Because they were in a strange place, Rochl actually dared to stand up to him.

Chapter 28

"So what shall I tell him?" Rochl asked her daughter again, hoping that perhaps she might think better of her decision. Jeannette looked at her mother, longing to pour out her heart to her, tell her the truth and ask her advice. She could see that her mother was dismayed and grieving that her daughter was going to marry the old man. Jeannette thought for a long time, but still could not summon up the courage, and instead shouted in hysterical anger: "What are you standing there for? I have *told* you I'm going to marry him. I like him! I like him! I like him, and if you don't like it you can go to hell!" She started laughing like a mad woman: "Tell him that I find him attractive and I want him! Do you hear me?"

Rochl was horrified. She was sure that her daughter had lost her mind and she started to cry.

"Well, what's the news?" Berman was pacing back and forth on the soft carpet of the neighbouring room, waiting. He had heard his daughter laughing and his wife weeping, and had even peered through the keyhole, but had only taken in disjointed fragments of conversation.

"I think she has gone mad. I tell you, she's ill, she doesn't know what she's saying. She says she wants him, that she's yearning for him. Or perhaps, like you, she really believes she *has* to sell herself to that old carcass," said Rochl, turning her rage on the fiancé.

"Is that so? Well, it looks as if I did know what was right for her after all! I always said that, with God's help, I would be proud of her!"

"Proud of her!" Rochl turned away from him. "Well, it's all the same to me now. My heart's broken in any case. This is just the last straw."

Berman went in to see his daughter.

"*Mazl tov* to you Jeannette, my dear daughter!"

He embraced her, pressing her in his big strong arms like a lover,

251

kissing her on the cheeks and forehead.

"You don't know how happy you're going to be. You will be the richest woman in Antwerp when, God willing, we return home after the war. And in London there aren't many husbands with hundreds of thousands of pounds in their pockets either!"

Jeannette wept all night, and then stopped. Gradually she began to convince herself that it was a good match after all. Nevertheless she kept running from one doctor to another, getting the same answer everywhere she went:

"That's a criminal offence, Madam!"

So she started trying to find some way to speed up the wedding, not realising that her father, afraid she might change her mind, was doing this in any case.

At the engagement party, Jeannette sat at the head of the table, wearing a black, silk dress which shimmered in the electric light. Her fiancé looked really festive in his new suit, with neatly combed white hair, polished pince-nez and elegantly manicured fingernails. The skin of his face had a brownish tinge, the tiny blue veins on his temples were pulsating and his rather elongated nostrils quivered. He sat beside Jeannette, wallowing in delight.

A girl like this, fresh and innocent, this was what he had been waiting for all the time. These idiots of matchmakers just hadn't understood what he meant when he said that he didn't want to get married because he didn't trust modern girls. They thought he was just making excuses. But *this* one was different! Such a sweet child; just weaned off her mother's milk, a young sapling, slender and graceful, a new Queen Esther. Yes, it really had been worth waiting. There was only one thing which spoiled his pleasure: he was angry with his prospective father-in-law.

Every time the large diamonds on Jeannette's long fingers and the brooch in her décolleté flashed, he felt a new surge of anger. Berman had insisted on selling the stones to him, and had demanded a ridiculous price, as if he, Rubin, had been a simple schoolmaster and not a diamond merchant himself. But what could he do, when Berman fastened onto him like a leech? *Oy*, what a sum he had had to pay for these diamonds! Oh well, he consoled himself, it was too bad, but for a girl like that anything was worth it. That father-in-law of his was a bastard, but never mind! And to console himself all the more, he kept running his cold, dry fingers over Jeannette's bare back. Jeannette shuddered.

The matchmaker was also there. In honour of his great triumph he had, for once, taken off his overcoat with its sheepskin collar, and was sitting at the table in a greasy, greenish frock coat with two worn buttons over the split in the back.

Rochl had dressed herself up. She smoothed down her best *Shabbes* wig and smiled at the bridegroom as bashfully as if she had been the bride, while Berman sat stroking his silky beard, trying not to see how the old rogue never took his hand off Jeannette's back for one moment, and how his daughter vainly kept trying to move away.

The hotel owner helped to bring in the supper. She was a small pale woman with a little snub nose and light grey, widely spaced eyes. A piece of sticking plaster covered a spot which had appeared on her forehead, but despite this she was an attractive woman. She never took her eyes off the bridegroom, thinking that this was the kind of match she herself would have liked to make.

The matchmaker looked her over thoroughly, knowing that she was a widow.

"Hmm ... not a bad-looking woman! We'll have to do something for her." Today Reb Beynish was confident that whatever match he undertook to negotiate would have a successful outcome.

Shapiro sat opposite the bridal couple. He was sighing with envy - look what money could achieve! *He* had sold himself to an ugly bitch for money, and here was a father selling his lovely daughter - such a beautiful young girl being wasted on an old blackguard like that!

Madame Shapiro envied the bride. In her view, a woman should always take a husband who was a lot older than herself. "Certainly, today's young women have sense," thought Madame Shapiro wistfully.

"It's agreed then. The wedding, God willing, will be at the beginning of the month of *Adar.** So let's drink another toast!" Berman raised his glass above his head. "*L'chaim!** To the bride and groom! *L'chaim!*"

Everyone in Hatton Garden knew about the engagement. When Berman went in the next day, dozens of hands stretched out to congratulate the lucky father, whose business was now doubly secure.

"*Mazl tov!* May the marriage be successful!"

"That kind of luck doesn't happen often!" confirmed all the merchants.

"Who would have thought that Rubin would get married!" the fathers of grown-up daughters said enviously to each other.

"I hear that Rubin has been unusually generous?" said Kuper, coming to greet Berman with a smile and a *mazl tov*. "Those diamonds must have been a nice surprise, eh?"

Berman stared at him: "What do you mean?"

"Oh, nothing at all. The setter showed them to me, that's all. After all, no one would give a bungler stones of *that* quality to set, so they want people to know about it."

"Indeed? So he is showing *my* stones all over the place? Nice to know! Those workers have nothing better to do than gossip!" said Berman, thereby betraying what Kuper knew already, namely that he had sold his own diamonds to the bridegroom.

Old Reb Mordecai sat down at Berman's table. "*Mazl tov* to you, Herr Berman! May God bless this union! God willing, you should have joy of your only daughter!"

Berman smiled, thinking: "He probably thinks I'll take out my purse and hand him a fiver, the old ruffian."

When Rubin came to Hatton Garden a few days later, the same ritual repeated itself; outstretched hands, *mazl tovs*, hidden smiles and unspoken jests.

Rubin glowed. Let them burst with jealousy. Some merchants who were much younger than he had landed up with wives who were already bloated, faded old women, and here was he, Rubin, with a lovely young girl.

The wives of the diamond merchants were making more extravagant preparations for the wedding than the bride's mother. Each one wanted to outdo the others, and they all spent days going round the expensive shops in the West End.

Meanwhile, the war was raging. Young, middle-aged and even elderly men, among them many Jews, were besieging the recruiting offices to volunteer "for King and Country." Columns of uniformed recruits marched through the streets, their thin legs wrapped in khaki puttees. Their army boots were new and shiny, and their eyes shone with a mysterious glow - the anticipation of victory. They were fresh-faced and happy, as if they were going to a ball, and as they marched, their hob-nailed boots ringing rhythmically on the road, they merrily sang: "It's a long way to Tipperary ...."

Both Gentile and Jewish women and girls on the pavements stared at the soldiers with admiration and curiosity. Elderly women turned their failing eyes heavenwards and piously asked for blessing on them, their thin lips murmuring prayers that God should protect the "boys." Girls blew kisses to them which the soldiers caught with their hands, and returned in the same way. Then their song rang out even more loudly: "... it's a long wa-a-y to g-o-o-o-o ..."

The sky had now cleared a little, revealing patches of blue here and there among the masses of heavy clouds. On windy days, wide tracts of sky appeared ... and the soldiers carried on marching.

Rochl and her daughter had samples cut from different silks, velvets and laces, and Berman inspected everything and gave his verdict. Not relying on the women's judgement, he accompanied them when they went to buy furs. The amount of money he was spending did not concern him at all. "She must have a dowry which is fitting for Berman's only daughter!"

Jeannette tried on the clothes, twirled in front of the mirror and was absolutely delighted with herself. Her passion about clothes made her forget her situation, her fiancé and everything else. She floated around among silk and satin, raised her arms and spread them out as if she were about to fly off, making the silk shimmer, when suddenly she felt a sharp pain in her side. For the first time she felt nauseous, retched, and started vomiting. Her eyes were bulging and streaming with tears. The dress was stained.

"Jeannette, what's the matter with you? God forbid you should be ill!"

"I'm ...." Before Jeannette was able to reply, she had to be sick again.

By the time she arrived home she looked green and gaunt, as if she had lost pounds during those few moments. A thought crept into Rochl's mind, but she tried to banish it: "*Feh!* How can I suspect such a thing! Since Dovid's been away there have been ill winds blowing round our home. I must stop this: just thinking dark thoughts can bring on bad luck."

But nevertheless she sensed misfortune creeping closer, like a venomous snake. "*Feh, feh!*" However much she tried to banish the thoughts from her tormented mind, the heaviness lay on her heart. Without exactly knowing why, she suddenly began to feel relieved that her daughter was getting married, even if it was to old Rubin.

The wedding day arrived. The large room was brightly illuminated by electric lights, shaded by yellow bowls, which hung from the ceiling. The light was gently diffused over white tablecloths, glowing silverware and vases of flowers, which stood all along the tables. It lingered on the powdered faces of the women, and on their bare arms, breasts and shoulders, making these boldly exposed bodies look very white. The light awakened the glittering fire in diamond earrings, bracelets, brooches and necklaces, and made white shirtfronts and bow ties appear more dazzling. The tailcoats and silk skullcaps on the men's heads appeared even darker by contrast.

Jeannette and her bridegroom stood in the wide doorway welcoming guests, smiling at them, kissing them, smiling again, kissing again.

Then the guests sat down to the meal. Jeannette sat there tightly corseted and pressed her lips together so that she would not be sick.

Afterwards the couples went into the ballroom and danced, whirling to the music. Burly men pressed their fat fingers into even fatter female backs, young men had their arms round the waists of slender girls. Then suddenly, before she had time to reach the anteroom, the bride vomited violently in the middle of the dance floor. The music stopped and the couples stood rooted to the spot, as if turned to stone, with arms around waists and hands on backs.

This frozen silence lasted for a moment, then noise and confusion broke out. Rochl was wringing her hands and the bridegroom turned as white as a sheet. His right leg started trembling like it belonged to a very old man. People were fetching water, vinegar, lemonade and chairs. Rochl felt she was about to collapse, which would cause yet another scene. Her previous suspicions had now turned to certainty and only her dread of the imminent scandal enabled her to stay on her feet.

Berman alone did not lose his head. Looking pale, he came in from the dining room where he and some other pious Jews, who were not joining in the dancing, had been sitting at the tables, conversing. With his new black frock coat, dazzling white shirtfront and elegant, long beard, he was an imposing figure. He advanced with measured tread towards the chair where the bride sat.

The room went deathly still.

"I told you," he said, addressing Rochl, "that she shouldn't be allowed to fast! You know this always happens! But she is a stubborn lass," he finished in a fatherly tone, stroking his daughter's head and the white tulle of her veil. "Oh well," he carried on, addressing his wife: "it is her wedding day after all and because she really *wanted* to fast, the *mitzvah* will be all the greater." He even managed to smile.

The women stopped staring and even the bride smiled, strengthened by her father's reassurance. His words freed her from the fear that people would suspect. She threw back her veil, powdered her face again, and the rest of the wedding passed off smoothly.

Though Berman was now fairly certain what the situation was, he started grilling Rochl as if she had been the bride, insisting that she should find out the whole truth from Jeannette.

Rochl protested. Perhaps Jeannette was simply unwell. How could she voice such a suspicion to her daughter? Jeannette would bite her head off. But Rochl's fears were unfounded, for instead of biting her head off, Jeannette put her arms round Rochl's neck, and in floods of tears, she begged her mother to help her and tell her what she should do.

When Rochl got back home from Jeannette's, she crept into her bed with all her clothes on and wept until she had no more tears left.

Berman came in from Hatton Garden that evening with his pockets full of cards of congratulations and his heart full of apprehension - as if he were weighed down by stone instead of his diamonds. What would happen if his suspicion turned out to be true? He would have a grandchild from a *goy*. And how far gone was she? What would his son-in-law say? What would the world say? He still hoped that Rochl would meet him with a beaming smile and scold him for his suspicions: this time he'd be happy to be the fool.

However, seeing Rochl lying in bed still wearing her clothes, not even having taken off her coat, he shuddered and woke his wife.

Rochl opened her eyes wide and stared at her husband for a moment or two as if she didn't recognise him, then started rubbing her red eyes.

"Now come on then! Out with it! Come on! Tell me!"

Rochl carried on rubbing her eyes. One of her cheeks was as red as fire, the other creased and pale as death. During the last couple of hours, all that she had suffered over the years had appeared in her face. She had, all at once, turned into an old woman.

"No! No!" yelled Berman. "So I'm to have no pleasure from my disgusting brats! Whenever there's a celebration in other families, they laugh with joy. In this household, we weep. They should both have perished in your womb. *You* should have perished before I met you. Let her be struck down on the spot. She and her bastard should die a horrible death, right now, this very day! And I hope that he doesn't come back. It would be for the best if a bullet finished him off over there!" Berman broke down and sobbed like a woman.

Rochl's eyes were dull, lifeless and unseeing; everything had grown dark. All she heard was Berman's torrent of curses against his own children - against Dovid. She listened to his sobbing.

Jeannette carried on seeking a solution to her problem, but all the doctors gave her the same answer:

"It's a criminal offence!"

She tried bring up the topic delicately in conversation with other young wives, expressing the opinion that it was better not to have a baby too soon after getting married, that one should have the chance of having a good time with one's husband first, because apart from anything else, Jeannette asserted, having a baby really ruined one's figure.

The women all agreed with Jeannette and gave her lots of advice. She tried everything, but nothing worked. A piece of iron would have melted, but still the baby lay contentedly in Jeannette's womb, as if these efforts didn't concern it at all. Time was marching on and it began to look as if she would give birth six months after getting married.

She tried to talk to her mother, who just looked at her in a way that made her flesh creep.

Quite unexpectedly, however, her maid Mary saved her mistress, Jeannette's parents, and her husband from a great misfortune. Jeannette had occasion to tell her that she was not doing her work well. She said it in a kindly fashion, because her own situation made her more considerate of her maid's weaknesses. The maid promised that in two or three weeks she would be able to work like a horse, and that her present lethargy was because she had just had treatment in a clinic.

"What's wrong with you?" asked Jeannette.

"*Now* there's nothing at all wrong with me," sighed Mary, and, kneeling on the floor with a scrubbing brush in one hand and a piece of carbolic soap in the other, she told her mistress that her "young man" had left her to join the army, when she was three months gone. "He had nothing to eat, the poor devil, so he had to join up, but I was left in that state – so what could I do? I had to get rid of it," the girl explained, and a tear dropped into the soapy water.

Jeannette's eyes lit up. "And have you actually done it?"

"I had to!"

"Who does that, Mary? Tell me, my dear!" Jeannette went into one of her affectionate moods and started kissing her maid as she used to kiss her father's beard.

Mary thought her mistress had gone mad.

"Mary, I'll give you two pounds if you let me have the person's address!" insisted Jeannette.

"Madam, it's illegal, I can't!"

"Mary, I'll never mention it to a living soul, I swear! Come on, give it to me!" and she pressed two pounds into the maid's hand. Mary, trembling, gave her the address.

"I wouldn't have done it," she carried on, trying to justify her actions, "if my mother could have looked after the child, but my father has joined the army too, he just left my mother with all the children and went off, and she has to go out washing floors. So what else could I do?"

Jeannette went there with her maid. The "clinic" consisted of a middle-aged woman with a wrinkled face, thin grey hair and a strange, unpleasant glint in her eyes. At first the woman, frightened off by Jeannette's fur coat, wouldn't hear of it and couldn't remember having met Mary. "I don't do such things!" she protested. But Jeannette offered a fee that the woman could not refuse, and it was arranged that she should come to Jeannette's house.

When Rubin came home that evening, his young wife was lying in bed. The doctor whom the old woman had brought with her, explained to Rubin that his patient had fainted. Now the danger was past but she must rest, and on no account get out of bed yet. Rubin was bewildered; "A child like her, being so ill?" he thought. He ordered a car and rushed off to tell his parents-in-law about Jeannette's illness. Berman glanced at Rochl and started to say: "May she ..." He was about to burst out with an oath again, but managed to stop himself and accompanied his son-in-law to visit his sick daughter.

Jeannette looked gaunt and exhausted. Her maid, Mary, was attending to her. She put the florins and half-crowns* which her mistress had given her into her bosom, and kept silent.

Jeannette smiled weakly at her parents and husband.

"Well, at least the problem's solved, that's the main thing," growled Berman when they got back home. "But that slut isn't my daughter any more. I don't want to have anything more to do with her. That ... that ..." He trembled. He was full of conflicting emotions.

Rochl could not cut herself off from her daughter, and as any mother would, she went every day to look after her during the period of her recovery. She wandered round the luxurious rooms of Jeannette's house, spitting to drive out the evil eye and weeping incessantly.

Jeannette smiled weakly but affably at her husband. She let him kiss her endlessly and did not even wipe her lips with her hand afterwards. She was as sweet and nice to him as she had been just after their wedding, with the difference that then she had used her charms to keep the old fellow in a state of perpetual excitement, whereas now she didn't allow him into her bed. She had the excellent excuse that the doctor had forbidden it.

Rubin, believing her, groaned with disappointed resignation. He had waited for so many years for a wife, and now, when he had tasted such bliss, he was again deprived of it. He hoped that she would get better, and in the meantime he consoled himself with the fact that he had a home and a faithful, loving wife. Rubin had always been a quiet man, who had never talked about himself, but he suddenly became loquacious and bored everyone with endless accounts of Jeannette's merits.

"Let me tell you, after waiting so long, I've found a wonderful woman! Do you know how much she loves me? I come home and find my wife in bed, looking so ill that I nearly faint from shock myself. When I say to her: 'You silly, little woman, why did you not send for me? I would have rushed home immediately,' she just smiles like a little child, with such affection in her eyes that your heart would melt, and says so lovingly: 'sweetheart, I didn't want to frighten you.' I'm her 'sweetheart'! Even though she's an only child she doesn't have a crumb of egotism in her nature. You don't find that nowadays. Most women today run around all day nibbling sweets, stuffing themselves and flirting. Even though they are as healthy as horses, they're constantly mollycoddling themselves and running to doctors. And there's my wife lying ill in bed, and she doesn't even send for her husband because she doesn't want to frighten him. Such an innocent child - she knows nothing of all those womanly wiles, she just knows that it's a wife's duty to look after her husband the way our mothers used to do."

261

Chapter 29

Leybesh had long since stopped working for Mr Marks, the "Torah reader", and had gone to work in a large workshop in the West End. He was a proper presser now, not just an under-presser. The firm was flourishing. The electric motors and two long rows of sewing machines in the long bare hall were humming and vibrating all day. The girls' crooked, pricked fingers flew and the needles flashed as they sewed khaki trousers for the soldiers. The foreman drove them on.

"Hurry up, faster! it doesn't matter if you miss a stitch. The main thing is: get a move on! The trousers don't have to be perfect. They're only for lying in the trenches with - as long as we get them done!"

The girls worked their fingers to the bone and sang all kinds of sentimental and bawdy war songs to fight their exhaustion and to drown out the clattering of the machines, the dull thumps of the heavy irons, and the hissing steam spreading round the room. So the needles flew over the work and the girls told stories about their flirtations with soldiers standing by the walls of buildings and lying on the grass in Hyde Park. They laughed and joked about it openly, without any feelings of shame or embarrassment, as if they wanted to experience life now, and felt they had a right to, because their fiancés might well die on the battlefield and they would die as old maids. Those who were children now would grow up and get married, but they, the girls sewing the trousers, in which their own fiancés might die, would be left all alone.

So they sang and laughed and kept throwing more pairs of trousers onto the huge heap of finished work which lay on the floor in the middle of the room, waiting to be ironed. Beside them was stacked another pile of already pressed trousers, which Leybesh and his comrades added to all the time. The foreman would come and inspect them, giving his verdict: "All right, these'll do for fighting in. Faster now, come on!"

As they worked and sang and laughed, the machines clattered and the irons thumped and the girls' voices mingled with the general din:

"I want some lo-o-o-o-ve just right now ...."

Leybesh worked all week and in the evenings he went to English language classes. He was the best student in the class, and the teacher was very pleased with him. As soon as the teacher saw him coming into the cold, green room with, high, barred windows, his lips drew back into a smile which showed his teeth.

"Good evening, Mr Bruckner. You're early again this evening!"

Leybesh was pleased and embarrassed all at once, like a schoolboy:

"Well, I've got nothing much else to do so I just came here." Leybesh sat down at one of the long empty tables.

The teacher started organising the books and exercise books, but there was still no one there apart from Leybesh. Eventually a few refugees trickled in, all older people, as the young people had better things to do in the evenings. The room remained almost empty and the lamps burned brightly under their green tin shades, making the room look like a hospital.

The lesson began. It really was very simple: how could anyone not grasp it?

"I remember, I remember,
The house where I was born ...."*

Even so, they just couldn't manage to learn it off by heart. Someone would start and say the first few words, but couldn't continue. Just as he nearly had it, the words flew away like a bird when you're about to catch it. Leybesh was the only one in the class who could soon speak English. He was very well informed about politics. He read all the English papers with the help of a dictionary. If people in the hotel were arguing about politics, they would look round for Leybesh: "It's a shame Mr Bruckner isn't here! He would soon tell you that I'm right!" Each person was certain that Leybesh would assure him that he, and not the other person, was right.

But Mr Bruckner was never there. He was working, studying, thinking. Recently he had been thinking a great deal.

Whenever he had a little free time, he would walk round the streets, and cover every inch of Hyde Park. He really loved this vast

263

unkempt park in the most affluent district of London. It lay there like a slovenly housekeeper, with all its possessions scattered around. The benches were all over the place and the deckchairs were not in rows like in other parks, but spread around in a higgledy-piggledy fashion. The trees also grew where they pleased, popping up here and there, all over the place. There was a huge, grassy area which lay empty under a cold, grey sky in the winter days, and in summer was covered with people, young men and girls, who rolled around wantonly on the grass, free to do as they liked, as if they were in their own bedrooms. Their ringing laughter could be heard all around.

On Sundays Leybesh felt he was at a fair. Early in the morning he walked like a leisured gentleman in Rotten Row. On the long stretch of well-trodden earth, rode ladies and gentlemen in black close-fitting riding coats, with stiff hats on their aristocratic heads, and shiny, elegant boots on their feet. Both the ladies and gentlemen wore riding breeches, so that it was difficult to tell the difference between them. They rode along in the fresh early morning air, on glossy horses with small hooves, dainty, intelligent faces and eyes which seemed to sparkle with laughter. Some galloped, while some walked slowly alongside each other, the riders chatting and laughing. Their laughter was so melodious, merry and carefree, that you would have thought there was no war on at all.

Leybesh stared and stared at them, then he spat in disgust and walked off to the "madhouse" at Hyde Park Corner.* Listening to the speakers, he didn't *entirely* agree with the entrenched pacifist standing on a soapbox, bawling his head off. The man was trying to make such important points that he wanted everyone to hear them. He tried to drown out the neighbouring speakers who were standing less than three feet away from him. He was sweating, the veins in his temples and long skinny neck stood out as thick as rope, and his wrinkled skin was brick red. But he had a calm expression on his face, and he even smiled at the dissenting shouts from members of the public. He seized the moment when the listeners were quiet and continued:

"Don't you see the stupidity of it? You'll join up, you'll be crippled, you'll be flayed like a carcass, or you'll die. Your children will be orphans, your wives widows, or perhaps even the mistresses of those

264

for whom you have sacrificed yourselves. It is an imperialist war. The capitalists are fighting each other; what they steal from us every day, they are now trying to pinch from each other. And they send *us*, the victims of their theft, into the battlefield to fight their wars for them. They convince us that it's 'for King and Country', and even if it were, what has all that to do with us? Whose 'country' is it? Not ours, at any rate. Do we get a great deal from the country? All we have is the right to work our fingers to the bone and to starve. And if we can't get any work, then they just let us die like dogs. They take the cream. They send their children to university – they should send the brats off to the battlefields and let *them* get butchered. What can they do to you, if you refuse to go? The worst they can do is put you in jail. Well, I ask you, is it not better to sit out the war in prison, and then come home to your wives and children as healthy men, and be able to start your lives again? What have you got to lose?"

Voices in the crowd shouted:

"Get him off! He's a traitor! He's betraying his own country! He's a spy! Arrest him: he wants the Kaiser to win the war. String him up!"

"Comrades!" shouted Leybesh suddenly, "Friends! Just one word! A single word!"

The din was deafening but someone shouted:

"Let him speak! Let's hear what he has to say!"

It was impossible to say how or why it happened, but suddenly everything went so quiet you could hear a pin drop, and Leybesh started speaking:

"Friends! Everyone is shouting the same thing: defend your own country! Certainly we have to defend ourselves. We should remember though, that the world belongs to those who toil, those who build it. Only those people and nobody else have the right to enjoy the fruits of their labour."

Clapping was heard. The pacifist shouted "Down with the war-mongers!"

"Go to Rotten Row," continued Leybesh, "and you'll see healthy young men galloping around on horses, flirting with girls, breathing in the fresh air, in order to sharpen their appetite for all the good food, which someone else prepares for them."

The policeman on duty was listening with a quiet smile. It didn't cross his mind to put a stop to any of the speakers. Let them talk, what did it matter? The English policeman had broad shoulders.

Beside the skinny pacifist stood another Englishman, a tall, hefty, fresh-faced man with ruddy cheeks, he stood on a tiny, wobbly platform. He spoke in a relaxed manner, with a clear voice. From time to time he wiped his face with a clean handkerchief and smiled with sparkling, blue eyes. He preached nationalism, arguing that it was the sacred duty of every Englishman worthy of the name to join the army and defend his homeland:

"It is your sacred duty to fight to the last man for your King and your country," he said, warming to his topic, "If you want to be worthy to bear the name of Englishman. Think of Lord Nelson!" He looked round triumphantly, with a smile, which seemed to say, "Can anyone claim that I am not correct?"

Again there were clapping and shouts of "hear, hear!" and of "down with him!"

The pacifist urged one of his supporters to cause a bit of a riot to drown out his opponent.

Slightly further off, a young Indian doctor was speaking. He had white, even teeth and large, laughing, black eyes, whose whites looked dazzling in his dark face. He maintained that it was the duty of all good Indians to make use of this moment of opportunity and fight heroically for India's liberation.

A bit further on a young Jew with a gold pince-nez on his fat white nose was talking, more with his hands than with his mouth, which had thick crimson, girlish lips. He was explaining how important it was for the Jewish people to have their own Jewish legion.

A priest with a shiny, round collar was saying that in a time of war, people should go to church more often. There was a nun with a dark, wrinkled face, in a black habit and veil, and someone with a long grey beard, whose thesis was that he was a member of the ten lost tribes, and that, although he was not a Jew, he was really a Jew. "We," he insisted, "are the only true Jews." Taking his sparse beard, which reached his waist, in both his skinny hands, he swore that this was true.

Mrs Pankhurst was also speaking, surrounded by hundreds of women and a few men. She stood there, speaking with great feeling:

"We will not rest, we will not stay silent, we will speak and agitate, never letting the matter rest and never resting ourselves, until they give equality to us women. Did you see how our dear friend threw herself in front of horses and was trampled to death in order to draw attention to our cause? We are prepared to bring many, many more sacrifices in order to liberate women, and we *will* liberate them!"*

Voices were heard:

"Hear, hear!!"

"Good old Mrs Pankhurst!!!"

Chapter 30

It was the winter before the Armistice. The city was shrouded in fog all winter long. The sky was hardly ever visible. When it occasionally did manage to free itself from the fog, it looked like a heavy sheet of iron, which was just about to fall on the city, and its people, destroying both.

Berman had already bought a great deal of goods. He had decided he was not going to buy anything, apart from rare bargains, and he was not going to sell, but rather wait and see. He was not worried about how much the market in diamonds was going to fall; he did not fear for *his* goods. But it was prudent to live frugally nevertheless.

He was content in his warm house, which seemed even cosier because of the bad weather outside. Since he didn't have anything else to do, he sought useful occupations for himself. He put on his white smock and busied himself during the evenings, cooking the next day's midday meal. From his Gentile neighbour on the first floor he even learned how to mend shoes. He bought himself the necessary tools and set to work. When there weren't any shoes to mend he tried to read a religious book, but somehow he did not have the taste for it any more. In Antwerp, when the children were still at home, when people were always coming and going and he had a thousand different business matters to attend to, he had really enjoyed reading holy texts, because it had calmed him down.

Now things were too calm. It was so quiet that one could hear the buzzing of a fly. The moment he started looking at a book, the sizzling sounds in the black, iron stove gradually faded, his head sank down and his snoring could be heard throughout the house. Often, the only thing which interrupted his delightful nap, when he rested his head on the table, was the sound of a whistle and the cry: "Take cover!"*

Berman knew this whistle well, and he would rub his eyes, focus

268

his startled gaze, and, a moment later, he would be sitting in his usual corner of the cellar, with both hands tucked into the wide sleeves of his warm dressing gown, his broad skullcap on his head; his nose looked pinched and livid, and his eyes stared blankly, like those of a dead fish. Then the danger was past, the enemy had been driven away. They could again mount the few steps from the cellar to the bedroom. But Berman would carry on sitting there with a bewildered air, fear in his dark eyes, and aching all over his body as if someone had broken his bones. Rochl would rouse him:

"Gedaliah, it's over, thank God!"

Then he would drag himself up the steps and sit on his bed. With his fringed undergarment draped over his stomach he would recite *krishme*, saying earnestly "threescore valiant men ... of the valiant of Israel."* Then he would go to sleep.

And so it went on throughout that long winter. The only things Berman still got a little pleasure from, were earning a little bit of money on a weekday - once in a blue moon, and taking an occasional walk up Whitechapel Road on a Sunday afternoon. On these Sundays, Rochl had to put on her expensive, black fur coat with the big, brown skunk collar, a broad border at the hem, and deep cuffs round her wrists. This coat really drowned her now. Her face had become pinched and grey. She wore a pair of white leather gloves, which were now too big for her thin hands. When she completed the outfit with a broad-brimmed hat on top of her wig, Rochl herself was hardly visible at all.

Berman, in his expensive, black overcoat with its beaver collar and lapels, and his elegant beard, looked like a king as he strolled among the Jewish men and women who had come out into this wide street for a Sunday afternoon walk. All the burly, corpulent men in their good winter coats somehow seemed ordinary and workaday in comparison with Berman. His coat was neatly buttoned, while theirs flapped open. From their fat stomachs hung thick chains with dangling, gold coins or Stars of David, diamond pins glittered in their cravats, and large, gold signet rings adorned their stumpy fingers. And yet they lacked the true stamp of affluence. Somehow they all looked like paupers who had come up in the world and wanted to show off their fortune. Their wives, with their double chins and black fur coats which were also trimmed with skunk fur, wobbled along on their fat legs wearing high-heeled shoes, which pinched their feet. They held their gloves in their hands to show off the thick rings on their fingers, which were coarsened, from too much peeling of potatoes and frying of fish. They, too, looked like jumped-up servant girls in comparison with the shrivelled little figure of Rochl.

Gradually, the Bermans became a focus of interest for the regular Sunday afternoon promenaders of Whitechapel. People couldn't fathom what sort of people they were and they decided that he must have been a rabbi from St. Petersburg, and began to give him the title of "Rabbi".

"Look, there's the rabbi," the wives would say, pressing up against their husbands in order to make way for the Bermans.

Berman didn't realise that they were talking about him, and he just walked on with Rochl to visit a niece of hers, a restaurant owner, whom Berman had come across here in London. The niece received them with a broad smile on her greasy face. She felt great delight and pride that Berman was visiting her, and served them portions of hot salt beef with pickled cucumber, positively beaming with pleasure: "Eat it in good health!" she said.

She had a waiter bring large chunks of apple cake and clear, red tea in sparkling glasses. Whenever she managed to find a free moment, she came over to have a chat, asking if they wanted anything more to eat, begging them to have just a little bit more for her sake.

The diners at the other tables kept looking over and trying to guess who the two people at the private table were. Rochl's niece didn't leave them in suspense for too long. "They're my uncle and aunt. He's extremely wealthy, you know, very, very rich!"

"Is it true that he's a rabbi?" the customers asked.

"He was before the war," she answered without hesitation, transforming Berman into a rabbi so that she would get even more reflected glory as payment for the free meal she had served to them.

Berman didn't stay long in the niece's restaurant. The latter protested: "Why are you in such a hurry, auntie? Let uncle stay for a little while." But Berman was in a hurry to get home: "We don't want to make ourselves cheap!" And if the niece insisted, he had a good excuse: he had to get back because of his father, even though, in fact, he had taken his father in to a neighbour, a man who would have given away everything he owned for a game of cards. Every Sunday he sent his wife and children out somewhere, and a crowd of his friends came in; they all rolled up their sleeves and started playing okey or sixty-six.* They were so absorbed in their game that they completely forgot old Chaim Yoysef, who sat by the stove reading a prayer book or dozing.

Rochl longed to stay on in the cheerful, brightly lit restaurant, watching the people coming and going. It helped her to forget her problems for a while. But Berman was in a hurry. He always had to go home just when things were getting really lively in Whitechapel, just when the young people began to erupt out of the narrow lanes. From the dark, crooked, little houses, which seemed in danger of collapsing and burying the Jewish poor under the earth, young men and girls appeared, all dressed up, noisy, buzzing like bees, making the streets echo with merry laughter, and dazzling the eye with bright clothes and cheap make-up.

Berman turned up his nose at them. He detested their long ball gowns which swept along Whitechapel Road, and their too-tight jackets, which they wore in order to look slimmer. With his expertise he could judge the quality of their silver fox furs. Nor could he stand the young men with tight shirt cuffs, patent leather shoes, yellow suede gloves and thick, rolled umbrellas à la Prince of Wales.

"They think they're fooling everyone!" he said to Rochl. "Have you ever gone into the little lanes where they live? There's hardly room for a person to walk along them. It's really disgusting, the way they're parading through the streets, showing off in front of the *goyim* at a time like this! Berman seemed to have forgotten that he and his wife were also parading around, all dressed up.

Rochl, however, really liked the hubbub of the street. The shops, too, were all open, with light pouring out of their windows. The dainty shoes in the big shoe shops were so nicely arranged that they seemed to be calling out to the people: "Come in, try us on!" There were furniture shops with bedrooms, dining rooms and salons fit for a king.

Red and green satin and silk cascaded down amid the furniture, as beautifully draped as in the most elegant West End shops. The charming wax figures in the clothes shops were dressed in expensive ball gowns, furs, or flowery silk frocks, which reminded Rochl of summer and of lovely flowerbeds. There were fine men's shirts, ties and gloves. And, equally elegant, was the waxen young man with slick, black hair in a dark red silk dressing gown, sitting in a relaxed posture in the shop window. His carefree, sophisticated smile attracted the customers.

Looking at him, Rochl forgot everything for a while; even Dovid Berman looked at him in amazement:

"Who buys all these expensive things? After all, the alleyways around here are simply packed with poor people, Jews and non-Jews alike."

The smartly dressed Jewish men and women had managed to make a little money because of the war, and with the few shillings they had earned through working like slaves all day and half the night, they bought some bits and pieces of jewellery, to have something set aside "for a rainy day." And in the meantime they dressed up in this finery, put on their rings, wore their brooches on the décolleté of their old dresses, and pushed their way along the crowded pavement. On the opposite side, the pavement was deserted and forlorn, and the few shops there were so huddled together that one could hardly distinguish one from another. The most prominent position on that side of the street was taken up by a large black church built in the Gothic style, with a spire which stretched up into the sky. It seemed to have a kind of fearful mystery about it. The building was adorned by all sorts of lacy tracery, where flocks of skinny pigeons had made their nests. It cast long spreading shadows which swallowed up the surrounding area into its blackness.

Even tramps avoided that side of the street. They were to be seen shuffling through the crowd: a pair of inflamed eyes, a swollen scabby mouth, tufts of matted hair surrounding a black, crumpled rag, which was the face, and old newspapers, secured by dirty string, wrapped round their loins. They only stopped to pick up a cigarette end or a bit of crumpled paper, in case there was something inside it. If they found nothing, they carried on along the brightly lit pavement to claim a place under a bridge somewhere to lay the bundle of newspapers which was their bedding, and prepare for the night. Among the well-dressed people they looked like heaps of dirt, which the road sweeper had swept together, then left lying there.

Berman looked at them, and it occurred to him that Dovid would look like them in his old age, if he couldn't provide for him, or find a solution to his problems. God willing, he *would* provide for him. As soon as Dovid came home, he would take him into the business and try his best to make a man of him. He would provide for him in his will. If only he came home safely, he would, with God's help, make him into a respectable person. Dovid could still become a diamond merchant.

This thought gave him such a warm feeling in his heart that he suddenly felt full of kindness towards humanity, which led him to sing the praises of Rochl's niece:

"A fine woman!" he said, and Rochl was thrilled to hear him praising one of her family, for once.

Chapter 31

Winter was drawing to a close. The square patch of sunlight on the floor of Rochl's kitchen got bigger every day, and the shadows in the corners ever smaller. The black range was cold. It was not needed during the warm weather leading up to Passover.

Just like the range, Rochl's face looked darker as the days got brighter. She was not needed either, and so she wandered aimlessly round the flat. She felt that Passover didn't really have anything to do with her, and apart from her aged father-in-law, she had no one to talk to. Her husband was taken up with his business dealings again, and when he came home in the evenings, she didn't dare to mention Dovid's name. Dovid was the only subject that interested her now.

If she went to call on her daughter, the cheerful atmosphere there irritated her. Jeannette dressed her maid in a black satin dress and the daintiest cambric apron a servant ever wore. She had the finest muslin collar and cuffs and the most beautiful cap to be found in all of London. Every afternoon, the moment she finished her work, the maid dressed up and manicured her fingernails. These were Jeannette's wishes.

Jeannette had bought herself a little curly-haired dog just like those belonging to the heroines in her French novels, and she wandered around all day in dressing gowns of silk, satin and velvet, embroidered with dogs, monkeys, opium-smoking Chinamen, Arabian women with flasks of wine balanced on their heads, and French dancers.

She was the best of friends with her maid, so that the latter almost forgot she was a servant. The mistress and the maid exchanged all sorts of confidences. They laughed and joked together and played with the little dog. Sometimes, however, in the middle of some game or other, Jeannette would suddenly have a fit of madness and start screaming at her in such a rage that the maid soaked the kitchen with her tears. But just as suddenly Jeannette would call her back and make up with her, blaming it on her nerves, and they would be good friends again.

Rochl seldom went to her daughter's house, but when she did, she would observe all this and she felt that Jeannette was even wilder than she had been before. She didn't feel at ease here, but she didn't feel at ease in her own house either. She preferred, however, to be in her own kitchen with her old, crippled father-in-law.

But her daughter would prevent her leaving, swearing she *did* usually get dressed and it was only that day that she was going around all day in her dressing gown. She begged her mother to sit down and even sent the maid out to buy something nice for her to eat. Rochl saw her reflection in all the mirrors at once, looking more dead than alive, and it seemed impossible to her that she would ever have the strength to walk back to her home.

"Oh, Mama, you look awful, you're wearing yourself out." Jeannette greeted her each time with what she thought was an appropriate remark.

"I don't need to wear myself out; they've done it for me already. The doctor says that it's nothing, that I have a weak heart, and that's all, he says. But I have a feeling I won't last very long. If only my death could save my son, I'd die happy!" She cried hot tears of pity for Dovid and for herself.

When Jeannette scolded her mother, telling her to drive away these melancholy thoughts, Rochl sobbed all the more, just managing to get out the words, which Jeannette already knew by heart:

"I hope I'll be proved a liar! But I tell you, my heart's giving me warning signals!"

When her son-in-law took her home after finishing his supper, she begged him not to try to console her, because that made her even more agitated. So they walked in complete silence along the quiet streets of North London. Their every step echoed on the empty pavements. The houses were just as silent, all the windows covered with expensive curtains and heavy shutters. The different scents of spring rose from the front gardens. Green spikes of tulips appeared in the flowerbeds, trees were full of sap and new life, ready to burst into blossom at any moment. Some already had plump buds and little, bright, green leaves, as tiny as match heads.

This scent of resurgent life irritated Rochl. It was as if she begrudged the trees their rebirth, and she started to walk more quickly, wanting to get back to her house with the black range and the crippled father-in-law. The chirping of the birds grated on her and she pulled her hat down over her ears and turned up her collar, trying to shut out the birdsong.

"Are you cold, mother-in-law?"

"No, no!" the mother-in-law (who was considerably younger than her son-in-law) answered agitatedly.

On the first floor, above the Bermans, lived a family who had experienced the same tragedy as many other families had. Their son had gone off to the front, hale and hearty, and all that came home was a package of clothes, a couple of medals and an accolade from the Ministry of War, which stated that he had fought as a hero and died as a hero. From that moment, every time there was a knock at the door, Rochl thought it was the postman with a black-edged envelope. It didn't help when her family reassured her, telling her a thousand times that more soldiers came home safely than were killed, that, like everything else in the world, it was just a matter of luck: that if it was your destiny to enjoy a long life, you would come back, even from the Other World, and if not, then you would, God forbid, fall sick and die anyway.

Rochl listened to what they said, agreed, and did actually realise that because it had happened to the family upstairs didn't mean that it would happen to them. She spat to ward off the evil eye, and tried to drive out the bad thoughts, but they kept on gnawing and boring away at her. The stone she felt lying on her heart wouldn't budge.

Berman prepared the Passover meal by himself. He ordered matzos,[*] chose the fowl at the butcher's, ordered wine and all sorts of other drinks. He cleaned the house, making sure it was kosher for Passover.[*] He went around in the evenings dressed in his white smock, boiling and frying food, and showing Rochl all the good things he had bought

276

for the festival; he wanted her to feel the hens, and he examined the eggs, with one eye shut to check their purity,* with just as much interest as he checked the purity of his diamonds.

Rochl wouldn't touch or test anything, but nodded in agreement to everything, wishing he would leave her in peace.

When the Passover arrived, the long table in the front room was covered with a white starched tablecloth for the first *seder.* There were three bouquets of flowers which Jeannette had got her maid to deliver. All the silver was spread out on the table, and a decanter of glowing wine surrounded by golden goblets stood on a golden tray, with some dusty bottles of wine from the Land of Israel beside them. In the open grate a fire burned brightly, giving out a lovely, intimate warmth and a feeling of comfortable affluence. All the lights were lit and shone brightly. Tall candles were burning in the silver candlesticks, making the atmosphere festive.

Berman sat at the top of the table wearing a white robe and a white skullcap with silver embroidery, and opposite him, sat his old father, similarly attired. They looked like two kings. Berman's daughter and son-in-law also sat at the table.

Rochl was wearing a festive dress, but she looked downcast. Jacques sat at his father's right side, ready to ask the Four Questions.* Suddenly there was a soft knock at the door and the neighbour from upstairs came in, dressed in mourning, with a thick crêpe veil over her hat, covering her face. She carried a basket in one black-gloved hand and in the other she held a letter. The woman lifted the veil slightly from her pale face, and was about to say something, but before she was able to get out a single word, Rochl stood up, made a grab for the letter with her outstretched hand, but couldn't get quite near enough to take it. She gave a sob and screamed: "God help me, it's my son!" then said softly "I'm not well." Then she swayed and fell to the floor like a stone.

There was great confusion. Everyone started shouting, pulling her, pouring brandy between her clenched teeth. They pinched her and tried to coax her back to life. The neighbour's husband and children, all in black, came running down from the floor above.

Forgetting that he was a cripple, old Reb Chaim Yoysef rushed towards his daughter-in-law, stumbled, and pulled down the tablecloth. Dishes clattered everywhere with a silvery ringing sound. The wine splashed out of the gold goblets. The tablecloth caught fire and lay blazing on the floor beside the dead woman.

The shouting and wailing rose heavenwards. Jeannette's maid brought a pot of water from the kitchen and tried to put out the fire. Jacques was the only one who had the presence of mind to call the doctor, who lived nearby.

The doctor was bewildered at the strange scene which met his eyes: two Jews dressed all in white, a family in black, gold and silver dishes lying about the floor, and a dead body lying in a pool of water and wine, with fire burning round it. The living, who themselves looked like corpses were coaxing her or wringing their hands. A small woman dressed in black was standing in a corner, staring with glazed eyes at one spot.

All the doctor could do was to certify that Rochl was dead, and that the probable cause of death was a heart attack.

For the duration of the festival the house was full of good friends. Jeannette kept horrifying the already traumatised family with fainting fits. Reb Chaim Yoysef went to bed and lay there like a lump of clay, not moving a muscle. He had become completely paralysed, though he could still speak. He had forgotten that the doctor had pronounced her dead, and kept asking "Well, how is she? How's Rochl?"

"Better!" they grunted at him and turned away.

"Better? God be praised!" The sight of the old man's yellow, wrinkled face, and the dead smile in his dull eyes, frightened them. It seemed as if death itself was smiling at them.

It was some time after the funeral that Berman came across the letter which the woman had been given by the postman as she was coming in from the street. It hadn't occurred to him till then that this letter had caused his wife's death and his father's complete paralysis. Now he turned the envelope over and over, looking at his name on it. A shudder went through his body when he opened it. The letter began in German:

Sehr geehrter Herr Berman,
Please inform me immediately of your price per carat. If you agree to the price I have offered, the parcel is as good as sold. If not, I should like to know your price. Please reply immediately. My best wishes to your wife, and I wish you a kosher and happy Passover.
Hochachtungsvoll,
Julius Shapiro

Chapter 32

After the war Berman went home to Antwerp. It was the middle of summer, and the city looked completely different: wider and brighter. The sky seemed higher than in London, higher than he remembered it in Antwerp before the war.

The city smelt of clay, lime, brick and concrete, and almost all the houses were covered with scaffolding. Workers in white overalls spattered with paint and lime were plastering, painting and cleaning everywhere. Some were throwing bricks up onto the scaffolding, which were skilfully caught by the workers above. There was the sound of shouting up from below and down from above. A new life was being constructed.

Berman opened up his house. It smelt like a tomb, and the darkness filled him with terror. He opened shutters, windows and doors - it was a ruin, not a home. The carpets were trampled down, torn, full of cigarette burns, their colours obliterated. The plush sofas and chairs were scattered around, sagging, threadbare, with wires and stuffing sticking out of them. The table was scratched and the piano was ruined. Wallpaper was peeling from the walls, which were covered with greenish mould. The tiles in the kitchen were brown and filthy, and some had fallen off. The crockery was broken and everywhere there was dust, dust and more dust. Dust and cobwebs, in which fat flies were caught. The spiders had tirelessly spun themselves new webs.

"Papa, I don't like it here, I'm scared," said Jacques. He now looked like a young man, yet he spoke to his father like a child: "Ugh!"

Berman rented a house. He soon calmed down, corresponded with lawyers, kept writing and running around, moving heaven and earth, until he was awarded a handsome sum in compensation, after which he began to renovate his home.

When the renovation work was finished, Jeannette came over from

London. When she saw the new, white-painted house, she exclaimed:

"Papa, don't dare to buy one single piece of furniture without me! Nowadays you can get modern furniture which is totally different from the old rubbish. You won't know what to buy. Do you hear me, Papa? You must rely entirely on my judgement!"

Dovid came home. He had aged. His jet black hair was streaked with white and his face was lined, like an old man's, which gave him an earnest, dignified appearance. He did not move into his father's house, but went to Brussels. In Austria, where he had been a prisoner of war, he had learned a trade. He had become an electrician. He had written the same answer to all Gitele's letters:

"I will provide for the child, but it's all over between us."

One Sunday morning Jacques came to see Dovid and begged him to let him come and stay with him.

"I can't stay there. I have to get away. It's horrible in that house. Everything is new. That madwoman has bought the most expensive stuff. She's off her head! She has forgotten Mama already, as if it was just a bad dream. And she keeps on kissing him all the time."

"Whom?"

"Our father."

"You can stay here with pleasure, Jacques. You can stay right now; you don't have to go back home." Dovid was pleased Jacques had come because he was finding the loneliness difficult to bear.

Dovid made tea and asked Jacques to relate once again exactly how it all happened, how their mother had died. Jacques told him everything, not just how she died, but what her life had been like since Dovid had left. And so the brothers remembered their dead mother, whom they had deeply loved and respected. The eyes of both filled with tears, and they vowed not to have anything to do with their father or his money.

Berman was alone in the house. He had no one to speak to. He stared at the furniture, the elegant wallpaper, the mirrors, which showed him that he was an old man with a white beard. He felt he really didn't belong in these surroundings.

Everything was so new and so different. Not only his house but the city was new, shining and cared for. Even the Jewish district was fresh and new, with no sign of its original dark appearance. But all this newness annoyed Berman. He could not stand it.

When he went into the Fortunia he found even that had been changed. They had installed some kind of strange machines. All day young merchants threw coins into them, and coloured balls started whirling round. The merchants stood shoulder to shoulder around these machines, as if they had all gone mad, peering with stupid, staring eyes to see where the mighty ball would land, as if this were their only aim in life.

All this drove him back home. He sat down and the image of Rochl floated in front of his eyes. Ah, she had really looked after him. She had treated him like a Kaiser. And now?

"*Oy!* It's horrible being alone. My sons don't want to know me, my daughter's in London living with that old man. How will it all end?"

He was filled with self-pity and Reb Beynish, the matchmaker, with his sheepskin collar came into his mind. Yes, thank God, he, Berman, was still a vigorous man, and Gitele was really a rather fine woman. It was as easy as spitting nowadays to get a divorce from a husband in Russia.* So he sat down and wrote a letter to Reb Beynish, which he intended to send to him in London. He felt a lot more cheerful. Gitele would certainly be delighted, suddenly to come into wealth like his!

Having posted his letter, he paced around in his elegant, modern dining room, and a little smile stole across his face and got tangled up in his grey whiskers. Yes, he thought, with God's help he would start a new life.

He was full of satisfaction at this prospect, and then it came into his mind that he had to ... no, he didn't *have* to, but nevertheless to-morrow morning he *would*, God willing, send for the monumental sculptor and order tombstones for Rochl and for his father. Yes, God willing, he would do that before his wedding. And another thing: he would overlook the fact that Dovid had fallen out with him. He would send for him and Jacques and give both of them money to start up in business. They should also have a good life.

The little smile hiding among his whiskers broadened, spread into his eyes and came to rest in his beard. The smile became a burst of joyful laughter, and a feeling of happiness came over him. Delighted with himself and his plans, he started looking among his father's things, which they had sent him from the "home of rest" for old people in London. It occurred to him that it was possible that his father, despite his illness, had managed to write a will of some sort. He wanted to carry out his father's wishes to the letter. And indeed he found a note.

It was a crumpled little piece of paper. The handwriting zig-zagged and the letters were shaky, some big and clumsy and others tiny and round, just like his father's handwriting had been when he was still in good health. Peering at the piece of paper, Berman made a great effort to read it. The more he looked, the more his face darkened, and his eyes became larger and more melancholy:

"I ask you to respect my last wish. In God's Name, do not put up a tombstone for me. I rue the day when I came to live with you. I do not want a tombstone bought with your money. Chaim Yoysef ben Rivke."*

All night Berman paced up and down his luxurious, modern dining room, back and forward, back and forward. He didn't even think about going to bed. He didn't think at all. The crumpled piece of paper lay on the polished table, staring after his every step. Only at daybreak did he collapse exhausted into the deep plush armchair and fall asleep. When he awoke in the morning, the letter was still lying there, grubby and crumpled as before. He looked at it. It seemed to him not like a piece of paper, but like a dirty, tattered life lying spread out before him. It drove him out of the house. He grabbed his hat, put it on his grey head, and went out into the streets and lanes of Antwerp.

The piece of paper didn't take its eyes off him.

Glossary

Chapter 1

"In het park van de nachtegaal": a slightly risqué popular Flemish *kermis* song of the time, referring to the Nachtegaalenpark to the south of the city, which would then have been on the edge of the city and is now in a residential district of Antwerp.

Spa: a popular resort to the southeast of Antwerp.

Chapter 2

the Keyserlei: de Keyserlei (named after a 19th century painter, Nicaise De Keyser) is a busy street in the commercial centre of the city.

the pious Hassidim: The populist movement known as Hassidism, to which Esther Kreitman's father belonged, arose in Eastern Europe in the middle of the eighteenth century. Its adherents, the Hassidim, grouped themselves round a *rebbe* or charismatic religious leader. Hassidism placed great emphasis on personal, ecstatic communication with God through prayer, music and dance.

shnorrers: a Yiddish word for a scrounger, commonly used in English too.

Chapter 3

shtetl: The word describes the small towns in Poland and Russia where communities of Jews lived.

Talmud: a collection of Jewish writings which make up the basis of Jewish religious law, consisting of early scriptural interpretations (*Mishnah*) and the later commentaries on them (*Gemara*).

Reb Elyohu Kornhendler: "Reb" is the Yiddish term for "Mr"

*shtibl (*plural: *shtiblekh):* a small Hassidic prayer house. The term is commonly used by Jews in English also.

The boys and girls called each other "du": du is the familiar form of address in Yiddish. Normally the formal *ir* would be used by adults until they knew each other very well. Freethinking groups like this would always use the familiar *du* as a matter of principle.

Chapter 4
to light a memorial candle: Jews light a memorial or *yortsayt'* candle every year on the anniversary of the death of a close relative.

Chapter 5
Melkboer (Flemish): milkman; *Dag menieër* (Flemish) "Good day, sir".

Borgerhout: Until the 1980s Borgerhout was a separate municipality to the east of Antwerp, near the old Jewish diamond district. Now it is a district of the city in which many Jews still live today.

Kosher: Ritually pure according to certain religious laws, suitable for consumption by Jews.

Sint-Anneke: at that time the village of Sint-Anneke on the left bank of the River Scheldt, with its seafood restaurants, spa and beach was a popular destination for tourist excursions. Now a dormitory town for Antwerp.

Chapter 6
mazl tov, mazl: good fortune. Both terms used when congratulating someone and wishing someone good luck.

Shabbes: the Jewish Sabbath, the day of rest which begins at sundown on Friday evening and ends at sundown on Saturday evening. Traditionally Jews light candles and eat a special meal with wine on Friday evening. The extra expense was often a problem for poorer families.

ken eynore: (from Hebrew: *ayin hora*), literally "no evil eye". Said to ward off bad luck, especially when making some optimistic assertion or praising someone.

krishme: The prayer beginning "Hear, oh Israel, the Lord our God, the Lord is One", which is said in the morning and evening, and before retiring for the night.

Chapter 7
shikse: rather derogatory term for a non-Jewish girl or woman.

bar mitzvah: the ceremony which represents the entering of the thirteen year-old boy into religious responsibility. At his *bar mitzvah* the boy is called up to read from the *Torah* (the Pentateuch, the first five books of the Hebrew Bible), in the synagogue, and a celebration follows.

Zurenborg: a smart district on the eastern side of Antwerp, near Borgerhout.

Vogelmarkt: a large market in the centre of the city, where all sorts of things can be bought including birds, dogs and other animals.

Gemara: a collection of commentaries on the Talmud (see note for chapter 3). The term *Gemara* is often used to refer to the whole Talmud.

Chapter 8
kugel: a dish made with noodles or potatoes.

Goy (pl. *goyim*): a non-Jewish male.

Chapter 9
loupe: the magnifying glass through which diamonds are examined.

Chapter 10
Shprintse: a Jewish female name.

Chapter 11
kaddish: the mourners' prayer, said at a funeral and on the anniversary of someone's death.

goeie koop (Flemish): a great bargain, *charmant* (French): charming.

"Lift up your hands ...": Psalm 134, v.2.

shochet: a ritual slaughterer, who kills animals according to Jewish Law to ensure that they are *kosher*, suitable for consumption.

mohel: the man licensed to perform the circumcision of Jewish males.

tefillin: phylacteries. Small leather boxes containing biblical verses on pieces of parchment. The phylacteries are bound onto the forehead and left arm by leather straps during morning prayers.

"thou shalt not suffer a witch to live": Exodus 22:18

Chapter 12
a Gerer Hassid: The various groups of Hassidim are known by the name of the place from which their *rebbe* originated. The Gerer Hassidim originated in the town of Ger, in central Poland.

Sfas Emes (literally "language of truth"): this was the name given to Yehuda Leyb Rottenberg, the second *rebbe* of the Gerer Hassidim, who reigned from 1870-1904.

Chapter 14
cheder (literally "room"): a Jewish school for young boys, teaching Hebrew language and Jewish religion, which was usually held in the teacher's house.

Torah: the Pentateuch, the first five books of the Hebrew Bible.

yeshiva boys: yeshivas are institutes for the study of the Talmud attended by pious young men, known in Yiddish as "*yeshiva bokherim*" ("yeshiva boys"). They studied long hours and were usually poor and undernourished.

Rashi: Rabbi Solomon ben Isaac (1040-1105), one of the most important commentators on the Bible. ("Rashi" is an acronym of the first letters of the Yiddish version of his name: <u>Ra</u>bbi <u>Sh</u>loyme <u>Yi</u>tskhaki)

Chapter 15
Cogels-Oyslei: An elegant street in Antwerp with beautiful *art nouveau* architecture.

mayrev: the evening prayer.

Chapter 16
High Holidays: the ten-day period encompassing the two most important Jewish religious festivals, *Rosh Hashana*: (the New Year) and *Yom Kippur* (the Day of Atonement), which falls in the autumn.

feast ... every Yom Kippur: Yom Kippur is a strict day of fasting, where neither food nor liquid may be consumed, from sunset on the eve of *Yom Kippur* until sunset the following day. Jewish secularist and socialist movements sometimes demonstratively ate during that period to register their rejection of the religious practices.

... to pluck white hens in the kitchen: They are making the preparations for the meal which will end the *Yom Kippur* fast.

the atonement ceremony: an old rite in which a live cockerel is swung round the head before being slaughtered, and the words are recited "This is my substitute, this is my vicarious offering, this is my atonement. This cock will go to its death, but I shall have a long and pleasant life of peace." This rite was rejected by scholars of Jewish law as early as the thirteenth century, and is seldom practised nowadays, except in some ultra-Orthodox communities.

this grey fortress: This is the Castle Steen on the eastern bank of the River Scheldt. Built sometime after 900 C.E., it is one of the oldest fortresses in Europe and functioned as a prison for several centuries. The artist Pieter Paul Rubens lived in the castle during his old age, and it is now home to the Scheepvaartmuseum (Belgian National Maritime Museum).

Lehavdil (literally: to divide one thing from another): This is said by pious Jews when a sacred and a profane thing are mentioned in one sentence, or immediately after each other. The girl is embarrassed that her traditional religious upbringing has slipped out in this way in the presence of her new secular comrades.

Chapter 17
Kheshvan: The eighth month of the Jewish year, falling in October/November.

Chapter 18
Galician Jews: the province of Galicia was part of the Austro-Hungarian Empire. Traditionally, there was enmity or at least rivalry between the Galician and Polish Jews, as there was between the Russian, Polish and Lithuanian Jews (see below in the next paragraph). Now, in addition to this, as subjects of the Austrian Emperor and the Russian Tsar respectively, the Galician and Russian/Polish/Lithuanian Jews found themselves on different sides in the conflict.

Efroim Yossel's kingdom: the speaker is referring ironically to Kaiser Franz Josef of Austria through a comic Yiddishised version of his name.

landslayt: people who come from the same area or *shtetl* in Eastern Europe.

Chapter 23

tailors' pressers: those who ironed the clothing in its various stages of manufacture.

yecke: term commonly used by Jews for German Jews (sometimes thought to be derived from German: "Jacke", a jacket, because the assimilated German Jews wore short jackets in contrast to the Eastern European caftan).

"*Rejoice, oh young man, in thy youth!*" Ecclesiastes 11:9.

Nicholas the Third: the then Tsar, the repressive Nicholas II, was particularly feared and hated by his Jewish subjects.

Chapter 24

the café: The Diamond Bourse in Hatton Garden did not open till 1940. Until then business was conducted in the street or at Mrs Cohen's café in Greville Street. (I am indebted to Carole Timms for this information. HV)

mezuzahs: small boxes containing a small piece of parchment with biblical verses, which Jews attach to the doorposts of their dwellings.

Chapter 25

ha'pennies (halfpennies): a very small coin in the old British currency pre-1971. There were 480 halfpennies to the pound sterling.

bloaters for a change: kippers and bloaters are in fact both smoked herring, prepared in slightly different ways.

bima: the platform in the synagogue from which the *Torah* is read.

Eyn Yankev: "The Fountain of Jacob", a popular religious book from the 16th century.

Chapter 28

Adar: the twelfth month of the Jewish year, falling in February or March.

L'chaim! (Hebrew): "to Life!" Words used in a toast.

florins and half-crowns: British currency before 1971, the equivalent of ten pence and twelve and a half pence respectively in modern British currency.

Chapter 29

I remember, I remember... a popular poem by Thomas Hood (1799-1845).

the "madhouse" at Hyde Park Corner: At Speakers' Corner on the edge of Hyde Park, anyone who wishes can speak on any issue, so that there is usually a cacophony, as speakers on themes from the conventional to the bizarre compete for the audience.

... we will liberate them: The struggle for women's suffrage in Britain was led by Emmeline Pankhurst and her daughter Christabel. The suffragette martyr who is mentioned here was Emily Wilding Davison who deliberately stepped in front of a horse owned by the king, shouting "Votes for women" at the Derby race of June 4th 1913, in the presence of the Royal Family and the elite of society.

Chapter 30

take cover!: In 1915 there were German Zeppelin raids over London and in 1917 bombing raids using aircraft. Both types of air raid caused casualties.

threescore valiant men: This is part of a verse from the Song of Songs (3:7), which reads: "Behold his bed, which is Solomon's; threescore valiant men are about it, of the valiant of Israel."

okey, sixty-six: *okey* is played with coloured tiles, *sixty-six* is a card game. Both were popular with Eastern European Jews.

Chapter 31
matzos: crackers made from unleavened flour which are eaten instead of bread during the eight days of Passover.

kosher for Passover: Religious Jews clean their homes thoroughly before Passover in order to make sure than no leavened bread or food with yeast in it remains in the house.

examined the eggs ... to check their purity: an egg which has even a speck of blood in it is not *kosher*.

the first seder: the first of two ceremonial meals on the first two evenings of the Passover, during which the story of the exodus of the Children of Israel from Egypt is retold.

Four Questions: Near the beginning of the Passover *seder* the youngest child present asks four questions about the festival of Passover, each beginning with "Why is this night different from all other nights?"

Chapter 32
A husband in Russia: from this we can infer that Leybesh, like many enthusiastic young socialists, went to the emerging Soviet Union at the end of the First World War, or that he joined the Russian army, like Avrom Kreitman, under the 1917 agreement (see introduction).

Chaim Yoysef ben Rivke: "Chaim Yoysef, son of Rivke", the traditional form of Jewish names, emphasising the matrilineal descent.

Bibliography

Works by Esther Kreitman:

Yiddish:
Der sheydim-tants. Warsaw: Brzoza, 1936.

Brilyantn: London : W. and G. Foyle,1944.

Yikhes: London: Narod Press, 1950.

In English translation:
Deborah: [English version of Der sheydim-tants]. Transl. by Maurice Carr. London: W. and G. Foyle, 1946; reprinted London:Virago, 1983; reprinted New York: St Martins Press 1984; reprinted London: David Paul/New York: Feminist Press, 2004.

Blitz and Other Stories [Yikhes]: Transl. by Dorothée van Tendeloo. London: David Paul, 2004.

Esther Kreitman's published translations into Yiddish:
Charles Dickens: *Vaynakht* [A Christmas Carol], Warsaw: Farlag Helios, 1929.

George Bernard Shaw: *Di froy in sotsializm un kapitalizm* [The Intelligent Woman's Guide to Socialism and Capitalism]. Warsaw: Goldfarb, 1930.

Secondary Literature :
I.J.Singer: *Fun a velt vos iz nishto mer.* New York: Farlag Matones, 1946. [English: *Of a world that is no more.* Transl. Joseph Singer. New York:Vanguard Press, 1971.]

I.B.Singer: *Mayn tatns bezdn shtub.* New York: Der kval, 1956. [English: *In my Father's Court* Philadelphia: JPS, 1966.]

293

S.S. Prawer: "The First Family of Yiddish". In: TLS, 29 April 1983.

Janet Hadda: *Isaac Bashevis Singer. A Life*. Oxford, New York, 1997.

Faith Jones: "Esther Kreitman: Renewed Recognition of her Writing". In: *Canadian Jewish Outlook*, 38 no. 2, Mar./Apr. 2000, pp.17-18.

Dafna Clifford: "From Diamond Cutters to Dog Races: Antwerp and London in the Work of Esther Kreitman". In: *Prooftexts*, Vol. 23, No. 3, 2003.